SHE SAID NOW

Queen of the Universe, she lounged back in the SUV on her elbows. She'd rolled her pinstriped trousers up past modesty, exposing yards of firm, toned legs that challenged his self-control.

"God, Kelsy."

"Yes, darlin'?"

Never taking her smoky blue eyes off his, she held her arms out, then said in a throaty, lounge singer voice, "My favorite cop."

Her blouse, unbuttoned to the waist, claimed his attention. He ran his hand inside the opening, down bare skin, back up to her bra.

"You've got ninety minutes, Finn."

BOOK YOUR PLACE ON OUR WEBSITE AND MAKE THE READING CONNECTION!

We've created a customized website just for our very special readers, where you can get the inside scoop on everything that's going on with Zebra, Pinnacle and Kensington books.

When you come online, you'll have the exciting opportunity to:

- View covers of upcoming books
- Read sample chapters
- Learn about our future publishing schedule (listed by publication month *and author*)
- Find out when your favorite authors will be visiting a city near you
- Search for and order backlist books from our online catalog
- Check out author bios and background information
- Send e-mail to your favorite authors
- Meet the Kensington staff online
- Join us in weekly chats with authors, readers and other guests
- Get writing guidelines
- AND MUCH MORE!

Visit our website at
http://www.kensingtonbooks.com

BARBARA PLUM

Queen of the Universe

ZEBRA BOOKS
KENSINGTON PUBLISHING CORP.
www.kensingtonbooks.com

ZEBRA BOOKS are published by

Kensington Publishing Corp.
850 Third Avenue
New York, NY 10022

All Kensington titles, imprints, and distributed lines are
available at special quantity discounts for bulk pur-
chases for sales promotion, premiums, fund-raising, ed-
ucational, or institutional use.

Special book excerpts or customized printings can also
be created to fit specific needs. For details, write or phone
the office of the Kensington Special Sales Manager:
Attn. Special Sales Department. Phone: 1-800-221-2647.
Kensington Publishing Corp., 850 Third Avenue, New
York, NY 10022.

Zebra and the Z logo Reg. U.S. Pat. & TM Off.

ISBN 0-8217-7774-2

First Printing: September 2005
10 9 8 7 6 5 4 3 2 1

Printed in the United States of America

For David,
Thanks for being with me through thick and thin.

Chapter 1

"Kelsy Chandler, Channel Three Top of the Morning News, hoping we've helped get *your* day off to a great start." Kelsy gazed directly into camera one and put on a happy face.

Lord, she must look like a recently revived corpse— with bags the color of stewed prunes under her eyes.

At least she wasn't having a bad hair day. With any luck, the overhead lights added soft glints to her naturally blond hair. She held her knock-'em-dead smile for a heartbeat past the all-clear signal, then quickly removed her lapel mike and yawned.

Jeeze, what sadist invented early morning news shows?

Her bright-eyed, barely-out-of-diapers producer gave her two thumbs up, then called, "Brad wants to see you . . . ASAP."

"Uh-huh, and I want to see Brad as soon as they start serving milk and cookies in hell. Till then, Brad can go suck—" The vibration of her cell phone interrupted the rest of her rant.

Her heart fluttered. Jogging off the set, she ducked into the ladies' room and flipped open the phone. *Go to the back of the line, Brad.*

"Hey, Finn." She collapsed against the nearest wall as lust hit her in the pit of her stomach and ignited.

"There you go, being eager again."

"Aren't you glad?" She laid a hand over her galloping heart.

"I'd like to show you just how glad." He made panting sounds into the receiver. Kelsy laughed, clutching the cell phone.

"I believe," she said primly, "obscene phone calls are illegal."

"As a cop, I'll decide what's obscene. I want to see you. Naked. For exactly ninety minutes."

"Ninety minutes. Is that all you can take?" It was lame, but Kelsy's mind was racing. *When? Where?* Hot all over, she shivered.

"We'll see how much I can take. One hour. E-Z Sleep Motel on East El Camino Way. That's in Palo Alto."

"Don't you mean Paradise? Sounds like the perfect place for a nap." First, though, she had to sneak past Eagle-Eye Brad.

"Who said anything about napping?" Finn chuckled.

"Promises, promises." She glanced at her watch. 7:00. The height of morning rush hour from San Jose, north into Silicon Valley. "Where are you?"

"On my way to the station house. Our department meeting should take half an hour, max. Any chance you can meet me?"

"Brad wants . . ." She paused, remembered she worked part-time in a dead-end job, then said, "Are you kidding? I'll be there. With bells on."

"Forget the bells. We've only got ninety minutes." Laughing, he hung up.

Kelsy laughed, too, then started giggling as soon as she hung up. God, she'd missed him. After his six weeks undercover, she was beginning to feel like a nun.

Nuns don't use pink vibrators.

No, but for lots of women without a guy in their lives, it was either the big M or a vibrator. Too bad she hadn't known about both with Sam, her lying, toe-sucking, skirt-chasing, cheating dickhead ex-husband.

Don't go there. Think about Finn.

Easy enough, since just thinking his name made her wet. A natural result, she figured, from sex deprivation. Without warning, resentment spiraled upward, out of the dark place where she normally buried such feelings.

Okay, call her immature, but she'd hated the nights alone in the king-size bed. Sleepless, she'd tossed and turned, obsessing over whether insomnia would age her. She did *not* want to look any older than the eight-year difference between her and Finn. Terrified she'd end up looking like his mother instead of his lover, she'd felt sick without him.

So, a meeting with Brad right now jeopardized her mental and physical health. Fun with Finn ensured she'd retain the TV-genic glow you couldn't buy in a bottle or from a plastic surgeon.

Anticipation exploded deep inside her and made her knees loose. Unsure she could walk to her desk, she inhaled deeply and didn't bother checking her mirrored image. The glow radiating inside her might break free any minute and blind her. Smiling like a woman about to meet the love of her life, she slipped into the newsroom.

"Hey, Traci." Plan in place, Kelsy waved at a nineteen-year-old intern with chartreuse cotton-candy hair and thick, black glasses. "Grab my bag and bring it to the restroom, would you?"

Traci clapped a hand over her heart and intoned, "Mr. Hall's waiting for you." She rolled her eyes so far back Kelsy saw only the whites.

Poor kid. Someone should tell her to forget Brad and invest in a vibrator.

Speaking reverently, Traci added, "He came in at least ten minutes before you signed off. He watched you like he was hypnotized!"

The hair on Kelsy's neck prickled. "Ten minutes?"

"At least. I can ask him to move so I can get your—"

"Thanks, anyway." Kelsy knew how to handle Brad, who imagined women everywhere were dying to go down on a TV executive—even though he managed a no-rep station in a Nielsen dead zone.

Five minutes and I'm outta here. She threw her head up and sailed into the newsroom.

Perched on the corner of her desk, staring at several reporters in the glassed-in break room, Brad dazzled her with his alligator smile. "Super, super show this morning, Kelsy."

"Glad you liked it, boss." Could she knock him off her desk, grab her purse and make a run for the lobby?

Still playing Mr. Nice Guy, he said, "After all that energy you exuded, I bet you could use a cup of coffee. Why don't we go back to my office? I have fresh espresso."

Kelsy's mouth watered. Damn Brad. He knew how much she loved coffee. She forced a smile. "Love to, right after I get back from my doctor's appointment."

The lie rolled off her tongue easier than the truth.

He frowned, his black eyes hard as marbles. "Did you tell me about a doctor's appointment?"

"No. This just came up." She felt a twinge of conscience, but immediately rationalized that Finn was her private mental health professional. "It's easier for me to get my purse, Brad, if you move."

"Let's go to my office first. We really need to talk."

"I really need to leave. Rush hour. Can't be late." She nudged his leg with her hip. He stayed put.

Sitting, he had a good four inches on her, so she took a step backwards, straightened to five foot ten on her three-inch Pradas and said coolly, "It's a female thing, Brad. Would you like details? Maybe a note from the doctor when I get back?"

"Of course not." Red-faced, he leaped off the desk as if he'd just discovered a stick of lighted dynamite up his butt. "Absolutely not." He patted his silk handkerchief but didn't take it out, even though Kelsy saw bullets of sweat above his black eyebrows. "No note, no details."

She pressed her lips together so she wouldn't laugh. Wait till she told Finn he'd become her GYN. "I expect everything to go well, so I should be back around 10:30." She pulled her purse out of her bottom drawer and slung it over her shoulder. "How does that work for you?"

His jaw clenched, but he said, "As long as you're going to be around for the rest of the afternoon."

"That's the plan, Brad." With a scream building inside her chest, she sidestepped where he stood.

He rocked back on his heels. "Jason's still in Montana, right? So you don't have to pick him up this afternoon?"

Pushing past him, she called over her shoulder, "I'm all yours for the rest of the afternoon."

". . . CHP clearing a four-car pile-up at Highway 85 North and 101. Expect a ten-minute delay."

"Damn, damn, damn." Kelsy smacked the off button on her car radio. "What happened to the economic turndown?" she yelled, surveying the gridlock.

Damn Brad, too. Like a faithful hunting hound, he'd loped along beside her to the sunny parking lot, then wouldn't shut up. She'd left him, his mouth running. About what she had no idea.

In an effort to forget Brad, she punched coordinates into her GPS system. Why were cars on both sides of her trying to inch to the right? Peering down from her Lexus SUV fueled her confidence. Without signaling, she edged out a new Mercedes. The driver flipped her off, then fell in behind her. Winning, and the robin's-egg-blue sky, made her magnanimous. She ignored the jerk.

Moffett Boulevard, the nearest exit, flashed on her GPS.

Her stomach churned. There was only one problem. Moffett, a logical exit, was closed for construction.

Sometimes, it actually paid to listen to the news she read off the teleprompter between five and seven each morning.

Disappointment seeped into her stomach like poison. Along with hundreds of other edgy drivers, she'd have to wait till she got past the pile-up to get off the freeway. Commuter vehicles would then clog the surface streets and make the five-mile trip to the E-Z Sleep as slow as stop-and-go traffic on the 101. She bit back a sigh and reached for the phone.

Finn swore that drivers who used cell phones for non-emergencies should have their mouths wired shut for a year. Was feeling horny a real-deal emergency?

Before she decided on an answer, her phone beeped. Her heart sank, then soared when she saw it wasn't Finn calling to cancel. Which he'd done twice before. *Third time's a charm.*

She didn't recognize the phone number or the area code. Another beep. Bored with going nowhere fast, she clicked the phone on and soothed her conscience by splitting hairs.

Technically speaking, she reasoned, with traffic at a standstill, she wasn't driving.

"This is Kelsy," she said, thinking she could always hang up if the call wasn't worth her time.

"Hello, Kelsy. This is Dane Jensen. Are you still looking for a change in your life?"

* * *

"You better run around the block a couple of times, LB."

Finn whirled around in the police station parking lot. "Shut up, Livvie." LB, Lover Boy, he hated the nickname.

"Sorry." A guy-magnet with her high cheekbones, wide, sexy mouth and buff bod, Olivia hated her nickname too.

"Yeah, like Hannibal Lecter was sorry he got caught."

"Just slipped out," Olivia said as if Finn Bishop didn't recognize crap when it hit him in the teeth.

"So did 'Livvie'," he said with the same degree of sincerity.

"Don't ever play poker. Everyone in that room's gonna *know* you're heading for the best damned lay—"

"Shut up." Finn stopped less than five feet from the front door of the station house.

"You know I'm right." She tugged on one of the dozen earrings in her right ear.

Breathing hard, Finn held his temper in check. "My personal life is nobody's business. Nobody means you and the rest of the department."

"*Bzzzt.*" Olivia shook the ultra-short curly mop she'd dyed coal black for this job. "You know the loo's take: we can't work undercover without enough sleep."

He opened his mouth to say he'd get a lot more sleep if he saw more of Kelsy, but Olivia talked over him. "This meeting's already cutting in on our sleep time. Then, you're trotting off to get laid."

Shaking his head, he said, "You don't know shit."

Despite her mirrored shades, she shaded her eyes against the glare of early morning sun. "Personally, I prefer a partner who knows his service revolver from his dick. Just in case," she added, "the bad guys decide to use us as target practice."

Finn snapped his fingers, then made a gun with thumb cocked, index finger extended. "If I get confused, I'll take 'em out with my secret weapon. Never fails."

"I'm sure Kelsy appreciates your humor. I don't," Olivia said through her teeth.

"For God's sake, Olivia." Finn looked up at the electric-blue sky. *Patience. Give me patience.* "Six weeks, and we've never seen one of our guys with a weapon."

She snorted. "Fine, genius."

"Ahhh, unbridled female admiration does turn a man's head."

Pushing her glasses on top of her head, she got right in his face. "Why the hell should Matthews give you hardship leave?"

His jaw cracked. He flexed his fingers at his sides. "What the hell do you know about hardship leave?"

Another snort told him he needed a brain transplant. "This is the most important case the CVPD has ever handled. Word gets around."

Squared for battle, he growled, "Thank you, Preacher Olivia." God, she'd missed her calling.

"Uh-huh." Olivia's mouth twisted. "So here you come, the new guy, and want personal time off."

In his gut, he knew he was wasting his breath, but he said, "The new kid has his priorities straight, dammit."

Her onceover stopped at his balls. "Give me a break. You walk around looking happy as a well-fucked clown, then you want time off?"

Slammed right between the legs, he pulled his shoulders back. Shiiit. Self-righteous as she was, she had a point.

"Time off for a vacation in Montana. With Kelsy. Biiig hardship." Teeth gritted, Olivia rushed on. "You're not even married to the woman, for cryin' out loud. Jason's not your kid."

Every nerve in Finn bristled. "I consider Jason my kid."

"Okay." Olivia rolled her eyes. "But how do you think the guys with families feel? They don't whine about time off."

Her accusations struck home. Finn crossed his arms so he wouldn't grab her, shake her, make her take *whine* back. Instead, he lowered his voice as evidence he was in control. "I'm not whining, dammit!"

Olivia didn't back down. "Does Kelsy have a clue what you're doing? How you're jeopardizing your career?"

Before Finn could take Olivia's head off, the desk sergeant stuck his head out the door and yelled, "Yo, you two! Matthews says get your asses in here. Now."

"So what're you going to tell Kelsy?" With legs as long as Finn's, Olivia easily kept pace with him into the building.

He strolled through the door she held for him. "Today's Tuesday. She doesn't leave till Thursday. A lot can change in three days."

"Was that gasp a yes? You are ready for a change in your life?" Dane Jensen spoke as if he and Kelsy had known each other forever.

"Definitely, Mr. Jensen," she whispered, her heart going ninety. "Sorry, but it's been so long since I sent you my portfolio. . . ." Ooops, did that sound blaming? "I mean, I'd given up ever hearing from you."

The rumble of his laugh sent goose bumps up and down her arms. "You should never give up."

"Oh, I don't," Kelsy hurried to erase any idea he'd formed of her as negative. "Ask anyone who knows me. They'll tell you I always get what I really want."

The car ahead of her crept forward, and Kelsy inched her foot off the brake. Glare from the sun, reflected in a rearview mirror, momentarily blinded her.

Blinking, she kept her foot on the brake and her mind on the goal. "I just mean I decided a busy man like you had higher priorities."

"I was out of the country when your audition tapes arrived. A month ago, wasn't it?"

"That's right." Exactly two weeks after Finn went undercover.

"I was in Scotland—playing golf." He chuckled, inviting her into his world, and she went, cooing, "Oh, you poor man." She pushed aside the memory of how bored she'd been without Finn.

He laughed. "You forgot to mention empathy as one of your character traits."

"Thank you." *Did this guy get wet when he walked in the rain?* "It's just that I do understand someone has to make the sacrifices. But I never gave up on getting a response from you."

"And here I am, responding."

Kelsy thought she detected a note of mockery, but was too busy blocking the Mercedes from sneaking in where no space existed. "Back off, you idiot," she mumbled.

"Pardon?" She heard shock tinged with anger in Dane Jensen's baritone, and said quickly, "Not you. Really. I was talking to a driver who dogpaddles in the shallow end of the pool."

Lame, lame. Her ears stung, but then Dane chuckled and she felt a little blip of excitement in her diaphragm.

"Is this a bad time? Talking on a cell and driving take special skills—"

"I do it all the time." Unbidden, the lie fell out of her mouth.

"Can people actually get anything done if they don't talk on their cell while they drive?"

"Life in the fast lane." Kelsy glanced at the sea of

cars. If she ever got off the 101, she'd pull over, call Finn, and—

"So you can handle life in the fast lane, Kelsy?"

Behind the steering wheel, she sat up straighter and lifted her head higher. "As I said in my letter, Dane—move over, Savannah, move on, B.J."

He laughed—maybe a beat too long for sincerity, then said, "You do dream big, Kelsy. Savannah Jones hits the big 3-0 this year and just signed a five-year, twelve-million-dollar deal with ABC. At thirty-five, B.J. Thomas pulls in well over three mil a year."

"I know," Kelsy said, feeling ancient at thirty-seven. But she wasn't so ancient that she'd spent every night of Finn's undercover assignment wallowing in self-pity. "I've done the research."

A pause, during which a driver behind Kelsy leaned on the horn. She jumped, her heart beating wildly. Had she blown it with Dane? Sounded too know-it-all? Throwing caution to the wind, she said, "I'm committed to advancing my career, Dane. I'll work hard—do whatever it takes."

Even tell Finn?

Blinded again by a splinter of sunshine and intimidated by Dane Jensen's silence, Kelsy nodded. When the time was right, after Finn finished this damn undercover assignment, she'd tell him she wanted it all: marriage, family, *and* career.

The sound of Dane Jensen clearing his throat broke Kelsy's trance. ". . . golf till 5:30. Then drinks, a shower. I'm not sure how long it takes to drive from the peninsula to the coast."

Mind churning, Kelsy didn't answer. Sheesh, she'd missed something. He bridged the awkward silence. "Do you know the Ritz-Carlton in Half Moon Bay? You can't see the resort from Highway 1, but—"

"Yes, I know it. I've been there." With her ex—not

with Finn, who didn't golf or enjoy dinner at places where the bill cost him a week's pay.

"Does seven work for you?"

"Seven's fine." Her heart fluttered, then revved up. *Oh, God, this was it. Her chance. Move over . . .*

"Any earlier," he chuckled, "and you'll find me in the shower."

The bubble of happiness inside her didn't pop, but it started leaking air. Whatever his intentions, she should inform him that she saw no one but Finn in the shower. She managed a lackluster chuckle, then said as primly as a nun, "I wouldn't want to embarrass you."

"You'll find," he said, never missing a beat, "I'm not easily embarrassed. You need a thick skin for success in our business."

Our business? The happiness bubble inflated again. Kelsy mentally counted to two, then said, "I look forward to meeting you tonight, Dane. I'm sure I can learn a lot from you."

His chuckle—maybe it was a nervous habit?—morphed into a gong clanging *danger.* Before she could edit her stupidity, he said, "That kind of attitude will take you far. See you tonight."

"But not with bells on," she said to the buzz in her ear.

She wasn't about to change her life *that* much.

Chapter 2

Should be a law against meetings. Finn tore out the front door of the station house. God, it was too hot for October. Eau de sweat would definitely not turn Kelsy on.

"Finn! Wait up!"

Jogging across the police department parking lot, he glanced over his shoulder, then waved at Olivia. "Later."

He was already late, thanks to the damn meeting that had lasted a decade. For forty-three unending minutes, Matthews had acted like Finn was invisible. Then, he'd hightailed it to another meeting. Of course he never mentioned Finn's request for vacation. Or leave without pay.

Dammit, no way he'd beat Kelsy to the E-Z Sleep.

So much for planning.

God, he hated meetings worse than undercover work.

Out of breath, he slid under the 'Vette's steering wheel. *Breathe, breathe.*

An invisible wire sliced through his lungs. Before his resentment took root, he reminded himself he'd volunteered for this assignment. Not to put too fine a point on it, he'd jumped at the career move. The first step on his way up.

As he peeled out of the lot, Finn caught Olivia's reflection in his rearview mirror. Hands on her hips, legs apart, she stared at him like she was memorizing his plates. As his senior partner, he had no doubt she'd give him an earful tonight.

If he still worked for the department by tonight.

At the stoplight on Foothill Expressway and Edith, he gripped the steering wheel and heard his jaw crack. Dammit, why had Matthews let the damn meeting run so long?

So he didn't have to veto your request for time off?

Ticked as he was, Finn recognized the wrongheadedness of that conclusion.

More likely, Matthews hadn't decided yet.

Even more likely, Matthews figured everyone at the meeting needed a chance to vent. After six weeks of 24/7 stakeouts, they had zip on the gang of South American boosters who, in a single month, had shoplifted a million bucks of PDAs, software, cell phones, iPods, and cameras. Everyone on the undercover task force, including Finn, was frustrated. Venting hadn't changed a damn thing, but somehow it helped.

Except Finn had sat there checking his watch and saying zip.

The light changed to green, and he shot ahead of the SUV next to him. The older female driver was yakking on her cell. Your lucky day, he thought. If Kelsy wasn't waiting . . .

Pain shot through his cock. He groaned. Christ, almost ten months with Kelsy, and he still couldn't control his crazy hormones. Olivia thought he shouldn't get three days in Montana for health reasons—for any reasons—but little did she know. And he sure as hell didn't intend to explain it to her. Matthews would either believe Kelsy and Jason needed him back in their lives 24/7 for the next three days, or he'd tell Finn to take a hike.

Either way . . . Finn swung into the parking lot at the E-Z Sleep and damn near rammed into Kelsy as she rocketed in on two wheels. Tires screeched, raising the hairs on his arms. She barely missed him and a giant potted bougainvillea. His heart went through his skull.

"Jesus, Joseph, and Mary." He twisted the 'Vette's steering wheel hard to the right.

Her face lit up with wonder when she saw it was him. She waved, taking both hands off the wheel to throw him kisses.

Finn cringed. Driving was not Kelsy's strong suit. Why she'd never had an accident mystified him. Right now, though, he didn't give a damn about that particular mystery. Fire ignited in his groin. Should he tell her about Montana first, or make love first?

Duuuh.

First things first. He motioned her to stay in the car while he raced into the office. Turning his baseball cap around so the bill hid his face, he paid his money and grabbed the card key. Wide-eyed, the clerk wished him a good day.

Or maybe it was a good lay. Finn laughed.

Out in the parking lot, it took all his willpower not to rip the door off Kelsy's SUV. Instead, he got in the 'Vette, drove around to the back of the motel with her tailgating him. Blind with lust, he killed the engine. He didn't give a damn that he'd parked in two spaces. Why? The lot was deserted. He'd seen the cleaning ladies on the front side of the building.

He fell out of the front seat, drawn to Kelsy like a planet to the sun.

Queen of the universe, she lounged back in the SUV on her elbows. She'd rolled her pinstriped trousers up past modesty, exposing yards of firm, toned legs that challenged his self-control.

"God, Kelsy."

"Yes, darlin'."

Never taking her smoky blue eyes off his, she held her arms out, then said in a throaty, lounge singer voice, "My favorite cop."

Her blouse, unbuttoned to the waist, claimed his attention. He ran his hand inside the opening, down bare skin, back up to her bra. "No bells?" he said.

"You've got ninety minutes to find out." Her lacy black bra served no purpose except to drive him crazy and distract him.

Mute, though mercifully not struck blind, Finn stood paralyzed while she dragged a fingernail down between her breasts. Then the bra broke open, and the luscious fullness of her taunted him.

"What's wrong, officer?" She pouted. "Aren't you going to arrest me for . . . indecent exposure?"

Finn swallowed convulsively. "Yes, ma'am. But first . . ." The fire between his legs whooshed through him, leaving him dizzy with lust, stupid with desire.

"Yes?" Mocking him with a sly smile, she slid out of the SUV and sashayed away from him, her hips undulating, her head cocked over one shoulder. Birds twittered in the bougainvillea hedge.

"First, first, first I-I—" His throat clogged. Jesus, she blew him away. "First," he said, his heart in overdrive, "I'm going to fuck your brains out."

"Oh." She turned and pressed her breasts into his chest and damn near seared the buttons off his shirt. "You want to do it right here—or in a bed?"

After forty-five minutes of teasing, heart-stopping, highly creative lovemaking, Kelsy forgot the drab motel room.

A sense of urgency, impending separation, hot hands, hotter breath, and spur-of-the-moment gratification left her too aroused to think about anything but enjoying every second of reuniting with Finn. Tingling from having him deep inside her, she reveled in the clandestine cocoon they'd created.

On the cusp of her sixth orgasm in the king-size bed, she sighed. Guilt faded. Dinner with Dane Jensen was a non-problem.

"Damn, I'm good." Finn kissed the crook of her neck.

She gasped, then whispered, "And so modest for a cop." His dark red stubble, grown for his undercover assignment, tickled.

"I'll show you modest in a sec." He pulled her to his chest, and it was like lying down on a live wire.

"Ohhh." She sighed, inhaling his hot, reassuring scent.

"There you go being eager again." His lips singed the spot above her nose, between her eyes. He touched her between her legs. She closed her eyes, biting back a scream.

"There you go being a silver-tongued . . ." She nipped his ear and ignored "Yankee Doodle Dandy" on his cell.

"Biting a police officer? That's a felony." He reached over her shoulder which, just for the hell of it, she raised, blocking him from the phone. "Oh-oh. Now, we add obstruction of justice. More than enough reason to bring out the handcuffs."

Desire lit up her eyes. "You, me, and handcuffs. Sounds fun."

"*After* I violate—er, read you your rights." He lunged over her, grabbed the phone, then swung his feet over the edge of the bed, speaking in hushed monosyllables she didn't really hear.

"Promises, promises." She ran a fingernail down his spine.

Half glad when he didn't turn around, she caught her breath, stretched, then pulled the sheet over her. God, what if someday she couldn't keep up with him anymore? When he was thirty-six and she was——. She stared at her wobbly triceps.

What if by forty-four she needed liposuction? What if she couldn't wear sleeveless blouses anymore? She'd have to stop going to bed naked, wear long sleeves, and beg Finn for sex. She took a deep breath, releasing it silently.

He cradled the phone closer, and she fought the urge to grab him, smother him in kisses, make *him* beg.

After ten months, she still worried when the earth tilted on its axis every time they made love. Admiring the tiny red curls grazing his ears, she felt dizzy. Worry about her triceps evaporated, but the anxiety she'd been carrying around with her since Dane Jensen's phone call spiked to panic.

Phone pressed against his ear, Finn turned, nodded, then blew her a kiss. She returned a weak smile. She had to tell him about dinner. Because a business dinner with another man really was no big deal. Her heart thudded against her rib cage.

As soon as he finishes.

Before we shower.

Shivering, she pulled the sheet under her chin. Life was a timing problem, but she couldn't put off telling him. He was undercover; she might not see him again for days. Might not see him before she left for Montana.

What if, after she and Dane had dinner tonight, he wanted her to meet him again? Or go to Seattle to check out the job?

Her chest tightened. She stared into space. A snapshot of roses and lilies flashed. The lobby arrangement at The Ritz came into focus. She'd gone there half a dozen times with Dickhead. The Ritz was light-years from the E-Z Sleep. Sweat pooled between her breasts. She pushed up to sit.

"Earth to Kelsy." Finn pulled her into his arms, and

she blinked back scalding tears and mumbled, "Work, right?"

He took her hand, laid her fingers over his, then kissed them one by one. "Bingo. Gotta go. Bad guys are out there."

"You said ninety minutes!" She sounded like a spoiled brat, her voice rising on a thready note.

"I know. You probably think I'm a wham, bang, thank-you bastard, don't you?" Grinning, he cupped her face and held her gaze. Dark gold flecks floated in his midnight-blue eyes.

Afraid he'd see her soul, she looked away. "I'll be glad when you finish law school. No more undercover work. No more—"

"No more fun like this." He hugged her, a gesture that usually made her feel cherished and protected. "I've got four minutes to shower. Care to join me? I've got a surprise."

Pout? Ruin everything by blurting out about dinner? Or take advantage of their quality time together?

With a whoop, Kelsy smacked him on the bare butt, then raced for the tiny bathroom. "Last one in is the Back Scrubber."

"Foul!" Gentleman that he was, Finn let her win.

In the shower, she offered a consolation prize. "You can scrub my back double the next time."

"Next time, you'll beg to do me," he countered and slathered soap from her neck, down her spine, to her knees, then stopped. "How about in Montana? This week—"

She screeched. "You're coming? This weekend?" The perfect time to tell him about meeting Dane Jensen. "When?"

"Flying up with you and Risa. 'S what you wanted, 's what you're getting. You know me—"

"Finn!" Forgetting everything but the happiness ex-

ploding inside her, Kelsy pressed against him, banged
into the faucet, and yelped.

He turned off the shower, fussed over her, then cocked
his head. "Either my ears are ringing or that's your
phone."

She groaned, then said through gritted teeth, "I'm
going to kill Brad Hall."

"Careful how you talk in front of a cop." Being
macho, Finn swiped soap off his chest, stepped onto the
bathmat, and handed a neon-blue cell to Kelsy on its
second ring.

"And if I'm not careful? Will you finally bring out the
handcuffs?"

Drying off, he laughed, then said, "If it's Jason, let
me say hi, okay? I want to know how his riding lesson
went."

"You're sure?" Kelsy held the phone between her
breasts, awed once more by the love Finn gave so freely
to her six-year-old son. "He'll be wired," she warned.
"You'll need more time than a minute."

"I'll make time." Finn pulled on baggy jeans over his
sleek, hard body. *What a pity to hide those assets.*

"Don't say I didn't warn—" Kelsy glanced at the LED
and flinched as if she'd picked up a cobra.

"Sam!" she hissed, clearing the call a breath before
Finn reclaimed the phone. He tossed it aside without a
glance.

"That guy's got the worst timing." Extending a thin
towel, Finn wiggled his eyebrows as he dried Kelsy off.

Her breath caught. He nuzzled her ear. "Has he ever
called when we weren't in the middle of making love?"

Weak-kneed with relief, she laughed. "Who cares?"

"Not me. Not when you put it that way."

Taunted by her second lie to him, she tucked the
corner of the flimsy towel between her breasts, then
grabbed his wonderful, sweet face and brought his lips

down to hers once more. When they finished kissing, she said brightly, "Better go, big boy."

"Not without you." He jammed a baseball cap on his head—backwards.

To Kelsy, he now looked about eleven. *Except he's a grown man who loves me and deserves the truth.*

Her stomach churned. *No big deal.* Quickly, she said, "I should make a phone call before I leave."

He frowned.

"Work," she said. "Five minutes. It's important. No driving and yakking on my cell, right?"

"The future wife of a cop? Don't think so." He grinned, dropped a kiss on her nose and waved on his way out the door. "Maybe I'll catch up with you tonight."

For a nanosecond, she couldn't breathe. Finally, she said, "No. I know how hard it is for you. Besides, Risa and I'll probably go out to dinner."

"Okay," he said sweetly, never doubting her truthfulness. "Drive carefully tonight, okay?"

"Always."

Miraculously, her mouth turned up in a smile that slid off her face as soon as the door shut behind him. Excitement erased her guilt. Hands shaking, she dialed the number from memory.

Yes, yes, yes. She'd hooked Dane Jensen for sure. Otherwise, why would he call her twice in less than two hours?

Carrying the memory of Kelsy inside him and feeling more optimistic than earlier in the morning, Finn showed up at the station house at 10:20. Not bad, given the circumstances.

Circumstances he wasn't about to explain to Matthews, who'd called and ordered him back ASAP. His stomach growled repeatedly as he cooled his heels outside Matthews's office. Making love to Kelsy burned a lotta calories. Heat still pulsed off him. Ready for anything, he didn't bother rehearsing what he'd say to Matthews. Maybe he wouldn't get a chance to say anything more than, "I quit."

One way or the other, he *was* going with Kelsy to Montana, day after tomorrow.

Twenty minutes after Finn's arrival, Matthews appeared in the door and nodded Finn inside his office. Without a greeting or any attempt to put him at ease, Matthews said, "How many more law courses before you finish?"

Caught off guard, Finn reined in his imagination. "Three, sir."

"Think you'll make it as a lawyer?"

"If I decide to, yes, sir." What the hell?

"You haven't decided yet?" Matthews made him sound as if he should consider a vocation—like plumbing or electrical work. Garbage collector, maybe.

"I still like being a cop, Lieutenant."

"But not an undercover cop." Matthews squinted at Finn over the top of his half-rimmed glasses. "What happened? You find out going without sleep and getting chummy with scuzz puppies isn't as much fun as you thought?"

Ears scalding, Finn said without hesitation, "Yes, but more importantly, I'm away from my family too much. Phone calls don't take the place of me being there for soccer or show and tell."

Not to mention sleeping next to Kelsy. The memory made Finn hot all over.

Matthews gazed at the silver frame on his otherwise clean desk. "You got married? There's a Mrs. Bishop?"

"Not yet. We were waiting for me to finish law school, but I'm thinking we should go ahead."

"I've known guys go undercover for six months with no break," Matthews stated.

"Yes, sir." And Finn knew guys whose marriages collapsed, pushed beyond repair because the job came first with them. No job excited him enough to give up being with Kelsy, touching her, smelling her.

"You know there's a buzz about you being top cop one day."

Surprised that Matthews listened to gossip, Finn nodded.

Arms crossed, Matthews stared up at the ceiling. "Taking time off in the middle of the job's not the way undercover works, Bishop. What if I just give you an indefinite break permanently?"

Finn felt a tiny pang. Regret? He wasn't a quitter. He let the emotion go. "I could live with that, sir."

A vein bulged over Matthews's left eyebrow, but he sounded calm when he finally said, "Take your three damned days. Don't be surprised when you land in Traffic the middle of the month."

It was all Finn could do not to jump up and click his heels together. But Matthews wasn't finished. "We can't keep up these 24/7 stakeouts. I'm taking out two other guys besides you. That's confidential, by the way. Do I have to define the word?"

"No, sir." Drunk on happiness, Finn didn't give a damn Matthews had jerked his chain.

"One other thing." Matthews, his mouth tight as a kid with new braces, did an eye-slide past Finn. "I wouldn't count on the top cop thing. Taking vacation in the middle of this sting operation won't look any better on your record in ten years than it does now."

Acid seared the back of Finn's throat. He swallowed, his eyes hot. "I can live with that."

Being with Kelsy and Jason beat out ambition every time.

* * *

Throwing on her clothes, Kelsy tried Dane's cell three times from the E-Z Sleep. On the third forward to his voice mail, she left a terse message.

"You called at 9:39 this morning. If we need to cancel tonight for whatever reason, please leave me a message before 4:30 this afternoon."

On the way back to KSJC, Kelsy mentally reviewed her message, but slow-motion frames of her in bed with Finn derailed her train of thought. She entered KSJC at 10:10, and Brad pounced on her. Smiling his alligator smile, he whisked her into his cave, shut the door and waited—smiling, smiling—while she settled into a chair shaped like some kind of car from the Fifties. From her description, Finn had once guessed it was a '55 Chevy.

"Guy obviously thinks he's a hotshot." Finn had gone on to suggest he show up one day and give ol' Brad a ticket. "For parking too close to a wild animal," he'd said solemnly, then grinned while Kelsy laughed till she felt drunk.

The other seating alternative was in the mouth of a humongous stuffed alligator.

Afraid she'd start howling, Kelsy averted her eyes from the reptile. She and Finn had concocted an elaborate plan to slip into Brad's office one night and make love in the alligator.

Until then, let her out of Brad's office. If she worked through lunch, she could leave at four—during gridlock again. It'd be close, but she'd still get home with time for a shower. Luckily, she already knew what she'd wear for her meeting with Dane Jensen.

Tired of waiting for her boss to get off the dime, she demanded, "What's up, Brad?"

"You, I hope."

She turned a full death stare on him. He added, "I mean you must've gotten a clean bill of health because you look positively radiant."

"Excuse me, Brad. Did I sign away my constitutional right to privacy when I signed my contract with Channel Three?"

"I simply meant you look energized." He stepped back from the car-chair, scuttled around his desk, and sat down in a leather executive chair. "You look up for anything. For the biggest assignment since you started with us at Channel Three."

"Really?" Kelsy didn't roll her eyes, but she figured he recognized her suspicions because he rushed on, "This is the kind of assignment that could kick-start your career, Kelsy. Make you a star. Right here in San Jose."

"A star in San Jose?" She cocked her head at him. "Isn't that an oxymoron?"

He squinted at her, a sure sign he was losing his patience. And so was she. "Just spit it out, Brad. What do you want?"

With his thin, sandy hair moussed into submission, he sat behind his parabolic glass desk, both hands patting air in front of him. He worked mightily, trying to arrange brows, eyes, and mouth into a semblance of empathy as he explained that Erica Parker, host of *The Afternoon Show* had called in sick. "Food poisoning. Up all night. Went to the ER at dawn. You can imagine."

"Uh-huh." Kelsy could see where this was leading, and she didn't need the headache. "You want me to take her show."

"You should be flattered."

Try that con on B.J. Thomas and Savannah Jones. Inching her legs out in front of her, Kelsy pinned him with a glare. "I should be flattered."

"Absolutely. Your first full-hour interview, done on the fly. Very impressive."

"I'm sure." Did she give a damn if she impressed Brad? Her pulse sped up. How about Dane Jensen?

Stared down by Kelsy, Brad gave up the facial contortions and said softly, "Believe me, I know it's an imposition."

"Really? How do you spell imposition?"

He sighed, long and deep. "Wouldn't you think Erica would know better than to eat sushi at a new restaurant?"

Teeth gritted, realizing he was dead serious, Kelsy demanded, "Why don't *you* host the damned show?"

Brad reared back in his chair. For a heartbeat, he looked as if she'd asked him to shove a little old lady into traffic. She spit out each word. "Erica does fluff interviews. Yoga gurus and aerobics instructors aren't my style." Style was what Kelsy had to offer Dane Jensen.

"Weren't you listening?" Pouty. Accusing. "The interview's with Victoria Moreno. She's the most powerful female techie in Silicon Valley."

Victoria Moreno? Kelsy sat up a little straighter. "What's Erica's angle?"

Brad shrugged. "I'm not sure. Her notes should help, and you've got three hours to showtime."

Against her better judgment, Kelsy glanced down at the papers he spread in front of her. "Oh, these are perfect."

Squiggles filled the top page. Nothing legible appeared on the second page, either. "Oh, great. Hieroglyphics help tremendously."

Chapter 3

You can do this, Kelsy reminded herself ten minutes later. Teeth gritted, she searched the Web, directed two interns, and ignored her pounding head. A minor point Brad had conveniently forgotten drove her: Victoria Moreno was coming with the president of her company, Steele Hood. He, too, was considered a force of nature. Two high-powered guests meant twice as much work digging out facts, separating trivia, developing snappy questions.

By noon, Kelsy felt close to meltdown. Enough of mentally kicking herself. She decided to ignore the first vibration from her phone. Then common sense over-ruled the idea. With Ben, Risa's husband, alone in Montana caring for triplet toddlers, plus five-year-old Molly and Jason, ignoring her calls wasn't an option. Kelsy glanced at the caller ID, saw Finn's number, and felt a spurt of angry relief.

"Hey," she said, rationalizing that stress made her edgy.

"This a good time?" he drawled.

"Sure." Any other time, she'd die to have him call her in the middle of the day. "Why aren't you asleep?"

"Guess," he whispered. "And the first one doesn't count."

Her edginess evaporated, and she shivered, recalling their earlier lovefest. "Think Thursday." She stared at hundreds of Internet search results on her monitor.

"No good. Just makes me horny. If I knew you'd slip over here around 3:30—about the time the alarm goes off—and crawl into bed, I could go to sleep."

"Darlin'. I can't." Panic uncoiled in her stomach. "Remember I told you Brad wanted to see me?"

"Vaguely." Finn yawned.

Pressed for time, she blurted, "Erica's sick. So, I'm hosting *The Afternoon Show.* It starts at two and—"

"Great! Three's even better. Shouldn't take you more than half an hour to swing by here after you sign off."

Kelsy rolled her eyes, took a deep breath, then lied through her teeth. "Brad will probably want to review the show around 3:15. . . ." At which time she'd be in the car, headed home no matter what Brad said or did.

"Oh." Finn sounded so disappointed, Kelsy wanted to reach across the miles and hug him.

"What about tomorrow morning? I can get away at seven—"

"Won't work." He sighed. "Olivia and I agreed on breakfast tomorrow. According to her, it's been a while."

If Kelsy hadn't been so mad—not jealous, mad—she might've recognized the perfect segue to having dinner with Dane Jensen. But she was too mad to think—about why she was mad or about dinner with Dane. Which might never come off, anyway.

Afraid she'd dump on Finn, she lied, "Here comes Brad."

"Love you," Finn said.

Frustrated and nagged by guilt, Kelsy stuffed her emotions into a hole she imagined in the pit of her stomach. She'd make it up to him. Her edginess. Her jealousy. Her lies.

First, though, she had to get a handle on Victoria Moreno. Too bad the official company picture was so blurry. Blinking, Kelsy scanned more Internet entries. Lunch arrived, but her throat was so dry she didn't think she could swallow roast turkey on sourdough bread. One of the interns brought her a new copy of Erica's notes. After reading them twice, Kelsy gave up. She had no idea what angle Erica had been developing.

Maybe I can't figure her angle, Kelsy thought, because I can't figure my own angle. Maybe I'll just let the guests drive the show.

Her phone vibrated. Thank God, a break. She recognized Dane Jensen's number. The buzz in her head grew louder.

If he was calling to cancel dinner, she'd miss her opp to give him the interview tape. Sure, she could send it, but she'd have to forego singing her own praises. Kelsy Chandler, KSJC's answer to B.J. Thomas.

"Hello," she said stiffly and kept her gaze glued to her monitor.

"Busy?" he asked without identifying himself.

"Very." Frost set in, but she regained control by saying brightly, "Big show this afternoon, and I'm subbing at the last minute."

"So you're a team player, are you?" He sounded as if he were smiling.

"No," she said, suddenly deciding she'd make her own opportunities. "I'm KSJC's answer to B.J. Thomas."

His laugh, warm and sexy, melted the lump of ice in her throat. "For the record, B.J. has no sense of humor."

A sense of humor and Finn keep me going, she thought,

but said, "Pay me what she earns, and I can be serious, too."

Another laugh, longer, warmer. "Of course, it's too early to discuss money tonight. Don't you think?"

Her heart felt like a racquetball ricocheting off her ribs. "Absolutely," she said, then whispered, "Believe me, money is *not* why I work at KSJC."

"No? Maybe you'll tell me the details tonight. Because I'm calling to say I definitely am *not* canceling tonight. Nothing short of getting beaned by a golf ball will cause me to cancel."

"Let's not borrow trouble." For the owner of four indie TV stations in Seattle, this guy sounded downright human. Maybe he'd become her mentor. Guide her career. Take her to the top.

"Sorry." He actually sounded sincere. "Gotta run. I'm at the top of my game today, thanks to you."

Her heart caught. She squeaked, "To me?"

"Absolutely. Your enthusiasm's contagious. See you tonight at seven."

"I'll be there. With bells on," she said, but luckily he'd already hung up. "I meant with my tape," she whispered.

"Air time in half an hour, Kelsy." Erica's skinny blond intern hovered a few feet away. "Shouldn't you touch up your makeup?"

Kelsy tore four more pages off the printer and hissed, "That question makes it sound as if I need a mortician." Which, if her heart didn't slow down, might be necessary.

Red-faced, the intern shook her head. "No, no. No! I didn't mean it that way."

"Oh." Damn. Kelsy realized she'd let her nervousness spill into hostility toward this kid. She said, "I know. Sorry."

Reading her printout, sure she was going to throw up, she said, "Did you see the show where one of Erica's false eyelashes fell off?"

Mikayla's mouth dropped—as if Kelsy had insulted the pope. Mouth tight, arms over her chest, the intern didn't get so much as a nod from Brad as, arms waving, he rushed into the newsroom like the Mad Hatter. A major pile-up on Highway 101. Traffic was backed up to Mountain View. Brad repeatedly tapped his Rolex. "No way Steele Hood'll make it by air time."

And you thought nothing would go right today. Kelsy bit her lip.

Brad raked a hand through his moussed hair. "I told Erica we should've taped this show."

Without waiting for the fallout from his bomb to settle, he rushed on. "Here's what we're going to do."

The adrenaline that had kept Kelsy moving at warp speed evaporated. Damn, damn, damn. She wanted that tape for Dane Jensen. Savagely, she ripped her notes to shreds. She shoved the pieces at Brad. Then, she stalked onto the set and introduced a taped interview, kept for such emergencies.

While she waited in some kind of fugue state to close the segment, Brad kept repeating, "My hero."

After the hundredth repetition, Kelsy said, "If you don't back off, I'm going to yark all over you."

Her threat worked. He scuttled out of her way as she dragged back to close the show. She spared Brad's life because there were witnesses and because she needed to conserve the last of her energy to drive home. The canned theme music swelled. Two thumbs up, Brad remained on the sidelines. Kelsy smiled into the camera. *You will pay, Brad.*

* * *

As Kelsy sailed into the Navio Restaurant at 7:13—thirteen minutes late—the yeasty smell of fresh bread went to her head.

Or maybe it was the sweet smell of success, so close she could taste it.

After her day, entering The Ritz was like entering heaven. She even floated on a cloud behind the broad-shouldered maitre d'. *This is it*, Kelsy thought. *Tonight could change my life.*

Head up, she borrowed a technique she'd read about, from HM the Queen. She gazed into middle space but, surprisingly, she still took in the polished mahogany walls and floor-to-ceiling windows. Golf course floodlights lit up the nearby green. Beyond the cliff where the hotel perched, breakers pounded the beach.

Two men at an ocean-side table caught her attention. Resisting the urge to pat the chignon she'd spent thirty minutes styling and spritzing, she didn't gasp. But she did feel dizzy: Clint Eastwood and Bill Murray.

Here for the golf tournament, she decided.

Bent over menus, they didn't notice she'd morphed from HM the Queen into head-spinning Linda Blair in *The Exorcist*.

Terrified one stupidity would lead to another, Kelsy tore her eyes off the famous duo. Wait till she told Finn.

He'd flip. Then he'd want details. Lots of details.

And what details will he swallow—hook, line and sinker?

A flash of tangled sheets sent her reeling. She plowed into the maitre d'. A pro, he didn't miss a step. Or look back.

Think B.J, think Savannah. Kelsy pasted on a smile and lifted her head higher. If she really expected to join those stars in their faraway galaxy, interviewing power brokers and newsmakers, she couldn't walk around, mouth open, catching flies after a near encounter with celebrities.

Shoulders back, she met the admiring look of a blond, sun-tanned thirtysomething in a tuxedo. The tension in her chest eased. All right. She wouldn't tell Finn about Clint and Bill. Not till she could tell him everything.

Kelsy shot her admirer a TV-genic smile. Head cocked, he raised his champagne glass to her. His brunette companion, wearing industrial-strength mascara and falling out of her tacky red satin bustier, bared her teeth.

The needle on Kelsy's confidence-o-meter went off the chart. She put a little sway in her walk, strutting her stuff in the black Valentino knock-off, and sailed past the brunette.

Move on, Savannah, move over, B.J. Absently, Kelsy touched her ring finger.

Dammit. She'd left Finn's tiny oval sapphire and diamond-chip engagement ring at home in the bathroom.

"Dane." She extended her hand across the white tablecloth and pitched her voice low. She enunciated the single syllable clearly. Mumbling killed more TV careers than bad hair.

"Your audition tape doesn't do you justice, Kelsy." Tall and blond as his Viking ancestors, Dane Jensen appraised her with the narrowed eyes of a cameraman. He smelled discreetly of Chanel for Men, shook her hand with a firm grip, and made her rethink her childhood images of the devil as dark and goateed.

"Thank you." Goosebumps cha-cha-ed on her bare arms. Surprisingly, he didn't point out—as almost everyone did on first meeting her—her striking resemblance to Nicole Kidman. God, what if he realized her dress wasn't an original?

"Now I see," Dane said in his TV baritone, "why KSJC's ratings have gone through the roof since you joined them."

"Not through the roof yet," Kelsy said, her heart

bouncing up and down as she returned the handshake with equal firmness.

Saucers at the next table were half as big as his pupils.

Without warning, a snapshot of Finn wavered behind Dane's head. Kelsy blinked, reclaimed her hand, and slid into the plush chair the maitre d' held for her. Finn's image faded. Shivering, she drank in the room's paparazzi intensity.

"Champagne okay?" Dane nodded at the maitre d'. His electric-blue gaze held Kelsy's. "We can celebrate your show today, and I'll celebrate my golf score."

Her heart fluttered. "I'm glad your golf score's worth celebrating. My guests never made it. We ran a tape."

Dane nodded once. "That's too bad. But I predict you'll have many successful interviews in your future."

"You do?" She knew she sounded pathetic and bit her tongue so she wouldn't ask him how he knew this.

"With total confidence." He laid a cool hand on top of her scalding wrist. She flinched like a Regency virgin.

The sommelier appeared instantly with a bottle he showed Dane. Remembering this kind of deference to Sam, her ex, Kelsy waited till her companion indicated his approval before she said, "I'm sorry I missed the bagpiper."

"You'll have to come back," Dane said smoothly, then sipped his bubbly, his fair skin slightly flushed.

Kelsy put her glass to her lips, but took only the tiniest sip. If she didn't want to get drunker than a goose, she'd have to pace herself for the drive home. How many drinks had Dane already had to celebrate his golf game? Was he drunk?

He didn't sound drunk as he chatted about his travels, his home in Bellingham, and his apartment in Seattle. Touching the rim of his glass for a refill, he asked, "Do you like Seattle?"

"Very much." Maybe introducing Seattle was his segue to the purpose of this interview. The reason she could justify lying to Finn.

"Most people do—till they spend the winter there." Dane grimaced.

"Better a winter in Seattle than Siberia." Kelsy smiled. Great, conversation dies, fall back on the weather. Move over, Savannah.

He didn't seem to notice her gaffe or that her stomach growled. Stuffing bread into her mouth, Kelsy didn't hear much of what he said. When was he going to interview her? Would he invite her to Seattle?

"You went to Bezerkley, right?" The corny mispronunciation caught her ear, and she nodded. Only people who said San Fran said Bezerkley.

"Loved every minute of my time at Berkeley." *She was*, prodding him subtly, educating him maybe, adding loudly, "I'll never forget the biology paper I wrote: *The Long and Penetrating History of Condoms*. My professor—"

Total silence crashed down around them. Kelsy froze. Heads turned their way. Dane didn't choke, but his cool blue eyes widened before he said smoothly, quietly, "My son applied. His mother says over her dead body."

"So did my mother."

He had said *his son's mother*, Kelsy noticed, her jaw quivering, her brain erasing *condom* from short-term memory. His son's mother. Not *my wife*. How old was he—with a college-age kid? So old that the mention of condoms freaked him?

"You'll have to tell me how you won her over." Brows knit, Dane twirled his flute and watched bubbles as if he'd never seen them before.

"Simple: I wore her down." A weak buzz started in Kelsy's head. *Condom erase now complete*. Picking up her champagne glass again, she checked out Dane's ring finger.

"I'd stand a better chance wearing down glaciers in Patagonia." No wedding band. No tell-tale circle of paler skin.

"So she's a formidable lady." Half the married men in America didn't wear wedding rings. Those who did could still cheat. They probably viewed condoms as—

Focus, focus, focus.

"Formidable." Dane stared past Kelsy into space.

She studied her own ringless finger. Talking about his ex or her mother didn't figure into her agenda tonight. Either might lead to the bad idea of talking about Finn. She said, "Berkeley's a great place."

Dane flinched, checked out their fellow diners, then spoke very slowly, "Jennifer and Andrew live in Boston. She's the ten o'clock anchor at WBN. She's produced a couple of award-winning programs and now really wants a Peabody."

Duuuh. Curious, more to the truth, envious, Kelsy sat up straighter. "She must be good." How old was she?

"Very good. Started in the business seventeen years ago—the first month she was pregnant with Andrew."

Seventeen years ago? Kelsy did the math. Jennifer Jensen must be pushing forty. "Was she on air during her pregnancy?"

"No." Dane brought his gaze back to Kelsy. "She was a gopher, then got a break when Andrew was a year old. At thirty-eight, she's a fixture at WBN. She'll never leave Boston now. Which is why Andrew *will* go to Harvard." He sighed. "And since I'm the absent dad, what can I do?"

Another test? As the ex-wife of a very absent dad, Kelsy could blister Dane Jensen's ears informing him exactly what he could do. *Go postal,* she thought, *you can forget the job interview.* Forget replacing Savannah and B.J.

Hell, if she spoke her mind, she'd be lucky if he ordered dinner.

Ticked at her cowardice, she said huskily, "I'm sure you do your best."

His eyes brightened. Sheeeesh. Was he tearing up?

"I try." He threw off a white-hot heat that smelled like sex to Kelsy.

Are you insane?

Before she could decide, he touched her wrist again. She froze.

"No one gets anywhere without trying." she said. The champagne flutes wavered in and out of focus.

"Thanks. Your empathy will take you to the top, Kelsy. Now, let's order. Shall we talk about scheduling a visit to KSWA over more champagne?"

To his credit, Dane took no offense when Kelsy refused the champagne. Determined to cut back on the booze, she suggested a shiraz. She usually detested red wine. Her first sip evoked thoughts of nectar. Halfway through her truffle-infused foie gras and review of possible dates for a Seattle trip, her cell phone beeped.

Finn! Kelsy kept smiling at Dane like a beauty queen contestant. The restrained clink of silver and crystal focused her. Was she nuts? A job interview wasn't illegal, illicit or immoral. Finn would understand she couldn't interrupt business negotiations for a late-night chat.

What if there's a problem with Jason? Chest tight, she reached for her purse. About the same time she saw Dane wiggling his fingers at her, she realized it was his phone—not hers—that had rung. So much for her concern about interrupting their business negotiations. Cell phones offered escape in lots of embarrassing situations. Surely, Dane realized he'd crossed a line revealing so much family info. Maybe he even realized he'd revealed too much.

* * *

Unwilling to sit there tempted by more wine, Kelsy slipped out of her chair. A wave of dizziness came and went. Carefully, she put one foot in front of the other. Was it her imagination, or did fewer male heads turn in her direction?

Maybe they were embarrassed by her condom remarks.

Maybe, because getting to the restroom had turned into a spiritual test, she didn't give a damn if heads turned.

Thank God someone had installed tiny, tiny recessed lights in the ladies' room. A corpse would look good in here, she thought. Taking no chances she was wrong, she turned away from the mirrors as she turned on the cold water.

WHOOSH. A geyser stunned her, spraying her face and chest.

Yipping, she jumped back and threw an armload of clean towels over the faucet. She danced in place, trying to avoid the runoff, and finally wrenched the handle shut. Triumph died quickly. A steady stream of water dripped over the side of the marble lavatory directly into her only pair of Manolo Blahniks.

She glanced down at her feet, then stared at her reflection in the mirrored wall. "Sheeesh!"

On the cusp of bawling her eyes out, Kelsy laughed. Admittedly, she sounded hysterical, but still she laughed. As the laugh rose to the cackle of an escaped lunatic, the door opened.

"My, my," said the brunette with too much mascara. "Look what the cat dragged in—wearing a knock-off Valentino."

"Yes, but my boobs are real." Kelsy sailed past the snooty fashionista, into the nearest stall, shut the door, and sat down, knees shaking.

"Real boobs and condoms. You really have the gift for gab."

"And you really have the gift for tons of mascara." Wet feet frozen, Kelsy slipped off her stiletto heels.

"Tons of mascara beat your pukey pink lipstick."

"Huh," Kelsy sniffed. She took four of the Egyptian-cotton towels to fashion bulky slippers. "You should re-think the blue eyeshadow."

Silence. Good. She needed a sec to regroup. Figure out if she should apologize. But why? Condoms weren't illegal. She scrubbed the inner soles of her sandals with more towels.

"A smart woman wouldn't leave that hunk alone," Kelsy called, mildly surprised by her outrageous needling.

The brunette hammered the door. "What's the matter with you? Are you drunk?"

"Not so drunk I don't recognize ugly mascara." Kelsy blotted her dress from neckline to hem with more towels.

"Are you a guest here?" The brunette rattled the handle.

"Sure am. I'm just waiting for my chauffeur to bring the Rolls around. He's informed me it rolled over the cliff, don't you know?"

A snort. "Anyone ever tell you you've got a mouth on you?"

"You mean anyone besides my lying, no-balls ex-hus-band?"

"Does he thank his lucky stars every day he's your *ex?*"

In the stall, everything went red. Kelsy jerked open the door and schlepped out in her towels. "Don't you have a life?" she demanded.

"I knew it!" The brunette pointed a finger at Kelsy. "You're Kelsy Chandler. Channel Three News. I told my date I recognized you, but he said Kelsy Chandler's got better hair."

For a heartbeat, Kelsy felt as if she'd stepped in front of the camera naked. She conquered the urge to pat her ruined chignon. "Go suck a toad," she said sweetly, then added, "Watch it, so you don't impale yourself on those eyelashes."

Chapter 4

Dane Jensen could give Savannah and B.J. a run for their money, Kelsy realized over a second glass of the shiraz.

With less than ten minutes of persistent poking, gentle prodding, and intense listening, he finally got her to open up about the disaster in the ladies' room and the bitchy brunette.

Halfway through her rant, Kelsy stopped in mid-sentence. God, she sounded drunk. And demented. Heat stung her face.

Dane's steady blue eyes never left her face. No wonder the Vikings had ruled the world, she thought. They probably hypnotized everyone they laid eyes on. If just half of them had been as handsome as Dane, no woman anywhere could've resisted the fair-haired conquerors.

Disgusted because her mind had turned on her, Kelsy gulped more wine than she'd intended. A vision flashed before her eyes: a scantily dressed woman lying in a long boat, her gaze riveted on a reddish-blond, bearded, muscled Norseman.

"God!" Kelsy blinked in awe. "I sound so—so pathetic."

Dane smiled. "Want me to kill her for you?"

Caught off guard, Kelsy slammed the glass down too hard. It teetered. She and Dane grabbed for it at the same time. Their hands collided. His skin crackled. Kelsy bit her lip.

"Sorry." He righted the glass. "Didn't mean to scare you."

"You-you didn't." She put her hands in her lap so he couldn't see them shaking. "I was . . . surprised."

Surprised because Finn had made the same offer almost ten months ago after a fight with Dickhead, her soon-to-be ex-husband.

"Me, too." Dane smiled. "I consider myself a pretty buttoned-up kind of guy. Losing control's a character flaw in my book."

"Mine, too." Kelsy clamped down on the memory of her meltdown the night Dickhead informed her their marriage had ended.

"Self-control's an absolute requirement for a successful TV journalist. Imagine Lance LeHayne crying on the Evening News."

"I can't." Kelsy breathed.

"Pandemonium." Dane shook his head. "As TV journalists, we have a sacred duty to remain objective."

The flaw in his logic teased Kelsy, but she couldn't latch onto it at that moment. Not with her head swimming and the room spinning. The rest of the meal passed in a blur. Which was too bad since it would be years before Finn could afford dinner at The Ritz.

So maybe I'll bring him here, she decided. If—*when* I get the job in Seattle, we'll come here and celebrate. Play golf, have dinner. Even spend the night, she thought dreamily.

"C'mon." Dane snapped his fingers under her nose. "Share the secret. You're smiling from ear to ear. Why?"

"Oh—" Her mind went blank. "I was thinking what a good time I've had." She patted her lips. "But all good things—"

"No, no, no they don't." He put his finger over her mouth. "The night's young."

"Uh-huh, but five o'clock tomorrow morning comes way too early. I can't go in front of the camera with duffel bags under my eyes." When he didn't pooh-pooh her concern, she hurried on. "Besides, my sitter will not be happy if I'm late." A small white lie, but it hurt no one.

"I forgot you have a son." Dane narrowed his eyes, so Kelsy didn't stand but said brightly, "He's a great kid. My biggest fan."

She wanted to leave. She didn't want to get into a conversation about Jason. She pitched the Brightness Meter higher—up to weather person peppy. "Since I leave before he gets up in the morning, I like to be at home for his bedtime."

Too late, she remembered she was interviewing for The Late Night News at KSWA. Determined that Dane wouldn't think she turned into a pumpkin after dinner, she smiled at him. "Besides, if I don't leave soon, I'll be fighting the fog."

"So spend the night." Cool, eyes unreadable, he studied Kelsy.

Her heart slammed into her chest. Blushing, she licked her lips, caught herself, and swallowed. *Stop acting like a born again virgin, for cryin' out loud.*

"I'm sure the hotel has a room," he said.

Kelsy winced. Duuuh. And if they didn't, guess who'd offer his room?

"I'm sure you're right," she said, surprised fire didn't shoot out of her mouth because he hadn't heard a damned thing she'd said about Jason's schedule. "But my son's waiting."

Time sped up. Dane pushed away from the table and stepped behind Kelsy's chair in one fluid movement. "I'll send for your car."

Taking her cue, Kelsy said coolly, "White Lexus SUV, 2001."

He relayed the info to the maitre d', then glanced over his shoulder. He whispered, "Miz Snooty's still here. I'll walk on the inside. If she goes for me, run. Save yourself."

The twinkle in his eyes provided Kelsy with a second clue. He was joking. His attempt at letting her know he had no hard feelings about her leaving?

Whatever, she'd give him the benefit of the doubt. She jutted her chin, then whispered, "My hero."

"If you'd talk to me—about the case, the weather, yada, yada, instead of sitting over there mooning over Kelsy—"

"Don't go there, Olivia." Making eye contact, Finn stretched in the front seat of the '98 Beemer. Not the most comfortable car for a twelve-hour surveillance. "Nature calls," he announced, opening his door.

"Sure." Olivia, staring at the same scene they'd been staking out for six weeks, didn't turn her head. Maybe she expected some action.

Finn kept his hand on the door handle. In the Nimitz Park Apartments, the blue and white glow of a TV flickered in Apartment 301. Maybe the boosters, from Colombia and Ecuador, were learning English while they waited to feed their stolen goods into the black market. Finn pushed the door open.

Fingering one of the three gold earrings above her left eyebrow, Olivia said, "Thank God you oiled those damned hinges. It's a wonder our baddies don't hear us every time we take a break."

Pulse steady, Finn decided he'd take the change of subject as an apology. He got out, shut the door, then leaned in through the window. "Give me eight minutes—"

"Take ten and call her." Olivia waved elegant fingers stacked with five, six rings on each digit.

"You call me if there's any action." Neck muscles tight, Finn sauntered toward the restrooms. At least Olivia hadn't asked him if he had his key. She was only a year older than him, but sometimes she treated him as if he couldn't zip his pants without instructions from her.

Undercover work did that to you. Made you get bossy and double-check every detail. Would he miss Olivia after he went back to Traffic?

The jury was still out on that one.

Straining to hear anything—mosquitoes buzzing or Olivia going *mano a mano* with the perps—Finn worked the key into the heavy lock on the restroom door. Citizens of Cielo Vista demanded that municipal parks close at sundown. As a cop, Finn thought the curfew made policing a helluva lot easier. Having a key to the john made this undercover assignment tolerable.

Finished with his business, he dried his hands, then squinted at his glow-in-the-dark watch. An adrenaline zap went straight to the brain. He had plenty of time. Call Kelsy. Tell her how much he'd loved their fuckathon this morning. Tease her with Matthews' pronouncement. Make her beg. Riiight. Kelsy begging?

Not the independent, outspoken, passionate babe he knew and loved. And he only needed one minute. One. Exhaling, he stepped outside before he weakened.

Two steps, and he pivoted, retraced his steps and jammed the key into the lock. Dammit. This was Olivia's fault. Telling him to call Kelsy was like Eve telling Adam to take one bite of the apple. Now he couldn't think of anything else.

Exactly the kind of cop you wanted on a stakeout.

Disgusted, Finn narrowed his eyes and studied the park, the apartments overlooking the lagoon, the Beemer behind the bushes. He snorted. What'd he expect? Olivia out in the street, clapping on the cuffs?

" 'Lo?" On the fourth ring of the phone.

"Damn, Risa! I woke you up. Sorry."

While he mentally kicked his ass, she mumbled something that ended in ". . . problem."

Okay, she didn't sound ticked. He said, "Even though I'm an idiot, can I speak to Kelsy?"

"She's not . . ." A yawn. "Not . . . here." Another yawn.

"At 10:54?" Finn didn't panic, but his heart missed a beat. "I thought you two were going out to dinner."

"Not sure where she is," Risa continued, talking over him. "I worked late. Till nine. Kelsy left a message at the office."

"Saying—" he prompted, reining in his impatience.

"Oh . . ." A pause that dragged on a decade. "Not much."

In his mind's eye, Finn saw Risa, her carrot-red hair flying in all directions in the guest bed of the house she rented to Kelsy. After a heartbeat, Risa said, "Her message said she was going to be late, and . . . I shouldn't wait up."

"Any chance she's there and didn't hear the phone?" Finn asked neutrally. He didn't want to scare himself or Risa.

"Possible. It's a big house."

"Yes, it is." The master bedroom, as he knew from many memorable visits to Kelsy, was at the opposite end of the hall from where Risa slept on her weekly trips to her pediatric practice in Silicon Valley.

As if speaking to one of her four-year-old patients, Risa said, "We know how Kelsy sleeps. She falls through a hole into another galaxy once she goes down."

"Tell me about it. I know she was kinda frazzled at work today."

Muffled noises rang in Finn's ears. Risa must've switched the phone from one ear to the other. Maybe gotten out of bed. "Hold on. This room doesn't have a portable phone. I'll go check."

"Thanks, but don't wake her if she's asleep, okay?"

"Thank you for that small mercy. Getting Kelsy up's harder than getting a teenager up for school."

Even so .... Inwardly, Finn groaned, feeling stupid and brain dead. All this fuss and he still wouldn't get to talk to Kelsy.

Not her fault she was a woman who believed no day should begin before nine. Yet, she managed to roll out of bed at 3:30 every morning and arrive at the TV studio looking gorgeous and alert. God, how was he so lucky that this woman wanted to have his kids?

Risa was gone so long that Finn stepped back to the door of the restroom and studied the Beemer. Still there. He doubted Olivia had moved a muscle since he'd left.

He glanced at his watch. In one minute, he'd exceed his eight-minute break. He never took more than eight minutes. Guilt nipped him. Dammit, Kelsy was worth breaking his stupid, self-imposed rules.

Edgy because Risa was taking so damned long, Finn did a couple of squats in place. Squats were part of his daily exercise routine at home, and he'd learned to do them anytime, anywhere. Great tension release, squats.

"I'm coming, Finn." Risa's throaty voice came from a long way off, and he realized she was trying to reassure him as she walked back to the phone.

Fumbling, then her voice clearly, "Sorry. The light and fan were on in the master bathroom, and I thought Kelsy was in there taking a bath. She wasn't, and she's not in her room." On a roll, Risa didn't pause. "I checked downstairs, too. That's what took so long. I should've picked up the extension down there, but my brain's not firing on all cylinders."

"You're doing fine. It's my brain that's not firing on all cylinders," he said. "Go back to sleep." Poor woman. With ten-month-old triplets, did she ever sleep?

Probably when she came back to her thriving Silicon

Valley pediatric practice two nights a week and jerks didn't call her at eleven o'clock.

By way of reassurance for them both, he said, "I'm sure there's no problem or Kelsy would've called."

"Yes, she would have." Risa used the soothing tone he'd heard her use with Molly and Jason. Five-year-olds, they often needed soothing.

"Okay. We agree." Semi-soothed, he said, "No need for worry. You go back to sleep, and I'll go back to watching the grass grow."

Risa laughed, and for some reason, Finn felt better even though his anxiety hadn't evaporated.

"Want me to leave a note, ask her to call you?"

"No," he said. "I work till five, then my partner and I are going for breakfast—if we can find enough tooth-picks to pry our eyes open. I'll catch up with her tomor-row for sure."

For sure if he and Olivia didn't report in early. Both the day shift guys were expecting babies any day so he and Olivia tried to give them a couple of extra hours with their wives.

"Sometimes I think if we all got more sleep, we'd find a solution for world peace in a matter of days," Risa said.

Finn chuckled. "A good discussion topic someday. Maybe when I come to Montana this weekend we—"

"You're coming with Kelsy? No wonder we can't find her! She's probably floating over the moon about now."

Definitely soothed, Finn said good night, checking the sky on his way back to the Beemer.

Dane towered over the kid who brought Kelsy's Lexus around. Jasmine and salt perfumed the night air. Hundreds of bee lights turned the deserted portico into an island. Wound a little tight, Kelsy watched Dane palm a folded bill into the valet's hand.

"I'll help the lady," Dane said, reviving Kelsy's image of a Viking chieftain.

"Yessir!" The kid all but bowed before he trotted inside.

"Thanks." Not sure she wanted help, Kelsy didn't pull her elbow away. Some of the pavers in the driveway looked downright treacherous.

"You're sure you're okay to drive?" Dane blocked her door.

In no mood for chit-chat, she said, "Totally sure."

"Doesn't that skirt present a challenge—climbing into the front seat?"

"Not at all." Her heart banged into her skull and brought a moment of clarity. Thong. Careful. Or he'd catch a peek.

"Call me when you get home." He kept his eyes, shiny and hot, on the slit in her skirt.

Her hands shook as she gathered the two pieces of the slit together. Could she leap into the front seat in her Manolos? "It'll be late. At least twelve-thirty."

"All the more reason—"

"No!" She straightened with a jerk, letting the slit fall away and revealing miles of leg. "Don't think so," she said, dizzy from her sudden movement.

All concern, he said, "You don't sound too sure."

"I am." Her head felt like a top spinning out of control. "I'll drive with all the windows wide open. I'm a big girl. I'll be fine."

"You are fine. Very fine." He moved closer. So close, she smelled the shiraz on his breath.

If he was so worried about her driving, why was he keeping her there?

Why, indeed, Berkeley grad?

Pasting on her happy face, Kelsy stuck out her hand. "Thank you for a wonderful evening. I look forward to hearing from you soon."

"Soon," he repeated, with a kind of tomcat purr.

Then he grabbed her elbows and bussed her right
cheek.

Eeeuuk. Kelsy jumped back, and he nipped the tip of
her right ear. It stung, but she didn't touch it. "Am I
bleeding?"

"Of course you're not bleeding."

A murderous expression flitted across his marble face.
God, he looked like a wasted vampire. Kelsy laughed,
then punched him in the shoulder. "Okay, okay. I'll call
you. I promise."

Too damn bad if he expected a smile. Mouth running at warp speed, she apologized profusely for her reaction. "I work out, you know. Tai chi. I could've really
hurt you."

"Kelsy, Kelsy. I'm a big, strong guy. You didn't hurt
me." Despite his protests, he practically shoved her into
the SUV.

Mercifully, she kept her insane worry about a hernia
to herself.

Certain she'd blown all possibilities for the job, she
told herself she didn't care. He shut her door. She
goosed the Lexus. The SUV shot forward with tires
squealing.

No problem, the drive's perfectly straight. Shaking, she
slowed down anyway, then stopped before she turned
onto the road that led to Highway 1. She should not be
behind the wheel. But she was. With no other options
and no way home.

Okay, if she wasn't smashed, why was she weirding
out?

It was a buss on the cheek. Not his tongue down her
throat. People in the TV industry gave air kisses and
cheek busses every day. Brad would if he dared.

All right, she'd had too much to drink. His move had
surprised her. Still embarrassed by her condom confession, she'd felt self-conscious, awkward, unsure.

She'd felt the same way the first time she'd let Rob Parker put his hand up her dress.

Don't forget excited.

She made a face. Rob had been her first teen-age crush.

Dane was a semi-stranger. Maybe her soon-to-be boss.

Her heart beat high in her chest, making it hard to breathe. Should she share all the details with Finn?

Absolutely. On the day she appeared buck-naked on *Oprah*.

Chapter 5

"What's wrong?" Olivia asked as soon as Finn opened the damn car door.

"Nothing." He slumped down in his seat till only his shoulders and head touched the leather upholstery. He pulled the bill on the baseball cap around and over his eyes. Hint, hint.

"Don't tell me you two lovebirds had a fight." Olivia tapped the steering wheel.

The woman probably wouldn't know a hint if it bit her in the ass. Finn went for direct. "Don't tell me I asked you to butt into my personal life." *Kelsy's fine. Probably home by now.*

"What'd you fight about?" Olivia sounded happier than Finn had ever heard her. "Money?"

"Money?" He thumbed the bill of the cap up enough to stare at her. "You ever thought about donating your brain to science? I bet—"

Talking over him, she said, "After two divorces, I know a lot about fights over money."

"Money's not a problem for me and Kelsy." Finn jerked the cap back over his eyes. Olivia could bring the pope to his knees. "You, on the other hand, are a pain in the ass. Jesus!"

Despite a cool breeze drifting into the Beemer, Olivia fanned her face with her hand. "You and I must make about the same salary—"

"Will you give it a rest?" A rest might mean he'd really start worrying about Kelsy, but Olivia shot the rest idea to hell by saying, "My paycheck always runs out two days before the end of the month. Does yours? If not, why not?"

"I live with my mother." Disgusted he'd caved, Finn clamped his jaw shut. From under the cap, he watched her finger a diamond ring smaller than the tip of his shoelaces.

"Both my exes thought if I worked, I should earn more money. That's why I'm in law school. Someday, sooner than later, I'm gonna be one hell of a DA."

"Not me." Finn shook his head, having no doubts about Olivia. "The more I think about it, the more I think I may bag law school."

"Get out of town! Are you insane? You're in the law school league of legends."

He slapped a hand over her mouth, surprised when she didn't bite through to bone. "Stop. Screaming. You want the neighbors to call the cops and blow our cover?"

Her eyes were bulging so he took his hand away, and she started right up, never missing a beat, still loud enough to raise the dead. "Every prof I've ever had holds you up like you're a revered teacher and they're total dummies."

Finn's ears rang. "That's a crock."

She jutted her chin at him. "How do you know what they say about you when you're not in the class?"

"Santa Clara's a small school." Dumb answer, but he didn't know what to say.

"So what? Seven months from finishing, why quit? I know the profs bent over backwards to accommodate this undercover sting for you."

"And you know this how?" Was there anything she didn't know about him?

"They did the same for me. Quitting law school can't be Kelsy's idea." She didn't even bother trying to hide her contempt.

Pissed, Finn said coolly, "Kelsy and I support each other in our careers. She knows there's more to life than bringing down the big bucks."

"Uh-huh. But does she actually know how few little bucks you bring down? She wears Manolo Blahniks, for God's sake." Olivia straightened the collar on her blouse.

"What the hell are Manolo Blah-Blah's?" He didn't give her a heartbeat to reply. "Unless they're illegal, I don't care what she wears."

"They're shoes. And just wait till you see the bill. The plain ones cost about two hundred and fifty bucks."

"A pair?" Finn croaked. "Two hundred-fifty—"

"Apiece." Smug—a DA crushing the prosecution's strongest witness.

"You mean five—" His mind froze.

"Bingo!" Olivia wiggled five fingers. "Do the math. Five hundred bucks. Five big ones, fifty small ones. That won't include back surgery when she hits forty."

Wary of any discussion about age, Finn blinked. Was Olivia playin' with his head?

Her smile had him speared like a fresh tuna. "Five hundred bucks," she repeated, then gave him a bigger smile.

Her smile didn't mean a damned thing. Not with Olivia, who could lie with the straightest face he'd ever seen.

She patted his arm. "See why you better finish law school?"

The slow, careful rhythm of her speech hit him between the eyes. People talked to kids or adults with low IQs the same way. God knew, he wouldn't go up against a one-celled organism right at that moment. Why didn't he know Kelsy wore shoes that cost almost what he paid every three months for insurance on the 'Vette?

Olivia snapped her fingers under his nose. "Helll-oo?"

"Stop that." He brushed her hand away, tempted to swat it.

"Testy, testy." Olivia gave him a look of pure pity.

"Wrong. I'm bored. With this conversation. With this damned stakeout." Had Kelsy ever worn those shoes with him?

Since he usually tore her clothes off as soon as they were alone, would he have noticed? Five-hundred-dollar shoes ought to glow and sparkle like Cinderella's glass slipper.

Out of left field, he said, "I want a job that makes a difference. Lawyers don't, cops do."

Olivia sighed and threw her hands up. "Heard any lawyer jokes lately? Jokes help pass the time."

Finn shrugged. He never remembered punch lines. That was Kelsy's talent. And Olivia's. Ignoring his silence, she threw out one lawyer joke after another. Occasionally, he laughed.

Olivia loved the sound of her own voice. No problem. As long as she wasn't yakking about Kelsy or his life, he could go through the motions and still think.

Someday, on their six-month wedding anniversary maybe, he'd ask Kelsy to come to bed naked except for the shoes . . . whatever the hell they were called. He knew there were guys out there who got hard as cement stakes at the mention of shoes.

For all Finn knew, a five-hundred-dollar pair of shoes might do the same for him.

* * *

Kelsy massaged her pounding head and sat through four green lights at Fairway Lane before she pulled onto Highway 1 at 11:15. Caffeine. She needed caffeine before she hit 92. God, Finn would kill her. *Never drink and drive.*

"Hindsight is such an exact science," she mumbled, checking the rearview mirror. One set of headlights. Good. Late at night. No fog. One car . . . some wine . . . no problem.

Except her head felt woozy. Champagne-woozy. Even the good—very good—stuff always gave her a headache. Not to mention the shiraz.

Had Dane expensed the whole evening? She considered it a professional meeting. Right up until his unprofessional goodbye. She'd swear he'd had even more to drink than her. She buzzed both back windows down to the max. Dammit. This was his fault. He'd plied her with booze, teased her with a job, and then—

"Didn't get laid," she finished. Her heart missed a beat, but after a second miss, returned to normal.

Nothing happened, Finn, I swear. She cranked up the A/C.

In the distance, lights from a convenience store glowed on her right. Easy exit. She slowed. Coffee and a pee-break . . . that should revive her. Alert, she had to be fully alert for Highway 92. Even in broad daylight, it was a killer highway.

A pickup, crumpled into accordion folds, flashed in her mind. She'd covered the accident last week. The driver had escaped, but no one knew how.

Finn would kill her if she had an accident.

What a cheery thought. She turned in to the convenience store parking lot. Riding the brake, she eased into a spot in front of the plate-glass window. As she cut the ignition, a car pulled in next to her on the left.

"Hey! Dummy." She checked out the five empty slots

on her right. Didn't you have to have the brains of a goose to get a driver's license in California?

Apparently not. Jerkoff had made it almost impossible for her to get out without banging her door.

"Miz Chandler?"

She screamed, clutched her chest, and felt her stomach drop like a 747. She saw herself: stringy-haired, no lipstick, hollow-eyed, in an orange jumpsuit with *San Mateo County Jail* stenciled over the right pocket.

"Miz Kelsy Chandler?" In the blaze of gas station lights, a blond, baby-faced, Half Moon Bay cop stood a few feet from the passenger window. He held a PDA in front of his chest.

"Busted," she whispered. Damn technology. Cops and their damn traffic databases. Something loose cannoned around inside her head. Her brain?

On with the happy face. "I'm sorry, officer. Is there a problem?"

Never open with an apology or ask if there's a problem. Finn's advice clanged like a gong in Kelsy's mind.

"Yes, ma'am. You sat through four green lights back at Fairway."

"I see." What could she say? That fending off a stranger's come-on had shaken her up? She wet her lips. Her stomach did not like eau de gasoline.

Certain her face would crack, she blasted the cop with her biggest smile. Big mistake. The slit in the Valentino had turned on her, exposing thigh up to her waist.

Never come on to a cop if you get stopped.

"I-I think I'm going to yark," she whispered, her face on fire, her hands freezing.

Instantly, Baby Face leaped further away from the window.

Kelsy squeezed her eyes closed, gripped the wheel, and concentrated on not passing out. The Lexus rocked back and forth. The taste of salt flooded the back of her throat. She snapped open her eyes. No more rock 'n rolling. Inside the convenience store, a couple of night geeks, scenting excitement, peered out, their faces framed by hands the size of suitcases.

What if one of them recognized her? *Please God, do not let me upchuck in front of them.*

Someday, everyone would recognize her. But tonight, she wanted to get home without losing her last shred of dignity.

A scarier thought punched her right in the diaphragm. What if Finn dumped her?

A small, involuntary noise escaped her throat. Almost at the same second, Baby Face pulled open her door. She tumbled out. Wedged in the crack of space between his hulk and her open door, she shimmied past her worst nightmare to the back of the vehicles.

A stinking mixture of champagne-laced shiraz, port, and coffee spewed from her nose, spraying the tips of her already ruined shoes. Baby Face jumped back; she groaned. After a decade or so, she stopped puking. Her nose and throat burned, but not half as much as her blistering pride.

Beyond the line of fire, Baby Face extended a bottle of cool water and a pile of paper napkins. "Looks like you drank a little too much, Miz Chandler."

No, she'd drunk a lot too much. Rinsing her mouth, Kelsy didn't quibble. Her throat closed. She whispered, "Are you issuing me a ticket?"

"That's about it."

"God, you're not hauling me off to county jail?" Tears stung her eyes. What if the story made the morning news? Would she lose her job? Would Finn dump her?

"You missed a spot on your shoes," Baby Face pointed out in the middle of her small breakdown.

Determined to grasp at any straw, she said, "Can you arrest me if there's nothing left in my stomach?"

"Yeah, sure can."

The radio in his car crackled. From a long way off, Kelsy heard "accident." Baby Face leaned into the window, adjusted the volume, then switched over to his headset. *BA-bum. BA-bum.* Didn't her galloping heart interfere with transmission?

God, Finn was going to die of embarrassment.

Regret shook her, sobered her. Her headache didn't evaporate, but she could feel the wheels of thought start to turn. "Okay," she said, standing on one foot. "Let's do an FSE." Field Sobriety Exam. Finn talked about them all the time. Pass it and she'd be home free. "FSE," she repeated. "Bring it on."

Baby Face wagged his finger at her, listened some more, nodded. Kelsy wagged back, pointing to her perfect posture.

An eternity later, he clicked off his headset, narrowed his eyes at her, still on one leg like a lost stork, then said, "An FSE's an option, but here's another alternative."

Long story short—during which Kelsy's pulse climbed to two hundred, higher than any pulse rate she'd ever registered in any aerobics step class—he followed her to a nearby bed-and-breakfast. Twenty minutes before midnight, registered and exhausted, she thanked Officer Tony Miller profusely.

He said, a little crisply, "Thank me by staying here at least two, three hours. Get some sleep before you take off." He cleared his throat, "I'm alerting CHP. If we see you out there, and you deviate a hair from an absolute straight line, you will go to jail."

Her heart jammed her throat. He was already at the front door, but she nodded her understanding. He stayed in the hall while she slipped into her room and kicked off her ruined shoes in the dark. The smell of her own puke overpowered the smell of rose potpourri. She groaned softly, working her toes up and down, imagining Finn administering one of his exquisite foot rubs.

Before or after he wrings your neck?

The reek of regurgitated booze turned her stomach. She dropped onto the bed. What a mess. All because she'd gotten bored being alone night after night. With too much time on her hands, she'd begun to rethink her whole life. She stared into the dark and came to the same conclusion she had weeks ago.

Like Risa, she wanted it all: marriage (to Finn, of course), family (she had Jason, the light of her life, but she was iffy on the two other kids Finn wanted), and career (anywhere besides KSJC).

So, which did she tell Finn first? Her doubts about more kids or the interview with Dane? And when did she slip in an oh-by-the-way announcement about her close encounter with Baby Face?

"Auuuugggh!" She rolled over and nearly fell out of bed.

No wonder. Her teeth and tongue tasted like road kill.

"Ohhh, God!" She sat up, but waited till the room stopped spinning. No matter what Baby Face said, she had to get out of here. She'd never make it to work if she fell asleep for a couple of hours. Worse, she'd never be able to cry enough tears, make enough promises, or call in enough favors for Risa to cover for her dragging home just before sun-up.

Say you got bitten by a vampire and spent the whole night club hopping. Say the pope granted you an exclusive interview. Say— She swallowed convulsively. Was she still drunk?

As proof she wasn't, she hauled herself to her feet. After a moment of swaying, she marched boldly to the lace-curtained window. One peek was all she needed.

"Thank you, God!" She dropped the curtain. Too excited to bother with a light, she raced for the bed.

The crack of bone against solid wood sent her mind

into a downward spiral. Stars twinkled in the dark room. Neon-blue pain raced up her leg and slammed into the top of her head.

"Owwww!" she doubled over. Her big toe felt as if she'd dipped it in scalding cement.

Remember, she thought between gasps, women got off the Titanic. She'd for sure survive a sprained toe.

Around midnight, the TV still flickered against the curtain in Apartment 301. Finn couldn't take one more of Olivia's lawyer jokes. He suggested she catch a nap. Five more hours of death by boredom stretched ahead of them.

Olivia said, "No way I'll ever sleep. But you go ahead. You need sleep more than I do."

"What the hell does that mean?" Finn snapped.

"It means getting laid—"

"You don't know anything about me getting laid," he growled.

In the light from the dash, he saw her eyes flash. She said tightly, "You do think I'm an idiot."

"Close. If I so much as breathed a suggestion you'd gotten laid, you'd have me up on sexual harassment."

"Jesus!" Olivia smacked the steering wheel. "You'd think we're married the way we bitch at each other."

"Believe me, I wouldn't think we're married."

"Gee, thanks." She didn't give him a chance to apologize but rushed on, "So, did Matthews give you time off or not?"

"I can't—"

"That means he did. If he'd turned you down, you either would've walked or you'd be mad as a bull."

"Draw your own conclusions, Olivia."

"Does Kelsy have a clue what a lucky babe she is?"

Accustomed to Olivia's mind jumps, Finn sighed. "Yes, I believe she does. And I have lots of clues what a lucky guy I am. End of subject." Finn massaged his chest. If he didn't talk about Kelsy, he wouldn't worry about her for the next five hours.

Leather squished as Olivia turned to face him, her face green in the dash light. "Are we still on for breakfast this morning?"

"Sure. If you're okay with Kelsy joining us."

"Dammit, Bishop!" For a second, Finn thought she was going to hit him. Instead, she pounded the steering wheel again. "It's not okay. I want to talk to you. I have my own problems. I don't give a damn that most Americans get their news from TV. Who the hell watches TV news anyway at five in the morning?"

Her fury hit him right between the eyes. Jesus, she sounded like she hated Kelsy. Making an effort not to jump to any conclusions, he said, "I think Kelsy only accepted because I asked her to come. If it's so important to you, I'll cancel—"

"It is so important to me." Each word fired out of her mouth like bullets.

It occurred to him to ask why. Get into it with her right now. But they'd agreed from the beginning to discuss personal problems after their tour of duty ended. Olivia might forget their agreement, but Finn would not.

Without sighing, he said, "All right, all right. I'll call Kelsy in the morning. Before she leaves for work. I imagine she'll actually be relieved."

"I have no doubt." Olivia slugged water from her water bottle. She stared at Apartment 301, then said, "If you're not going to sleep, what're the chances you can stop thinking about Kelsy for two seconds?"

Finn shot back, "What are the chances you can hold off your next mood swing for two seconds?"

To his surprise, she laughed. "I know guys have feelings too. But like . . . who cares?"

All stressed out and no one to choke, Finn thought, then shrugged. "Spit it out, Olivia."

Head back, she looked down her nose at him, waited a beat, then said, "I love this kind of give and take, Bishop. I don't know what's going on with you and Kelsy—"

"Please don't make me kill you," he said, chest tight.

"Okay." Olivia shrugged. "This case is bumming everyone. Matthews wants action in the worst way. You and I could be heroes if we put our heads together."

"Sounds interesting." About as interesting as an old tennis shoe, but Finn wasn't up to another verbal battle with Olivia.

"You're game?" Sounding suspicious, she stared out the windshield.

"I'm game." For two more days, why not? As long as Olivia didn't mean literally put their heads together.

Kelsy was, he reminded himself, a strong, capable, independent woman. If anything had happened to her, he'd know it by now. She'd listed him as her contact in case of an emergency.

There is no emergency.

He ignored the fire in his gut. "Here's an idea."

Chapter 6

The ugly stepsisters must've been nuts.

For Kelsy, no way she was slipping into her right Manolo. Not even for a prince.

Fresh air. Fresh air would revive her. All she had to do was float from her room, through the hall, and out onto the spacious front lawn.

"No whining." She bit down on her bottom lip. Think of the Donner party. They had survived. There was a peppy thought.

Bag and shoes presented a problem of balance as she alternated between hops and lurches forward. She paused to catch her breath. Sweat dripped down her sides and pooled between her boobs. Realizing the knock-off Valentino was probably ruined made it easier to toss the Manolos on the bed. Barring a miracle, her toe, now as big as a stretch limo, would never fit into anything but high-top sneakers after tonight.

There is a God, she thought, as she crept onto the front porch. Not because of the star-filled sky. Or the peaceful, predawn hush. But because the innkeeper had slept through Kelsey's lumbering trek across the living room.

More uplifting, Baby Face wasn't parked outside.

Air whooshed out of her lungs. *Finn still loves you.*

Momentarily fueled by a spurt of optimism, she stepped down on her right foot. A white flash of pain destroyed fantasies that she'd someday regale Finn with her small adventure.

She whimpered. God, if Baby Face came back. . . . If he was anything like Finn, he'd toss her butt in jail, then throw away the key.

Call Risa. . . . Brilliant idea, but she'd left her phone in the Lexus.

Drenched in sweat, she refused to check her watch as she shuffled toward the Lexus parked only a hop, skip, and a jump away at the curb. Shuffling and shambling took longer. As in forever. When she finally beeped her key and opened the door, she felt like screaming, *Mission Control, we have a problem.*

Pain was not her thing. Climbing into the SUV could rank up there with giving birth to Jason.

She almost laughed at her own melodrama, but her toe didn't appreciate levity. Her toe felt like a lighted stick of dynamite.

Call a cab.

Surprise, surprise, a logical idea. Doable, too. By holding onto the door, keeping her right foot off the ground, she could just stretch far enough to reach the cell phone. As her fingers closed around the phone, she felt it vibrate. Who said coincidences happened only in bad fiction?

"Finn!" She wasted two seconds staring at the LED before she actually saw the number.

"Dammit!" She punched the on button. "Let me guess," she said, snippy as hell. "Could this be Dane Jensen, calling to see if I'm still alive?"

There was just one blip of silence, then he said, "No, this is Dane Jensen calling to say good night. Why wouldn't you be alive?"

"Maybe a ghost kidnapped me," she blithered. "I worried about vampires, but the alcohol in my blood—"

"Did the local gendarmes pull you over?"

"Not exactly." Her right foot felt like a chunk of ice. "I—I've had an accident."

"Where are you?" He sounded concerned. Didn't he?

She told him, briefly, because her foot hurt too damn much for more than sound bites. He vetoed the idea of a cab. "The Ritz has a limo. At this time of night, I won't have to wait."

Some of his confidence seeped into Kelsy. Her toe didn't miraculously shrink back to normal size, but at least she could stop worrying about gangrene. What to tell Finn now leapfrogged to the top of her Worry List.

Forty-five minutes later, the ER doctor assured her gangrene wouldn't set in as long as she used common sense. She didn't point out her common sense had dried up. Otherwise, why'd she walk around in a strange place in the dark?

Too dumb to live?

Eyes hooded, face unreadable, Dane stayed right next to her. Kelsy tried to pretend he was Finn, but quickly gave it up.

When it came to TLC, Finn was in a class by himself. Last year, when she'd had the flu and was stressed out to the max because of the divorce, their age difference, and his insistence he wanted to marry her, Finn had persuaded her to let his mother take care of her.

What a stroke of genius. Despite the bad-as-they-get experiences she'd endured with her own mother and mother-in-law, she and Maeve Bishop had bonded like cement.

The doctor gave her a shot, and she floated on a

cloud of hazy flu memories while he cleaned and wrapped her toe. Last, he fitted her with an ugly blue, toeless, soft boot.

"My gosh, where have Velcro straps been my whole life?" She extended her foot, then winced from the effort.

Vicodin, she was assured, should help manage the pain. "See your regular doc tomorrow or Thursday at the latest."

When Kelsy said she didn't have any questions—a lie, but so what?—the ER doctor gave her and Dane a jaunty two-fingered salute. *He thinks we're married.* So did the orderly who chatted to them as she pushed Kelsy's wheelchair to the waiting limo.

Mister Efficiency, Dane told the driver to take them to the hotel, but she said, "No, to the Lunada."

"You can't drive home, Dane protested, sitting next to her—not too close, though—Kelsy noticed.

She blinked, trying to focus. "The doctor didn't say I couldn't drive."

"No, and he didn't say you couldn't ice skate, either." Dane raised one of his exquisite blond brows. "I've already checked with The Ritz—"

"My news show begins at five." Kelsy tapped the glass, nodding at the kid behind the wheel.

"I'll call Brad Hall for you. He and I go way back."

Kelsy jutted her chin. "I can't call him three hours before air time."

Dane cocked his head and looked at her as if he was seeing her for the first time. She propped her foot on the opposite seat, laid her head back, and sighed. The hot pins and needles shooting up her leg became bearable.

Cutting through the awkwardness, Dane said, "Let me see if I can get someone at the hotel to drive you home, then."

"That would be wonderful—but I'm not really your problem."

"Problem? Who said anything about problem? I believe in taking care of my people. Ask anyone."

In the end, they both got their way. Through a series of complex negotiations with The Ritz, negotiations Kelsy couldn't follow, Dane would return the limo. The driver would schlep her over the mountain in her Lexus. Somehow, he'd get back to Half Moon Bay. Buckled into the passenger's seat, Kelsy didn't give a damn about such details.

Dane moved closer to her window. *He's going to try something sneaky.* Groggy from her mind candy, tired, and in no mood for a witness to Dane's sneak attack, she inched closer to the driver.

Dane didn't take the hint, and short of Kelsy rolling up the window, she figured he probably wouldn't. He leaned inside. "Sorry to give you more bad news, but you've got a scrape on your right front bumper I don't remember."

"Finn called," Risa said before Kelsy even had the kitchen-garage door closed. It was 2:37, and the taxi had just taken off to return the limo driver to Half Moon Bay.

"What're you doing up?" Kelsy stalled. The ache around her heart hurt more than the one in her toe.

"What happened to your toe?" Risa opened the fridge and pulled out coffee beans.

"Did you tell him I was asleep?"

"Are you insane?" Risa slammed the beans on the counter.

"How'd he sound?" Kelsy inched toward the downstairs bath.

"How do you think he sounded?" Risa pressed the on

switch, and the noise from the coffee grinder sent a flash of blue pain up Kelsy's right leg.

"Are you going to work?" Risa sounded pissed, and Kelsy felt a nervous flutter in her stomach. She said, "Why wouldn't I go to work?"

"Because you can't walk? Because you look like road kill? Because you—"

"Okay, okay." Kelsy felt the sting of tears as Risa's voice dropped lower and lower. "I'm sorry I scared you. I should've called. I—I thought about it once . . . then time just got away from me."

A plus-size woman, Risa whirled around with amazing speed. Scroungey purple robe flapping, she jogged across the kitchen and threw her arms around Kelsy's neck. "I am so mad at you I could strangle you."

Sniffling, Kelsy said, "Can you wait till I get home from work?"

"No, and what about Finn? Shouldn't you call him?"

Kelsy shook her throbbing head. "Only if it's an emergency. Those are the rules, and Finn respects them totally." She sucked in a deep breath, then said, "Besides, what would I tell him?"

A while later, after some argument, Risa insisted on driving Kelsy to KSJC. Located in downtown San Jose, the station was the opposite direction from her Cielo Vista office and ten miles, round trip, out of her way. Risa, who'd given Kelsy and Jason a place to stay before, during, and ten months after the divorce, shot Kelsy a questioning look as they pulled onto I-280.

"I'm multi-talented, you know," Risa began. "I can drive and talk at the same time."

"This is probably one of those times when the less you know, the better off you are," Kelsy said, adding, "These blue ice bags are great. Thanks."

Finn will understand.

"Give me a break!" Risa slid into the commuter lane,

going five miles faster than the car to her right. She spoke slowly and crisply, "You have to stop squeezing my arm, Kel, I can't drive when it's numb. Just tell me, and you can relax."

"I wish I believed that." Kelsy released her death grip on Risa's upper arm.

Finn will understand.

She'd been clutching her best friend's flesh off and on since Risa had helped her dress, hobble out to the Volvo, and then settle into the passenger's seat. All the while, Risa fired question after question at Kelsy.

"I'm really tired, La Ti Da." Kelsy used Risa's nickname, hoping to push a few empathy buttons.

"Uh-huh. Dragging home at three in the morning makes most people tired."

Finn will understand.

"See!" Kelsy stared out her window at a stretch limo probably headed for SJC. "You already know too much. If Finn asks, it would be better if you just said I got home late."

"I imagine it would, and I imagine Finn, being a cop, would never try to pin down *late*."

Yawning, Kelsy wasted a few more seconds stonewalling, hoping to get her pulse down to a gallop. Risa drove in silence before saying, "I won't be home tonight, so this is the only time we can go over what happened."

So, throat dry, hands clammy, Kelsy told her. In a rush. Beginning with the job interview but jumping all over the place, trying to sidestep her first good-bye with Dane. The barf episode she related in one sentence. "I was so scared, I upchucked my toenails."

Finn will understand.

Risa, adored by the parents of her patients because she listened more closely than God, didn't interrupt once. Finished, Kelsy said, "That's it. The end. Curtain's down on the soap opera. Finn will understand."

A slight bottleneck at Guadalupe Expressway required Risa's attention to driving, so she didn't say anything for about a mile. Instead of feeling reassured, Kelsy felt the ashes in her stomach ignite. Two cups of coffee—strong enough to revive the dead—had started to boil. *Of course, Finn will understand.*

Finally, about three miles from KSJC, Risa said, "I think you should tell him this morning. After breakfast. As soon as Olivia leaves. The two of you go someplace quiet. Someplace where you can't make love *before* telling him."

Figuring she should be embarrassed, Kelsy felt a flare of excitement. "Quiet places are open territory for making love."

Risa took a hand off the wheel. "Some details I don't need. I suppose I could let you use an exam room—"

Kelsy cleared her throat. Risa stopped. "Don't tell me—"

"Okay." Kelsy pressed her lips together, trying to repress a grin. "I'll just say this: Playing doctor is a lot more fun if you actually play in a doctor's office."

Risa's jaw almost hit the horn before she got control of herself. She shook her head, but her mouth twitched. "You two!"

Straight-faced, Kelsy hugged her waist. "I appreciate your pearls of wisdom, La Ti Da." *No doubt. Finn will understand.*

"If you don't laugh, you're going to explode."

"No, I won't. I'm a mature, level-headed—" Kelsy giggled, made the sign of the cross to deflect Risa's glare, then laughed. *Finn, Finn.*

Risa clenched her jaw and held out for about two seconds. Then, a deep, infectious laugh rumbled out of her. Shoulders shaking, Kelsy buried her face in her hands. Hooting, Risa eased up on the gas. They came to a stop. With a deep, relaxed sigh, Kelsy laid her hands in her lap.

As Risa pulled in front of the TV station, she said, "Maybe with your toe, making love becomes a moot point."

"Or a challenge. Most twenty-nine-year-old cops love a challenge."

"Yes." Risa sighed. "Not the least of why you love your twenty-nine-year-old cop, right?"

"Closer to the most important reason I love him." Kelsy couldn't help it, she grinned, and the ache around her heart definitely eased. "That's why he'll understand about Dane. Finn knows I don't have eyes for anyone but him."

"Exactly why you have to tell him, Kel." Risa cut the motor, met and held Kelsy's gaze. "Show him you won't jeopardize his trust."

"I know." Translation: Okay, okay, La Ti Da. You've made your point. I'm not an idiot. Back off.

Because Risa was Risa, she opened her mouth, and Kelsy felt her patience slip. She waited, and La Ti Da said, "I'll admit I'm not giving up on Harry, Tom, and Charlie being big brothers to a couple of kids. Yours and Finn's."

"I didn't say I absolutely don't want kids, La Ti Da."

"I know, Kel . . . and my fantasies don't have to mesh with yours at every single point in our lives. I'm sorry I pushed your guilt buttons. I'm surprised you didn't tell me to mind my own business."

Relief flooded Kelsy. "Thank you. And I know how ga-ga Finn is about having two more kids. I just hope . . . I know we'll work it out."

For a second, Kelsy thought Risa would fight her on the point, but then the second passed.

Five minutes later, aided by a cane Risa had unearthed, Kelsy leaned on her best bud's arm for the trip to KSJC's front door. "I appreciate your advice, La Ti Da."

"And I appreciate your pink bedroom slipper and blue boot with a charcoal, pinstriped Armani pants suit."

"I fully expect Finn will too." The *whap whap* of her footwear was driving Kelsy nuts. The confession to Risa, lack of sleep, and worry about Finn were taking their toll. She could barely put one foot in front of the other.

"Miz Chandler! What happened? Do you need help?" Nick, the white-haired guard at KSJC, rushed through the plate-glass door.

"Don't give her a football today, okay?" Risa grinned at Santa's clone, handed over Kelsy's bag, bussed her cheek, then left.

"What happened, Miz Chandler?"

Get used to that question, she thought, and dodged it by saying, "Nothing that will make the morning news, Nick."

Kelsy waited while he opened the door for her. Most mornings, she chatted with him when she signed in— between 4:11 and 4:20. This morning, to escape his pre-occupation with her feet, she hightailed it as fast as she could for the safety of the elevators. She'd get used to stares and questions, but not at 4:19 A.M.

Her stomach, still tender from her barfathon, dropped as the elevator climbed. She peered down at her feet. Suppose she swept into breakfast with Finn and Olivia and acted as if she'd shown up in Pradas or Manolos?

Olivia, of course, would open her mouth. Say something cute. Something veiled and nasty. Something that would sail right over Finn's head. And Kelsy would have to bite her tongue. Because her sweetie liked his part-ner. Thought it would be great if she and Kelsy were friends. "Like you and Risa," he'd said, so innocent that Kelsy wanted to cry.

"Risa and I've known each other thirty-four of our thirty-seven years, darlin'."

"I know. But I think Olivia looks at you as a role model."

"You think so?" As a role model for the last woman on earth Finn should marry, Kelsy had thought.

The elevator made a noise, and Kelsy returned to the present. Suppose—the elevator stalled? Or stopped completely? That would save her. No toe explanations necessary. No explanations about Dane. Better . . . what if the cables suddenly snapped?

Who would do the Morning News then?

Brad would drop a microphone down the shaft and expect you to give a riveting, over-the-top, eyewitness account.

Worried she'd teetered out on the cusp of melodrama again, Kelsy stared at her reflection in the mirrored walls and groaned. Damn, damn, damn. She touched one cheek, then the other. At Risa's, she'd all but laid on makeup with a trowel.

The elevator doors opened, and she escaped into the hall.

It's not like I'll stop clocks or scare dogs, she thought as she hobbled toward the set. After a night in hell, no amount of foundation could enhance her cheeks with the blush of roses. There simply wasn't a big enough bottle of concealer to cover the bags under her eyes.

What would you expect on road kill—eyes like sapphires?

No, but Finn would notice, maybe wonder: *Will she look older than Ma before we even tie the knot?*

When, after two, three heartbeats, she couldn't make the thought go away, she had another thought: Wait till tomorrow, then tell Finn everything. On the plane ride to Montana. Perfect, because at thirty thousand feet in the air, Risa would give them all the privacy they needed.

She smiled at her brilliance. The plan was beyond perfect, she decided, because Finn couldn't get pissed and stalk out before he forgave her.

Chapter 7

"Why are you answering your phone?" Finn almost dropped his cell when, at 4:40, Kelsy picked up on the first ring. "This time of the morning, I expected your voice mail."

"Are you okay?" Kelsy whispered.

"Fine, fine. Sorry if I scared you, babe." With Olivia at the wheel, taking in every syllable, Finn tried not to sound like a pussy-whipped fool apologizing, but he felt bad for scaring Kelsy.

"I-I wasn't expecting you. I thought you worked till five."

"We do. We got a break today. How about you? Everything okay with you? Isn't it time for you to be on the set?"

"Um, I have a few minutes before air time. Just checking my makeup. Where are you?"

"On the way to the station. Olivia and I are picking up our cars. That way, after breakfast, we can go straight home." Any other time, he'd have made a crack about going home to dream about Kelsy. Or, he'd invite her home with him.

"Shiiit!" Throwing her arm out in front of him,

Olivia slammed on the brakes at Main and California. Their headlights picked up a black cat streaking across the deserted intersection.

"Sorry," Olivia muttered.

Finn sucked in air between his teeth, swallowed, and eased back into his seat. Mr. Cool, he said to Kelsy, "A little excitement. We just had a close encounter with a cat. It couldn't tell a red light from green. Thanks, to Olivia, we're none the worse for wear."

Instantly, oxygen evaporated in the car. "Shut up!" Olivia hissed.

His gut clenched, but Finn reined in his temper. Give her a minute. Some space. Lots of people lost their cool after a close call. He shrugged, signaling no bad feelings on his side.

"Who's driving?" Kelsy asked.

"Oliv—" He heard a sharp intake of air, sharper than a hiss. He glanced at Olivia's livid face, a spooky green from the dash light. What the hell was wrong with her the last couple of days? She was pissed at him for sure, but what else was going on with her?

Watching her out of the corner of his eye, he said to Kelsy, "Oh, Love of My Life, how'd you like a pass on breakfast this morning with me and Olivia?"

He sorta stuttered on 'Olivia'. Would she hiss, howl or run the squad car up the nearest tree? His mind shied away from more speculation because Kelsy sighed in his ear.

"Surely that's relief I hear and not regret?" He teased.

"Guess you'll never know now." Soft, breathy.

"Oh, I wouldn't say *never*. I have my ways—"

"You mean handcuffs?"

"You, me, and—"

"Is Olivia listening?"

"Yep." His ears stung. Jesus, he became a blithering idiot around Kelsy.

"Shut uuup," she chanted. "Hold that thought, and we'll pick it up tomorrow. In our own private jet—with only Risa."

Then, before he was ready, she hung up. He listened to the dial tone for a few seconds. Before Olivia figured out he'd lost his mind, he snapped the phone shut.

"Wanna tell me what that was all about? Why I couldn't mention your name?" he drawled, determined to give her a chance to explain.

"Is Kelsy coming to breakfast?"

"No." Mentally, he counted to ten. "Now, what's up?"

"We're almost at the station. We can talk at breakfast."

We can talk at breakfast, Finn said in his mind, mocking Olivia's bossy tone. Jesus, he'd be lucky if his eggs didn't curdle in his stomach.

"Thank you, thank you, thank you for the invention of cell phones." In the restroom at KSJC, Kelsy fastened her gaze on the ceiling and pinched the inside of her arm. She felt like dancing. Instead, she hurried back to the set. Amazing how one phone call could change your life.

Her producer pointed at her feet and mouthed, *"What happened?"*

"Later," Kelsy whispered, then carefully eased into her chair behind the high desk. Thank God, she didn't have to move for a full fifty-nine minutes. Life had never looked brighter.

Fifty-nine minutes later, she signed off. As soon as she got the all-clear sign, she pushed away from the desk.

No gazing directly into camera one today.

No holding her knock-'em-dead smile for a heartbeat past the all-clear signal.

Her plan, formulated during breaks, still made sense: Slip out past the producer, the cameraman, and— Brad?

Pins and needles slam-danced up her right leg. She leaned against the desk for a second, then hobbled off the set, pretending Brad was invisible. Unfortunately, Brad didn't get the message that she'd rather kiss a snake than talk to him. He sidled up next to her.

"Accident?" He took her elbow, escorting her into the hall.

"I was just on my way to see you." She jerked her elbow out of his grasp, throwing her arms out when she stumbled.

"See how our minds work in sync? I saved you some steps." Brad picked up her cane, then tagged alongside her, closer than her shadow. "What can I do for you, Kelsy?"

Silently, tiny, invisible antennae behind her ears shot up. Careful, she thought, making an effort to think before she spoke. "I wanted to let you know I need the rest of the day off."

"Because of your toe?" His tone was so kiss-ass Kelsy wanted to puke. That triggered the ugly image of her barfing champagne on her Manolos in Half Moon Bay. Quickly, she said, "The doctor says I should keep it elevated today."

"We can probably work out a deal."

Probably? "Probably?" Kelsy stared at him. "Definitely, Brad. And you can fire me—"

"Fire you? Didn't I just say we'd work out a deal?"

Puzzled by his oily tone, Kelsy decided to hang him on his own words. "You sure did. So, I'm outta here."

"First . . ."

Kelsy snorted. "First, what?"

"First, Erica's still sick."

"I'm sorry to hear that." Kelsy punched the DOWN

button on the elevator and jabbed Brad in the ribs with her elbow. *Not my problem.* "Who's covering her show today?"

"We'll run another tape. Caroline Reed's hosting."

His lips moved, but Kelsy felt her brain shift into watching-the-world-go-by gear. Colors and lights dimmed. Breathing decreased to slo-mo. Sounds faded to underwater glugs.

Déjà vu. She'd been here, heard this spiel before.

As soon as Brad's lips stopped moving, he gazed at her like a cocker spaniel waiting for a pat. Her brain shifted again, and sights, sounds, and breathing returned to normal. Without actually knowing *what* Brad had said, she knew exactly what he wanted from her.

"Sorry, Brad. I told you I'm beat." To hell with expecting concern from the idiot, but her conciliatory tone nearly gagged her.

"You don't look beat. You look great, Kelsy. By tomorrow afternoon, you'll be ready for anything."

Ready to tell Finn what a mess she'd made?

"Ready for a kickboxing demo, right?" He didn't so much as glance at her foot. She said flatly, "Tomorrow's a short day for me, remember? I'm flying to—"

"Do Erica's show tomorrow, and I'll give you Friday off."

The elevator pinged, then the doors opened. Brad jumped in, mashing the OPEN button for Kelsy. She limped in after him, waited for the doors to close, then said, "I have Friday off. With pay. In case you've forgotten, I worked full days Monday and Tuesday."

"Yes, but don't forget your doctor's appoint—" He must've seen how close she was to cracking his head with her cane.

"Okay, take Monday off." Desperation shone in his eyes. "Tuesday if you need it. You've already done the research for Victoria Moreno and Steele Hood. All you have to do is show up, right?"

He grabbed her arm. She flashed him a murderous grimace and he let go of her. Sweat dotted his hairline like diamonds. "Chat them up for an hour, and you get two days off with pay."

With pay nearly choked him, but the elevator dropped so fast, taking Kelsy's stomach down without her body, she couldn't enjoy having him by the short hairs.

Or maybe the laugh was on her. *Déjà fucking vu.*

"If this interview bombs, don't blame me."

"Kelsy, you're a pro. You won't bomb."

Was that a smirk when he said *pro?* She cocked a brow and dared him to give her any more crap.

What the hell? Situations like this built reps in the world of TV.

Not as dumb as he looked, Brad fell all over himself when she finally gave in. No problem if she wanted to work at home. And there was no problem when she wanted Erica's intern to call her there.

Hmmm, what else did she want?

Power tingled in her blood. She had Brad right where she wanted him. He made a few more comments about gratitude. She stopped listening. Did she give a rat's posterior what he said? Dane on the other hand . . . . Despite her toe, she made a production of leaving the elevator.

Sunshine bathed Kelsy in Indian summer glory when she fell into the back of a cab fifteen minutes later. Yakking to the bitter end, Brad waved from the sidewalk. She exhaled deeply.

Lord, putting up with an idiot boss required the patience of a saint.

Maybe, just maybe, being a stay-at-home mom offered its own rewards.

As the cab passed Naglee Park, a couple of Starbucks-toting mothers, pushing expensive strollers, ambled toward an empty bench. In the early morning sun, their huge diamond rings flashed like traffic lights. Kelsy twisted Finn's tiny ring. She loved the depth and various shades of blue in the antique sapphire. Loved knowing his dad had given it to his mom. *Call him. Right now. Tell him you love him.*

Common sense said he'd already gone to bed. How long could breakfast with Olivia last?

If he was in bed, calling was a bad idea. This undercover assignment had put way too much on his plate. He needed his sleep.

She didn't need to tell him about her big chance on Erica's show. Not this minute. Tomorrow. *Stick to the plan.* She smiled, imagining his joy for her. He'd go berserk. Anything good that happened to her he ranked with a cure for cancer.

Only one of the big differences between him and Dickhead. In ten years of marriage, it had always been about Dickhead's wheeling and dealing. Celebrating Kelsy's moments in the sun never appeared on his radar. Because he'd never credited Kelsy with an idea, job, or accomplishment worth celebrating.

Finn, on the other hand—

Stick to the plan. Tomorrow, Erica's show provided the perfect bridge to new career hopes. Then, she'd segue into explaining everything: dinner with Dane, her close encounter with Baby Face, her broken toe.... Plus, she'd convince him that having more kids didn't fit with a fast-track career. By the time she finished, he'd understand.

With a deep sigh, she relaxed enough that her toe stopped screaming. The stop and go of the taxi in rush hour traffic lulled her like a rocking chair. After the third time her cell phone vibrated, she finally answered it.

Dane Jensen purred, "Wanted you to know I delayed my tee-time this morning and caught your show." His TV announcer's baritone caressed her ear. The intimate undertones woke her up with her heart hammering.

"What-what'd you think?"

"You looked great. Absolutely in control. If I didn't know about your toe—any reason we can't get together tonight for dinner, discuss my impressions?"

Caught off guard, Kelsy jumped. Her right foot bumped against the seat in front of her. Pain shot up her leg. She cussed in silence.

"I'll come over there," he said. "Pick you up since your toe—"

"I can't!" She didn't bother controlling her deafening shriek. "I have plans. My housemate's birthday." The lie came through the pain with perfect clarity. "It's her thirtieth. She threw a marathon party for me, so I have to reciprocate."

"I love a good party."

Funny, she hadn't noticed his cement head last night. "Ohhh, this is just us girls. Eight of us. No guys."

"I see." She could hear the repressed laugh in his voice. "What if I came as the male stripper?"

Say what? Kelsy recoiled from the phone as if it was a rattlesnake. Holding the phone at arm's length, she said, "It's not that kind of party. We're all profess—business women." What was one more big, fat lie? "We only do this for major life-events. Big birthdays. Promotions. That kind of event."

"Oh, well . . . another time."

Dream on. That male stripper comment crossed the line.

"I leave for Seattle tomorrow," he continued. "I'll be in touch. Careful no one steps on your toes tonight."

"Thank you," she said stiffly, hating the heaviness in her chest, hating more her disappointment he hadn't offered a job.

* * *

At the last minute, Olivia changed her mind about breakfast at McAfee's. Too many other cops there. Cops had big ears. She wanted privacy.

"Let's stop at Starbucks on Miramonte," she said in the police parking lot. "We can buy pastries and coffee. Go to Cuesta Park. No interruptions."

Grudgingly, Finn said, "Sure. I'll only have to do about a thousand squats to offset one apple fritter."

"Try being a woman." Olivia slid under the wheel of her vintage Mustang. "Six weeks in that damned BMR, and I've put twenty inches on my butt."

From Kelsy, Finn knew this was the kind of comment that invited a response. He gave Olivia full palms up. "I never noticed."

Her face, below her shades, sorta fell—like a kid who wanted skis for Christmas and got wool socks.

Like a fool, he added, "Honest."

She snorted. "Good thing you gave up your PI fantasy, Bishop."

He grinned. "What can I say?"

"Say, 'See you at Starbucks, Olivia.'" She backed out without looking behind her and nearly ran him down.

"Awww, shit," he said under his breath after his heart rate came down to about ninety miles per hour. *Men can not win when women start in on their body parts.*

Somehow, he beat her to Starbucks. Had she been wearing lipstick in the parking lot? He didn't know and didn't ask. He just gave his order: tall, black coffee and a blueberry muffin. At 7:03, they were out of apple fritters. Olivia ordered a grande latte, picked up a yogurt, and paid as Finn fished out a twenty.

"I asked you, so I pay," she said. "You know the rules."

He did, so didn't argue. Ever the senior partner, she said she'd lead the way. No big deal. The fragrance of coffee mellowed him out. Macho Cop, he didn't give a damn if she took the lead. He followed her the three blocks to Cuesta Park.

It didn't surprise him that she bypassed the benches near the playground. Too early for kids, but avid joggers took that route when it was deserted. Silently, she led the way to a secluded bench. The faint *pop, pop* of tennis balls on a backboard punctuated the quiet. Personally, he'd have preferred a spot that might catch some rays, but he hoped they'd be long gone before the fog burned off.

Within seconds after they sat down, half a dozen small birds landed nearby in the grass. The bigger, braver birds hopped up to the bench, chirping at each other and ruffling their feathers at the smaller ones.

Focused on them, Finn opened his mouth, but Olivia talked over him. "No small talk. If I don't get right to the point, I'll bag this whole idea."

"You sound a little edgy." He went for the soothing tone he used with accident vics. "You're probably hungry. We've got time. Eat your yogurt first." He unwrapped his muffin, and a couple of hopeful sparrows hopped right up to his shoe.

Swinging her arms viciously at the birds, Olivia pressed her lips together. "Just setting the ground rules."

Finn brought the muffin up to his mouth and winked. "Fine. As long as there's no rule against eating."

Eyes flashing, she snapped, "Do you think you could be serious for just one damn minute?"

Finn blinked. "Whoa! You don't sound edgy, you sound like you went over the edge an hour ago."

"Thank you, Dr. Phil."

Jesus! He held up one hand. "Sorry. I forgot I have the right to remain silent. I will now SHUT UP."

"Please do. Don't make me kill you." She looked away from him, shooed a bird off the back of the bench, then kept her back to him.

A decade or so later, Eagle-Eye Finn noticed her shoulders shaking. The muffin in his gut tasted like sand. Scalding sand. Shiiit. She was crying. Not out loud, but the quiet weeping only women did. He laid the muffin on the ground several feet from the bench, and the birds immediately descended.

Determined not to be cute, he imagined he was speaking to Kelsy. "You better tell me what's going on, Olivia. Whatever it is can't be hopeless."

Her cackle raised the hairs on his arms. "Forget that pearl of stupidity," he mumbled.

"Thank you." She still looked at the trees behind them.

"You're not sick?"

An inelegant sound, more guttural and harsh than a snort. "You mean cancer? A brain tumor? PMS, even?"

"Yeah. Anything like that." He crossed his fingers. God, not PMS, please.

"Relax." Olivia faced him. "I'm sickeningly healthy."

"Great! That's great." Kelsy, he'd take into his arms, hold her tight, thank God. With Olivia, call him a bastard, but he'd rather hug a porcupine.

She must've read something in his expression or his body language. She shot him a phony smile, then hid her face with one hand. "You know what, Partner? I think I'm sleep deprived. Could we erase this whole scene? Pretend it never happened?"

"Like hell, *Partner.*"

Her mouth twisted like she was holding back pain. Finn hesitated, then he grabbed for her. "Olivia? What the hell's wrong? Is it your heart?"

She slid away from his touch. "Coffee . . . down . . . wrong way."

Without warning, she jumped off the bench. Wings flapping, the birds flew into the cloudless sky. Finn damn near fell on his ass.

"I'm going straight home. Straight to bed." Hands in front of her chest, Olivia scurried backwards. "I'll be myself by tonight. I promise."

Since this wasn't a soap opera, where characters' feet

were nailed in place in similar situations, Finn got his feet firmly under him and stood up.

"No, no. I mean it. There's nothing you can do."

"Thanks for the ego boost," he said.

"How about my ego?" She pounded her chest so hard Finn winced. "I'm embarrassed to death, and you, typical male, worry about *your* ego."

"That's not what I meant." He took a step toward her, and she recoiled like he was some kind of creep.

"Sorry if I look interested." She yawned.

Afraid he'd grab her and shake her, Finn took a step backwards. Touch her, and whatever mutant cell had broken loose in her brain might really run amuck.

"Since you want your space, I think I'll wait here till the fog clears."

Expecting a zinger, he felt strangely disappointed when she turned around and left without another word.

Chapter 8

Ass-deep in alligators, Kelsy didn't answer Finn's call at 4:30 that afternoon. "Sorry," she said out loud, "I'll make it up to you tomorrow."

Somehow, cyberspace had eaten her notes from the day before. Erica's intern had no clue what had happened. She'd had a root canal late yesterday and kept whining that Kelsy expected too much. With troubles of her own, Kelsy simply cracked the whip.

At nine that night, Risa tiptoed into the family room and found Kelsy asleep on the sofa. Dr. La Ti Da immediately ordered bed. Imagining Savannah Jones in the same situation, Kelsy protested. She insisted she felt refreshed.

Not refreshed enough, though, to confess she hadn't talked with Finn.

Two hours later, she threw in the towel. Her eyes felt like fried eggs, and her toe hurt so much she popped another Vicodin. In bed, she was too tired to think about Finn or the upcoming long weekend together. She tossed and turned, dreaming about the interview. A knock-out interview with Victoria Moreno and Steele

Hood could cement her future. Dane would have to hire her if she pulled this off.

For once, Finn arrived at the station ahead of Olivia. His chest was tighter than usual. For whatever reason, he hadn't reached Kelsy before he'd left the house. He'd wanted a woman's view on the breakfast in the park. Should he ask Olivia how she felt? Should he let her start the conversation? Should he just talk about the case?

With no input from Kelsy, Finn took his cue from Olivia. It didn't take a genius. Senorita Cool, she started yakking about the case as soon as she got behind the Beemer's wheel. They were going to play Let's Pretend for twelve hours. Which suited him just fine.

Breaks came and went. Olivia never stopped talking. Finn figured it was only a matter of time before his ears started bleeding. Finally, around midnight, she shut up. Without warning, she morphed into a sphinx. Again, fine with Finn. The silence provided the perfect backdrop for daydreaming about vacation with Kelsy and Jason.

It wasn't till later, when he called Kelsy right after her show ended, that he realized Olivia had sighed from time to time.

Hyper as a hyena, Kelsy limped out of bed before the alarm went off at 3:30. After a shower, her toe felt considerably better. Good enough to drive.

Or maybe she felt better after spending extra time on her makeup. If they didn't look too closely, she thought, no one would suspect she was Queen of the Dead.

Dressed in her smartest Ann Taylor pantsuit, every

hair cemented to her head, she bundled each brush, jar, and bottle into two hefty cosmetic bags. To look her best with Victoria and Steele, she'd need all her magic wands. Especially since she was condemned to her pink bedroom slipper and blue shoe.

To her astonishment, Risa wasn't standing guard at the door to the garage when Kelsy sneaked into the kitchen. Gotta be a sign, she thought, needing two trips in and out of the house to load her makeup stash into the Lexus.

Without the benefit of Vicodin, hauling her butt into the front seat took her breath away. Finn would kill her, but what he didn't know wouldn't hurt him.

The thought momentarily shocked her. She smothered a pang of guilt. After today, she never intended to keep another secret from Finn in her life. Until she divulged all, she'd drive as if a cop was tailing her. The first time she put her foot on the accelerator, the engine revved. Her heart jumped. She let up on the gas. By the fourth time, she whispered, "Just do it."

Her uneventful commute she took as a sign. The planets had moved into harmonic convergence. The stars pointed to a memorable interview with Victoria Moreno and Steele Hood.

One more sign was the ease with which she sailed through Top of the Morning News. Lord, Lord, she was on a roll.

That giddy feeling of being able to handle any damned thing that came her way didn't let her down when Finn called at 7:04.

A brilliant plan popped into her head: Take a tape of *the* interview on the plane. What better way to make her career argument? So, instead of mentioning this afternoon's show, she said brightly, "How was breakfast with Olivia?"

A pause, before he said, "Okay."

"You don't sound very sure." Kelsy gave Brad the okay sign with two fingers as she entered the news-room.

A heartbeat's hesitation, and Finn said, "Olivia—I don't know. I don't think she likes having another part-ner while I'm gone."

"Why would she?" At her desk, Kelsy flipped on her computer. "You're the best. She knows the real deal when she sees it. Besides, Olivia has the hots for you."

"Babe! You need a vacation. I drive Olivia nuts."

"I believe I've made my case." Kelsy tried one more Internet search for a good picture of Victoria Moreno and Steele Hood.

"We can talk about it later. Or not. I'm just calling to say hi, before I hop in the sack." He howled like a dog at the moon. "Just think, we'll wake up in the same bed this time tomorrow."

Since Kelsy shared this same fantasy, she laughed. "If Jason doesn't roust us out at dawn, I don't know my son."

"You're right. But we'll wake up together—for three days. God, I feel like I took the wrong exit and ended up in Paradise."

Kelsy felt her throat clog. "It's only Paradise because you and Jason are there. I love you."

"I hope you're prepared for me to show you how much I love you."

Two minutes from crawling into the sack, Finn heard his phone ring. High on adrenaline from talking to Kelsy, sure she was calling back, he answered.

Olivia didn't identify herself. For a nanosecond, Finn didn't recognize her low, husky voice. Running her words together, she said, "Forgot to say I hope you have a great time in Montana."

"Thanks, Partner." Once Finn recovered from his initial shock, he added, "I appreciate the sentiment."

"If you go up there to Montana and become a cowboy—"

"Not a chance." Unsure where they were going in the conversation, he said, "Kelsy would die of boredom. She'd move to Patagonia first. It's all she can do to work in San Jose."

"Call me crazy, but I like life in the 'burbs." Olivia sounded so sad, Finn wondered if she'd been drinking.

"Yeah, me, too. Man, am I one lucky fool or what?"

"Off the top of my head, I'd go with fool. See you on Monday."

Finn stared at the buzzing receiver. He figured he should be ticked, but what the hell? He threw back his head and laughed right up until he climbed into bed.

Pleasant dreams, Olivia.

At 1:15 that afternoon, Mikayla announced that the guests were waiting in the greenroom. Kelsy was ready. *Here I come, Victoria and Steele.* She'd absolutely stun them with her intelligent grasp of their lives. *Move on, B.J. Move over, Savannah.*

Hallelujah, Erica was still sick. Interviewing the most powerful woman in Silicon Valley didn't happen every day.

Anticipation hummed in Kelsy's veins as she chatted with the small audience. She deflected all questions about her toe. She'd not visited the greenroom because she'd been doing research up until show time. More importantly, she didn't want any comments, later, about her journalistic objectivity.

Especially since she intended to focus on the fact she

and Victoria Isabel Moreno had in common: They had both immigrated to the U.S. when they were three. The piece of trivia filled Kelsy with a sense of . . . sisterhood.

Of course as soon as Dane saw *this* interview, she'd be a shoo-in for the KSWA job.

Visions of pinch-hitting for Savannah Jones fueled Kelsy during her opening. She concluded her glowing intro, "Now, it is my great pleasure to welcome, President Steele Hood and CEO Victoria Isabel Moreno."

Luckily, Kelsy remained seated as they came onto the set. Otherwise, she was sure her knees would've given out. Victoria Isabel Moreno sported an apple-red Armani pantsuit that would stop traffic. Long, black hair flowing, she charged ahead of her boss in red Pradas. The glare from her diamond chandelier earrings and tennis bracelet momentarily blinded Kelsy. She blinked repeatedly as her heart slammed into her chest.

The brunette bearing down on Kelsy still wore too much mascara. She still wore a tacky, boobs-popping red shirt, totally sluttish for the occasion. She showed zero resemblance to the only picture Kelsy had found of her.

Inches from the wing chair next to Kelsy, Victoria Moreno stopped. She slapped one hand on a cocked hip and thrust the other hand out. Steele Hood bumped into her, but recovered gracefully.

"Pay-up time." Victoria gazed into camera one like a cobra.

Someone in the audience tittered. The opening remarks Kelsy had rehearsed floated out of her head. She stammered, "Uh, pl-pl-please, sit down, Miz Moreno."

Victoria tossed her head. "Your chair looks more comfy."

The show's producer made a rolling sign, hand over hand. Kelsy stood, her toe on fire. Dizzy from the sudden pain, she forgot smiling. "Wherever you'd like to sit," she said, between gritted teeth. "You're the guest."

"What about him?" Victoria pivoted to face Steele Hood. "Is he chopped liver?"

"I certainly hope not." Grinning, he stepped around Victoria. Despite the unforgiving studio lights, his blond hair gleamed, sun-streaked and artfully tousled.

In an aside to Kelsy, he said, "I hate chopped liver. Foie gras, on the other hand . . ." He studied the three chairs. "Pay no attention to Victoria. She's always sitting in my chair. I tell her she reminds me of Goldilocks."

There was a snicker in the audience. Tongue-tied, Kelsy blushed. Did he mean Victoria hopped from bed to bed?

"Isn't that just the kind of remark you'd expect from someone named 'Steele'?" Victoria nudged Kelsy aside without comment on Kelsy's mismatched footwear.

" 'Steele Hood'!" She snorted, turning to the audience. "Can you imagine naming a kid 'Steele Michael Hood, *Junior*'?"

The audience laughed as if they were getting paid. Kelsy fought the panic squeezing her chest. She tried to catch her breath. Steele clapped his hand over his heart and mimed a man removing a knife. The audience roared.

In a small, pathetic, voice, barely audible over the laughs, Kelsy said, "Stay with us, we'll be right back after a break."

Given the all-clear signal, she felt her patience shatter. "Are you drunk?" she yelled the question because Victoria bumped her toe again. An accident?

"You mean like you were the other night?" Victoria asked.

"You're insane," Kelsy hissed, feeling faint when Brad stepped out from behind the cameraman.

"Depends on who you ask." Victoria batted her blackened lashes. "Also depends on what day of the week. Since today is Thurs—"

"Shut. Up." Fighting tears, Kelsy waved Brad away and indicated with a nod she'd seen the ten-second signal. If her toe wasn't broken, she'd kick this idiot woman.

Steele Hood patted Kelsy's wrist. "Don't let her throw you," he said. "She's really not so bad."

In fact, she was worse. Much worse. So much worse that Kelsy gave up before the second commercial and sat between her two guests in silence while they played their off-the-wall game.

Whatever the game was.

With the mother of all headaches destroying her brain cell by cell, with her toe hurting worse than labor pains, Kelsy didn't have Clue One. What's more, she didn't care.

After a century, the hour dragged to a halt. Humiliated beyond her worst nightmare, Kelsy refused to shake hands on-camera with either of the devil's spawn.

Let Brad do the honors. She hobbled off the set as fast she could—before the credits started or before she threw up.

No way she'd give Brad the chance to slice and dice her in front of the crew and the devil's spawn. *They are the devil's spawn.*

A red haze fell over walls, carpet and her skin. She slunk into the scarlet newsroom. She avoided the red-faced embarrassment her co-workers couldn't hide. *Finn.* She wanted his arms around her, his mouth on hers, soothing her, promising her it would be fine.

Blinking back tears, she nearly dislocated her shoulder tearing open her desk drawer. Talk about your Thursday from hell. Kiss any job at KSWA good-bye— except sweeping floors.

Someone called Brad's name. She froze. Her heart stopped.

Get out. Move. Before he escorts you out of the building. She grabbed her purse and limped out of the station at warp speed—as if her hair was on fire.

Reason warned she couldn't drive. Not because of her toe, but because she was losing the battle with her tears.

Get outta here. She lurched faster across the parking lot.

The fuzzy pink slipper fought her every inch of the way. Terrified Brad had followed her out of the building, she wobbled and careened onward.

Key! Where was it? She fumbled in her purse, praying, *Please, please.* Did she leave the damn key on her desk?

If she did, forget going back inside. You could hold a gun to her head, and she still wouldn't go back inside.

Aware she teetered on the cusp of hysteria, Kelsy found the damn keys. Then, she couldn't remember where she'd parked. Everywhere she looked, there was another white Lexus. The sun, a fiery red ball in a cloudless sky, bounced off chrome and glass. Her mind kept veering back to the interview. Knowing where that led, she pitched up one aisle and down the other.

Walking restored a little oxygen to her brain. Her pulse came down to a gallop, and the knot in the pit of her stomach closed up to awful instead of unbearable. Her toe simply pounded. She wasn't calm or composed, but at least she wasn't falling apart. She believed she'd survive when—after the third time around the same SUV—she recognized it as hers.

Hands on her hips, she stared at the dent in her front bumper.

How paranoid would it be to stomp back inside on her broken toe and accuse Victoria Moreno of backing into her car?

* * *

Clean jeans. Five pairs of socks. Two wool shirts. A new bottle of Old Spice. It drove Kelsy wild.

Ten minutes ahead of schedule, Finn backed out of the drive, mentally ticking off the items in his gym bag. The exercise kept his mind off Kelsy. Despite their E-Z rendezvous on Tuesday, he felt higher than a kite about seeing her again.

Risa had assured him that she, Ben, and their four kids lived a very homey existence in the wilds of Montana. Translation: He and Kelsy would have plenty of time to catch up on making love. He could hardly wait to see her appreciation when he dropped his hints about returning to Traffic.

Self-discipline gave way to self-indulgence at I-280 and Highway 85. Looking for a break in the bumper-to-bumper traffic, he broke his cardinal rule and called her.

"Hi." Her greeting had all the enthusiasm of an egg-plant.

"What's wrong?" He checked for a break in the fast lane.

"I'm tired." White noise offered no clues.

"Rough day?" In his book, TV people didn't know what a rough day was, but he sure never let Kelsy know how he felt.

"It's not worth discussing right now."

Wonderful. He choked the steering wheel and cut in front of a guy trying to beat him to the metering light. "I'm trying to get onto to 280."

"We're ten minutes from the airport. See you in a few minutes." She hung up.

Half an hour later, he shook off the memory of her frostiness as he bounded up the steps into the private jet. Quint Ferguson, former father-in-law of Risa's husband, owned it. Risa had told Kelsy, who told Finn, that the old man rarely used the plane. He was too happy being "Granpa" to five-year-old Molly, his only grandchild. Happiness, and Risa, had cooled his anger toward his son-in-law for the accidental death of Molly's mother. In the happiness equation, the jet made it a piece of cake for Risa to come to Silicon Valley, then return to Montana, with less hassle than most people's daily commutes.

I could get used to this. Finn took in the easy-chair seats. They made first-class seats look like instruments of torture. Soft lights, fresh flowers, and polished tables reminded Finn of a small, luxurious apartment. Like a kid who got all the toys on his Christmas list, Finn was so busy examining his surroundings he almost missed Kelsy's shoes.

Frowning, he stopped in his tracks. "What—"

"It's worse than it looks." Kelsy shrugged. Just my toe."

Fantasies of amazing sex evaporated as worry took root. "When did you hurt it? Is it broken? Why didn't you tell—"

"It's no big deal, Finn." Her stare got under his skin. Ridiculously, he felt her watch his every move.

Trusting his instincts, he stared at Risa. She refused to meet his gaze. *What the hell's going on?* "And what kind of deal does our esteemed Doctor La Ti Da say it is?"

"Dammit, Finn!" Kelsy's voice stung like a live electrical wire. "Don't put Risa in the middle. It's my toe, and *I* say it's no big deal."

Something in her voice warned him to let it go. Just for the hell of it, to prove he didn't think only with his dick, he said, "If it really is no big deal, why are you making it such a big deal?"

Her mouth dropped before she caught herself, and he was a hundred percent sure Risa smiled. He resisted the wild urge to press his point. She sputtered, "That's the silliest logic I ever heard. This is what happens when we're separated so long."

"Since we agree on that point, can I kiss you? Or are you too mad at me?"

"I'm not mad at you, Finn." Her voice sounded full of tears, but her eyes reminded him of the blue ice he'd seen in Alaska.

"Okay, then." He sat down in the chair next to her. "I'm taking you at your word." He grabbed her and felt like he was kissing an ice cube.

Not particularly surprised, he released her. "And they say absence makes the heart grow fonder."

Wisely, Risa made a beeline for the back of the plane. She and the leggy, brunette cabin attendant went into a huddle. Kelsy could've gone to jail for the murderous thoughts dancing across her face. She tried to kill Finn by directing a hard, laser-stare at his balls. When he didn't keel over immediately or morph into a dancing monkey, she said, "I'm not in the mood. Today's been about the worst day of my life."

Finn swallowed a laugh. God love Kelsy. Part of what fascinated him about her was her amazing sense of drama. "Let me guess. You don't want to talk about your very bad day."

"Bingo."

"Would you love it if I went up with the pilot?" Most women he'd known bored him.

"You don't have to stay up there the whole trip." Kelsy didn't bore him. She never bored him.

"Thank you, Your Graciousness."

"I don't feel like laughing right now." Just enough drama for an Academy Award.

"Not a problem. I don't feel like making you laugh."

She frowned, looked so scared for a minute he almost backed down, but she said, "Risa and I had a-a misunderstanding in the limo. I need to patch things up. You understand, right?"

"Uh-huh." Just when he thought he had her figured out, she surprised him big time. Instinct told him, surprisingly, there was a kernel of truth in what she said. The whole truth he'd have to wait for till she was good and ready.

Risa, who couldn't boil water without burning it, broke out a catered dinner ten minutes after Finn joined the pilot. The food rivaled anything Kelsy had ever eaten in the air.

Or on the ground for that matter. On the ground included her dinner at The Ritz, since she remembered only the champagne.

"Are you going to tell him?" Risa set a tray of Brie-stuffed mushrooms with red pepper aioli next to Kelsy.

"That I crashed and burned today?" Making no effort at curbing her impatience, Kelsy snorted, then rolled her eyes for good measure. "I think that news-flash can wait."

At thirty thousand feet, the hors d'oeuvres smelled divine. "Besides, he's more interested in keeping me barefoot and preg—"

"Oh, Kel. That's not true." Risa opened a bottle of spring water even though Kelsy was eyeing the bottle of champagne. "What about the job offer in—"

"For cryin' out loud, La Ti Da!" Kelsy stared out the window, unimpressed by the splash of magenta from the setting sun. Spectacular sunsets, rare in the Bay Area, didn't fit with her Thursday from hell. She said, "You gave me the same sermon in the limo."

"And you weren't listening then any more than you're listening now."

"For the record, I probably won't say anything to him till tomorrow. If that's okay with you, of course."

"Are you being sarcastic because you're hungry or because you're still mad?"

"I don't know." Kelsy grabbed a mushroom. "My toe hurts. I'm hungry and—"

Embarrassed for dumping on Risa, she said, "Excuses aside. I'm sorry I bit your head off in the limo, La Ti Da."

"I know." Risa stopped arranging food and hugged her. "I'm sorry we didn't have more time together while I was home this week. I miss you, you know."

"Really?" Kelsy hated sounding so small and needy.

"Really. Why do you think I ask you to come up to the ranch every time I come back to California? Molly and Ben miss you, and I swear Charlie, Tom, and Harry still expect you to rock them every night."

Kelsy felt the hollow in the pit of her stomach shrink. "I remember taking care of Charlie and Tom as if it was yesterday."

"To me, it feels like a lifetime ago." Risa and Ben had stayed with Harry before, during and after six consecutive heart surgeries. Stretched to the breaking point, they'd depended on Kelsy to run Risa's home, get Molly and Jason off to school, *and* feed, bathe, entertain and rock Tom and Charlie when they cried non-stop for hours. She'd done it all while carrying on a white-hot lovefest with Finn, and before she started working at KSJC.

"Finn's beat," Kelsy said slowly. "His job—he doesn't need grief tonight. I'll tell him tomorrow. Everything. Okay?"

At that moment, the door to the cockpit opened and Finn joined them at the table. Sniffing, he said, "Figured now that I have us safely in the air, I'd join you ladies."

Love washed over Kelsy. Lightheaded with longing, she got up and wrapped her arms around his neck. "You're sure you didn't smell the crab cakes?"

God, he smelled good. Excitingly familiar and sexy. Too bad she couldn't jump his bones right there.

"Crab cakes?" he said, all feigned innocence that sent lust channeling through her.

"If the pilot needed you, you'd forget your stomach, right?" Her voice quavered with wanting him, teasing him, hoping she could surprise him with her apology. "You'd go back in there without a second thought to save me and Risa, right? Me first, of course."

He looked at Risa. "Is this a test?"

She laughed and shook her head. "Better have a couple of crab cakes to help you think about it."

"Uh, uh, uh." Kelsy grabbed the plate and held it away from him. "Not yet. I don't want those incredible little tidbits to burn a hole in your stomach."

"Why would they burn—"

"Because it's not healthy to eat during emotional upheavals. Right, Risa?" She didn't turn her head but gazed directly into Finn's eyes, sure she saw a deep vein of forgiveness. He loved her. Of that she was certain.

"I think I'll take Cody some mushrooms," Risa said from a distant planet. "He says they help him stay on course."

Grateful for her tact, Kelsy said, "Hurry, please. I've been off course all week."

As Risa passed by Finn, he grabbed a mushroom and stuffed it in his mouth. "Hope this doesn't destroy your image of me," he mumbled.

Kelsy nibbled his ear. "What about me? Don't you worry about destroying my image of you?"

"Are you kiddin'?" He fell into a chair, pulled her down with him and walked his fingers under her blouse, then under her bra. "I know exactly what your image of me is, and it's illegal in all fifty states."

"In case you haven't noticed, we're in a jet plane." Breasts tingling, she kissed his mouth, tasting the earthy aroma of mushrooms and salty cheese.

"In case you haven't noticed . . ." He pushed against her, his erection burning her hip, his pupils huge.

Hot and cold all over, she whispered, "Risa won't be long."

"We can check out the bathroom." He grinned slowly, and the space between his front teeth made him look devilishly innocent. He cocked a brow. "I've always wanted to test that urban myth about the mile-high club."

Kelsy sucked in air. "We . . . Are you serious?"

"Are you game?" His eyes gleamed with mischief.

"And ready," she said, standing on wobbly legs.

Chapter 9

Finn wrapped his arms around Kelsy's waist and glued his body to her back. Christ, how could a column of bones evoke such erotic fantasies? How could walking ten feet feel like a dance of seduction? Hot enough to self-combust, he closed the bathroom door and shoved Kelsy up against the sink.

"There's not a lot of space," she whispered.

"More than in the backseat of your Lexus."

"Point taken."

He shifted his feet. She said, "Watch da toe, Big Boy."

The button on her jeans required attention. Head ducked, he said, "It's not The Ritz—"

"What?" Her whole body went stiff, the blood drained from her face.

"I said—"

She made a noise, sorta doubled over, clipping his chin.

"Kelsy! Sweetheart! What's wrong?

For the rest of the trip, Kelsy lay on a bed Risa and Finn made by extending the foot-rests on two seats that faced each other. She elevated her toe, but she didn't moan. She felt too embarrassed to go that far with her charade. She did keep her eyes closed. She couldn't face Finn. He'd worried she had food poisoning till she reassured him she wasn't going to throw up.

Truth was, she wanted to barf. Purge herself of all the lies she'd told so easily in the past few days.

God, how was she ever going to tell him about dinner at The Ritz? Would hearing the name of the place always turn her stomach upside down?

From time to time, a laugh broke the quiet hum of Finn's and Risa's conversation. Wishing she could join the fun, Kelsy lay on her bed—hard as cement. Penance, she thought, for her deep stupidity.

Luckily, she trusted Risa completely. Risa would never betray her, never tell Finn about her pathetic secret hopes and dreams. *Trust him, Kelsy. He loves you.*

Yes, but like most cops, he was a stickler for the truth.

By the time they landed in Kalispell at 8:48 in total darkness, Kelsy had talked herself out of her funk. Jason hadn't seen her for a week. She wasn't about to show up and rain on his parade. None of the mess she'd made the past week—including a broken toe—was his fault.

In fact, his delirium was contagious during their nightly phone calls. For some reason no one understood, Molly's grandfather had taken Jason under his wing, taking him fishing, teaching him to ride, and giving him checkers lessons. Kelsy fully intended to pop off the plane filled with questions and high spirits—even if it killed her.

"Mommy! Mommy! Finn! Finn!" Arms wide, Jason broke away from Ben in the well-lit arrival lounge and charged like a baby rhino.

He was too big for her to pick up even without a bum toe, but she whooped his name. Her heart swelled with love.

"What's wrong with your foot, Mommy?" He hung back as she tried to pull him in close.

"A little bruise. A kiss would make it lots better." Finn shot her a look that squeezed her chest. Translation: What's the truth about that *little bruise?*

Half a dozen kisses later, watching Finn out of the corner of her eye, she said, "You've grown a foot!"

"I caught a fish, Mommy! Mine's was bigger 'n Molly's. She's afraid of worms, but I'm not. We ate it for dinner. Finn, we hafta to go fishin' in the mornin'. Early. Before the birds are awake. You 'n me 'n Ben and Quint."

"Just us guys, huh?" Finn gave Jason a high-five.

"Right!" Jason grabbed Finn's thumb. He'd have bumped into Kelsy if Finn hadn't caught him.

"What about me, honey?" Kelsy told herself the knot in her stomach wasn't jealousy.

"You're not a guy, Mommy. 'Sides, you won't like it. Fish are smelly. We'll go before you get up and bring a big sucker home for breakfast."

"Big sucker?" Kelsy glared at Quint Ferguson, off to one side, while Risa hugged Molly, Ben and her triplet sons as if she hadn't seen them in years.

"Howdy, Kelsy." Quint came forward, hand extended. "Finn. Good to see you again. Jason's quite the fisherman. And quite the rider."

Cheeks crimson, eyes shining, Jason reported in enamel-shattering tones his success on a pony and his intentions to ride a horse someday when he and Molly were bigger. "Will you take a picture of me on Ole Paint, Mommy? I wanna send it to Daddy."

A wet-blanket silence settled on the lively welcome. As always, whenever Jason mentioned his father, Kelsy felt as if she were falling through space. Her cheeks burned, and her heart pounded too fast. Tears clogged her throat. She felt helpless and scared, like a little girl who'd discovered a monster asleep under the bed. She knew if she moved, she'd wake the monster. If she didn't move, the monster would wake and eat her up.

Next to her, Finn squeezed her elbow. His eyes telegraphed his love, and she released the breath she'd been holding. She said to Jason in the lightest tone she could summon, "You want to hold the fish while you sit on Ole Paint?"

What's wrong with this picture? Everyone in bed, Kelsy in the bathroom. Finn lay on the king-size bed of Risa and Ben's humongous guest room. Flames in the stone fireplace had died to gray-tipped embers. Fresh wood-smells blended with flowery soaps and lotions wafting in from the bathroom. He'd invited Kelsy to share a shower, but she'd refused.

Her toe.

Of course.

It's not as if we've been celibate, Finn.

Kelsy's comment echoed in Finn's mind. For the hundredth time, he snorted. Ninety minutes of love-making in six weeks?

That sure felt like celibacy, but Kelsy's edginess warned him to keep this opinion to himself.

Silently, the red digits on the bedside clock turned over to 11:10. *Enough with patience.* Finn tried to keep his voice steady when he called, "I'm dying in here."

Two heartbeats later, she stuck her head around the corner, patting cream on her pale face. Her blue eyes glowed in the dying firelight. Lord! She could pass for a goddess with her long, blond hair skinned back and tied at her nape.

So she wasn't dawdling. She'd just made it easier for him to kiss her neck—a pleasure that always sent both of them into orbit. His throat felt tight, his mouth dry. God, he never got tired of looking at her.

"That bed squeaks," she said.

"Who cares?" He rolled from side to side, then declared, "Superman *might* hear that squeak."

"Why don't we go into the living room then if you don't care?" She made no move toward the bed.

Finn kicked the covers back. "I'm ready."

"Oh, stop it, Finn. Grow up." She retied her robe.

Ouch. Not a man to act on assumptions, he shoved his feet out of the bed and stood, naked, his erection a sure sign he hadn't yet given up hope. "Okay. I exaggerated. As you can see, I am not dying. The bed squeaks. The sofa works for me."

"Well, it doesn't for me. My back hurts from sleeping on the plane and carrying Jason. I told you that, but you don't listen. Since you have your agenda, I won't mention my toe."

"Kelsy?" A surge of adrenaline propelled him across the room. He pulled her, resisting, into his arms. "What's wrong?"

"Nothing," she mumbled. Her apathetic tone scared him silly. Especially when she ducked her head like a little girl. Whatever her peccadillo, he'd bet she hadn't broken all ten of the Commandments.

"Hey!" He tried again, without success, to tilt her head back so he could gaze into her eyes. "I'm a cop. I know nothing's the same as something major."

"Are you accusing me of lying?" Her tone could break glass.

Confused, he said, "I was trying to sound . . . sensitive. Isn't that what every woman wants? A sensitive guy who—"

She snickered. "What every woman wants is a man who listens to her. A man she can trust and confide in."

Finn's heart slammed into his chest. He didn't drop his arms, but his neck prickled. "You know you can trust me."

"Do I?" She took a step backwards, and he let her go. "I'm tired. Tonight's not the time to get into an argument."

"Why should we get into an argument?" The back of his throat felt raw. They'd never argued till today.

Another snicker. "What're we doing right now?"

"Wasting time." He leaned a shoulder against the door jamb. "Why don't you want to tell me what's wrong?"

"I said nothing." She lifted her chin, but he wasn't buying that any more the second time than he had the first time. He said through clenched teeth, "Fine. Since nothing's wrong, let's go to bed. Let me hold you—"

"Oh, that'll be the day." She rolled her eyes.

He looked down at his cock. Erections came, erections went. With a little cooperation from Kelsy, his would rise again.

He smiled at the image, and she demanded, "What's so funny? You and I fuck like rabbits. Any time, anywhere, since Day One together, and you expect me to believe we'll climb in bed and you'll hold me? I don't think so."

He didn't have to look down to see why she'd doubt him. For some reason, her fiery denunciation had the effect of twenty minutes of foreplay. Go figure.

"Involuntary reaction." He hoped she took his comment as a compliment. "Perfectly normal whenever I'm around you."

Her primped mouth brought a flash of discouragement, but his mind raced as he mentally searched and sorted for a few credible words to hook together. "I can choose to take a couple of options here. I can pretend I'm not aroused and hold you. Or, I can admit I'm aroused and hold you. Neither involves making love to you if you don't want me to."

Tempted to add *trust me*, he shut up.

"You could also sleep on the couch." She pointed at it. Did she think he didn't know where it was?

He shrugged. "Whatever you want. After six weeks of sleeping in the Beemer—"

"Stop that!" She wagged a finger at him.

At a loss, seeing they were going nowhere, he figured at that second, he could sleep standing up. "Stop what?"

Loving her, but wanting to wring her neck?

"Stop trying to manipulate me. I know you're a hero. I know you've single-handedly been keeping the good citizens of Cielo Vista safe. But give me a break."

Finn's jaw dropped, and his erection shriveled to the size of an overcooked hotdog. He bit back a yelp of surprise and fought the urge to clap his hands over his balls.

"Finn! I'm sorry."

He kept his distance. Just in case her moodometer swung back to *Men are the Enemy* without any warning.

"I-I don't know what's wrong with me." Her mouth trembled. "I'd swear it's hormones—"

"Oh, I figured it was your toe." He heard his jaw crack. Too much adrenaline was pumping through him for PC chatter. She'd crossed an invisible line, dammit.

"Please, please, don't take what I said personally."

"Don't take it personally." He made a face, shook his head and shrugged. "Of course not."

"I about took Risa's head off earlier. I blasted Ben, too." Shaking so hard he thought she'd break in two, Kelsy reached for his hand.

The muscles in his neck and arm stiffened, but he felt his mouth and jaw soften. "What you're saying is you're on a roll?"

"What I'm saying is—" She swallowed convulsively, and his own throat ached with love for her.

"Take your time," he whispered and took her in his arms.

"I don't want to fight with you. I love you. I—"

"Shhh, Kelsy." He pulled her even closer, adjusting himself so her breasts didn't push into his chest or his cock didn't push against any part of her. "You're wired to the breaking point. You need some sleep. Jason's gonna be a wild man tomorrow."

She sniffled. "Do you think he was glad to see me?"

"He wants to get up at the crack of dawn and bring home a fish for you. Just one of the limited ways we guys show our women we love 'em. Bring 'em somethin' ugly and stinky."

It wasn't that funny, but she smiled. He thought about scooping her up and carrying her to the bed but decided that was too clichéd. And dumb, since he was hard again.

"Crawl into bed," he said. "I'll tuck you in."

Hesitating, she swayed against the bed. Steadying her jerked his dirty mind away from the mental riff on tuck-and-fuck.

"Do you—do you hate me?"

"Never." His erection could make her hate him if he wasn't careful. He smoothed the covers, then arranged a pile of pillows for her foot. "I love you, and I'm not mad at you." Confused, nervous, and horny as hell, but not mad.

"I'm sorry . . . for that hero crack." A sigh shuddered through her.

"You mean I'm not?" He nudged her, and she toppled onto the bed and into his arms.

"I didn't mean to hurt you." She bit her lip.

"I know." He helped her position her foot on the pillows, then pulled the sheets up around her.

"Thank you for giving me a break."

"My pleasure."

Finally, he lay on top of the covers and pulled her close, smoothing her hair, crooning her name till sleep dragged him over the cliff into a dark cave.

* * *

Eyes squeezed shut, Kelsy felt as if an elephant slept on her chest. She wanted to scream.

How dare Finn fall asleep when they hadn't settled anything?

What'd he think the fight was about—squeezing the toothpaste in the middle?

Seething, she tried to roll over, but couldn't budge. He knew something was wrong, yet he'd given up and gone to sleep while her nerve endings jumped like water on a hot skillet.

What'd she have to do? Beg him to make love?

She poked his ribs. "Are you asleep?"

A snort, then he turned his head the other direction.

Hating her need for him inside her, Kelsy put her mouth on his ear, then flicked her tongue. "Finn!"

Arms wide, eyes wider, he sat upright, Frankenstein's monster with red hair and a space between his front teeth. "What? What?"

Nervous he might ram her foot, she threw the sheets back so her toe was visible. "Are you awake?"

"Huh-uh. I'm pretty sure I'm having a nightmare." He scrubbed his eyes, then ran a hand through his hair. A longing to tweak his rooster's tails shot through her.

"Can't you sleep?" He yawned.

"Not really. My toe hurts."

He cocked his head as if evaluating this. "Will you still respect me in the morning if I have my way with you?"

"Depends . . ." Kelsy came up on her elbows, and her nightgown slid of her shoulders. "What do you have in mind?"

He eased down next to her and put his scalding lips in the hollow of her throat. "Sucking your big toe for starters."

"Eeeuuuk!" She punched his bicep. "That's disgusting."

"Oh. How do you feel about this?" He slipped two fingers inside her, deep into her wetness.

The bed tilted. When she moaned and threw her arms around his neck, he removed his fingers. Hot all over, she whimpered, arching her back, pushing against his leg, lust pulsing off her.

"Want more?" he whispered. "Or should I stop?"

"No!" She grabbed his hair and pulled his mouth to hers, running her tongue along his bottom lip. "Do *not* stop."

"I don't want to hurt your toe." He grazed her breast with his tongue, and her heart missed two beats in a row.

Out of breath, she said, "You're still mad, aren't you?"

He blinked. She laughed, surprised how good an emotion besides guilt felt. "You're mad," she repeated, "because I didn't want any toe-sucking."

"Oh, right." On fire, he pressed into her. Shimmering heat shot into her brain. Healing heat entered her toe.

Awkwardly, she rolled on top of him. "Why don't I show you some other ideas?"

"Ummm." His stubbly beard tickled her breasts. She giggled. He said, "Something new sounds wonderful."

"Wonderful." She took his balls, felt him flinch but held on gently. She couldn't stop smiling—especially when he lifted her up, supporting her arched body, and dragged a slow, hot kiss from her throat down to her belly button.

After that, he rolled her onto her back, straddled her and slipped into her with such ease she said, "You are wonderful."

When they lay in each other's arms afterwards, fighting for breath, he said, "How's your toe?"

"What toe?" she murmured, grateful Finn was forgiving enough to love her again before they slept.

As proof that love had transformed her, Kelsy opened both eyes at 6:17 when Jason cracked the door, stuck his head in and whispered, "Time to get up, Finn. Early worm gets the fish."

"Gotta love that Quint," Kelsy mumbled, her eyes gritty, her mouth dry. "C'mon in, Honey."

"You forget I'm naked here?" Dragging a sheet around his waist, Finn pushed up to sitting.

Jason marched into the bedroom. "No time for a shower." He clapped his hands together. "Let's move it, Finn, or we won't be back in time for breakfast."

"Oh, yeah," Finn whispered. "Gotta love that Quint."

Ten minutes later, Kelsy stood on the back porch, shoulders hunched against a brisk breeze. Dressed in thick socks, jeans and a flannel shirt, her hair uncombed, she waved at the men as they tromped up a dirt path toward the mountains. Jason took the lead, but he looked back twice and waved at Kelsy. She threw kisses till they disappeared, then she hobbled into the warm, coffee-oatmeal-scented kitchen. Risa sat at the oak table taking turns ladling oatmeal into her three sons' bowls. Molly was in her room.

"She's a little miffed she got excluded from the fun," Risa said.

"I thought she didn't like fishing." Kelsy swiped Tom's oatmeal-encrusted hands, and he kicked his heels against his chair. "Okay, Handsome," she said. "Don't give me any trouble."

"Hates fishing, but loves being the center of attention." As if he understood the conversation, Charlie giggled, then sent his bowl crashing to the floor.

Risa sighed, picked up the bowl, and set it on the table. "Molly reminds me of you when you were her age."

"Me?" Kelsy grabbed the dripping spoon Charlie raised over his head.

"You don't remember wanting to be the center of attention?"

Heart fluttering, Kelsy said, "I was a brat, wasn't I?"

"Sometimes." Risa's smile took the sting out of the truth. "All kids are brats at one time or another."

"Yes, but I'm not a kid anymore." Kelsy flew the spoon toward Harry, popping it into his mouth. "Even if I act and feel like one most of the time."

"Did you and Finn talk last night?" Calmly, Risa started cleaning out Tom's yucky high-chair tray, then moved on to her son's sticky fingers and face as he made noises of resistance.

"No, he was tired." Kelsy stopped, realizing the lie had rolled off her tongue without a second thought. Quickly, she added, "That's not why we didn't talk."

"I see." Risa moved on to cleaning Charlie's high chair.

Despite her rough day yesterday seeing patients, she'd arrived home with two additional house guests to a huge, rambling home that welcomed kids and adults with a warmth that couldn't be faked. On top of raising four kids under the age of six and monitoring the evolving relationship between her husband and his former father-in-law, she never whined or lost her temper. Radiant with happiness, she told everyone she had it all—career, family and a husband straight out of a romance novel.

In the company of such success, failure obsessed Kelsy.

Of course, lots of money helped. Kelsy shook her head as the thought, pesky as a mosquito, buzzed in her head. "How do you do it, La Ti Da?" She waved her hand in front of her, expecting Risa to follow her train of thought.

"With Ben, of course. We're in sync on everything that matters. Kids. Where to live. Careers." She lifted Tom out of his chair. "Don't misunderstand me. Ben's money helps. Being able to travel back and forth on a private jet helps. Living up here, we could manage without either."

Kelsy shuddered. "But you live in the middle of nowhere!"

"And I *love* it." Risa grinned and set Harry on the floor. "Will we always live here?" She shrugged. "Don't know. I pretty much don't care where I live as long as Ben and the kids are with me." The other two toddlers whimpered to be put down.

Risa's sincerity boomed with trumpet clarity to Kelsy, but a feeling of dissatisfaction persisted. Until she figured out what she wanted, what price she was willing to pay and what exactly she'd tell Finn, Kelsy doubted she'd recognize magic if it bit her in the butt.

Chapter 10

Jason's excitement over his "awesome" fish was contagious.

So, when Kelsy limped outside, laughing, admiring the catch, Finn put it down to pride in her son.

She smothered Jason with kisses. Just as Finn started feeling left out, she kissed him with even more enthusiasm. Egged on by Risa, Ben, and even Quint, the kids whooped and cheered like they'd never seen a kiss bring a grown man to his knees and beg for mercy. It took a while, but Kelsy finally agreed to mercy if he cleaned the fish, then helped her fix it for breakfast.

Suspecting she wanted time alone with him, Finn agreed to her terms without a second thought. His soul brothers dispensed plenty of advice, enabling him to enter the kitchen. Risa stuck her head inside. "We're all going for a walk, maybe find some wildflowers for the table. Back in an hour."

Kelsy didn't even wait till the door shut before she jumped Finn. She slammed him up against the sink and tore his shirt off. Her eyes glittered with a feral passion that had him hard as new wood. All fingers, blind with lust, he yanked her shirt up to her neck. More grateful than surprised that he didn't have to bother with a bra, he thumbed her taut breasts, then buried his face in their pillow softness.

Arching into him, she unzipped his jeans. Her hand burned through his skivvies, down past skin. "God, Kelsy."

"We've only got a few minutes." She nipped his ear.

"We've got all the time in the world." He shoved her cell phone aside and slipped his hand inside her waistband, past her panties, straight to the spot he wanted.

"I'm already wet," she whispered.

"Are you now?" He inserted a finger. She cried out, calling his name, then came in a rush that shocked but excited him.

He held her hips, tilting her closer, disappointed when she pushed away. "I love you," he whispered huskily.

"Uh-huh." She dragged her burning tongue down to his belly button.

"Uh-huh?" he asked, eyes closed as she moved her mouth lower and lower.

"Uh-huh." Then she took him in her mouth.

They were worse than teenagers at breakfast, but no one seemed to mind. So Kelsy grabbed every chance that came her way to touch Finn. Thigh-to-thigh, she sat next to him, smiling at him like a lovesick cow, only half-listening to the talk at the table, sending silent screams of exultation to Risa.

Exactly what the doctor ordered.

Before the adults finished the last of their coffee, Molly and Jason started begging for riding time. Everyone except the triplets helped clear the table. Again, Kelsy made as much body contact as possible with Finn. God, she had missed him.

Their hands touched when she handed him the

plates for the dishwasher. Snickering, she pinched his butt when he bent over to load plates. He smacked her a couple of times with a dishtowel. The other adults, along with the kids, got into the game. Laughter and giggles filled the kitchen.

Consumed by happiness, Kelsy felt as if she'd left the mess at KSJC in another galaxy. Dane Jensen was a faint memory. This was the kind of life she wanted. She saw how shallow and silly she'd been, tempted by glamour and celebrity.

Arm-in-arm, she and Finn hobbled out to the corral. Sunshine danced on her shoulders. The neon-blue Montana sky really did stretch forever. For the first time since she could remember, no knots or kinks or aches nagged her. Even her toe felt okay. She could completely forget. *Too bad they can't bottle sex.*

"Mommy! Look, Mommy!" Jason, astride a gray pony with black spots, waved.

The aroma of horse wafted across the open space. Kelsy wrinkled her nose, waved, then said to Finn, "He looks as if he's levitating three inches above the saddle."

Finn focused his camera. "Go stand next to him."

After that, there were pictures of Finn next to Jason. And of course, he wanted a picture with Quint, then Risa and the triplets. By the time Ben and Molly sat next to him on their mounts, Jason wanted Kelsy and Finn to get on horses and ride around the paddock in the parade.

"Let me just watch, Honey." Kelsy shielded her mouth and spoke to Finn. "I've never been on a horse in my life. I prefer to keep my feet on the ground. Especially with a broken toe."

"Better stop floating around then, with that sign saying you just had the best lay in your life," Finn whispered.

"Technically, it wasn't a lay." She smirked.

"C'mon, Finn!"

"Is there a white steed left?" Finn asked and got a sour look from Quint. In an aside to Kelsy, Finn said, "I flirted with the idea of joining the San Jose Equine Division."

"Uh-huh. So why didn't you?"

"Self-preservation. Riding a horse is too sexy if you don't have someone to come home to after a long day."

"You are so full of it!" She reached up and kissed him.

"You love me anyway." He swaggered toward a black horse.

"Watch it. Your head gets any bigger, you'll fall off that horse as soon as you get on it."

Whether it was Kelsy's heckling or Finn's goofing around, he missed the stirrup and almost fell on his nose. Jason started giggling, and soon everyone joined in. Kelsy was laughing so hard she barely felt her cell vibrate on her waist. But the vibration persisted till she glanced down at the LED.

"Oh, hell." The last person she wanted to deal with today—after Brad—was Dane Jensen.

No, she decided, Dane Jensen was not a problem.

Moving out of earshot, away from Risa and the triplets, she said without an ounce of regret for lying, "This is Kelsy. I'm in conference."

"Brrrr. Where is it?" Dane asked in falsetto. "In the North Pole?"

"Would you like my voice mail?" She spit out each word. What'd she need to do? Spell it out for him? "It will be some time before I get back to you." Not till hell freezes over.

"Oh-oh. By then, they probably won't be able to thaw me with a blow torch."

Kelsy felt her mouth twitch and stared across at the mountains. Why was he being so nice—as if he still wanted her for a job at KSWA? Obviously, he hadn't seen the disaster with Victoria Moreno.

"Sorry," Kelsy said with a couple of degrees of warmth. "I appreciate your call, but we're looking at other offers."

"Damn! I knew it. I tried reaching you all afternoon yesterday. Of course, after that amazing interview you didn't return—"

"Wasn't it amazing?" she trilled, sickeningly sure Dane didn't mean *amazing* as a compliment. *So what does he want?*

A sudden gust of wind slapped her in the face. He said, "I've never seen anything like it."

"I'm sure." Her chest tightened.

"That was Miz Snooty, right?"

"I need to go." Kelsy took a step back toward Risa, who managed to keep three ten-month-old boys from crawling under the fence into the paddock.

"Whatever Brad offered you, I'm prepared to beat," Dane said in a rush. "Believe me he can't top the perks I have in mind."

Kelsy stumbled, caught herself, said, "What kind of perks?" She thought she sounded reasonably rational for a woman in shock.

"For one, how about two specials? One your subject, the other ours."

How about "The Short History of Condoms"? she almost asked.

Lightheaded, she covered the mouthpiece, yelling at Risa, "I'll be right there."

"How does that sound?" Dane persisted.

"That sounds . . . ." Out of the corner of her eye, Kelsy caught sight of Jason waving at her. Finn rode alongside him and threw her a kiss. Her mind raced, but she wiggled two fingers at them, then turned her back once more so she could focus. "This would be in the contract?"

"All spelled out. The i's dotted, the t's crossed. I'd look after you, Kelsy."

Something, the tone or the words, bothered her. She hesitated. "I'd want a lawyer to look over any contract."

"Of course. Exactly what I'd expect from an amazing, soon-to-be star like you."

Again, a little niggle of doubt, her heart pumping too hard. *Stop being such a cynic. Why would he lie?*

"So when can you come? Today? I can arrange for you to do The News at Ten tonight—if you aren't too tired. Or—"

"Wait, wait. Slow down." Kelsy laughed and her legs went weak. "You're moving too fast. Today's impossible."

"Because you're in conference?"

His tone implied they shared a secret. One he wouldn't tell. Despite the sun's heat, Kelsy felt a cold rush on the back of her neck. Risa would kill her . . . not to mention Finn and Jason if she left early. Risa knew about the *amazing* interview, so she wouldn't buy a work emergency. No matter what excuse—okay, lie—she manufactured, Jason and Finn would scream bloody murder.

Overhead, an eagle swooped across the gentian sky. Wings spread, he seemed to fly with some kind of built-in radar. Nothing distracted him. Kelsy sighed. She could take a lesson.

Temptation tantalized her. Dane's quiet breathing on the other end of the line added to her sense of excitement. God, it was fun being chased for her brain instead of for her bod. If she turned Dane down, would she ever get another chance like this one? Would any other TV exec look at that tape, see *amazing* and offer her the time of day?

Okay . . . . Dane might be a little more interested in her bod than she wanted to admit, but he was willing to take a chance on her. That counted for something.

Laughs from the corral decided her. In a rush, before she caved, she said, "I can't come this weekend. I promised my son we'd go away."

"I keep forgetting you have a son."

The comment struck a nerve. She snapped, "Well, I don't forget. I won't go back on my promise about going away."

"Seattle's away." Was she nuts, or had his voice deepened?

"We've already made plans." She allowed no hint of reluctance.

"You are a tough lady."

Not to mention a liar, she thought, but said, "I'll take that as a compliment. Now, I really need to get back to—"

"To your conference?" He made the question smack of an indecent proposal.

About to blister his ears, she heard Risa call, "Kelsy!"
Something's wrong. Kelsy whipped around, saw Risa running toward the corral and felt her heart lurch.

"I've got to go." She disconnected and took off as fast as she could move with her stupid toe and with her heart hammering in her ears.

"Mommy! Mommy!"

Four hours later, the immense Montana sky had already turned dusky at 3:45. Kelsy rode in Risa's Volvo with Jason asleep in her arms. His dark blond hair lay in damp ringlets around his hairline. The cast on his right arm rested on a couple of pillows Risa had unearthed. Finn drove as if they carried a car full of precious china.

In the backseat, Molly said for the third or fourth time since leaving the ER, "La Ti Da says Jason'll be fine, Kelsy. She's a pediatrician, you know. She takes care of lots of kids 'Sides me 'n Jason."

"I know, honey." Kelsy barely moved her lips. Her toe felt as if a bomb had exploded inside it.

She shifted Jason's dead weight. "I'm glad you're here to remind me, though."

Out of the corner of her eye, she saw Finn's mouth twitch. She blushed. He knew she was lying. Just as she'd lied when she agreed the accident wasn't her fault. Ben, Risa, Molly, Finn, and even stone-faced Quint had repeated it wasn't her fault Jason had fallen off his pony and broken his arm.

Watching kids every second of the day was impossible. Plus, overprotecting them destroyed their self-confidence. All kids needed lots of chances to try their wings. A broken arm wouldn't slow him down for more than one or two days, max.

Half a dozen more platitudes rolled in and out of her mind like subtitles at a foreign movie. None gave her any comfort. Because no one had asked her *why* she'd been on the phone instead of watching her kid go round and round the corral.

She knew they all wanted to know the answer. And she knew she wasn't going to tell any of them—especially Risa and Finn. Once she started, all her interwoven omissions, fibs, and lies would then unwind and end up strangling her.

"How you doin'?" In her trance, she hadn't felt Finn lay his hand on her knee.

"Fine." Tears thickened her voice. "Fine," she repeated, staring straight ahead at scenery she didn't see. She didn't dare look in Finn's eyes. He'd see her lies, her guilt.

"I'm fine, too," Molly offered. "Except I feel really, really bad for Jason. Do you think he'll ever want to come back and visit me?"

Kelsy felt her heart drop. *God, I hope not.* She rotated her numb shoulder, felt the silence thicken in the car and fought the desire to smother her sleeping son with kisses.

Finn jiggled her knee. "I don't think Kelsy heard."

"Yes, I heard you, Molly." Resentment surged through

Kelsy. She wasn't deaf. Why didn't he mind his own damned business?

"My mistake," Finn said quietly. "I thought—"

Talking over him, Kelsy said, "We'll have to ask Jason if he wants to come back." She took a deep breath, exhaled softly. "We'll ask him when he feels better."

"Are you mad at me, Kelsy?" Molly sounded close to tears.

"No, honey." Kelsy turned in her seat and tried to smile at the beautiful, loving child who, through thick and thin, had been Jason's best friend for the past ten months.

Fragments of memory melded. Kelsy clearly saw the pattern of Molly's generosity and her own liar's selfishness. She said, "Honey, I'm not mad at you."

She emphasized *not* and *you*, then added forcefully, "I'm mad at myself." Finally, the truth. "I'm sorry if I hurt your feelings." The tightness in her chest eased.

"You didn't hurt my feelings, but you scared me. Your face went all scrunched and scary. Didn't Kelsy scare you, Finn?"

"No, Molly. I don't think Kelsy could ever scare me."

An invisible knife stabbed Kelsy's chest. Shame caught in her throat. Squeezing her knee again, Finn flashed a smile into the rearview mirror. "But I'm a big person."

"Yeah, and I'm a little person," Molly said with great solemnity.

Heart banging, Kelsy felt about four or five. But since she was an adult, she tried to comfort Molly. "You are a little person, and I'm sorry I forgot and scared you. Want me to tell you a story?"

"No thank you."

Hallelujah! As much as Kelsy hated admitting it, she needed a second to regroup.

Another squeeze from Finn told her he understood.

Except, of course, he didn't know about her lies. The back of her throat burned. She already knew she was going to use Jason's broken arm as an excuse to avoid talking, really talking, to Finn. She'd already decided she couldn't go to Seattle next weekend, but she hadn't decided when she'd tell Finn about the meeting with Dane Jensen or his job offer.

Lord, no wonder people lied. Telling the truth hurt.

Out of the blue, Molly said, "I wish Jason could stay longer." Straining against her seatbelt, she said, "Can he, Kelsy?"

"No, Molly. He has to come home with me so I can take care of him."

"But La Ti Da said he'd be fine!" Molly wailed.

A muscle ticked under Kelsy's left eye, and she heard a little snap inside her head. Or maybe it was her toe. She said crisply, "Jason is going home with me, Molly. He has school on Monday, and so do you."

She ignored Finn's fingers tightening on her knee. "In fact, I think we may leave tomorrow."

"Tomorrow?" Molly flounced back against her seat. "Why?"

"Don't you think staying here with Risa for another couple of days makes sense?" Finn took his eyes off the road.

Kelsy gritted her teeth. "Right now what makes sense is a little quiet. We can't wake Jason. Risa said he needs sleep more than anything."

"Your face is all scrunched again," Molly whispered.

Finn escaped murder by coughing the laugh that almost got away from him. "I imagine it is," Kelsy said, blinking back tears. "Now can we ride the rest of the way without talking?"

As soon as they reached the ranch, Molly insisted Jason should sleep in her room as he always did. This was only fair, in her opinion, if he and Kelsy were really going home tomorrow. Half zonked from anaesthesia, Jason registered no opinion.

News of an early departure sent Risa into a dither of disbelief. Ticked because Molly had let the cat out of the bag, Kelsy capitulated on the sleeping arrangements, but specified one condition. She would sleep in Molly's bedroom as well.

Risa rolled her eyes but said zip.

Finn stared at Kelsy, then said, "Hey, Ben. How about keeping an eye on Jason while you read Molly a bedtime story?

To Kelsy's amazement, Ben, who kept his mouth pretty tightly zipped ninety-nine percent of the time, said, "Sure. I can watch Jason and read to Molly. But if you two are going to argue, don't upset Risa. Harry's teething, and she's had a rough two days in San Jose."

"Count on it." Finn led Kelsy outside where the temperature felt about minus ten degrees.

"Let's walk." He slipped a sheepskin jacket over her shoulders.

"That should be fun with my toe."

"Okay, let's sit on the front porch for a sec."

"I want to stay close enough I can hear Ben if—"

"For cryin' out loud, Kelsy!" Finn grabbed her hand. "Risa's one of the best pediatricians in the U.S. You think she lied when she said Jason will be fine? What is wrong with you?"

Jaw locked, Kelsy jerked away from him and stood planted a few feet from the back door. "What is wrong with you?"

"You are." He closed hard fingers around her shoulders. "I know I'm a Martian and you're female. But I'm an intelligent Martian. In case you haven't noticed, my knuckles don't drag the ground when I walk. I don't drool or pick my teeth in public. So tell me what the hell's going on with you."

The pasta, as tasty as cement rods, that she'd forced down at supper, lay undigested in her stomach.

"And don't even think about lying," he added, stopping her heart.

On the defensive, Kelsy blustered, "Why should I lie? Have I ever lied to you? You go ape, then accuse me—"

"Kelsy, Kelsy. Stop." In cop-mode, he held up both hands. As a cop, he could probably see with laser acuity into her lying heart. "I'm sorry."

It killed Kelsy he was apologizing when she should be on her hands and knees. She swallowed. "No. I'm—"

"I wasn't accusing you of lying." He fingered his three rooster's tails. "I didn't mean—"

"You said—"

"I know what I said, and I know you're upset about Jason. I know you're scared." He tried to pull her into his arms, but she went limp.

He sighed. "I also know there's something else going on. Is it because I've been neglecting you? Spending too much time on the job?"

"No!" She couldn't hold back the tears so she shook her head back and forth, reduced to a feeling like a kid. "I understand about your job. I work, too, remember?"

"Yes, but you keep your work priorities straight. I know I don't. But I plan to change that. I swear. I talked with Matthews yesterday, told him—"

"It's not your work." She almost choked on her own saliva.

"What is it, then? You're worse than a wild cat. Your claws are out. You spit at me and hiss at Risa. You scared Molly silly."

Heat stung her cheeks. "Thank you very much for that reminder."

"Jesus." He looked up at the moonless sky. "Did I fall asleep and wake up in some kind of alternate galaxy?"

"Why didn't I think of that?" She didn't bother softening her sarcasm. "An alternate universe could explain everything, make it so easy."

"No." He caught her hand, folded her fingers over his and kissed them. "We still have to talk. About taking Jason back home tomorrow. About why you won't sleep with me tonight. About—"

"I'm taking Jason home tomorrow because I think it's the best place for him. I'm not sleeping with you because I'm sleeping in his room tonight. You're a big boy who can live one night without sex. He's a little boy who needs his mother." She moved to go back inside, but he blocked the door.

"Funny he needs you now, but you were so busy on the damned phone this morning . . ."

For a heartbeat, her tongue stuck to the roof of her mouth. When she spoke, her voice was harsh. "That's below the belt."

Below the belt, but so close to the bone Kelsy knew she'd run out of wiggle room. And now that they'd finally come to something real, she realized she wasn't ready.

"No, it's not." Finn narrowed his eyes. "Guilt's eating you up, and you know it. The only way you'll ever believe I don't care if you were talking on the phone, filing your nails, or staring into space is to trust me enough to talk to me about whatever's bothering you."

Fear dripped into her stomach. Trust. That word again.

"I'm not Dickhead. I don't expect you to be perfect. God knows I'm not."

Maybe not, but he'd join a celestial choir while she begged for ice chips in hell. Which was exactly why she wasn't sleeping with him tonight. Or ever again. He was too good for her. He'd figure that out one day and leave her. If she didn't make the move first. She rubbed her aching head.

"You're ready to drop. You need rest. Take our bed. I'll sleep with Jason."

As much as she wanted to argue, she caved. Tomorrow. Tomorrow, she'd tell him there was no place in her life for him.

This much she knew. . . . Whether she took the job in Seattle or not.

Chapter 11

Just as Finn had suspected, Kelsy couldn't stay out of Jason and Molly's room. Between ten and midnight, she shuffled to the doorway every fifteen minutes. Barely breathing, Finn watched her through squinted eyes. Her white nightgown swirled as she walked. Her blond hair haloed around her shoulders, and teased him with an angelic sexiness. Every other trip, she bent over Jason, peered at him intently, then slipped out of the room as silently as she'd entered.

Finn felt invisible, and the feeling pissed him off.

Deciding enough was enough, he finally crawled out of his sleeping bag at midnight straight up. The witching hour held its own magic for the two of them. During their first two weeks together, he'd worked 1:00 P.M. till 11:00, then hightailed it to Risa's, where he and Kelsy officially welcomed in each new day.

Then, she took off to be with Risa in Nashville during the bad days after the triplets' birth. She stayed for a month. It felt like a decade. Amazing how satisfying phone sex turned out to be. If they'd survived the stress and anxiety of that separation, they could survive anything.

Even Kelsy ignoring him when he stood right next to her. "I love you," he whispered.

"Go back to sleep," she hissed, trying to push past him.

"Ha, ha." He stood his ground.

"If you wake the kids—"

"Nothing's gonna wake those kids." He put his mouth against her ear and felt her shudder.

"Get. Out. Of. My. Way." She slapped both hands on his chest and shoved.

"Stop that!" The youngest of seven boys, he'd been shoved a lot growing up. He didn't like it then, and he hated it now. Though, in a kinky way, it sort of turned him on when Kelsy did it.

Bathed in a circle of gold from the night light, she stared at him as if she could read his mind. Her huge pupils revealed her desire. "It turns me on," he said. "Big time."

She glanced down at his crotch. Her eyes widened.

"Did I lie?" He leaned in so close he could smell her, feel the heat pulsing off her.

She went rigid, then shouldered past him. "I don't have time for this."

"Make time."

With no idea what had happened, Finn dogged her into the hall as wide as a football field, past three closed doors. Future bedrooms for the triplets, Ben had told him on the house tour. Doors to the master bedroom suite and nursery, at the opposite end of the hall, were also closed. Short of an explosion, Finn doubted Risa and Ben could hear anything in the hall. Were they asleep? Making love?

Whichever, at least they're together. Finn heard his jaw crack. Frustration does that to a person, he thought. Makes them jealous, small.

A step ahead of him, Kelsy tried to slip through the

guest-room door and shut it in his face. He'd antici-pated this move and put his shoulder to the door. It opened immediately. She yipped. He said, "Did you want me to huff and puff and blow the damned thing down?"

"I want you to get out of here. We're not having sex."

"How about making love?" He shut the door.

"Damn it, Finn. I said no. Surely, young stud that you are, you have heard the word." She crossed her arms over her breasts, and he willed himself to hold her gaze.

"*Young* stud?" Certain body parts, he realized, didn't necessarily require visual stimulation.

No wonder she might doubt he loved her for more than her soft, curvy, sexy bod.

"Which word don't you understand?" Her look could drop a baby elephant.

"Is that what this is all about? The age thing?" He took a step which forced her to step backwards. How much of this tango before they made it to the bed?

"The age thing?" Her tone said he was robbing a vil-lage somewhere of an idiot, but the set of her mouth made him sure his wild guess hadn't totally missed the mark.

Where to go next?

"This is about you not understanding 'no'," she said.

Wherever he went, she wasn't going to help him fig-ure out zip—even though he was sure she was ready to snap. If he was a better man, he wouldn't push her. He'd let her think he didn't want to protect her or love her . . . that all he wanted from her was sex.

"Here's another newsflash, Finn. You're not irre-sistible." This statement carried the ring of truth and momentarily shook his self-confidence.

He ran his hand through his hair, ready to pull it out follicle by follicle. "Let's not waste the rest of the night. I, for one, can think of several more exciting—"

"You promised you'd get your excitement by staying with Jason. If you can't keep that promise, get out of my way."

"Call me insensitive, but I think Jason will survive for the next five minutes. Or . . . if you really want me back in there, then stop jerking me around. Trust me. Tell me what's wrong." He didn't give a damn if he did sound like he was pleading. Pride didn't matter a damn where Kelsy was concerned.

Shivering, she continued to stare at him. Her face hardened. Whatever emotions were roiling inside her, she managed to hold in check.

"Ten months together, and you still don't trust me."

She lifted her chin but didn't deny his statement.

Male pride said he could wear her down. She'd beg him to make love to her.

Common sense vetoed the idea. Calling himself every kind of fool, he opened the door. Before stepping through it, he said, "You win."

The next morning, edgy and exhausted, Kelsy got up at 6:00 and dressed without showering. She spritzed herself with Joy, reasoning Finn could knock the door down any minute. Sniffing, she realized Joy was his favorite perfume. Damn. She scrubbed her wrists till they were crimson.

By the time she reached Molly's bedroom, both kids sat at a small, red plastic table overlooking a side yard of ferns. Finn sat on the floor between the kids with Lucky Prince in his lap. All three humans wore chocolate mustaches. The dog barked. Kelsy winced.

"Good morning!" Miz Perky, she stared at a tree.

"Mommy!"

Exhausted, Kelsy jumped, then rubbed her ear.

"We saw a deer. A buck." The dog barked again, and

Jason shushed him but screamed, "He was humongous! My arm doesn't hurt at all."

Each statement went up a decibel, shattering Kelsy's nervous system. Coherent thought took a nosedive. It didn't help that Finn grinned up at her like an elf. He escaped murder because she couldn't move, she was sure, without her head falling off. Or without falling over her toe.

"A broken arm apparently doesn't affect the vocal cords," Finn offered from the floor

"Finn made us hot chocolate!" Molly screamed, and Kelsy bit back a shriek.

"A broken arm apparently doesn't affect the vocal cords of one's best friend, either." Finn saluted Kelsy with a mug. "Coffee?"

"Don't think so," she said, tempted to knock him over and grab the thermos next to him.

"It's free," he said. "No strings attached."

"I'm sure," Kelsy shot back, wanting to smack him. He'd orchestrated this whole damn setup.

"Doncha wanna sit down, Mommy?" Jason pointed at a spot on the floor next to Finn.

Infuriated by Finn's lame sneak attack, confirmed by his wide-eyed look of innocence, she started to refuse, then decided it was too early to engage in verbal ping pong and accepted Finn's hand to sit down. As if giving her room, he made a production of moving over. In fact, he didn't move an inch, but Molly and Jason giggled at his antics.

The humor escaped Kelsy. Every time he rocked back and forth, she tried to draw her arms and legs in closer. Somehow their knees touched anyway, and she felt as if she'd brushed an electrical wire. Which was ridiculous, she told herself. She had every intention of telling him she had other plans for her life, and those plans didn't include him.

The second Finn stopped his silly games, Jason announced, "I don't wanna go home today, Mommy."

White-hot fury at Finn exploded in Kelsy's head.

"We've got lotsa things to do," Molly interjected. "Finn said he'd play hide and seek with us."

Jason ran his tongue around his chocolate moustache. "I wanna come home when Finn does."

Gripping the edge of the low table, Kelsy shot Finn a look that should've popped the buttons off his shirt.

He poured her coffee with a steady hand. "Finn isn't coming home till Sunday." She wanted to blister his ears but held her tongue for Jason's sake.

"I know." Jason smiled sweetly. "I wish we could stay, Mommy."

"Please, Kelsy." Molly got up from her chair and wrapped her arms around Kelsy's neck. "I miss Jason sooo much."

"And I miss Molly sooo much," Jason added, not whining, simply letting her know, punching all her guilt buttons.

"You two." Kelsy inhaled.

Defeat had never had sweeter faces. When Kelsy and Sam had announced their divorce two weeks before Christmas, Molly had saved Jason. Dickhead then broke the news of his imminent move to Los Angeles. Momentarily caught in the past, Kelsy couldn't immediately return to the sun-filled room.

"Can I stay, Mommy?"

"Please, Kelsy." Without Molly, Jason would never have come through the divorce as well as he did.

Without Finn, you'd have hit the wall.

"Give her a second, kids." Finn laid his hand on her knee. No pressure, just there, warm, reassuring, wonderfully familiar.

Heat started in her stomach and spread. Feelings of inadequacy faded as her head cleared. She said, "La Ti Da says staying here's exactly what the doctor ordered, so yes, Jason, you can stay." She squeezed Finn's hand, met his gaze and telegraphed a silent thank you.

Midway through yips of euphoria, Jason screamed, "You, too, Mommy?"

Finn didn't move his hand. The grin he tried unsuccessfully to hide still melted Kelsy's insides. She punched his arm playfully. "Okay, but Finn is It for the first game of hide and seek."

After the screams died down, Finn shrugged. " 'S a toughie, but I bet I'll find you in two minutes flat."

"You're pretty cock–confident." Blushing, Kelsy made a face at the kids, who giggled.

Jason yelled, "Finn's good, Mommy. Real good."

"I know Finn *thinks* he's good," Kelsy taunted, her face hot, her heart fluttering.

"No," Molly said solemnly. "He *is* good." She slurped the last of her hot chocolate.

"Better pay attention to my fan club," Finn drawled.

"And if I don't?" Kelsy shivered.

"You'll be sorry." The kids immediately took up his sing-song chant. "You'll be sorry! You'll be sorreeee!"

Wiggling her toe, Kelsy declared, "Let the games begin."

Shrieks from Molly and Jason as they ran straight for the barn. Questioning her sanity, Kelsy paused at the barn door. She glanced over her shoulder at Finn. He looked like a million bucks in his hip-hugging jeans and blue-plaid shirt, his back to her, his head buried in his arms against a post on the corral. He yelled, "One, two, three . . ."

Seventeen seconds to find Jason. Without being too obvious as the overprotective mommy, Kelsy had no intentions of hiding. She intended to make sure Jason was okay. That he hadn't hidden somewhere he could hurt his arm. She closed her eyes against a mental snapshot of him on the ground writhing in pain.

". . . nine, ten . . ."

Limping slightly, she slipped into the dim barn and blinked. Smells of horses, hay, and leather enveloped her. A nicker intensified the silence. Whatever nook or cranny the kids had found, they must not be breathing.

"Fifteen!" Finn shouted.

Kelsy felt her pulse jitter. A huge black cat, lying under a sun-filled window, hissed and darted into the shadows as Kelsy moved deeper into the barn. Where the heck was Jason? She was a hide-and-seek novice. In her own distant childhood, she'd preferred dress-up in her mother's high heels, silky slips, and assorted costume jewelry. Risa, who played soccer and taught Kelsy to ride a bike, had rarely refused entering the pretend-world of grownups.

"Twenty!"

Tensed for the slightest sound that might reveal Jason's location, Kelsy ducked behind a bale of hay. The horsey smells made her dizzy, but she also felt strangely excited at the thought of eluding Finn. She held her breath.

A whisper of warm air on the back of her neck threatened to ignite her hair.

"Are you lost, little girl?"

"Yiii—" Her heart hit her skull as Finn clamped his hand over her mouth. Lust pulsed through her, and she shot into another dimension. God, was she lost. "Ummmm."

"Want me to show you a shortcut home?" He moved his head toward the loft several times, then winked broadly.

His erection told her exactly what kind of delightful dangers lurked on the *shortcut.*

Then, she remembered Jason and Molly. Were they watching? She plied Finn's fingers away. "My toe—"

Taking a chance the kids wouldn't emerge till they were sure it was safe, she ran her tongue along Finn's fingers. His moans reminded her how easily he forgave her lousy moods. How had she ever thought she could live her life without him?

On another planet, Kelsy heard a horse neigh, then giggles. Out of the corner of her eye, she saw Jason jump out of an empty stall. "Mommy's it!"

An hour later, after four games, Finn emerged the hide-and-seek champ. The exhausted kids and panting dog flanked him outside the barn. He swaggered a few steps away from them and clasped his hands high over his head. "I, Finn The Finest Funmeister found here or on foreign shores, reserve the right to decide my prize at a later time."

He locked eyes with Kelsy, declaring, "Probably after lunch. Or maybe during afternoon naps. Or then again—"

"What prize?" Kelsy demanded, shivering when he cocked a brow at her. "Nobody said anything about a prize."

"So?" Finn made a hand-motion to the kids, who parroted, "So?"

Lucky Prince barked, then jumped in the air. As if weighing in on the matter, a horse neighed. The kids howled, but Kelsy wasn't about to be distracted so easily. Whatever prize Finn wanted, she knew she'd end up the payee. She said, "I've never heard about a prize for winning at hide and seek."

"Yes, there is, Mommy." Jason held his cast in close to his chest but showed no signs of pain. He'd played as if he'd worn the cast since birth.

"We always play for a prize, Kelsy." Molly nodded as if this made her statement fact.

"Times have changed, Mom. There's always a prize." Finn winked, and Kelsy blushed.

Mentally, she whacked herself upside the head. "All right," she said. "I give up. Finn can choose his prize whenever he wants."

"How gracious of you, m'lady." He made a sweeping

bow, and Kelsy wondered why chivalry had died. Did men have any idea how women loved being the center of a man's attention?

Immediately horrified by this traitorous thought, she said crisply, "Graciousness aside, this mother says it's time for a quiet activity till lunch."

Whether it was her no-nonsense tone or whether Molly and Jason were simply exhausted, they headed for the house without protest. Bringing up the rear behind them, Finn hooked arms with her. "I suppose you feel compelled to go in and help Risa."

What she felt like—falling into his arms and begging his forgiveness—she didn't do. The timing wasn't right. Instead, she nodded. "It's only fair. I thought I'd suggest she and Ben take a break this afternoon. They don't get much alone-time with four kids."

"That's nice of you." Finn tucked a piece of hair behind her ear, then drew his finger across her cheek, then down the line of her jaw. "Since I don't want to come across as a self-centered, horny adolescent, I won't add that I'm disappointed."

"I'm starving." Laughing, Jason turned around, stumbled over Lucky Prince, bumped Molly, then missed a step.

"Jason!" Kelsy forgot her toe and lunged forward, but Finn leaped ahead of her.

He sidestepped the dog racing around in a circle apparently thinking they'd started a new game. In a flying tackle, he caught Jason, lifted him off his feet and held him aloft for a heartbeat before setting him next to Kelsy. "Inches to spare."

Choked by relief, she couldn't speak.

"You gotta be more careful, Jason." Molly made the tsking sound Risa often used to express concern. "You almost fell on your broken arm."

"Did not." Jason stuck his bottom lip out.

"Did, too." Molly jutted her bottom lip out even farther.

Little by little, Kelsy felt the adrenaline-rush ebb. Jason was fine. He hadn't hurt himself. Thank God, Finn had quick reflexes. She'd been too self-involved to watch out for her own kid. How could she ever manage the two other kids Finn wanted them to have?

Savvy as only kids testing distracted adults can be, Molly and Jason continued their bickering. Each recrimination was a nail in Kelsy's skull. She massaged her temples. Lack of sleep, the stress of the past few days and the constant bickering with Finn didn't make for a calm babysitter. Risa and Ben would come home from an afternoon out and find her ready for a padded cell.

Her meltdown vision was so vivid, she jumped when Finn put an arm around her waist. As good as she felt being so close to him, she couldn't shake her tension. He whistled, and she was sure her blood pressure shot off the chart.

"Oookay, " he said to the kids. "You two take this discussion over to the back porch for about five minutes. After that, if you can't settle it, adults will have to help you out."

"You're not the boss of me." Jason glared at Finn, shocking Kelsy.

Usually, Finn's slightest comment carried the weight of another commandment with her son. Sometimes, jealousy ate away at her. Yet, she wanted a strong man in Jason's life since Dickhead had basically gone AWOL long before the divorce.

While Kelsy hesitated, Finn said calmly, "You're right. I'm not the boss of you, but you aren't the boss of me and your mom, either. You and Molly know how to work out your problems."

Finn shot her a look. Translation: so do we. Fire shot from Kelsy's toe to her head. Sex had always worked with Dickhead—or so she'd thought for ten years of marriage. With Finn, it was different. He wanted to know what she thought. What she wanted. What she expected.

Her stomach clenched. Too bad she didn't know the answers. She had eight years on him, but his maturity, insight, and love made her feel younger than Jason and Molly. As she continued her study of deep space, Finn laced their fingers but spoke to Jason. "I know you and Molly are very good at working out your problems. But if you need a time out first—"

"We don't need a time out." Molly pulled Jason toward the porch.

Dry-mouthed, Kelsy watched the five-year-olds sit down in a puddle of sunshine and longed to rush over and hug her rigid son. Boy, did she understand how he felt. Molly and Finn should be canonized. Both were loyal to a fault. Both exuded patience through their pores. Jason and Kelsy exuded sweat. Finn and Molly heaped everyone with kindness. Jason and Kelsy accepted kindness as their due.

Next to her, Finn chucked her chin. "What say you and I take a lesson?"

A wave of resentment washed over her. Finn, the eternal optimist. She said neutrally, "You and I probably need more than five minutes, don't you think?"

Frowning, he shrugged. "Tell me what's wrong, and I might say yes."

Her heart started that stupid fluttering again. "You'll think I'm silly." She lifted her chin. Honesty mattered to Finn. He'd bared his heart from the first night he'd waited for her outside Risa's. What if he decided her lies were unforgivable?

His mouth tightened. She hugged her waist. "Silly." He pronounced it as if he'd never heard the word.

"Silly," she repeated. Was he making fun of her? That

had been one of Sam's favorite tactics, mocking her during arguments till she exploded, giving him an excuse to stomp out, calling her hysterical and out of control.

Hysterical had been one of Sam's favorite words. One he'd used the first time he and Finn met. The only time she'd ever seen Finn angry enough to lose control.

On a hunch, he'd waited outside Risa's, Kelsy's refuge after Sam finally confessed about Bimbette. She and Finn spent the rest of the night together drinking coffee. Before they finished the first cup, he declared he'd always loved her.

And she'd believed him. Despair over Sam's betrayal faded. The next morning, she and Finn showed up at Risa's one minute ahead of Jason's arrival with his father.

Sam exploded. Kelsy had better get over her hysteria from the night before. If she thought hysterics would keep him chained to her, she'd better damned well grow up.

Eyes flashing, hands fisted, Finn had stepped in. Sam's rage was no match for Finn's fierce protectiveness.

The memory of how protected she'd felt faded. Eyeing her, Finn said, "I like silly. Silly as in the silly guy who believed he'd someday get the woman he'd loved."

She swallowed. "I like that silly, too. That's a wonderful silly. That's why I think 'immature' hones in on the way I've been behaving. Hysterical probably works, too. Risa suggested PMS, but as much as I'd like to blame my hormones, I—"

"Kelsy." He grabbed her hands flapping in front of her chest. "Just tell me. Whatever it is, we'll work it out."

"You make it sound so simple."

"As long as you're not trying to dump me, I figure it's simple." His blue eyes, clear as the Montana skies, invited trust. "I love you. I know you love me. I know you're not sneaking around behind my back with some other guy—"

Her knees wobbled as the blood rushed out of her head. "Kelsy!" He caught her before she came close to falling. "You're not pregnant?"

Hysteria bubbled in her throat, and her chest felt as if a moose sat on it. "You should know," she said, unable to say anything comforting when disappointment flared in his eyes.

"Not a problem," he said quickly. "I didn't really think you could be, but you know us guys. We're always worried about the human race dying out."

His laugh invited her to join him in poking fun at himself, and she thought she managed to put an authentic ring in her chuckle. She knew how much he wanted two more kids. They'd even chosen names . . . long before Dane Jensen showed up and turned her life upside down. Which wasn't Finn's fault. Admitting she now wanted a career more than the life they'd imagined bordered on cruel when he was this vulnerable. On the other hand, she couldn't keep pretending. Not with Finn.

Determined not to hurt him, she pulled his face to hers, drawn into a bottomless pool of blue warmth. "This afternoon, while the kids nap, we'll talk. I'll come clean."

"Damn!" He snapped his fingers. "Sounds as if I shoulda brought the handcuffs."

Chapter 12

Getting five kids to take naps after lunch turned into a monumental feat, but Finn thought he and Kelsy managed pretty well, given their lack of experience. And zero coaching from Risa and Ben, who tore out in the pickup without a backward glance. By 2:45, Molly and Jason, who had made up, snoozed in the twin beds in her room. Lucky Prince lay on the floor, head on his paws. Down the hall, even the teething Harry had zonked out.

Sprawled on the sofa in the great room, Finn looked up at the pine ceiling and sighed. The golden wood filled the space with a radiant warmth. His mind drifted. Twenty years earlier . . . . Sean's prom. Kelsy in his parents' entryway. Next to Rob Parker—Sean's totally undeserving jerk of a best friend. The flash of cameras. Gazing at her, Finn had felt struck by lightning. So what if she was almost an adult and the most beautiful creature he'd ever seen? Silently, he vowed he'd always have her light in his life.

Kelsy, returning from a peek at the triplets, broke the spell. "Some day I'm coming up here and videotaping every movement Ben and Risa make. Maybe then I can figure out how they manage four kids."

To Finn's surprise, she sat down next to him without any encouragement and laid her head in the crook of his shoulder. As always, whenever she was near, he felt every nerve come to attention. The flowery fragrance of her hair always conjured up for him a hothouse of lilacs and roses.

"Ummm." He inhaled, unable to get enough of her.

"When was the last time we did this?" she murmured.

His chest tightened. "Too long. This damned assignment. I had the perfect life, so why did I want more? People are nuts."

She pushed away from him, a frown between her eyebrows. "You weren't nuts for wanting something more. How would you ever know if you were cut out for undercover work if you hadn't applied for this assignment?"

He groaned. "If I find a whip, would you beat me for a while? Or kick me. But be careful of your toe. Do anything you want, but don't sound so understanding, okay?"

A muscle ticked under her left eye, but he put it down to exhaustion. She hadn't slept last night. Then, they'd had the stupid blow-up outside. "C'mere."

He sat up and ran his hands down her spine. "Your muscles feel harder than Montana boulders. I know it's been a long time, but I still give a pretty mean massage."

She twisted away from him, but laced his fingers with hers. "We haven't had our talk yet."

"Do we need it?" He winked. "Talk's sometimes overrated as communication."

An ugly red splotch covered her neck. "And sex isn't the only form of communication," she said with an edge.

"Oh, shit!" He tilted his head and focused on the ceiling fan. "Here we go again."

"What's that mean?" Scarlet-faced, she clenched her hands into balls.

"Sorry." He meant it, though an eggplant probably sounded more enthusiastic.

"Yes, I can hear that." The way she narrowed her eyes should've shriveled his cojones but, pervert that he was, he liked it. God, she was gorgeous when she got edgy.

"Should I go down on my knees to prove I meant it?" He wiggled his eyebrows.

"You should stop being a smart ass and—" A tear leaked down her cheek. Viciously, she scrubbed it away.

Finn straightened with a jerk. "Kelsy!" He grabbed her hands before she could go at her eyes again. "Stop that. Hit me, don't hurt yourself."

For a second, he thought she was going to accept his offer. Then, she went limp—as if a wind had blown through her and blown out the light inside her. A rag doll shows more resistance, he thought, dragging her onto his lap.

"God," he said, stroking her neck. "Talk about your thick-headed Irish cop. Do I fit the stereotype to a T or what? If you'd hit me, I'd feel a hundred percent better."

"Sorry, I'm not into S and M for fun." The edge gone.

Accustomed to her energy and independence, Finn didn't know what to do. He'd never seen her cry—except when she'd bawled buckets at Ben and Risa's wedding. Mostly, she worried his mother and family thought she was psycho. In fact, Ma had, several times, warned him he should marry Kelsy as quickly as possible—before she realized his jokes and insane humor could drive a saint to blasphemy.

"I don't want fun any way except with you," he whispered.

"What about being serious—for just one damned heartbeat?" Seated in his lap, she stared at him, her jutted chin trembling. He wanted to grab her, hold her, and kiss away her fears.

"Will being serious get you in bed with me?"

"Go to hell." Fire blazed in her eyes.

Good, she was coming back to life.

He held up his hands. "It's the silver tongue in me head. I don't know how to be serious." He looked at her and cursed his stupid need to go for funny. "That's the truth," he added.

At first he thought she was going to start crying again. But she said, "The truth. Finally."

"Now, you're scaring me."

"Not half as much as I'm scaring myself." Early afternoon sunlight streamed through one of the uncurtained, floor-to-ceiling windows. Her pale face shone with an inner light that sent goose bumps down Finn's arms.

For once in his life, he was struck mute. In the split second before he made some lame comment, his cell beeped.

"Forget it." He didn't even look down at his belt. "I'm on vacation. Matthews knows that. Whatever you've got to say is more important."

"Take the call." Over his protests, she slipped off his lap and floated toward the bedroom wing. "I'll check the kids."

As always, he loved watching her walk. He'd never entered a public place with other men present where they all didn't study the sway of her hips. Nothing flagrantly sexy, just total confidence. Probably the way Eve moved to offer the apple to Adam. The phone beeped again, and his fantasy evaporated.

Olivia? He snarled, "This better be good, Stuart."

"Is Kelsy there?"

His neck muscles twanged. "In the other room."

"Don't say anything."

Mind racing, he felt as if he'd been whacked with a lead pipe. "You've been watching *Law and Order* too much, Stuart."

"Ha, ha. Anyone tell you you should be a stand-up comic?"

"Kelsy. About two minutes ago. *She* appreciates my rapier wit." He settled into the sofa.

"Rapier wit. I bet." Olivia paused, then said, "I don't have time to beat around the bush. So here's the skinny. If Kelsy comes in, let me know."

Acid bubbled in the back of Finn's throat. Tempted to crush the cell phone with his teeth, Finn said, "Tell me, dammit."

"Shut up and listen."

Surprised, he blinked. She rarely pulled rank on him. What the hell was going down? "Hurry up," he snapped. "Kelsy'll be back any second."

"If we get disconnected, don't call me back. Follow up on your own."

Ready to bellow like an enraged orangutan, Finn said through gritted teeth, "Gladly. But following up on my own would be a helluva lot easier if I knew *what* I'm supposed to—"

"A plate listed in a suspected hit-and-run is Kelsy's."

"What?" Finn roared so loud his head rang. "Hit-and—" Fury filled his throat. Cops everywhere hated hit-and-runs. They violated every code of honor and decency.

Before he regrouped, Olivia rattled off more info. "I was checking the CHP BOLO database for our perps' license plates. Kelsy's name and SUV plates are on the list."

"Shiiit!" Hadn't he known better than to leave her at the E-Z on that *business* call?

"The accident happened in Half Moon Bay—"

"Cheese and crackers, Olivia!" Some part of Finn's stunned mind realized he was so scared he couldn't swear. He inhaled, his brain clearing. "Christ, woman. You had me going long enough there for a major coronary. Kelsy lives in Cielo Vista. You remember? She housesits for Dr. Risa Macdonald. The two of them have probably been up every night this week shooting the breeze about this weekend."

As soon as he spit the words out, they sounded hollow, and he couldn't breathe right again. *They weren't shooting the breeze on Tuesday night.*

"Exactly why I'm calling you, Einstein. Right now, the Chippies haven't issued a warrant. They simply want to question her. Which means—"

"I know what it means," Finn snarled. "Some idiot probably keyed a wrong digit into the database or listed all the white SUVs within a hundred-mile radius of Half Moon Bay—"

The faster he talked, the faster the wheels in his head fell off. He knew Olivia was yammering on and on, but he heard mostly white noise. Kelsy had been so damned weird on Thursday. On the jet . . . never calming down even after they reached Montana. He'd figured her agitation was due to seeing Jason.

They'd had their fuckfest at the EZ and . . . . That phone call . . . as he was leaving . . . . Something strange there. Wednesday . . . she'd never given him a clue anything was wrong. He stared at the ceiling fan. Sweat dripped into his eyes. Then, the call here. Mr. Asshole. He'd completely forgotten it.

He interrupted Olivia. "When did the accident happen?"

"Wednesday morning. Early. An anonymous caller

reported the wreck at four-forty. The driver's unconscious."

"Four-forty?" Finn exhaled, so he wouldn't yell at Olivia. Instead, he swallowed, then said quietly, "Kelsy's on the air at five o'clock. She leaves home between four, four-thirty. It's at least an hour from Half Moon Bay—"

"Hey! Slow down. You don't have to convince me of a damned thing." Olivia raised the volume a couple of notches.

Uh-huh. They both protested too much, Finn realized, ignoring her bossiness.

Olivia, who'd met Kelsy twice, hated her. Most women did. On sight. Ma and Kathleen, Sean's wife, were the exceptions. They never let Finn forget what a lucky man he was to have such a beautiful, intelligent and genuinely nice woman love him. As if he didn't give thanks every day.

Ma and Kathleen aside, Kelsy had picked up immediately on Olivia's hostility, but she'd been nothing but gracious. Later, she told Finn she never got used to other women treating her as if she walked around naked as Eve.

"Babe," he'd drawled. "You're sexier dressed like an Eskimo than most women are in their sexiest negligeé."

Aware the silence on the phone had become awkward, Finn said, "Sorry I bit your head off, Partner. Thanks for the heads up. I'll run with it from here."

He hung up as soon as Olivia mumbled she *hoped* it was a computer glitch. What if she had it all wrong? A smart man would do a little preliminary investigating before he shot himself in the foot.

"Let's go see Uncle Finn." Kelsy tiptoed into the room with Harry against her chest, a wad of her golden hair fisted in one hand. Her T-shirt was wrinkled, the front tucked into her jeans, the tail hanging out.

Throat arched to accommodate the baby, she

stunned Finn, with her skin rosy, her eyes aglow, her full mouth curved in a soft smile. "Remember that saying about the best-laid plans?"

"Looks like ours are kaput," he said, more relieved than a cop should admit.

Harry's grumpiness quickly became contagious and started an epidemic when the older kids woke half an hour later.

Worried over coming clean with Finn, Kelsy tried to remain calm; but Jason's whines frayed her nerves to the quick. Unlike adults, herself included, who hid their darker emotions, her son made no bones about his resentment of Harry being cuddled.

"Harry doesn't have a broken arm, Mommy. You should hold me. Let Harry cry. A broken arm hurts more than crying."

Throughout this tirade, Jason stayed glued closer to Kelsy than wallpaper. She felt flattered for about two seconds. Then, arms and mind went numb. In their swings, Tom, and Charlie exercised their lungs while Lucky Prince ran around in circles barking as if in competition with the puny two-legged howlers.

Finn and Molly worked with the Trio Los Locos—which left Kelsy in charge of Harry and Jason. Whatever attraction she held for adult males, the two boys showed a marked immunity.

"This happens 'most every day after naps," Molly offered.

"I don't like it," Jason stated. "LP, you be quiet!"

Tail tucked, Lucky Prince threw his head back and howled.

"Maybe you should put him out," Kelsy suggested.

"Noooo!" Molly shook her head. "Sometimes he calms Charlie, Tom and Harry."

"He could start any time now," Finn said.

Kelsy laughed, a little surprised Finn didn't join her. "Don't tell me seven Bishop boys didn't raise plenty of bedlam."

"Huh. There's bedlam, then there's bedlam."

"Believe me, it could be worse." Kelsy caught him studying her with such puzzled intensity, she almost dropped Harry. If bedlam unnerved him, why was he so set on having two more kids?

Confident he suspected nothing about Dane, she dazzled him with a smile. *Please, please, don't let her hurt him.*

Whether he was dazzled, dazed, or simply dumbfounded, he stared at her, then said slowly, "I'll grant that watching kids requires more skill and patience than staking out bad guys."

Her heart fluttered. "I'll remember that."

The second time she intercepted his puzzled look, she focused her imagination on drawing a dragon on Jason's cast while she crooned to Harry and patted Jason's hand at the same time. Tempted to call Risa and Ben to come home, she repeatedly rebuilt her smile and imagined saying to Finn, *See how much blood, sweat, and tears two more kids demand. How can I have a career with two infants? By the time they start pre-school, I'll be senile. So old I won't know a teleprompter from a radish.*

The skin on her arms prickled. Finn was staring at her again. This time, despite her trip into la-la-land, she had no doubt something was eating at him. "What's wrong?"

"Now's not a good time." His refusal to meet her eyes gave him away and fanned the ashes of panic in her stomach.

"Okay." She squeezed Harry so tight, he screamed. Soothing him was a snap, but her own anxiety flared. Whatever troubled Finn, she'd bet it wasn't a declaration of happiness ever after.

* * *

To her disappointment, Risa's and Ben's return worked no magic.

Harry still clung to Kelsy as if she were his mother. Jason still wouldn't move two inches away from her. Lucky Prince still yipped and barked with the energy of a dog on speed.

Ben bussed Risa's cheek, then suggested he and Finn take over supper preparation. Instantly on his feet, Finn invited Jason too.

"No way."

Kelsy sighed, then whispered to Risa, "Remind me to get my head examined before I come up here the next time, okay?"

Listening to Molly's running commentary on her brothers, Risa changed Tom, but replied to Kelsy, "You think this is crazy? Show up when all four of them have colds."

"I don't have tummy aches anymore," Molly stated.

"Honey, that's great." Chronic stomach aches following the accidental death of Molly's mother, Kelsy remembered, had helped bring Risa and Ben together.

Lust had brought her and Finn together.

"Don't call her *honey*!" Jason tugged on Kelsy's hand.

"I've always called Molly—" Seeing her son's jutted chin, Kelsy recognized defeat and stopped. "You know what?" She put her nose on his, then widened her eyes.

"What?" Jason squinted his eyes.

"I think you and I could use a little quality time." Silently, she checked this out with Risa, who nodded. Mouthing thank you, Kelsy added, "Just you and me."

"Yay, yah." Jason supported his broken arm with his uninjured arm and jumped up and down. His face clouded. He came to a standstill. "Can Finn come, too, Mommy?"

There was no way Kelsy could say no to the eagerness in his face. Unnerved by Finn's grimness, she crossed her fingers and said, "Sure, if Ben doesn't need him in the kitchen."

"*And* Lucky Prince?" Jason started for the kitchen. "Ben won't need him for sure."

"I want LP to stay with me," Molly wailed.

"No, you come with us, too," Jason said, expansive in his role as Czar of the Universe.

Chapter 13

Fifteen minutes later, with the kids in jackets against the late afternoon nip, Jason led the circus toward the barn to say good night to Ole Paint. Kelsy automatically reached for Finn's hand, felt him flinch, and felt her pulse stutter.

"Are my hands too cold?" she asked as the kids raced ahead with Lucky Prince in hot pursuit.

"Of course not." He tucked her hand in the crook of his elbow, but didn't squeeze her fingertips or smile.

His smell of Old Spice had faded. The hollow in her stomach contracted. "Why'd you jump then?"

"Surprised," he said, with the ring of truth.

"Must've been an unpleasant surprise." Her throat was so dry, it hurt to talk. Why couldn't she smell him?

"No. Don't overre—" He stopped, shrugged. "I just wasn't expecting you to grab my hand."

"Grab—" She swallowed. "You always hold my hand when we walk. I love it." Feeling safe, protected, and always excited by his strong, tender fingers.

"You do?" His surprise jolted her.

"Haven't I told you that?" She frowned, her hands now icy.

"Yeah, you have. Sorry, I was thinking about something else." His hand felt damp, almost clammy, in hers.

Longing for a hint of his slow, sexy smile, she hung back from entering the barn. "About me, right?" Heart hammering, she stated, "Something bad about me."

Her ears felt hot. Too late, she wished she hadn't said *bad*. It was a word kids used. So, why wasn't Finn protesting?

"Helllooo?" The pressure grew in her ears as confusion in his eyes stared back at her. Barely breathing, scared because he was so quiet, she waved her fingers in front of his nose.

"Hello." His impersonal, joyless response sent a chill down her back.

Anemic sunshine slanted through a window in the barn, creating a wedge of whitish light just inside the door. Kelsy refused to step into its warmth. "Are you going to tell me what you were thinking?" she whispered.

Misery peered at her from his disbelieving eyes. He tugged one of his rooster tails. "Someone told me . . . something. I can't decide how much is true and how much is a mistake."

"Couldn't I tell you if anything you've heard me about is true or not?" She hated sounding so scared.

His hesitation pushed her heart into high gear. BA-bum, BA-bum, BA-bum. Her ears rang. *Do not cry. Do not cry.* She blinked, but a tear leaked out of her left eye.

". . . knew something . . . was wrong. You . . ." Palms up, he talked.

Her body tensed, but she didn't listen. She waited for him to grin. Wink, maybe. Then, he'd scoop her up and kiss her. Reassure her. Promise everything would be fine.

Maybe, in fact, that's what he was saying. She strained, focused on his mouth. It opened and shut, opened and shut, his tongue a pink reminder of exotic pleasures.

I can't hear you.

A soundless stream flowed from the mouth she'd kissed so many times she'd lost count. Rapid words. Steady words. Comfortless, because of his frown and worried eyes.

Hold me. Hold me, Finn.

She heard a crack. His jaw or hers?

Then silence. Thickening to a gel that stuck to them, the air around them, in her throat. The silence spread and took on a sense of rightness. She felt the fissure deepen. Passage across it no longer easy, but serious and dangerous.

Impossible now for him to hold her.

"Finn! Finn! C'mere, Finn!" Jason's ear-splitting screech plus the sound of his feet slapping on the wooden barn floor broke Finn's trance. Sweet Jesus, talk about bad timing.

Out of breath, cheeks crimson, Jason careened to a halt a few feet from Kelsy. "What's wrong, Mommy?"

Finn wasn't sure she'd heard, but he wasn't about to lie to Jason. He didn't have to. Kelsy shot him a warning look, then said to Jason, "Sorry, sweetheart. Finn and I were talking. What's so exciting? Where's Molly?"

"She's okay, right?" Finn felt a blip of guilt. Facing off with Kelsy, he'd forgotten the kids and still hadn't told her about Olivia's call.

"Molly's fine." Jason rolled his eyes. "Come see what we found." He pulled on Finn and Kelsy at the same time.

There was a moment of awkwardness as the three of them tried to stay in sync with each other. After a couple of missteps because of Kelsy's toe, Finn motioned her and Jason in front. He fell behind.

A biiiig mistake. As a nice guy who loved her, he

should be figuring out how to tell her about Olivia's allegations. As a red-blooded male who lusted after her, he couldn't keep his eyes off the rhythmic sway of her luscious hips. Finn sucked in essence of horses and hay.

Jesus, he had the attention span of a gerbil.

"Over here, Mommy." Jason tugged on her hand, and her laughter echoed off the wooden walls.

Pleasure crept into Finn. God, he loved watching her move—with and without clothes. Head high, shoulders back, she walked with the unconscious ease of a dancer.

Or a princess.

A princess who routinely pinched his butt—inviting a similar response from him.

The curve and arc of Kelsy's hips promised fleshly mysteries he never tired of exploring. But her jokes about his cute buns, her fondling and caressing his flat ass, still stunned him.

Maybe they should just hop in the sack. *Give her a good lay, right?*

Smell and fantasy blended, and his brain shifted infinitesimally. The vertigo passed as quickly as it came. He snorted. He was a total idiot if he thought their problems would magically disappear with a good lay.

Jason looked back over his shoulder. "Hurry, Finn. Ya gotta see this."

This was Molly hovering over a nest of tiny, mewing kittens, so young their eyes were still closed. "Ohhhh," Kelsy cooed, melting Finn's heart.

Instantly drawn to her tenderness, wanting to protect her, he moved up behind her just as she leaned down at Molly's level. Face aglow, she glanced up at Finn. His throat tightened, but doubt evaporated. Kelsy never left the scene of that accident.

"They're sooo cute," Molly whispered.

"And sooo helpless," Kelsy whispered, her eyes soft. "Where's their mother?"

"We don't know." Jason hunkered down and arranged his cast across his legs. "Me 'n Molly found 'em, but not their mommy."

"I think she's afraid to come out," Molly offered.

"I imagine she's scared of Lucky Prince." Kelsy stood, blocking Finn's view. "Maybe Finn can take him out while we look for her."

"I—" *don't want to* is what Finn almost blurted. But, hey, someone had to be the guy, so he said, "Not a problem."

"Maybe you can look around out there, too," Kelsy said, her back to him.

"Sure. Why not?" he boomed.

Lucky Prince woofed and inched out of his corner.

"Shhhh!" Molly and Jason glared at him.

Ears stinging, Finn noticed Kelsy's smirk and had to bite his tongue. "We'll be back," he said in an exaggerated whisper.

"Be still my heart." She bent over the kittens again, and he laughed since they were damned cute.

Besides, he deserved her small power play. He'd let her down earlier by not being up front about Olivia's call right away. *Live and learn.*

Twenty minutes of searching didn't turn up Mom Cat. Suspecting this news wouldn't sit well with the trio in the barn, Finn went into the kitchen for a flashlight. Dusk had reduced visibility, and he figured he'd make more progress without Lucky Prince sniffing every inch of ground.

The smell of onions and garlic made Finn's mouth water, but he ignored his base reaction, filling Ben in quickly on the situation. Lowering the heat on his pots and pans, his host volunteered, "Why should you be the only hero? I know a few hiding places we can check. Let me give Risa a heads-up."

Glad for any excuse to stop obsessing about Kelsy, Finn said, "Lead on, MacDuff."

The need to tell her what Olivia had found burned in his brain with the intensity of a fever. Outside, the first evening stars dotted the darkening sky. Brrrr. He blew on his hands. After halfheartedly peering under several bushes and shrubs, he said, "Did Risa mention anything about Kelsy's . . . moods while you were out?"

Ben directed the flashlight on a spot near a dead flowerbed, held the light steady, then moved on. "Risa and I didn't talk much while we were out. A 1964 Chevy pickup encourages other activities."

"Got it." Finn was glad the dark hid the neon-green tinge glowing on his hands.

"And even if we had talked, Risa would kill me if I breathed a syllable to you. Near as I can figure it, she and Kelsy have a blood pact. You and I are just lucky they like men."

"In my case, at the moment, that's debatable."

Ben laughed. "What'd you do? Open mouth, insert foot?"

"Right up to the hip. Not so far I think Kelsy's swearing off men any time soon, but don't ask her about swearing off me."

Off to their left, the bushes rustled. Ben swung the light around. Two yellow eyes stared at them. A deer, momentarily frozen. Ben lowered the beam, and the animal sprinted away.

"One thing I know for sure," Finn said. "If we don't find that cat, you and I can forget sleeping next to our women tonight."

"Would you have it any other way?" Ben swept the rose garden with light. "Our women have the biggest, tenderest hearts. What's a night's sleep?"

"Easy for you to say. I noticed your bedroom door was closed last night. I assume you were inside."

"Your point being?" Ben stepped off the path into

what Finn thought was a black hole. But he followed, grumbling, "My point being, I'm hoping for your kind of luck behind closed doors tonight."

"We find that cat, you can bet on it." Under his breath, Ben called the cat.

Finn joined in. After about five minutes, he said, "We can both forget sleeping inside if either of us mentions coyotes."

Within fifteen minutes, they'd searched around the entire perimeter of the house as well as around the barn, outbuildings, backyard, bushes and shrubs. No sign of the cat, but no fur or blood either. A ghostly moon bathed the stone path in a cool, filtered white. Neck prickling, Finn sensed night predators lurking, waiting for the humans to go inside.

Or maybe it was hunger he felt.

Despite the grumble in his stomach, he renewed his efforts. In truth, imagining Kelsy's gratitude, he renewed his efforts. Along with males everywhere, he and Ben communicated through grunts, growls, and snorts. Five more fruitless minutes, and they returned to the barn.

Eyes bright with hope, Kelsy must've seen their failure in his face. Damn, she could read him like a book. One with wide margins. The hunter come home to let the woman deliver the darker side of life. *Sorry kids. Daddy looked high and low, but he couldn't find Sweetie, your pet Mastodon.*

In the second he lost his mind, her shoulders slumped; and he thought she swayed. He took a step toward her, but she limped away from him.

"If both of you talk at the same time, it scares the kittens," she said to the kids in a calm, warm voice that made Finn want to go back outside and find that damned cat.

"Jessicat probably won't come back in, either, if

you're making so much noise." Finn expressed the male view confidently, thinking he deserved some credit for knowing the animal's name.

"We're not makin' noise, are we, Mommy?" Jason sent Finn a glare that told him he knew zilch.

"Maybe a little too much noise for the kittens." Pricklier than a porcupine, she silently warned Finn to keep his distance. "Since they can't see yet, they have extra-sensitive hearing, remember? Finn was just reminding us of how good their hearing is, right, Finn?"

She didn't turn around, but he jumped at the lifeline she threw him. He lied boldly, "Right. Exactly what I meant."

Maybe she wouldn't throw him to the sabertooths. He winked, telegraphing Kelsy his gratitude for salvaging his ego.

During the momentary lull in the noise level, Ben suggested dinner, then another search before bed. This suggestion, as Finn could've told his fellow Neanderthal, crashed and burned. There were no hysterics, but Molly and Jason begged—with eyes that brought back starving-children posters—to stay in the barn with the kittens.

Closing the barn door would, they reasoned, make it impossible for Jessicat to slip back inside.

Leaving the door open with no humans around meant a coyote could come in and eat the babies.

So much for trying to protect the innocence of children, Finn thought, figuring he'd look hard-hearted, unfeeling, and weak if he admitted a sissy need for food.

At age eight, he'd laid that judgment on his father after the family mongrel slipped his collar and broke for freedom. Dad took Finn to the local pound twice that first day, then helped him make and post LOST DOG signs throughout the neighborhood. Horrified that Dad could then go home and even put food to his lips till Rover came home safely, Finn had stayed in his room bargaining with God.

Ma tried tempting him with favorite meals and snacks. His older brothers called him a wimp and worse. Although his bargaining pivoted on abstinence from food, stealing his brothers' stash of porno pictures and giving up attempts at masturbation, he knew it was only a matter of time before he succumbed and ate.

Day Three, he finally accepted half a bowl of oatmeal without milk or sugar for breakfast. Mom broke the bad news. Rover had been impounded—and already adopted by a family in Palo Alto as the birthday gift for their ten-year-old son. The bottom fell out of Finn's universe.

The buzz of low voices brought him back from his trance. Straining to pick up the gist of the conversation, he mentally shook himself. God, he hadn't thought about Rover for twenty years. Or that Dad had brought the mutt home safely.

With her arms around Molly and Jason, Kelsy shot him an odd look. Her gaze was clear and absolutely steady. Was he okay?

Fine, he telegraphed her. How the hell could she take care of the kids yet spare a thought for him? He'd acted like a jerk.

The way she dealt with the kids must've triggered the Rover memories. He hunkered down next to Jason. One of the many reasons he loved Ma so much was because of the way she'd taken care of him as an eight-year-old. She'd let him feel his loss and sorrow while also encouraging his stubborn hope. Kelsy had that same touch. He'd tell her so . . . maybe offset Olivia's allegations and his stupidity.

Determined to restore Kelsy's faith in him, Finn volunteered to stay out with the kittens while everyone else went into the house. Her jaw dropped. Jason piped up,

"Ben already said he'd stay with them. Weren't you listening, Finn?"

To lie or not to lie. With Kelsy and the rest of them staring at him as if the mother ship had left him behind, he said, "Nope. I was thinking about your mother. Whenever I think about her, my mind goes."

Jason sighed. "It sure does."

"Can't help it, Jason. I love her, and I can't stop thinking how glad I am you and she are in my life."

The soft light in the barn hid most of Kelsy's blush, but Finn didn't need a searchlight. He'd surprised and embarrassed her. Good. He loved her and wanted everyone to know it.

"I understand the feeling." Ben picked Molly up and nuzzled her behind the ear.

"Is it kinda like me 'n Molly feel about the kittens and Jessicat?" Jason asked.

"Pretty much." Finn grinned. Did Kelsy realize *pretty much* didn't begin to cover the depth of his feelings for her?

Chapter 14

Back at the house, Kelsy shooed the kids off to wash up for dinner. On a mission, she joined Risa in the kitchen and asked about sleeping bags. "In case the guys don't find Jessicat, you know Molly and Jason will insist on sleeping in the barn."

Stirring spaghetti sauce while keeping an eye on the triplets in the family room, Risa said they had enough sleeping bags for all of Montana. "Sure you really want one for Finn?"

"I'm only sure you'd have to lock him in a closet to keep him in the house."

"That's goodness, right?"

Kelsy hobbled to the oven. She removed the garlic bread. Usually the pungent odor made her mouth water. Tonight, her stomach protested. Risa passed her a bread basket. "If Finn didn't love you, why would he want to sleep out in the barn?"

Heat stung Kelsy's cheeks. She arched a brow. Risa laughed. "Sorry, but sleeping on the barn floor with two kids and four kittens to feed every three hours will cool his lust."

"Did going out in that old Chevy pickup cool Ben's lust?"

"Point taken. But you and Finn have to talk. Neither of you will be able to lose control—or run away—out there with the kids asleep and the kittens—"

"Yada, yada." Kelsy shrugged. Dammit, Risa knew her tendencies to run when cornered. "I wish I had your confidence he'll understand about Dane. I figure as soon as I mention not wanting more kids—"

"You've absolutely made up your mind?" Risa bit her lip.

Kelsy shook her head. "I haven't *absolutely* made up my mind about anything. I'm exploring what I want to be when I grow up."

The garlic hit her empty stomach like poison. She swallowed. "Anyway there's something else wrong. Someone told Finn something about me. Whatever it was, it's not good."

"All the more reason to talk."

"We agree." Eyes watering, Kelsy backed away from the garlic bread. "But suppose he tells me, and the bad stuff's true?"

Confusion danced across Risa's face, but she smiled. "If it's true, you'll deal with it. You're not a bad person, Kelsy."

Just a liar. Kelsy licked her lips. His flinch—on the way to the barn—still unnerved her. What did he think she'd done? She hesitated, then said, "I miss sleeping next to him, you know? I sleep like a baby whenever I'm with him."

Risa removed her apron, then put her arms around Kelsy's neck. "Some day pharmaceutical companies will figure out how to bottle post-coital calm." They put their foreheads together—the way they'd done since they were Molly and Jason's age. "Tell him everything, Kel. You'll never sleep so well again if you don't."

In theory, Kelsy agreed. In practice, she asked Ben to take Finn's supper out to the barn. She and Risa then told Molly and Jason about the sleeping plans. The kids went nuts, kissing, hugging, and, of course, screaming. The triplets quickly got in on the act. Like mothers everywhere, Kelsy tuned out the noise. She tried to stay in the bubble of joy, but her mind kept veering away to the inevitable late-night discussion with Finn.

Please, please, let him believe she'd never intended to deceive him.

The spaghetti was wolfed down in record time. Kelsy then supervised hurried baths for Molly and Jason. Ben put the triplets down for the night, and Risa went out to the barn to spell Finn. He was loading the dishwasher when Kelsy entered, intent on making a thermos of hot chocolate.

She drew in a loud breath, then tried to speak naturally. "I think Risa wanted you to take a break."

"I'm fine. How are you?" He pivoted toward her, his face so tender her heart fluttered.

"I'm . . . not . . . sure." She propped a hip against a counter. *Whatever someone told him, he doesn't believe it— yet.*

Quick as a tango dancer, he placed his hand in the small of her back, pulling her into his body. His breath pulsed hotly against her ear. "By morning, you'll be fine. I promise."

The kiss he planted on her lips brought her right to the cusp of believing him. But teetering on the cusp didn't give her enough courage to demand point blank: Tell me what's going on. He left to search for Jessicat, and she stayed behind with the kids in the barn.

A heaviness in her chest made it hard to read *Goldilocks*. She suspected the long shadows from the lantern spooked Molly and Jason. They interrupted every paragraph of their favorite story with dozens of questions.

Where was Finn? What was taking so long? Shouldn't they check on the kittens? When was the next feeding? What if Finn didn't find Jessicat? What about poor Lucky Prince? Did he feel left out? Where would he sleep tonight with Molly in the barn?

For every calm, reasonable answer Kelsy gave, another nervous, uneasy question surfaced. Which made thinking about Finn impossible.

Well, not impossible. But more difficult. Straining to hear the scuff of his boots or catch a whiff of Old Spice, Kelsy admitted she was wound too tight.

Somewhere between the zillionth Q and A, she started to worry he'd been gone too long. What if he met up with a mountain lion? Risa had told her they'd seen a big cat's tracks less than a mile from the house. Remembering, Kelsy couldn't breathe. If Finn was hurt before she set things right with him . . . .

She fingered the cell phone in her pocket. The phone was Risa's idea. In case one of the kids got scared and wanted to return to the house. "In case you and Finn want to come back," Risa had teased. "You can always throw a blankie over the kittens' box and bring them with you."

Determined to stick out the vigil, Kelsy toyed with calling him. Would he think she'd lost confidence in him if she did? Unlike Dickhead, he wasn't a man who required constant ego stroking. Unlike Dickhead, he was quick to sing her praises. For some reason, she had never doubted his sincerity.

Why couldn't she marry him, have a career in another city, be happy, make a difference in the television industry, and have it all, like Risa?

"Kelsy!" Molly tugged on her hand before answers to these harder questions came.

"Yes, Honey."

"I heard something." Molly's eyes were the size of saucers.

Adrenaline sent a small stab of fear through Kelsy. "I didn't hear anything, Honey." She patted Molly's hand. "We're probably as safe in the barn as we are in the house."

"You heard Ole Paint." Jason's voice rose, sounding as dismissive as his father to Kelsy. She winced, but bit her tongue. Don't take her anger at Dickhead out on Jason.

"Shhh." Molly pointed to the kittens, snuggled into each other, their soft bodies folded into a black, white, and gray mosaic of fur, paws, and tiny pink noses.

"You shhhh." Eyes snapping with fury, Jason stuck his tongue out.

"Hey, you two." Kelsy used the mommy voice that left no doubt she meant business. "If we're quiet, maybe we'll hear whatever Molly heard."

Jason sniffed. So did Kelsy. Horsey smells flooded her brain, stopping up her ears. She, for one, couldn't hear zip.

"I don't hear anything now," Molly said, eyelids drooping.

"I don't hear anything, either." Kelsy glanced at her watch. Finn gone for nearly half an hour? It felt longer. "Maybe you heard Finn. He should be back any minute."

Wishful thinking?

"I like it better when Finn's with us," Jason mumbled.

Taking no offense, Kelsy said, "I know, Sweetheart. I like it when Finn's with us, too."

"Will he stay with us forever, Mommy? He won't divorce us like Daddy, will he?"

Two questions rushed together, each one causing Kelsy's head to pound harder than the other. Together, they formed an unending drum roll.

"Forever's a long time, honey." Another mental drum roll heralded this deep pronouncement.

"I know, Mommy." Jason had gotten his second wind.

Zebra Contemporary

Be sure to visit our website at www.kensingtonbooks.com.

To start your membership, simply complete and return the Free Book Certificate. You'll receive your Introductory Shipment of FREE Zebra Contemporary Romances, you only pay $1.99 for shipping and handling. Then, each month you will receive the 4 newest Zebra Contemporary Romances. Each shipment will be yours to examine FREE for 10 days. If you decide to keep the books, you'll pay the preferred subscriber price (a savings of up to 30% off the cover price), plus shipping and handling. If you want us to stop sending books, just say the word… it's that simple.

FREE BOOK CERTIFICATE

Yes! Please send me FREE Zebra Contemporary romance novels. I only pay $1.99 for shipping and handling. I understand that each month thereafter I will be able to preview 4 brand-new Contemporary Romances FREE for 10 days. Then, if I should decide to keep them, I will pay the money-saving preferred subscriber's price (that's a savings of up to 30% off the retail price), plus shipping and handling. I understand I am under no obligation to purchase any books, as explained on this card.

Name _____

Address _____ Apt. _____

City _____ State _____ Zip _____

Telephone (___) _____

Signature _____
(If under 18, parent or guardian must sign)

Thank You!

Offer limited to one per household and not to current subscribers. Terms, offer and prices subject to change. Orders subject to acceptance by Zebra Contemporary Book Club. Offer Valid in the U.S. only.

CN095A

ll..l..lll...ll.l.l..ll.l.l..ll.l.l..ll.l..lll..l

Zebra Contemporary Romance Book Club

Zebra Home Subscription Service, Inc.

P.O. Box 5214

Clifton , NJ 07015-5214

PLACE
STAMP
HERE

Maybe because Molly was out like a light, slumped against Kelsy, her chin almost to her chest.

Jason held Kelsy's gaze. He lowered his voice to a whisper. "Forever's like happily ever after, right?"

"Yes, a long time." After such brilliance, she felt herself floundering. *Where* did he come up with such questions? Maybe she should stop reading him fairy tales at bedtime.

Careful of her toe, he crawled onto her lap and put his arms around her neck. "I know forever's a long time, Mommy."

"I thought you did, Sweetheart." Her heart missed a beat as she hugged him. He probably knows more than I do. Poor kid, he definitely knows too much.

Divorce did that. Ruined your innocence. Took away your sense of happily ever after. Left you longing for *forever*.

"You know," she said, feeling her way, "Daddy didn't divorce *you*. He and I divorced each other."

Jason squirmed away from her, turning his face up to look at her. "I don't wanna talk about Daddy. I wanna talk about Finn."

Run, run as fast as you can. You can't get away from a Curious Young Man. From out of the blue, the mangled line popped out of her unconscious. She smiled weakly. "You want to talk about forever, right?"

"Will Finn always stay with us, Mommy?"

Every fiber in her wanted to yell, *yes*, but her tongue refused to cooperate. Lying had become a habit, but lying to Jason crossed the line. *What about lying to Finn?*

Her heart clenched. She drew in a breath, held it, finally said, "We'll have to ask him."

"When he comes back?" The anxiety in his voice tightened Kelsy's chest. "Yes, when he comes back."

Jason looked so relieved that Kelsy ignored the temptation to change her mind. Since she couldn't speak for Finn, she'd at least orchestrate the timing of the inquisition, let him catch his breath before Jason started deposing him.

"If I fall asleep, will you wake me when Finn comes back, Mommy?" A note of uncertainty crept back into his voice.

"Yes, I will. I promise." She laid Jason's head against her breast, held it there, crooning his name.

The sing-song rhythm lulled her, pulled her back to one stormy Sunday night. She and Finn had made love for the first time that afternoon. Too soon, he'd left for work. Totally stunned, she'd enjoyed being alone, anticipating Risa's shock.

The shock came when Ben arrived with the kids but without Risa. In the middle of their Christmas-tree adventure, she had received bad news. The birth mother of Charlie, Tom, and Harry had gone into premature labor.

Taking charge, Kelsy sent Ben to the soaked-in airport. *Take care of Risa.*

Kelsy took care of putting Molly and Jason to bed. Electricity hummed inside her. Calmly, she reassured the kids about the triplets. Time slowed.

No news from Risa. No calls from Finn.

Between checks on the kids every five minutes, Kelsy willed the phone to ring. God, she'd had sex on the floor. With a man eight years younger. A man she'd met when he was a kid. A man she'd known for less than twenty-four hours.

Chased by fears of loneliness and rejection, tormented by visions of Sam with his bimbette, she'd put her soul into sex on the rebound.

The phone rang at midnight.

Finn, on his break. His partner in a dive buying coffee.

Edgy and unnerved, Kelsy said, "Think he suspects you're calling your lover?" Saying *lover*, she shivered.

"Mike thinks I'm bedding half the women in Cielo Vista. He tells me constantly I should settle down, get married, have kids."

"What do you say?" Dry-mouthed, Kelsy couldn't swallow.

"That the woman I love doesn't know I exist." Finn laughed. Kelsy's breath caught. After a heartbeat, he added, "I tell him I'll die a lonely, unfulfilled bachelor if my mystery lady and I don't get together in this lifetime."

"This-this lifetime?" Kelsy closed her eyes.

"You and I have loved each other before . . . many times."

Jason shifted in her arms. Slowly, she came back from the past. Her hands felt clammy, and the drums in her head started up again. After that phone call, she'd believed totally that she and Finn were destined for each other. Throughout eternity. Forever.

What did lies do to forever? She shivered. Where was he?

Jessicat jumped out of Finn's arms the second Ben opened the barn door. Tail straight up in an exclamation mark, she made a beeline for her nest. Like a fool, Finn yipped triumphantly.

"Finn!" Kelsy's voice carried over a couple of soft neighs.

"The returning hero," he whispered loudly.

"Since I'm no use here, I'll go back to the house," Ben said. Over his shoulder, he called softly, "A smart man would milk that returning hero bit. You've got the battle scars to prove it."

Finn touched the small bandage Risa had applied to his left hand. "A smart man probably wouldn't have picked up a cat caught in a briar bush."

"Huh." Ben slipped back through the barn door. "Give her time. Maybe by tomorrow she'll appreciate you're her hero."

"As long as Kelsy appreciates me—" He realized he was talking to himself.

Call him Mr. Macho, but where the heck was Kelsy? Why wasn't she here to greet him with hot, passionate kisses? Why didn't she rip his shirt off, drag her tongue down his back, and set him crazy the way she always did with that move? Then, she could unsnap his jeans. . . . His fantasy revved into fast forward as he rounded the corner. *Forget Olivia's questions.*

In slow mo, Kelsy's head came up, golden in a pool of flickering light from the lantern. Doe-eyed, she held Jason in her arms. Finn's breath caught. A goddess. Pagan and wild for all her soft curves and angles. *His* pagan goddess. Innocent till proven guilty, dammit.

"What happened?" Her eyes widened.

"To me, or Mama Lion there?" Examining her babies, Jessicat had her back turned to them. Finn dragged his unbandaged hand across his face so the scratches wouldn't scare her.

"Mama Lion looks pretty good. But not as good as you." Kelsy held her face up, gasped at the scratch on his chin, but didn't turn away. "Want me to kiss it? Make it aaall better?"

"Uh-huh!" He breathed in her scent. Drunk on her nearness, he lied shamelessly. "Risa says it's pretty bad. So, I'll need lotsa kisses."

"I think I'm up to that." She put her lips to his ear, and heat surged through him.

"Isn't that my line?" He forgot how much the scratches around his eye stung.

Jason stirred. They froze. "I should wake him."

"Now?" Finn tried not to sound indignant.

"I promised." For a heartbeat, Finn thought he saw her bottom lip tremble.

Raw desire uncurled in the pit of his stomach. Tempted to drag his tongue across her lip, then move to the hollow of her throat, he said, "Hurry, then. The sooner you wake him, the sooner he'll go back to sleep."

"Don't count on it." She switched her gaze to the kittens. "He wants more than a recap of how you found Mama Lion, okay?"

"Okay! Whatever, I'm ready."

"He has something to ask you." Her wistful tone confused Finn. "Something important."

Careful, instinct told him. Don't blow this by being cute. "Okay," he said. "I won't even ask for a hint."

Her sigh surprised him. Relief—because he didn't ask her what was so important?

He could hear Jessicat licking her babies. The sound of her tongue on their tiny bodies soothed him, and he wondered why Kelsy held herself so rigidly. A muscle in her neck jumped.

"I love you," he said. "No matter what."

Tears sparkled in her lashes. "After you and Jason talk, you and I have to get some things straight."

"Fine. But that won't change loving you."

She swallowed, then whispered, "Jason. Finn's here."

Murmurs. Head turning. Mouth noises. Sleep pulled at the little boy Finn loved.

She touched Jason's cheek, patting it while Finn wrestled his green-eyed monster back into its dark, airless cave. Plenty of time for her to rip his clothes off later.

"Finn found Jessicat." Kelsy kissed her son's forehead.

Jason's eyes snapped open. "Is she okay?" He tried to scramble to his feet but couldn't get them under him.

The mother cat hissed, and her tail flicked like a cobra.

"Easy, Pardner." Finn caught Jason around the waist

and lifted him onto the floor. "We don't want to scare her."

Finn held him a few feet from the nest till his legs steadied. "She's fine. See? She's feeding her babies."

"Ohhh." Surprisingly, Jason kept his distance. "They act starved."

He held Finn's hand, leaning into him, mouth open as the kittens' paws kneaded their mother's side. Out of the corner of his eye, Finn watched Kelsy's face and body soften. Looking away from her, he felt his pulse thud. He stood there, willpower taxed to the max, and listened to Jason marvel over the kittens.

Squatting down, eyeball to eyeball with Jason, Finn shot Kelsy a smile. "Mommy says you have a couple of important questions for me. I'm ready whenever you are."

Jason tore his eyes away from the kittens, looked up, his face alight with radiance at the adults. He shook his head, "Not anymore. I already know the answers."

Kelsy's heart did a skip and a flutter at Jason's pronouncement. Mercifully, Finn didn't pry or prod. Maybe because Jason still had a zillion other questions to which he did want answers. Nervous one or more of the questions might turn out to be a bomb, Kelsy inched up close to Finn, Jason, and the cat nest.

From time to time, Finn squeezed her hand, melting bones and igniting a bonfire between her legs. Even with Jason there and her soul black with lies, it was all she could do not to jump Finn's bones. Maybe stick her hand down his jeans. Maybe break her other toe.

With a saintly patience that forced Kelsy to behave, Finn wove a tense but PG-6 account of his search for Jessicat. He showed his scratches, then his bandaged hand, with no trace of machismo.

"I bet those boo-boos hurt," Jason said, stars in his eyes.

QUEEN OF THE UNIVERSE

"Naw, not any more." Finn shook his head. "Mommy kissed them and made them all better."

Hot all over, Kelsy squirmed. Who said there was no such thing as a white lie?

"Really?" Jason the Doubter cocked his head.

"Really really." Finn winked at Kelsy. Her heart clutched. "Mommy's so sex—so smart, she knew exactly what I needed."

Kelsy blushed, saying lamely, "Should I start med school?"

"Forget it," Finn growled. "Jason and I are the only males that kisses work on."

"Yeah, me 'n Finn." Jason giggled.

Out of the blue, guilt seared her. *Don't forget Dane.*

Luckily, Jason demanded Finn's attention. He wanted a detailed replay of *The Rescue of Jessicat.* Despite constant interruptions and corrections, Finn replied with tongue-in-cheek remarks that sent Jason into gales of laughter.

Just as Kelsy expected, it was only a matter of time before the hilarity woke a couple of the horses. Their neighs roused Molly. After oohing and ahhing over Jessicat, she crawled into Finn's lap with Jason and demanded the whole adventure from start to finish.

More questions. A few answers from Jason.

More snorts from the horses. More giggles from the kids. More jokes from Finn. The Energizer Bunny, he apparently never ran down.

Fingers crossed, Kelsy hoped the silliness continued till dawn. Risa would kill her for letting the kids get so wired, but too bad. Contrary to popular opinion, Kelsy doubted that confession was actually good for the soul. She had no doubt her revelations would dampen everyone's high spirits.

Just what she needed—more guilt.

A buzz started in her head. She concentrated on the

irritation. The noise gave her something to think about instead of confessing about Dane. Or the wine and champagne. Or the job offer in Seattle. Or—*Buzzz, buzzzz.*

The smell of hay vied with the buzz for her attention. Neither worked. She wanted to join in the fun, feel as if she belonged. Hard to do when she felt like such a hypocrite.

Make that *terrified* hypocrite.

No, make that crazy. Unlike Finn, who'd written a cute, happy-ever-after modern fairy tale, she'd written her little drama with Dane into a mega-budget, technicolor melodrama. All she had to do was tell Finn the truth, for cryin' out loud.

Ease into the meeting in Half Moon Bay. He'd understand. He had career ambitions.

Explain she was rethinking more babies. He'd understand. He loved Jason.

A loud yawn from Molly interrupted the imaginary confession. Finn shot Kelsy a satisfied grin. Her throat tightened. The skin around her mouth felt like fresh cement, ready to crack from the slightest stress. Afraid Finn would notice her weirdness, Kelsy leaned forward and feigned interest in the kittens.

Without moving any other visible muscles, Jessicat opened one eye. Come any closer to my babies, she seemed to say, and I'll claw you to ribbons.

Kelsy shivered. They—whoever *they* were—said guilt unhinged the mind. Well, melodrama must at least crack the mind. Wrapped up in her own guilt, she'd forgotten Finn also had an agenda. Kelsy hugged her waist. A lifetime ago, he'd said . . . what?

The thought danced away. Whatever he'd said—or whatever she'd read between the lines—evaporated. She exhaled and came back to the barn. She could feel his eyes on her. In the past, she'd believed he could see into her soul. Now, she hoped she was wrong.

She sneaked a peek at her watch. Two o'clock. They'd all be zombies tomorrow. Edgy from lack of sleep. Not a good time to talk. How much longer could she stall? Jessicat lay absolutely still, her yellow-green eye unblinking, reminding Kelsy of some creepy horror story by Stephen King.

"Kelsy!" Finn hissed, a soft invitation. "Are you asleep?"

"No." Her blood sang, but she tamped down her excitement. "Just tired. My toe hurts." More believable than a headache.

"Not to worry," Finn said, his eyes dark with desire. "I have exactly what you need for a hurt toe."

Chapter 15

The lantern had gone out. How long ago, Finn could only guess. His nose twitched. The smell of horses. Darkness everywhere in the cavernous barn. Shadows around the cocoon of sleepers. The steady plink of raindrops invited snuggling in, shutting the world out. He closed his eyes, but at 6:15, no matter how hard Finn pretended he was dreaming, the equines didn't stop clumping their feet or snorting.

Asleep on his numb arm, face radiantly rosy from their lovemaking till almost dawn, Kelsy slept through it all. *Sleeping Beauty*. It took all Finn's willpower not to put his mouth on hers, wake her with a kiss, start the morning right.

Dream on, Prince Charming. The fire in his groin fizzled. Molly and Jason, sure to wake any minute, made the risk kinky.

Yes, he and Kelsy had behaved like kids in the backseat of a car less than four hours ago, but nothing short of an earthquake could've roused the kids. Someday Jason would walk in on him and Kelsy making love. He'd have a hundred, make that a thousand, no, probably a million questions.

The thought delighted Finn, and he chuckled. He'd read most parents got embarrassed and gave kids too much detail, confusing everyone. But not him and Kelsy. They'd be open . . .

The horsey noises and drip-drip-drip of rain irritated the hell out of Finn. If he was honest, he'd wake Kelsy up right now.

No touching.

No kissing.

Just blindside her with what Olivia had found.

Blindside her because last night, he hadn't been straight with her. He'd hustled her.

Yes, he'd wanted and needed her.

But, secretly, a part of him hoped, expected, she'd tell him about the accident—afterwards, as they lay there, trusting and pleasured in their cozy sleeping bag.

In his own defense, the sex had hit him harder than a freight train. Clothes pins couldn't have kept his eyelids open to discuss Olivia's phone call. Kelsy's toe, which she barely mentioned, must've wiped her out, too.

What was the story there? The full story? The part she hadn't told him? The part she might never tell him? Had her foot slipped off the brake when she hit the other car? Or had she really run into a bedside table? Who the hell was the joker who called the day of Jason's accident? *Asshole.*

Doubt squeezed his heart and spread to his throat. It hurt to swallow. Jesus, he needed a cup of coffee.

If he got up, called CHP and verified Olivia had seen the correct license number, what then? His pulse spiked.

Then, he'd have to take Kelsy and the Lexus into the nearest Highway Patrol location as soon as they got home. Adrenaline spurted into his veins.

Wasn't he a prince?

* * *

It made sense to Kelsy the sun wasn't shining. She could feel in her bones it was going to be that kind of day. The tension in Finn's forearm was another tip-off. If she felt a smidgeon of optimism, she'd simply conclude her head had cut off his circulation. If she'd told him about Dane right away, she might have room in her for guarded optimism. As it was . . .

Without warning, half a dozen hot needles set her big toe on fire. Eyes closed, she didn't make a peep. The pain had kept her awake half the night. During the other half, her conscience had done a number on her.

The fire in her toe raced up her leg. She fought back a gasp. No one liked a whiner. Not even if she couldn't stand. Sweating, she mentally counted to two.

The fire in her toe and leg went out as quickly as it had flared up. Even with a black cloud hanging over her, she might have a few minutes of relief before the next attack. She should let Finn know she was awake. But why? So he could grill her more about how she'd hurt it? She bit back a sigh and opened her eyes.

"Morning," she managed to whisper. Dammit, why did the day always start in the morning? She wasn't ready.

"Morning." In the dim light, his eyes blazed an electric blue. "Mind moving your head before they have to amputate my arm at the shoulder?"

She lifted her head. "Oh, you silver-tongued devil."

He laughed, but she could tell his heart wasn't in it. She felt her throat close. "I figure," he said, "our relationship can take the truth."

So there they were. "Yes, but what about you and me?"

He rolled over, so close she tasted his breath. "Just tell me, Kelsy."

She couldn't breathe.

He touched her cheek so gently she thought she'd imagined the feathery caress. Tears filled the back of her throat.

"I'm not Dickhead," he whispered.

In the sleeping bag next to them, a kid sighed. Kelsy put a finger to her mouth. Finn kissed her finger, sending a tremor through her hand and elbow.

"You know I'm with you for the long run, Kelsy."

She swallowed hard. "That's what I've been telling myself."

"Good. So tell me. Whatever it is, we'll handle it."

Goose bumps danced up and down her clammy arms. "I'm having some difficulty with that . . . pronouncement."

"Why? You don't trust me?" Angry, accusatory.

"I hate that kind of question. Yes or no." Don't look down, she thought, feeling scared and nervous, as if she was about to step out onto a high wire.

"For God's sake, Kelsy, stop being so melodramatic."

He didn't raise his voice, but she flinched, wishing she felt brave enough to take that first step. "Fine, I'll be brutally honest."

Her chest heaved—melodramatically, she supposed, as she tried not to think about hyperventilating. A bad idea, akin to not thinking about the elephant in the room. Now all she could think about was hyperventilating. The word replayed in her head. Think about being melodramatic instead, she thought as *hyperventilating* looped and relooped through her fears and insecurities.

Saved by a supreme effort at logic and pissed by the way Finn squinted at her, Kelsy said, "If we can handle anything, why haven't you told me what's bothering you? You started, but never finished."

He didn't move, didn't frown, or look puzzled, but she felt him draw away. Without asking what she meant.

"See?" she hissed, smarting from his crack about melodrama. "You tapdance around taking that first step, too."

"Kelsy?" Molly sounded more awake than asleep.

Heart pounding, Kelsy tried to do something with her foot so she could sit up. "Yes, Honey. You okay?"

"I need to go to the bathroom."

"Me, too." Jason sat up and waved his cast within inches of Finn's head.

"Watch out!" Kelsy shoved Finn. Had Jason heard them?

"Thanks. Hardheaded as I am, that could've smarted," Finn said, his voice strained.

"I'm sorry." Jason's lip trembled.

"A near accident." Softening his tone, Finn snapped his fingers. "But I can wait for the girls to go to the bathroom first. How about you, Jason?"

"I can wait, but hurry." Jason tottered as he stood, but Finn steadied him a second ahead of Kelsy, who opened her arms for a kiss.

"I can't wait another second." Molly crawled out of her sleeping bag, her dark curls wild as snakes.

Finn shone a light for Jason, who bypassed Kelsy's hug for a closer look at Jessicat and her brood.

"Lead on, Molly." Kelsy stuffed her surprise. She managed to lurch to her feet and grab Molly's outstretched hand. *Owww.*

Hunkered down next to the cat's nest with one arm around Jason's waist, Finn didn't glance their way. Afraid groaning would be construed as melodramatic, Kelsy lifted her chin.

Molly said, "Does your toe hurt a lot, Kelsy?"

"Not really, Honey." The absolute truth, since the dull ache in her chest hurt far more than the sharp twinges in her foot.

"Please tell me you haven't killed Finn." Risa, a coffee-and-hot-chocolate angel of mercy, came down to the barn a few minutes past seven. Jason and Finn were in the bathroom.

"Not yet." With her jaw clenched, her hands fisted and her legs trembling, Kelsy stood next to Molly, who oohed and aahed over Jessicat.

Risa immediately gave Molly a plate of cool scrambled eggs for the feline, warned her to save some for Jason to dispense, then pulled Kelsy out of earshot. A horse tossed his head at them and whinnied, but Risa wagged a finger at Kelsy.

"Tell me you told him about the job inter—"

"Not yet."

"Then, what in the heck's going on?" Risa glanced over at Molly, calling out what a good job she was doing in such a sincere way that Kelsy suddenly wanted to do something that would earn herself the same kind of praise.

Making no effort to hide her bitterness, she said, "If I told you the truth, you wouldn't believe it."

Risa hesitated.

Kelsy made a face. "This is where you're supposed to say, 'try me.' "

"No, this is where I say, 'since when don't I believe you when you tell me the truth?'" Risa nailed Kelsy with a green stare, and Kelsy slid her eyes away, saying, "Why don't men ever say that kind of thing?"

"Some men do. Ben does . . . a lot, as a matter of fact."

"Could he give lessons to Finn?"

"You're kidding, right?"

"Oh, for cryin' out loud, Risa!"

"Well, you sound grim as a hanging judge. I've met warmer ice cubes—"

"Okay, okay. I get the picture. What do you look like when you're hurt and disappointed? Like you just won

the lottery?" Kelsy waved her hands in a you're-out gesture. "Like you won the Nobel Prize for Medicine? Of
course with a husband like Ben, who says the right
thing a lot—"

"Kelsy, slow down." Risa put her hand on Kelsy's
shoulders. "I am totally lost. You're speaking faster than
the speed of sound. I think you're speaking English.
But I don't have Clue One what you're blithering
about."

"Fine." Kelsy sniffed. "Just tell me one damned thing.
Just one."

Palms turned out, soothing the mental patient
who'd gone off her meds, Risa said, "You know I will—if
I can."

"You are a true friend." From the back of the barn,
Kelsy heard the faint flush of a toilet.

Her heart sped up. Jason and Finn would be here
within seconds. Since she didn't give a rat's posterior,
she said, "All I want is the truth. Am I being melodramatic?"

"Kelsy!" Finn caught her a nanosecond after she
crashed into Risa. Rhett Butler scooping up Scarlett, he
fought the panic churning his gut when she didn't
open her eyes right away.

"She fainted." Stating the obvious, Doc held fingers
to Kelsy's forehead.

"Is Mommy okay, La Ti Da?" Jason forgot the cats.

"Honey, she's fine. A little overheated, but—"

"How'd she get overheated?" Jason demanded, his
anxiety pushing one of Finn's guilt buttons.

Asked the question four hours earlier, Finn would've
hazarded a guess. Repressing images of him on top of
Kelsy, totally unaware of her injured toe, he asked, "Is it
because of her toe? Maybe she hit it in the night?"

"It's possible." Risa shot him an unreadable look, then picked up a sleeping bag.

He decided she didn't understand his *real* question. He didn't take time to edit his thought processes, but blurted, "Would night-time exercise aggravate an infection, maybe?"

"Mommy doesn't exercise in her sleep!" Jason yelled.

Risa's eye roll, as she piled a sleeping bag on top of Kelsy, told Finn he was a moron. "Want me to explain, Finn?"

"Please!" Weighed down with Kelsy, he couldn't lift his shoulder to wipe the sweat stinging his eyes.

Intercepting a nod from Risa, he shuffled toward the barn door. Whatever she said—a question he would never ask her—apparently resolved Jason's concerns. Or maybe it was Molly leaving the kittens and walking back to the house with Jason and Risa. Maybe it was something else altogether. Finn, still staggering around with one foot in his mouth, didn't care.

"Kelsy," he whispered, glad she'd never know of his deep stupidity. "Babe. Open your eyes."

"Uhhhh?" Kelsy flailed, fighting to sit.

He tightened his hold on her and the sleeping bag. A wild swing caught him on the ear, almost knocking him out. "Hey, Risa," he called over his shoulder. "How high is her temp?" He ducked more bucking and thrashing. "She's out of her head."

"I don't think there's any cause for alarm." Sure he was out of his head, Finn thought for a nanosecond he saw Risa grin. Then, he realized she was simply trying to reassure Jason. She trilled, "Can you go open the door, Jason?"

The tone apparently calmed Kelsy as well. She went limp in his arms. Finn exhaled. Kelsy twitched.

His heart went through his skull. "Risa?"

A step behind him, she peeked over his shoulder. "A reflex. I'm sure she's fine. Just . . . get her . . . inside."

What the hell? Finn jerked his head up, a hundred percent certain this time that Risa was laughing. In fact, she was grinning from ear to ear.

"Molly, will you go tell your daddy we're coming?"

As happy as a kid joining the circus, Molly skipped off, but Finn still wasn't convinced. His invisible cop-antennae stayed on alert. Something was not right. Was Risa playing with his head? Why had Kelsy fainted? Why had she been so damned moody?

Something inside his head snapped. His legs turned to water. Two steps from the back door, he blurted, "Is Kelsy pregnant?"

"Whaaat?" Risa stared at him like a Eve musta stared at Adam when he asked why her belly was getting so big.

"If you ever pull that kind of trick again, I will kill you." Risa bounced several times on the guest bed. Each bounce was more violent.

"Stop!" Kelsy held her stomach. "I'll throw up."

"Don't you dare." Risa glared at her, bounced one more time, then stopped. "Not unless you want that poor man to think you're pregnant for sure."

Pushing up with her elbows, Kelsy glanced nervously at the door. "You're sure he's not out there?"

"From the look on his face, I'd say he's in the kitchen having a coffee transfusion."

"I thought maybe he was making an appointment for a brain transplant." Kelsy giggled.

"Kel! You should've seen his face when he asked if you could be pregnant." Disapproval dripped from Risa. "Probably the same way I looked when you *fainted*." She clicked her fingers around fainted.

"I'm sorry." Kelsy grabbed Risa's hand, then ruined her apology with another giggle.

"Are you insane?" Risa got off the bed. "What is going on with you?" The way she primped her mouth, a sign she was definitely stressed out, spoke volumes. At the very least, Kelsy had something highly contagious, and Dr. La Ti Da didn't want it.

Slightly miffed, feeling her own stress spike, Kelsy drawled, "Awww, c'mon, La Ti Da. I felt cornered. So . . . I did something a little . . . off the wall."

"Outrageous." Risa plumped the pillow next to Kelsy.

"Flamboyant." Kelsy cocked her head to one side.

"Out—" Risa stopped, stared at Kelsy for a decade, then said, "If you weren't my best friend in the world . . . if I didn't owe you—"

"You don't owe me." Kelsy shook her head. "You don't. Because if we're keeping tabs, I'm in the hole."

"Okay, okay." Risa sat down again, took Kelsy's hand and laced their fingers the way they'd done since kindergarten.

Tears stung Kelsy's eyes, but she said brightly, "Okay. See? We're in agreement on something."

"We're slipping and sliding around the real issue here. Which—" Risa narrowed her eyes to glittery green slits. "Is that your agenda? Keep me chasing my tail the way you have with Finn ever since that stupid job interview?"

"Will you stop saying *that stupid job interview*? You make me sound as if I'm applying for a job as a snake charmer or circus clown."

Risa grinned. "Busted. I'll stop saying *stupid job interview*, but you have to stop driving me crazy."

"You're my best friend. How can I drive you—?"

"You figure, sooner or later," wagging her finger, Risa talked over Kelsy, "a crisis will erupt. I'll be called to referee with Charlie, Tom, and Harry. Or, I'll have to give an opinion on names for the kittens. Or what-ever."

Heart fluttering, Kelsy knew when to hold and when to bluff. She said nothing. Didn't need to say a word be-cause Risa picked up the thread. "As soon as I take up my mommy's mantle, you'll go to sleep. Of course, you'll make a heroic effort to get ready for the plane. In the car, your toe will start—"

She broke off, jaw dropping. On the defensive on general principles, Kelsy drew herself up in the bed. "What?" she said, going for innocence.

Her effort earned a snort from Risa. Kelsy flushed. "Stop looking at me as if I eat my young!"

"Is your toe really broken? Is that part of this-this—"

"Charade?" Kelsy offered, then smiled sweetly. "You didn't question my broken toe the night I came home from Half Moon Bay."

"Because I only suspected you'd lost your mind. Now I know you have, and I don't put anything past you. I know you, remember?"

"Sometimes, the people we think we know best can still surprise us." Kelsy looked straight into Risa's eyes.

"How is she? Can I go back and see her now?" Finn jumped out of his kitchen chair so fast, it tipped over, barely missing Risa's foot.

Hand on her heart, Risa jumped back. She said shak-ily, "She's asleep. Her temp's normal, but her toe's pretty inflamed."

"Did she say anything?" Finn meant, *Did she say if she's pregnant?*

"I don't believe she's pregnant." Risa poured a cup of coffee, keeping her back to him. "Most of what she said made almost no sense."

"But she was making sense this morning—early, before the kids woke up." Finn righted his chair. Blood rushed to his head, leaving him dizzy.

"I think she's exhausted. Jason's accident took its toll."

"Not to mention her late night on Tuesday." Finn crossed his fingers and hoped Risa didn't notice his clumsy attempt at pumping her.

Instead of taking the bait, she held the coffee pot toward him. He shook his head. "I had three cups with Ben. He's down at the barn, by the way."

"Hmmm." She slugged back her coffee, rinsed the green-frog-with-a-crown mug, set it on the counter and then stared out the kitchen window so long Finn thought she'd forgotten him.

He cleared his throat. She swung around, and her braid flew out behind her in a red arc. "I probably should get down there. Five kids and five cats. That's a recipe for trouble."

Finn agreed. He rinsed his own mug. Risa didn't move, so noticing the erratic pulse in her throat was obvious since he wasn't blind. Almost as an afterthought, he said, "Am I missing something?"

She fixed her steady green eyes on him. "Probably."

"Because I'm male? Or is it something else?"

"Yes, and yes." Risa smiled, but Finn didn't feel comforted. He hesitated, then asked, "Do you know what?"

Putting her hand over her racing pulse, she didn't miss a beat. "Some of it."

"And you don't intend to tell me what you do know, right?" He tried not to sound blaming.

"Right."

"Ohh-kay." His stomach dropped, but he gave her a two-fingered salute. Ironically, he admired her loyalty.

"Fair's fair," he said. "I don't intend to tell you what I know either."

Eyebrows arched, she grinned. "Shouldn't you add, *yah, yah, yah, yah, yah, yah?*"

He laughed. "That would simply prove I belong to that half of the people in the world whose IQs are below average."

Chapter 16

The plane ride back to the Bay Area reminded Kelsy of a sit-com with the sound turned off. Jason slept, she pretended to sleep but really studied Finn through her lashes, and he stayed in his seat staring at her. After a couple of decades, the cute cabin attendant brought out supper and listened as Jason jabbered about *his* cat and Finn's bravery. Unable to eat more than a couple of mouthfuls, Kelsy spent most of the rest of the flight in the restroom.

Face it, she thought. Neither rain, nor sleet, nor aching toes will keep Finn from coming home with you tonight.

Her heart fluttered. He'd been there for her from Day One when Sam announced their marriage was over. He'd been there while she went to Nashville to help Risa with the triplets. He'd been there when she went back to work. Finn had been there . . . and now she didn't want him to be there anymore?

No, he she wanted him to be there, but with conditions. . . .

Shaken by her selfishness, she took her seat for the

descent, announcing she'd just brushed her teeth and washed her face.

"Now," she told Jason, "I can hop into bed as soon as we get to Risa's."

"I guess I should go brush my teeth, too," Finn drawled.

"Should I go brush my teeth now, Mommy?"

Kelsy flushed. She wanted to smack that smirk off Finn's face. "You can wait, sweetheart." She definitely didn't want Jason to leave her alone, or it was all over. "Maybe Finn will read you a bedtime story while I pick up my voice mail."

Finn cocked his head from side to side. "We're about to land."

Busted. In no mood, she said between gritted teeth, "Let's read a story, sweetie, then I can hop into bed as soon as we—"

"You already said that, Mommy."

"Mommy's so tired, she doesn't know what she's saying," Finn said, his voice dripping syrup. "Fainting takes a lot out of—"

She shut him up with an icy smile, then replied crisply, "Finn's right, sweetie. I'm so tired. I'm glad Finn understands how tired I am. I bet I'm asleep as soon as I get to my room."

Her nerves shrieked. She half expected Finn to ask how she'd manage the stairs with her toe, but he pulled Jason onto his lap. "I bet you're not too tired to undress, are you?"

Protecting his balls, Kelsy thought and tossed her head.

"Huh-uh. I'm not too tired to undress." Jason laid his head on Finn's chest, and Kelsy felt a homicidal urge to pull her son into her arms. "I can't sleep in my real clothes," Jason declared.

"Me, either." Finn winked, and Kelsy glared.

Teeth gritted, she tapped her cell phone. Winking

was so unfair. He knew it undid her every time. How did he come off being so honest when he pushed her buttons and winked?

He looked straight at her. "With your toe and fainting and all, you'll probably need some help undressing, right, Babe?"

For a second, she thought her hair was on fire. "No," she said in the firmest voice she could muster. "I will not."

"I will," Jason said. "Can you stay and help me, Finn, since Mommy's tired and could faint again?"

Kelsy couldn't keep her jaw from dropping, but she pulled herself together enough to say evenly, "We can manage by ourselves, Sweetheart."

"But I want Finn to stay." Jason tried to cross his arms, but the cast was too heavy for him to hold the pose.

Patience. Patience. Kelsy gave Finn a look that would fell a full-grown elephant. *What if this is his last time there?*

He gave her a look that would sour sweet milk. Knowing what was coming, she bit back a scream. He said, "I'll stay if it's okay with Mommy."

Over my dead body didn't seem justifiable in front of Jason. Neither did, *in your dreams.* Swearing was out. So Kelsy said lamely, "As long as you don't stay too long. I have an early start in the morning."

The lie popped out before she could stop it, but taking it back meant she had no hope of getting Finn out of the house tonight. *One battle at a time.*

"Yay, yay, yay!" Jason cheered.

Finn must've seen the blood in her eye. He said to Jason, "See those lights? I'll show you where you and Mommy live."

Hurtling through the dark, Kelsy shivered. She didn't know if she was mad—or glad—Finn had won the battle to stay with her and Jason. But let him even think *faint* and he was a dead man.

* * *

A screw-up.

That's what Finn called the ride from the airport to
Risa's. In the best of circumstances, the 'Vette was a two-
person vehicle. Between Kelsy's luggage—enough to
rival that of a movie queen—and Jason's, there was no
place for Jason in the back. Buckling him in the same
seat with Kelsy was, technically, against the law in
California. Not to mention uncomfortable, despite the
leg room.

There was no doubt in Finn's mind that fleas moved
around less than Jason. He squirmed, shifted, and wrig-
gled till Finn wondered why Kelsy didn't scream.

Probably figured they wouldn't hear her. Not over
Jason's barrage of questions and comments and asides
about his kittens, the pony, and the cockpit. The kid
jumped from one subject to the other till Finn admitted
defeat. He couldn't make heads or tails of any of it. A
convention of monkeys had nothing on Jason. A non-
stop talker, he rattled on at warp speed.

Staring out the window as if viewing a miracle on the
freeway instead of traffic, Kelsy sulked.

So much for winning the battle and losing the war,
Finn concluded. He gripped the steering wheel and felt
his patience unravel. She'd hooked him like a fish with
that *faint.* Jesus, he was an idiot. A smart man would
dump his passengers in Risa's driveway and take off for
wherever. At that moment, sitting for twelve hours in
the Beemer with Olivia promised a glimpse into
heaven.

The headlights flooded the garage door. "Opener?"
Finn prompted Kelsy, who didn't miss a beat. "In the
Lexus."

Mention of the SUV brought reality crashing down
on Finn. He snapped, "Wasn't that brilliant?"

Kelsy let out a breath, then said slowly, as if he had

difficulty with basic communication, "I had other things on my mind."

Say that again.

Jason looked from Kelsy to him, and Finn clamped down on his jaw, crunching bones. "Why're you mad, Finn? What did I do? Did I do something bad?"

Each question got smaller and quieter and softer, reminding Finn of the first days after Dickhead waltzed out of Jason and Kelsy's lives. The jerk hadn't seen his own son more than twice in the past ten months. Next to him, Kelsy sucked in a breath that broke his heart. Grabbing her hand and Jason's, he unhooked his seatbelt and turned around to face them, feeling as if he'd kicked two newborn puppies. He tapped Jason's cast gently.

"You didn't do a thing, Kiddo. I was a total butthead, and I'm sorry if I scared you. I lost my cool, but not because of anything you did. Okay?" He tilted Jason's chin up and stared in his eyes.

"Are you sure, Finn?" Tears leaked down his cheeks.

"Positive." Awkwardly, Finn crossed his heart with his left hand. "I'm a cop. Cops have to tell the truth, you know."

Kelsy swallowed loudly. Realizing he'd forgotten her, Finn glanced away from Jason for an instant. Their eyes locked. Unshed tears filled hers. Her chin quivered, and he could see how much self-control was costing her. His heart banged his ribs. *I love you. I love you.*

Neither of them spoke.

Breaking the silence, Jason said, "I want to be a cop when I grow up. Or maybe a fireman. Can I be a cop and a pilot, Finn?"

"You can be anything you want." Finn gave Jason a left-handed high-five. "Isn't that right, Mommy?"

"Anything." She buried her face in Jason's blond hair.

"Can't you break in?" Kelsy couldn't believe she'd left for Montana without her house keys on Thursday.

Okay, she could believe it, but she didn't want to admit her stupidity.

"The department frowns on cops breaking into the homes of the citizens we're sworn to protect." Finn slid back under the steering wheel. So he couldn't believe she'd forgotten her keys either.

Tough. She'd told Risa they needed an exterior keypad.

"I called the security company." Curiosity was written all over him—the sly way he studied Kelsy with narrowed eyes, the restraint in his tone, the delay of questions she could see burning through him.

"How long before they get here?" Jason asked.

"They said ten minutes, and it's already been two." Finn showed Jason his Timex watch.

Kelsy almost laughed with relief. Mr. Easygoing. It was killing him not to ask how she'd forgotten those damned keys. But after his apology, he was watching every word he said.

"Can we get out? My legs hurt." For once, Jason consulted Kelsy first instead of Finn.

Her toe now felt as if a semi had rolled back and forth over it, but she said, "Sure. This isn't the best car for a family."

"No," Finn agreed. "I didn't have a family when I bought it." He came around and opened her door. "Of course, I don't think your SUV's a family car either."

Her skin prickled. What was he really talking about? Unsure where the land mines lay, she said brightly, "Really?"

"I like our SUV," Jason said. "I like being up real high where I can see everything. It's like being a king."

"Nothing wrong with being a king. Being up real high, now that's a problem." With a hand on her elbow, Finn guided Kelsy around the front of the Corvette.

"Why?" Jason asked, as if Finn of course knew.

Sure she also knew the reason, Kelsy said, "Yes, why, Finn?"

"Lots of people think SUVs roll over too easy."

"Ohhh. I wouldn't like that." Jason shook his head.

Ticked by his not so subtle preaching, Kelsy said, "I drive very carefully, Sweetheart."

When you haven't had too much to drink?

The reminder smacked her upside the head. Throat clogged, she stopped to catch her breath. "My-my toe," she mumbled.

"Is it worse, Mommy?"

"I don't think so, Sweetheart."

"But it's not getting any better, is it?" Finn asked.

Warily, sensing a trap, but thinking she saw a way out of Finn staying more than five minutes at Risa's, Kelsy said, "I'm not sure."

"I think I'd better spend the night, drive you to the station in the morning," Finn offered.

Snap. Hellooo, Kelsy? She fumed inwardly.

"Yay, yay, yay!" Jason jumped up and down. "Then, can you come back and have breakfast with me 'n Gramma Bishop?"

Kelsy felt her legs unlock, loosen dangerously. But Finn was there, his arm around her waist, covering for her so Jason wouldn't be scared, having no idea why her old-lady legs trembled.

"Hey!" Finn hooted. "How about I pick up Krispy Kremes?"

Jason clapped his hands. "They're my favorite!"

Some days, Kelsy thought, it just doesn't pay to chew through the straps.

She leaned against the hood of the car. Come hell or high water, she and Finn *were* going to talk. She *was* going to come clean. About the trip to Half Moon Bay. About her ambitions and aspirations. About her doubts and fears.

Under the streetlight, Finn smiled glumly at her.

Jason's shouts receded to an echo. She smiled, in awe of the gentle man whose demonstrations of steadfastness toward her, empathy for Jason, and brash sincerity were the most obvious traits she loved.

Whether he understood her no longer mattered. His capacity to understand was the real deal. He had the biggest heart. It was up to her not to break it.

Ordered to sit down and rest her toe half an hour later, Kelsy collapsed on the family-room sofa with a cup of tea. Laughing and joking, Finn and Jason headed upstairs for a quick bath. A hundred percent certain she'd have a small breakdown if she stared at the fire and mentally rehearsed the story she had to tell Finn, Kelsy picked up her cell phone. Fourteen messages should distract her for a few minutes.

The first three messages—sent within five minutes of each other—were from Brad Hall. *And they say people in TV have short attention spans.*

Tempted to delete his messages without listening to them, Kelsy checked the time the last message was left.

Before she'd talked to Dane in Montana. Before he'd offered her a job. A dream job. Or, had she dreamed that? Hadn't the job Dane promised seemed too good to be true? She reached down and massaged her ankle. Her toe was starting to ache.

The next seven messages, amazingly, were from Dane. He'd left five before she took off for Montana on Thursday. The other two, he'd left on Friday when she'd turned off her cell after Jason's accident. Excited by his perseverence, Kelsy closed her eyes. Friday, another lifetime ago. And The Ritz? How long ago was that?

Her eyes snapped open. She pressed the SAVE key. Okay, give the man a gold star for persistence. If she hadn't talked with him on Friday, how many messages would he have left? *How many angels dance on the head of a pin?*

"... eleventh new message, Friday at 10:10 A.M. ..."

Laughter floated down from upstairs. Automated directions cued her to press 1 to hear the message. Kelsy hesitated, surprised by a spurt of jealousy. Finn had learned enough ventriloquism from Risa to build on what Jason already knew. Both males had spent hours teaching Kelsy. Patience, encouragement and bribes didn't work. She finally concluded a gun to her head wouldn't improve her lack of talent.

"... eleventh new message ..."

Admitting another moment of self-delusion, Kelsy pressed the phone against her ear. Lack of talent had nothing to do with learning ventriloquism. Lack of interest and motivation told the real story.

So being jealous of Finn made no sense. She might as well be jealous of Jason, the special bond he shared with Finn, the unspoken pact that drove her wild and left her dry-mouthed and feeling small.

As voice mail went into a third loop, she mashed 1 with her thumb, bypassing who'd left the message.

"Kelsy, it's—"

The devil.

Kelsy recognized the caller instantly. Heart thudding, she choked and jerked the phone away from her ear.

"What the hell?" She stared at the hateful neon-blue thing with loathing, then threw it at the other end of the sofa.

She hated cell phones.

No, she hated voice mail. Hated people she detested having access to her twenty-four/seven, mocking her, leaving prank messages. *You're losing it, Kelsy.*

With her good toe, she pushed the phone onto the floor. No, she was not losing it.

She was tired. Her toe hurt.

Nervous about talking to Finn, she'd gotten a nasty surprise.

But she sure wasn't losing it.

Not over a phone call from Victoria Moreno. Victoria Moreno didn't have that kind of power.

On the floor, Victoria's recorded message continued, audible but un-intelligible. *The woman does love the sound of her own voice.*

Smiling grimly, but strong again, Kelsy scooted to the other end of the sofa and picked up the phone. Just for the hell of it, she put the receiver to her ear.

" . . . home or private cell any time. As I said, our target date to begin is yesterday, but—"

"Say what?" Kelsy held the phone at arm's length and stared at it. What was going on? Victoria Moreno—a warm, sincere member of the human race? What happened to the cold, merciless alien who ate her young at birth?

Face hot, Kelsy couldn't smother the feeling of acute embarrassment. Embarrassment didn't kill people, even though she'd died a hundred times as Victoria sliced and diced her into little pieces during the *Amazing* Interview from Hell.

Victoria Moreno had had her fun. Why would she go to the trouble of searching for and finding Kelsy's private cell number, calling her, and—

A shriek from upstairs interrupted Kelsy's mental battle between logic and paranoia. She took a deep breath. Of course there was a reason for the personality transplant. Victoria was playing a trick, having her fun, getting her kicks.

Why?

"Five minutes, and here we come for a good-night kiss!" Finn shouted.

"Okay," Kelsy called, feeling the first stirrings of happiness. "I'm puckering up as we speak."

"Make that three minutes for me, five for Jason!"

Jason's shriek echoed through the house. Kelsy laughed. "Hurry up, then. I can't hold this pucker all night."

Her guilt didn't evaporate, but she felt her heart flutter instead of thud against her ribs. What a wonder. She could still feel guilty and enjoy the fire crackling, her son laughing, and Finn joking. Everything mattered more than the fiasco with Victoria Moreno. Accessing her phone mail, she said, "Come on, Vicki, give me your best shot."

The "best shot," stunned her, caught her by surprise—like the dragon in a kid's story apologizing for belching fire and destroying villages. Victoria suggested a business proposal.

Everyone who had seen the interview with Kelsy loved it. By everyone, Victoria meant the PR staff at SteeleBright, Inc. With a major trade show coming up, the company wanted a big production, featuring Steele and Victoria. The interview had wowed everyone—even after the fifth, sixth replay.

"So, please, please call me at your earliest convenience at home or on my private cell any time. As I said, our target date to begin is yesterday, but I think together, we can hit a home run here."

Uh-huh, when pigs fly, Kelsy thought, replaying the message twice. She shook her head each time. "Woman's demented," she muttered and picked up the next message.

"Name your price," Steele Hood said. "All expenses paid, best hotel, airport limo, you name it. You've got us by the cojones, Kelsy. We want you."

Suspicions confirmed that Victoria Moreno and Steele Hood were playing some kind of vengeful game, Kelsy listened to the last message.

Without preamble, Brad said, "Where are you? Why haven't you called Victoria and Steele back? Do you have any idea how many times they've called me since

Thursday? They won't believe you're taking vacation to-morrow. They swear they'll camp out at the station if they don't hear from you. For God's sake, Kelsy, call me or them! What is wrong with you?"

In a daze, Kelsy tried to grab a coherent thought whirling in her brain. Brad sounded desperate.

Hysterical.

On the other hand, the man could lie—

Her stomach clenched. True, Brad lied whenever it suited his purposes. Who didn't?

Finn doesn't.

Footsteps on the stairs struck a nerve.

Damn, she needed to think, regroup, and forget phone calls. Could she do it? Get ready for Finn? Could she really deflect his questions? Defend herself without sounding defensive? Or selfish? How long could she use Jason to postpone the inquisition?

Not long enough.

Face flushed, Finn stuck his head around the corner. "I'm a minute ahead of time, but I didn't want your pucker to dry up."

"Not a chance." She sat up straight, forcing a smile. "What's Jason doing?" *Why would Brad conspire with Victoria Moreno and Steele Hood?*

"Choosing a bedtime story." Kelsy stretched her legs out toward the end of the sofa, giving nothing to Finn, but he lifted her feet and made space. "How's the toe?"

"Better." *What benefit did Brad get from a conspiracy?*

"Want to put your foot on my leg? Get a little more comfy?" Finn patted his thigh, but locked eyes with her.

Her heart caught, but she said, "I feel better when I don't worry about banging my toe against something."

He shrugged. "Here I am if you change your mind."

"Thanks." Her toe twitched, but she ignored the twinge, visible through her tennis sock.

"Expecting more calls?" Finn pointed to the cell.

"Not tonight." She clutched the phone till her fingers went white, but she felt the bright light in her toe sharpen her thinking.

"You look exhausted, Kelsy. What can I do? More tea? A pillow? Ice?"

As irritating as static on a radio, his litany of concern interrupted the reception between her brain and thought. She smothered her annoyance. "Go check on Jason. Please." Conspiracy notions faded, overridden by echoes of Dane's enthusiasm. "I know my son. He's way too quiet."

"You're right." With the same exquisite care he'd shown earlier, Finn lifted her feet, then laid them back on the sofa. "Give me ten minutes."

"Take your time." Ten minutes? Kelsy's ears rang. She'd never figure out what she wanted in ten minutes.

Chapter 17

Act surprised. Finn tiptoed across the carpet, expecting Jason to jump out from behind his bedroom door. Act excited, too. Don't let Jason suspect something was wrong—that Finn was mad as hell at Kelsy.

Pale yellow light from the bedside lamp turned Jason's head of golden curls into a halo. Bushy eyelashes lay on crimson cheeks that looked as if they'd been scrubbed with a Brillo pad. On top of the covers, his bare feet exposed, arms at his sides, he looked so vulnerable that Finn wanted to wake him up and smother him in kisses. An illustrated book of fairy tales lay on the floor, dropped apparently when he couldn't hold his eyes open any longer.

Jesus, he was a great kid. Chest tight, Finn gazed down at the child he adored. He inhaled, then dragged the spread off a chair and unfolded it over the sleeping body. He snagged a pillow with an ugly purple frog on it from the same chair. He turned back to the bed. Per Risa's instructions, he should elevate the cast.

No problem except moving his arm could wake him. If he woke, he'd demand a story. Then, he'd traipse downstairs for his usual good-night kiss. He'd undoubt-edly ask about Kelsy's foot and give advice that echoed Risa. If there was a lull and he suspected bedtime was approaching, he'd ask for hot chocolate.

Kiss another half hour goodbye. Finn sighed. How long would Kelsy let Jason stay up since the next day meant school?

Long enough, Finn suspected, she'd then plead ex-haustion. And she'd sleep on the couch while he slept upstairs. Forget talking to her about voluntarily show-ing up at CHP headquarters.

Of course, there's the alternative.

"What a prince you are, Bishop," Finn whispered.

Disgusted he'd even think about letting Kelsy get picked up by CHP, he laid the pillow on the bed, then placed Jason's cast on top of it, gently spreading the tiny fingers out flat. Jason mumbled something. Finn froze. Five heartbeats later, convinced Jason was asleep, Finn left the room. At the foot of the stairs, he called, "Ohh-kay, Kelsy. Here I come. Ready or not."

"I was beginning to—" She sort of shrank into the sofa. "What story did you read him?"

"I didn't. He was already asleep. He's fine. I covered him and put a pillow under his arm. Now, have I missed anything? I'm sure I've missed something you want to know about your son that can't possibly wait. If not, we can always begin a scintillating conversation about the weather."

Frowning, she said, "You sound—"

"Edgy? Good, because I am edgy."

"Maybe you'd better sit down then."

"I think I prefer standing." Sitting made it too easy to smell her, touch her, kiss her.

"Well, I can't look up at you without getting a crick in my neck." She rubbed her long, elegant neck, and he had to fight a flash of lust not to bend over and nip her on the neck, which usually drove her wild.

"Are you doing that on purpose?" he demanded when she dragged her fingers from behind her ear down to the hollow of her throat.

"Doing what?" she sounded genuinely puzzled, but didn't stop tantalizing him.

"Offering me a bite of the apple, of course."

"What apple?" She pursed her lips.

Good. That meant he was getting to her. "You heard me."

She waved his comment away. "Words that make no sense."

"I've always figured the apple Eve offered Adam was sex. But I'm not going there because I have an agenda and theology isn't on it." Hands in his pockets, he rocked back on his heels.

"I am so glad."

"Not glad enough to ask what *is* on the agenda."

She shook her head as if trying to avoid a fly. "No wonder you're studying law. The way your mind jumps around, you'll stun juries. It would take a warped mind to follow your logic because I sure can't. Not with my toe—"

"Oh, yeah!" He smacked a fist in his palm. "Your toe. I knew it was only a matter of time before you trotted out your toe. But guess what? That pig won't fly."

"Finn!" She dragged his name out, each letter ringing with hurt.

Feeling himself about to cave, he stared into space beyond the sofa. "See Spot balk. See Spot refuse to roll over and beg for attention? See Spot demand a little respect."

She frowned, scratched her head, then shrugged. "I'm sure that makes perfect sense to everyone but me."

Nervous he'd confounded even his own twisted

mind, he took a breath. "Here's the bottom line. I am going to talk, and you are going to listen."

"Of course, m'lord. Whatever you say, m'lord." She folded her hands in front of her breasts, and he knew in his bones it was an invitation to jump her right there and forget getting to the bottom of anything.

The idea tempted him, but he dredged up enough willpower to say, "Short of you calling an ambulance and going to the hospital, you cannot escape. So stop that." She looked at him as if he'd crawled out from under a rock.

"Right now," he added for good measure.

She opened her mouth, but he said, "Please, Kel. We have to talk."

Blood drained from her face. In the firelight, her eyes were all pupils. She wet her lips. "You're not sick, are you?"

Breathy and husky, her voice could still knock his socks off. It was how she sounded after making love. Vulnerable. Awed. He chuckled weakly. "You mean besides in the head?"

"I-I-I'm serious."

Tears filled her eyes, but none slipped onto her cheeks. Ashamed of his smart mouth, he went down on one knee and pulled her hand away from her throat and held it against his cheek.

"Physically, I'm not sick. But I am worried sick about you, all the tension—" Her shirt gaped at the throat, revealing the swell of her breasts, and he felt his determination slip.

Damn, he knew he should've kept his distance.

Resolute, he shifted back a little so he wasn't peering down at her cleavage with adolescent excitement. "You can't keep everything bottled up, Kelsy. It's unhealthy."

"I know." The tears glittered, but she blinked them back. "I've meant to tell you so many times, but with all the craziness this weekend, it's been pretty easy not to tell you. At various points, I've convinced myself either my hormones or a brain tumor is the reason I've weirded out."

"Hormones, huh?" He stole a glance at her. God, he hoped she didn't plan on using PMS or early menopause or some other female complaint for leaving the scene of an accident. Cops, and he was sure CHP cops were no different, hated that plea.

"Hormones could explain . . . why I feel so strange lately. I sometimes feel as if I'm wandering around in another person's body."

"Really?" He loved her body. Was she talking an out-of-body experience now? That tactic would get her less sympathy than the hormone argument.

"You ever had that feeling?" She squirmed, moving her foot higher on the pillow.

"Let me think." All he could see was a patch of ivory skin above the ankle. Not enough to wreck his concentration, but enough to fire his imagination which already had ideas about his hands sliding up her sweats to the flimsy. . . . He groaned.

"Finn?" She tried tugging her hand out of his.

"No," he said as if he'd been thinking about what she'd said, but meaning he wasn't letting go of her hand.

"Your eyes remind me of a wolf with raw meat," she said, blame and accusation hitting high notes.

Heat burned his ears. "We're getting off track."

"One of us is getting off track." She lifted her chin. "The other one is trying to focus."

Duly scolded, he said, "One of us is waiting for the other one to come clean. We've stalled long enough. Tell me, dammit. What happened Tuesday night in Half Moon Bay?"

"How do you know—" She snatched her hand away as if she'd touched a snake. "Did Risa tell you?"

Finn felt his anger build, that she'd trusted Risa instead of him, that he'd persisted in thinking she was innocent, that there was a mistake he could easily fix if she'd told him.

Tightly he said, "Focus. *Who* told me is irrelevant. *What* you told Risa is the point."

"She didn't tell you a damned thing." Kelsy leaned forward on the sofa, her hands fisted. Just in case she took a swing, he kept his distance. She whispered, "You trapped me."

He flinched. "A behavior I'm not particularly proud of."

She snorted, contempt twisting the mouth he'd kissed so many times. "I've heard it's okay for the police to lie to suspects, twist the facts and pound on inconsistencies till the suspects confess to something they didn't do."

"Most departments video their interrogations so there aren't abuses."

She snapped her fingers. "Well, there you go."

Feeling ankle-deep in quicksand, Finn said doggedly, "The courts have upheld most of the disputed cases."

"Well, guess what? I never thought those techniques sounded right, and now, I can tell they don't *feel* right, either."

"If you'd trusted me in the beginning—"

"Trust is a one-way street, right?" Tears ran down her cheeks, gathered in a blob on her chin, then dripped down her throat.

"Of course not." Finn's heart galloped. He knew better than to touch her, so he handed her his clean handkerchief.

She stared at it. "Is there a hidden microphone inside?"

"Don't be ridicu—" Choked by the foot in his throat, he shut up.

"I guess they told you in Interrogation 101 that insults don't work, huh?"

"No, they told us insults work very well," he shot back, with equal sharpness. "Especially with people who keep dodging the truth."

Staring at him, she swallowed hard. "Do you want the truth? Or a confession?"

Finn shifted, trying to get blood to his feet and regroup at the same time.

Slowly, picking each word, he said, "I want you to trust me. No matter what, I'm here for you."

She laughed, and the sound tore into his guts. "*Bzzzt.* Wrong answer. You forgot to read me my rights."

As happened so often on TV, in the movies and real life, the phone interrupted the stalemate between them. Getting right to the point, Kelsy announced she wanted privacy. She expected a protest, but he said, "Okay. But we're not finished."

To her relief, he went upstairs instead of into the kitchen. Since Risa had called on her cell, Kelsy didn't worry about him picking up an extension.

He wouldn't do that, a part of her objected as she said hello to Risa.

Don't be too sure, the bruised part of her said before dumping on Risa.

When she finished, Risa said, "This is a misunderstanding the two of you could settle if you sat down and talked adult to adult."

"Thank you so much, La Ti Da."

"You're so welcome."

"For what? Bad advice?" Kelsy swung her foot onto the floor, hoping a different position would stop the throb.

"What's bad advice about sitting down and talking?"

"Talking, like sex, isn't the only part of a strong relationship." Kelsy laid a small pillow on top of her toe.

"No, but talking's a good way to let Finn know what's on your mind. You two have lost something or you'd never have gone to Half Moon Bay without talking to him *before* you went."

"You're right about losing something. Ever since this stupid undercover—" Unable to talk past the lump in her throat, Kelsy stared into the fire, squeezed her eyes shut, then said, "Déjà vu. Been here, done this with Sam—five-minute phone calls every other day. Not what I signed up for with Finn."

"Have you told him that?"

A kissing-sound came through clearly on the line and slammed Kelsy to the ground. She snapped, "Didn't I just say we don't talk?"

"Sorry," Risa said cheerily. "I felt the need to grab my lovin' husband and knock his socks off."

"Did he take his shoes off first?" Kelsy came back with the line said by Molly that had helped Risa understand she loved Ben.

"That comes later. Then, after that, we'll talk."

"If you're not trying to make me jealous, you must be trying to make a point, right?"

"Dang! The problem with being transparent is that people see through me. Talk to him, Kel."

Kelsy snorted. "You make it sound so simple."

"It's not. And don't think Ben and I haven't had several bumps in Paradise." Risa chuckled. "Several *big* bumps."

"I'm not talking about bumps. I'm talking about sink holes." Unnerved by the image of a gaping, bottomless pit, Kelsy replaced the blue ice pack Finn had brought her for her toe on the pillow.

On the other end of the phone, a door banged shut. Kelsy saw Risa setting the breakfast table for the next morning. Triplets required that kind of planning. "Did these sink holes exist before Dane Jensen came on the scene?" Risa asked.

"Maybe not sink holes," Kelsy admitted. "But I sent out my résumé a month before Dane arrived in Half Moon Bay."

"Two weeks after Finn went undercover."

The glop in the ice bag was mushy, so Kelsy pushed it aside as she explained, "About then. Writing a résumé gave me something to do at night."

"Didn't your mother fly in on her broomstick about then?" The clink of silverware put Kelsy in the kitchen with Risa.

"La Ti Da!" Kelsy bit back the laugh that choked her. "You know I met Monica at SFO. She had a four-hour layover and wanted to see Jason."

"Did she mention wanting to see her future son-in-law?"

Won't missing so many classes adversely affect finishing law school, Kelsy? Isn't Finn at a disadvantage beginning a law career at his age? Of course, he looks very young, doesn't he?

Muscles tightened in Kelsy's neck. She smothered the memories and said to Risa, "She knew he'd started a new assignment."

"How bad a time did she give you, Kelsy?"

Surprised by the tears stinging her eyes but grateful for Risa's sympathetic tone, Kelsy said thickly, "Not so bad."

"Kelsy." Risa sighed. "I know Monica, remember? I suppose being in a public place probably cramped her style. Did they have to call security?"

Going for perky, Kelsy said, "No. Really. She didn't cause a scene. Nothing compared to when I told her about the divorce."

"Oh, well, now I'm relieved. If she ever throws one of her famous Hungarian temper tantrums around Finn, I hope he throws her in jail and tosses the key out the window."

In an aside, Risa called for Ben to let Lucky Prince out, allowing Kelsy a second to regroup. She said, "I never told Finn about her coming. I saw her for less than four hours."

"Uh-huh, and after she left, you wrote your résumé and started seeing sink holes. Is there a connection, Dr. Freud?"

Using her ventriloquist-falsetto, Risa replied to her own question. "Not unless you think there's a connection between trains and penises."

"Risa!" Kelsy shrieked. "Is that your subtle way of telling me Ben's there?"

"Not subtle. Be straight with Finn, Kelsy. Get this whole mess out on the table. You can't hold back if you want honesty from him."

Kelsy's warm feelings of support and confidence lasted until she hung up. Then, like a balloon let go, her good intentions slipped away. Hot nails hammered into her toe, giving her an excuse to procrastinate. She wanted all her ducks in a row. The cliché didn't seem strong enough for what she needed to do before shooting herself in the other foot.

She smacked both her cheeks. *Enough with the clichés.*

Monica hated them. She'd raised Kelsy to think precisely. Clichés reflected small minds and smaller imaginations. For Monica, they ranked up there with slang.

But if Finn dumps me, Kelsy thought, it will make my mother's day.

Grimacing, Kelsy lurched over her knees. Damned if she'd go at it with Finn towering over her. She'd stand or know the reason why. Unsuccessful after two attempts, she bit her bottom lip. After two more tries, with sweat dripping in her eyes, pulse pounding, she stood. Good sign, she thought.

For a second, she thought the ringing she heard was in her ears. Then, she heard Finn's footsteps overhead. She glanced at her watch. 9:11. Who in the world?

Curious, but not curious enough to clump out to the hall, face a neighbor, and explain about her toe, she picked up her crutch and adjusted it under her arm. Determined she'd appear in control when Finn finished with the neighbor, she fanned her face.

The in-control smile she pasted on fell off as soon as he marched into the family room. The monuments on Mount Rushmore showed more emotion.

"Two people who might be smashed, Victoria Moreno and Steele Hood, feel certain you want to see them." He stared at her foot dangling above the carpet.

With every nerve in overdrive, Kelsy shook her head.

Finn nodded. "I feel certain I can convince them you don't want to see them."

Her jaw dropped, but he'd already pivoted around. "No," she croaked. "Wait. I will." Shaking his head, he faced her—as if she'd escaped a locked ward, so she added, "See them."

"Tonight?"

Meaning, she translated, *are you insane?*

"Now's fine." Hot pins jabbed her dangling toe. God, what if she fell on her nose in front of Victoria Moreno?

"Now is not fine. You're gonna hit the floor in about—"

"Now is fine." She waved her free hand in the general direction of the hallway.

He flushed a dark, ugly red. "Five minutes," he said. "Then, I'm kicking them out, and you and I are finishing our talk."

He was gone before she could come back with something that would shred his ego. Then, before she got sidetracked, Kelsy moved down to the end of the fireplace, away from the damned fire. She laid her arm across the mantel, then settled the crutch under her armpit.

Probably hokey, she thought. But at least I'm in control.

Chapter 18

Dressed in a long, flowing black skirt with a matching turtle-neck, Victoria Moreno swept into the room as if she owned it.

"Kelsy!" Movie-star cool, she extended her arm, palm up.

Fire from three diamond tennis bracelets nearly blinded Kelsy, who battled sudden panic. What if Victoria knocked her over, and she fell into the fire and suffered horrible, disfiguring burns?

"That's close enough." Finn stepped between her and impending disaster. He encircled Kelsy's waist, and despite the bad vibes between them, she felt safe, protected.

"She should be in bed," Finn growled, sending a shiver of desire flashing through her. "With her foot up."

"No!" Kelsy shook her head.

Steele Hood put a hand on Victoria's elbow. "We should go."

"Five minutes," Victoria said to Kelsy with palpable desperation.

"Take it down a notch," Finn ordered.

"Please." Victoria had a wild look in her black eyes

that reminded Kelsy of a neighbor woman. Mother of five, she'd thrown the kids out of the house one miserably hot summer day, then locked all the doors and windows.

"Then you'll leave." Kelsy remembered Risa's mom had taken the kids in, fed them, and kept them till the father came home and admitted his wife to the nearest mental hospital.

"Absolutely."

"Are you on some kind of meds?" Finn asked.

Kelsy gave him one thumb up, then said, "Five minutes—then you can go home and call your doctor for a new prescription."

Ignoring the insult, Victoria shouted, "Did you listen to my phone message?"

Finn dug a knuckle in his ear and stepped to one side, but still kept his arm around Kelsy's waist. She nodded. "I didn't call back. I'd rather kiss a snake than talk to you two."

"You think our call was a prank," Steele said flatly.

Faster than a cobra, Victoria jumped forward. "It's not!"

"It's not." Steele Hood clamped a hand on Victoria's shoulder and pressed her down into a chair. "Honestly."

"Show her the check," Victoria hissed, her eyes too bright.

He reached inside his beautiful tweed jacket. Next to her, Kelsy felt Finn's arm muscles contract. Her chest tightened and didn't loosen till Steele withdrew a check. Kelsy exhaled. What had she expected—a gun? Victoria grabbed the check and passed it to Finn. He fingered it for a second, but didn't read it. Apparently satisfied it wouldn't explode, he passed it to Kelsy.

Her gaze went straight to the amount line. "Seventy-five thou—" She swallowed.

"Whaaat?" Finn studied the check made out to Kelsy and drawn on the account of Victoria Pilar Isabel

Moreno. Her names started in the left hand corner and
missed by two spaces running into the transit and rout-
ing codes above the date.

What the hell? Finn telegraphed silently.

Dry-mouthed, Kelsy finally said, "Ha, ha." Did they
think she'd forgotten the interview from hell? Dane's
offer aside, the program would someday, undoubtedly,
be used the best example of The Worst Live Interview
in the History of TV.

Humiliation, toxic as poison, seeped into Kelsy's
stomach. Coldly, she said, "*Now* is the joke over?"

"Joke?" Victoria frowned, but somehow the frown
didn't diminish her dark, perfect beauty. Placing a
hand on the side of her face, she nodded slowly as if
seeing something clearly in the headlights of a 747. "I
don't blame you for being careful." She bowed her
gleaming head. "You have every reason to think we're
snakes in the grass."

"Actually, I think cobras and rattlers are sweet,
moral, compassionate creatures compared . . . ." Heart
banging, Kelsy let the sentence hang.

Victoria's blood-red mouth twitched. "I swear this is
no joke. Sign the contract—"

"And proceed directly to Hell?" Kelsy bit her tongue.

"Just a sec." With diamond bracelets throwing off
more sparks than the wood in the fireplace, Victoria removed a single sheet of paper and a black pen from the
saddlebag at her feet.

"Everything's pretty straightforward, but of course
you should read it. After you sign it, I'll electronically
transfer the money to your account. *Toute suite.*" She
snapped her fingers. "You can check your balance in
five minutes max."

"Yes," Kelsy said, "and I can show up for tea with the
queen, but how long before they figure out the mistake?"

"There's no mistake."

"Trust our amazing technology, huh?" The tic under Finn's left eye told Kelsy he'd arm wrestle Victoria into submission if she made a move.

"Technology has changed our lives," Steele Hood said as if he'd given deep thought to Finn's smart-ass comment. "Amazing's exactly the message we're trying to convey, Kelsy."

Wow, he's not just another pretty face. Finn shot him a cop look, filled with deep suspicion, mixed with what Kelsy bet was an assortment of murderous thoughts.

"Is there a problem?" Victoria moved the paper so Kelsy could see the X near the bottom of the page.

"Not for me." Kelsy shrugged. Not if she forgot her nerve- endings still stung from that damn *interview* four days ago.

"Nice paper," she said, trying to get inside their little fevered brains. "Quality bond. Embossed letterhead. Details like these give your 'contract' a nice, official appearance."

Tension arced like lightning between Victoria and Steele. She extended the pen. A signal the game was getting fun now?

Toe on fire, Kelsy didn't reach for the contract or the pen. For all she knew, the pen would spurt ink or blood or sugar-water in her face. Then the paper would self-combust.

Kelsy leaned into Finn, solid, his face a mask. "Tell me, again, what I have to do for almost triple my salary."

With someone as loony as Victoria, what normal, rational person could anticipate all the practical jokes?

Steele and Victoria started babbling, talking over each other, eyes shining, breathing hard. "You'd think they invented fire," Finn growled. "You tired of this?"

Kelsy nodded. Fingers at the corners of his mouth, Finn whistled. Once. A sharp, shrill demand for quiet.

Victoria and Steele shut up instantly.

They sat up straight, as eager as well-trained dogs

waiting for a new command. Kelsy smiled to herself. Too bad she couldn't unleash Finn on them.

Calmed just by thinking about such a move, she said, "Time's up. You've had your fun. Not as much fun as you expected, I suppose, since I didn't slobber on your check or get naked or—"

"And if pictures of her naked show up on the Internet," Finn interrupted, "I will have more fun than you can imagine cutting you off at the knees."

"He's a cop, for your edification," Kelsy said to the gawking pair. Not to mention her knight in shining armor. Blinded by heat rising off him, she felt hope stir in the pit of her stomach. He wouldn't defend her, would he, if he hated her?

"For Chrissake, do you think we're total morons?" Steele eyeballed Finn, snorted, then lowered his voice. "Don't answer that. Yes, we're total morons, but we're not skanks! We don't buy, sell, or create pornography. We *never* mentioned naked."

"He's right about that," Kelsy said grudgingly.

"Thank you." Victoria fanned her lovely face.

For the first time since they'd met, Kelsy detected no hint of aggression in the other woman.

"Believe it or not," Steele continued with his own agenda, "we came here with a legitimate business proposit—deal. If we all sit down, take a deep breath, I think I can show you in two minutes why it's worth your while not to flip us off."

It took more than two minutes, but less than ten, for Mr. Hotshot to make his case. Not bad, since Finn interrupted frequently. Kelsy asked diddly. Eyes glazed, she lost focus after the first sentence out of the guy's mouth.

"We want to hire you for a month to tape a series of interviews with us, and we'll pay you seventy-five thousand bucks as soon as you agree. We'll pay you seventy-five thou more for each completed interview."

Admittedly, Finn also had trouble focusing after that. "Why?" he asked, hoping he didn't come off as unsupportive.

"Exactly," Kelsy mumbled and squeezed his hand.

"Because we have great chemistry with Kelsy," the guy said.

"Make that charisma." Victoria smiled at Finn with the kind of detachment he associated with corpses or zombies who came to room temp slower than ice floes melted.

Brrrr. How long could Kelsy work with that kind of woman before her own charisma—which Finn believed he fully appreciated—turned to ice?

"It's as if Kelsy's a lightning rod," Victoria said smoothly. "She brings out my Inner Imp."

"Your Inner Imp," Finn repeated the phrase as if reading a line from Shakespeare—full of individual words he recognized, but together made no sense except to actors and English majors.

Avoiding eye contact with Kelsy, Finn waited for her to crack up. To his surprise, she said, "Was that your Inner Imp that came out during the interview on Thursday?"

"Yes, but it started coming out when we met in Half Moon Bay." Victoria sorta lit up.

Head cocked, Kelsy froze, reminding Finn of a deer sniffing the oncoming ten-wheeler a heartbeat too late. Or maybe that was the way he felt with his nervous system in meltdown and his mind in overdrive. Taking a breath hurt, but exhaling raised a concern about coronaries.

"What happened in Half Moon Bay?" The question to Victoria tasted bitter.

Blood drained from Kelsy's face, and Finn felt a wave of dizziness from holding his breath.

"I don't have a clue." Victoria laughed, shrugged and looked at Kelsy. "Do you?"

Wetting her lips, Kelsy hesitated, then said, "Not really."

"You came through the restaurant sizzling," Steele offered. "No one there could take their eyes off you."

Since Victoria possessed the beauty of a cobra, Finn assumed Steele meant no one could take their eyes off Kelsy, as fear slammed into his chest.

Feeling as if his diaphragm had collapsed, Finn said, "That must've stroked your ego."

Kelsy stared at her feet, but Steele said, "That's an understatement. It was more awesome than planets hurling through space, on fire, throwing off light so bright . . ."

He wound down, but not before Finn realized he didn't have the foggiest idea what the guy was saying. Victoria, looking a little dazed herself, patted Steele's hand, but spoke to Finn. "I think you really had to be there . . . to understand. Don't you agree, Kelsy?"

Pointedly, mouth clamped shut, Finn gave Kelsy the look that turned speeders into contrite citizens practically begging for a traffic ticket.

Without showing any signs of self-consciousness, Kelsy stared into space several beats, then said, "By Jove, Victoria, I do agree."

By Jove? Was insanity contagious? Finn didn't know. He knew the two women's giggling mocked him, left him out of the loop. Which might explain why the rage inside him was building.

"Bedlam, chaos, and trouble with a capital T." Finn exhaled. "Victoria, Steele—your work here is done."

Time sped up while Finn showed Victoria and Steele to the front door. Kelsy barely had time to arrange pillows around her hips and legs on the sofa before Finn stomped back into the family room. His face was flushed a bright orange, and the vein in his left temple pounded with a rhythm that scared her silly.

Knowing she had to defuse the situation, she said, "If any more smoke comes out your ears, the alarms will—"

"Shut. Up." He tossed the two pillows next to her hip onto the floor.

"My toe!"

"I'm not anywhere close to your toe. So lie back, shut up, and give me a second to calm down."

"You look ready to pop an artery." Too late, she bit her bottom lip.

"Thank you, for that encouragement." He wiped his face across a shoulder, which should have been a turnoff since he was sweaty and obviously out of control.

"Take a deep breath and hold it." Against all reason, she longed to hold him. "Count to five, then release your breath to the count of ten," she said softly while her mind churned, sifting and sorting the mess she'd made.

After four or five iterations of the exercise, he still looked awful. The backs of her knees began to sweat. "They say laughing's a good stressbuster."

Misery peered back at her. "Don't think so. I can't think of anything funny about what's going on with us."

"Maybe that's reason enough to wait till tomorrow."

"If I ever look back on this and laugh, I'll be a permanent resident in the loony bin."

"Me, maybe, but not you." She started to touch him, but thought better of it since her hands were clumps of ice.

"Why not me?" He sounded so bitter she flinched. "If you can be the drama queen, why can't I be the drama king?"

"I didn't—I only meant . . ." God, she hated this feeling that she had to examine every word, every gesture, every damned emotion. "I feel as if I'm living with Sam again. You and I fight more than we make love these days."

He winced—as if she'd dug her fingernails into his heart, but then he leaned toward her, smelling pissed and dangerous. "Now that you mention it, I believe I may have noticed a different pattern. I wonder why that is?"

"Sarcasm," she shot back, her heart about to crack a rib. "That's just one more service you offer, right?"

"A guy's gotta have a little fun," he said softly, almost casually. "Give me a few years, and I'll demonstrate more maturity."

"I'll hold my breath," she snapped. Lips pressed together, she glared at him. What was he doing? He knew how insecure she felt about being older than he was. Mr. Innocent, he gazed back at her. Neither intended to blink first.

"We can keep this up all night, Kelsy. Hurting each other. Sidestepping the real problem. Sooner or later, one of us will cross an invisible line. . . ."

Her heart clutched, then stopped. Her skin felt clammy. "And then what?" Her fear of abandonment burned white-hot in the back of her throat. "Is that when you say adiós?"

"I keep reminding you I'm not Dickhead." He edged closer on the sofa.

"Actions speak louder than words." She put her hand between her hip and his thigh. He grimaced.

"You want action?" His mouth tightened. "First, I'm still hanging in here—even though you've been acting as if I caught you with your hand in the cookie jar, while you insist there is no cookie jar."

Her heart missed a beat. He's fishing. Confident he didn't *know* anything, she said, "Guess what?"

He didn't take the bait, but waited till her nerves screamed. Finally, he said, "Just tell me why you've been acting so guilty, dammit."

He spit out *guilty* with such contempt she almost gasped. Resentful because he was right, she taunted, "Sooner or later, everyone puts a hand in the cookie jar."

His lips thinned. "Meaning?"

"Meaning I don't appreciate your judging me. Admittedly, you are a saint—"

"Yeah, that's me. We agree, so drop that subject." The crack of his jaw dared her to disagree.

On guard, she waited, kicking herself for being such a coward. Nearly nose to nose with her, he said, "Dammit, I'm a blind man feeling his way, Kelsy."

Despite the soft light from the fire, he looked haggard. Her heart twisted. Tell him, she thought. Trust him. *Lose him.*

In a quiet, level voice, he said, "Why didn't you tell me you went to Half Moon Bay to meet with The Loony Tunes?"

"I didn't." She swallowed, her pulse so fast she couldn't say more.

He rolled his eyes. "So, who'd they see on Tuesday? Your hologram?"

"No, they saw me. I was wearing a black Valentino knockoff, my Manolo Blahniks—"

"Your Manolo Blahniks?" he repeated as if the shoes meant something deep to him. "Was the guy you met Dane Jensen, Kelsy?"

Suddenly bone cold, she rubbed her arms, felt her heart clench, then felt relief, mixed with suspicion, roar through her. "How do you know Dane?"

"I picked up a call from him in Montana."

"On my cell?" Mind blank, she felt a little panicky because she couldn't remember when she'd been without her phone. "Where was I?"

"With Jason in the ER. They wouldn't let you go into his cubicle with it, remember?"

"If you say so." The whole ER scene was blurred, and all she remembered was the fear and guilt.

"*Dane* got a little mouthy, wouldn't say who he was, demanded to know where you were and who I thought I was. I told him to go play with his prick and hung up."

"Dammit, Finn. Why didn't you tell me he called?"

"He rubbed me the wrong way. He sounded like Dickhead's clone to me, so I forgot about him. I also had other worries, till you mentioned the shoes."

Her head hurt, probably because she'd crashed headlong down the same dark hole she'd just climbed out of less than five minutes ago. Wary now, she said, "What do my shoes have to do with Dane Jensen?"

"A lot. I don't figure you'd wear a pair of five-hundred-dollar shoes over to Half Moon Bay to impress a weenie. If he's not a weenie, I figure he must be someone you think either walks on water or doesn't get his pants wet like the rest of us mortals. Probably some TV bigwig."

His deductions—or were they inferences?—were dead-on. Eerily so. In a rush, she blurted, "He's from Seattle. He came down for a golf tournament at The Ritz. I met him there for dinner. Just to see if there was a mutual interest."

"A mutual interest in what?"

"In a job! What else?"

"Want me to tell you what else?"

"He was a perfect gentleman." Face hot, she smothered the memory of the fumbling kiss. Five days later, she had a clearer perspective of his good-night peck on the cheek.

"A perfect gentleman." Finn repeated her words with no attempt at hiding his derision. "That must be why you didn't tell me about going over there."

Before she could explain about her toe and the interview *and Baby Face,* Finn continued. "A perfect gentleman left you moody and preoccupied, not to mention wired. When do I meet this perfect gentleman?"

When she opened her mouth to blister his ears, he

interrupted. "What really happened to your toe? Did the perfect gentleman take you to a doctor?"

His intuition regained some focus, putting Kelsy on the defensive. "Have I ever told you how much I hate it when you go into cop mode? I bet you go easier on criminals than you do on me."

He shrugged. "Why don't you save that distraction for another time? Right now, I'd think the woman I love would have no problems volunteering lots of information."

Nodding, she pursed her lips, hoping he took this as a sign of agreement instead of confirmation she was guilty. While she dug her fingernails into the underside of her arm, he said, "Volunteered info almost always gives me peace of mind."

"Almost always? How encouraging." Realizing she'd hit a brick wall she couldn't climb over, she hugged her waist. "All right," she said and stared at her sweaty hands. "I screwed up. I should've told you about going to Half Moon Bay. I should've told you about Dane Jensen. I meant to."

Expecting no sympathy from Finn yet, Kelsy lifted her gaze and smiled. Maybe, just maybe, he'd smile back. Maybe he'd cut her a small break. Stone-faced, he crossed his arms over his chest. Her mind churned as she reconnected with the point she wanted to make.

"I didn't say anything at the motel because you were so happy about beating Lieutenant Matthews—"

"You didn't say anything at the motel because you were so busy lying and staying behind to call *the perfect gentleman*. That was him you called as I was leaving, fat, D-U-M and fucked, wasn't it?"

Her heart lurched, but she met and held his blazing eyes. "Yes."

He flinched. "This is one of those times when volunteered information goes a long way."

"There's nothing to volunteer—if you're talking about sexual attraction."

"Uh-huh." He pressed his lips into a grim line, and his mouth worked as if about to spit out something bad.

Rage uncoiled in her stomach. Through clenched teeth, she snapped, "Here's a piece of *volunteered* info for you. The neon sign I wear says, 'Not Available'."

His gaze dropped to her lip, then traveled down to her throat, and finally stopped at her heaving chest. "Your sign must be on the fritz," he said. "I can't see it."

Close to tears, she wailed, "I only wear it in public."

With fingers cold as icicles, he touched her engagement ring. "Let's take a break. I need a time out. Can I get you anything?"

"Nothing, thanks," she said in the cool, polite tone of a stranger not wanting to feel indebted to another stranger.

Chapter 19

Clarity came for Finn in the kitchen with his second cup of black coffee.

Determined to act before his nerve slipped away, he didn't bother rinsing his cup. To his surprise, Kelsy wasn't asleep when he returned to the family room. Neither spoke. The silence was uncomfortable, but he resisted the impulse to ask about her toe. At the same time, he ignored the impulse to sit in a chair instead of next to her on the sofa.

Reminded of his gut-wrenching terror the first time he went off the high dive, he jumped right in.

"This isn't helping—me withholding info from you." The dying firelight lit her pale face with an incandescence that shook his resolve enough he couldn't meet her eyes.

Thank God, she didn't use her power and reduce him to a babbling fool with one word. Weakly, he continued, "If my male ego hadn't hijacked my brain, we'd be in bed together right now."

Maybe it wasn't worthwhile arguing the obvious. He didn't spare more than a thought to his bruised ego. Without mentioning sources, he pretended Kelsy was

Matthews and recited Olivia's account of the accident in Half Moon Bay. He watched Kelsy carefully out of the corner of his eye, noting she blanched as soon as he said CHP.

His lungs stopped, but he took a deep, aching breath and let his mind float to the ceiling. He didn't really feel the sofa under him or his mouth open and shut.

Disbelief, confusion, anxiety, and terror flashed across Kelsy's face like headlines in a newspaper.

Get this over, he thought. Then, make it up to her.

Furious at his stupidity, he picked up speed. The Lexus was still on the CHP's "Stop List." He knew this because he'd checked with a buddy seconds before The Loony Tunes had shown up.

Staring at him out of her soulful blue eyes, she listened as he ranted on about the very lucky hit-and-run survivor. She didn't interrupt. She just listened.

Listening, Finn realized, dumping more and more accident crap on her, was one of her best qualities. Before they'd fucked each other's brains out the first time, they'd spent eight hours talking non-stop.

Mostly, he talked. Non-stop. About being a cop. About finishing law school. About karma.

Mostly, she'd listened even though Dickhead had just turned her world upside down and inside out.

As his mind crash-landed in his body again, Finn fought a wave of self-disgust. Here was this beautiful, smart, funny woman he could talk to about anything. Now, ten months later, when he didn't openly attack her or pass judgment on her, she still listened as if pearls of wisdom dropped from his lips.

Since he couldn't think of a logical segue from his rant to enlightenment, he said abruptly, "The Highway Patrol wants to talk to other owners of white SUVs besides you."

"How lucky for me," she flared, "since I never hit anyone."

Despite the web of lies she'd woven, her show of spunk had the ring of truth. "I know," he said.

Chin jutted, she sat up straighter. "How?"

"You just told me. You said you didn't hit anyone. I believe you."

Her chin trembled. She raised her chin, stretching her neck longer than a giraffe's. "Surely you want rock-solid, irrefutable proof I didn't hit that man."

He'd seen drivers as guilty of traffic violations as Hannibal Lecter was of bad taste try this 'tude, and it generally pissed him off. In Kelsy's case, he said, "I only want to know what you want to tell me."

"Shhh." She put her finger over her lips. "Don't tempt me with an easy out."

The resignation in her voice tempered the relief filling him up. Out of respect for her wishes and payment for his arrogance, he didn't kiss her, but slipped her hand into his and laced their fingers. Hers felt as if they hadn't received blood for a couple of decades.

If he expected a smile, he was disappointed. She looked ready to cry, and he almost repeated she didn't have to tell him a damn thing. Forget the fuckin' details.

As if sensing the argument boiling inside him, she waited till he nodded, then gave him a rundown, with times, on leaving The Ritz, getting sick, going to the B and B. She hesitated, but finished. "I checked into the ER a little past midnight and was back at the B and B by 1:45. Dane Jensen arranged for the limo driver from The Ritz to bring me home. We drove into Risa's at 3:07."

His stomach dropped. "Uh-huh," he said brilliantly. "I'd say that pretty much clears you, then."

"Two people can corroborate my alibi."

The limo driver and Jensen? Consumed by homicidal jealousy, Finn bit his tongue. He'd swallow it before he asked.

"The hospital must have a record," Kelsy said. "Officer Miller didn't give me a ticket, but he'd know what time he left the B and B."

What can Jensen confirm? An empty hole expanded in Finn's aching stomach. He made a few noises, apparently received as encouragement, then tried to block out the story Kelsy told. He couldn't let himself take in all the details or he'd hit something. Maybe bang his head against a wall. She'd been in trouble, and she hadn't called him. What did that tell you?

From long practice he kept his face impassive, succumbing to her vulnerability even as he called himself a fool and worse. Eyes squinted, chest rising and falling too fast, she looked every shade of sorry for the hell she'd put him through.

Her defiance hadn't disappeared, but it was tattered. She whispered, "I was an idiot, but I didn't drive the car that hit an old man."

Nodding, colder than he could ever remember, Finn said, "If you want, I'll go with you to CHP."

Surprised by Finn's offer, Kelsy thought she sounded sincere when she thanked him. Her first instinct was to throw her arms around his neck, drag him down on top of her, and make him forget her deep stupidity. But when he made no move to kiss or hug her, she distrusted her instincts. In a neutral tone, he did volunteer to set up the CHP appointment. The lame joke she made about being in his debt for eternity bombed.

Instead of discussing a time for the appointment, Finn stood. In a series of slow, clumsy movements, he shuffled toward the fireplace. Shoulders slumped, he banged his shin on the coffee table, swore, then limped across the room.

My God, he looks as old as I feel. Too much adrenaline, she thought. Guilt squeezed her heart. Too many surprises and disappointments in one day.

For a lifetime.

Without thinking, she blurted, "Are you okay?"

"Sure. A couple of hours sleep, and I'll be a new man."

Biting her tongue, she let the new man comment slide. She said, "Take more than a couple."

"Don't you have to be on-air at five?" Eyes glazed, he glanced over his shoulder at her.

A memory flashed. Finn asleep. Red hair tousled. Hot, so hot. "Not this morning."

"How come?" He turned his back to her.

Her mind stayed with the memory of him asleep. She adored his freckles. Thick-tongued, she said, "What?"

"You taking The Loony Tunes' offer?" He poked the ashes.

"Brad owes me after I covered for Erica." *Turn around.* God, she loved waking up next to him, his body soft, warm, ready.

"With everything going on, I don't suppose you called Ma."

"I-I forgot." Feeling defensive, jerked out of her fantasy, she tried not to read too much into his preoccupation with the fire.

"No problem. I'll call." He checked his watch. "I'll let her finish *Law and Order.* She never misses that program."

"I've never seen it," Kelsy said just to keep up her end of the conversation.

Finished with the fire, Finn removed her teacup to the kitchen, opened and closed the dishwasher, then ran water into the sink. No jokes, no I love you's. Just silence—awkward and embarrassing. *Probably terrified if we talk, the other shoe will drop.*

Heart thumping, Kelsy adjusted her toe on a pillow and welcomed the burst of fire up her leg. The pain helped her focus. Until she told Finn about Dane's offer and her doubts about wanting more kids, there were still too many loose ends to say *I love you* and expect him to believe her.

Through blurry eyes, she watched him check the doors, then heard him go into the garage. Double-checking the alarm? Any other time, she'd tease him about his compulsions. Not tonight. Tonight, she didn't have the right to tease him.

She also didn't think she had the right to ask for help to the bathroom. More to the point, she was too damned proud. Once he was upstairs, talking with his mother, she'd manage with the crutch. She wasn't helpless.

"Anything else I can do?" He paused in the doorway, backlit by the hall lamp, looking hard and inviting. "Another pillow? Water?"

Hold me, she screamed silently—a heartbeat before she pasted a smile on her face. "Not a thing. Good night."

For the first hour after Finn went upstairs, Kelsy checked her watch every ten minutes. During each check, her pulse leaped, her stomach clenched, and her hands sweat profusely. *Get a grip, Kelsy. He's not coming.*

Not fair, she argued with her brain. Paste a red L in the middle of her forehead. Parade her through the streets of Cielo Vista so everyone could see what a liar looked like. Exact a pound of flesh. Just start her sentence tomorrow. Right now, let him come down and hold her, tell her he loved her and always would.

At two, she started crying. Silently at first, then snuffling because the tissues were in the bathroom. Tears pooled in her ears, and she tilted her head to each side, whacking her temples, fighting the panicky sensation of drowning.

By three, she stopped crying. Her eyes felt gritty and tender. Dry-mouthed, nose stopped up, she chugged water. The burn in the back of her throat eased. *He's not coming.*

Her body went into a kind of shock from adrenaline overload. It was as if she'd been running on a treadmill as fast as she could, and suddenly, the electricity went off. The treadmill stopped, throwing her off.

Time to regroup. She wasn't worried about a chat with CHP. They'd check the Lexus, find nothing and take her name off their list. Telling the truth about her stay at La Lunada had been a no-brainer for her and a stick in the eye for Finn. Choosing her career over having his baby wouldn't destroy him, but would it destroy them as a couple?

Her heart banged high in her chest. Life without Finn? *Do not go there.* Not till she was thinking clearly. Not till—

Her head dropped. Sleep wrapped around her in a warm, cotton cloud. Her body floated toward the softness, sank into it, and relaxed. Later, later, she'd—

Her head snapped upright. Determined to consider Victoria and Steele's offer, Kelsy blinked, trying to zero in on a few of the ideas darting through her fuzzy mind. But as soon as she grabbed a fragment, it slipped away, deeper into the darkness. She snatched at more thoughts, then gave in to the soft clouds surrounding her.

At 7:13 the next morning, Finn and Jason sneaked out of the house as quietly as cat burglars. The promise of Krispy Kremes drove Jason. The hope of escape drove Finn. Fully dressed and shaved, his bloodshot eyes bleak, his face a patchwork of cat scratches, he knew he couldn't go through the motions of happy, happy at breakfast with Kelsy in front of Jason.

Going through the motions with Jason alone was a piece of cake. First, the kid never shut up during the three-mile drive to the doughnut shop. *He is his mother's son.*

High-octane enthusiasm challenges your apathy, Finn thought as he leaned back so Jason could scream his order into the mike at the drive-through window. Pressed for time, Finn had suggested drive-through when it looked as if half the commuters in Silicon Valley had stopped off for a heady fix of grease and sugar. Accepting a box of warm goodies, he wondered if inhaling the fumes alone didn't clog enough arteries for triple bypass surgery.

It wasn't a question for five-year-olds, so Finn handed over the box of doughnuts to Jason. The cast gave him a little trouble with the unwieldy container. But not so much trouble he couldn't rip the box open and grab his sugar fix.

After taking part in a few seconds of sighs, groans, and shrieks of gluttony, Finn swallowed half of his first doughnut then said, "You should probably rethink going down the slide. You know, for a day or two. With your cast."

"Did Mommy say so?" Jason said around a mouthful of chocolate doughnut.

"Nope. My idea." Finn stuck a straw into a milk carton and passed both to Jason.

"Oh." Jason slurped. "I promise I'll be real careful."

"I know." Finn grinned, feeling some unidentifiable bond with this kid he loved and didn't want to scare or turn into a sissy. He shrugged. "Sometimes, though, accidents happen."

"Like at Molly's?"

"Exactly like at Molly's." Kelsy thought she could've stopped Jason, but even if she hadn't been on the phone, that seemed improbable to Finn. He owed her a big apology there.

"Everybody's supposed to be real careful on the

slides," Jason said solemnly. Quoting Ms. Forrest, his teacher?

"Understand. I'm not saying forever." Proud the give and take felt so damned good, Finn selected a glazed doughnut. Since he was bonding with Jason, he ignored the napkins. "A day or two," he said. "That's all."

"A day or two's a long time."

"Not as long as three or four days," Finn countered. Look at what had happened in the last four days.

Afraid thoughts of Kelsy and the accident would lead to putting her in the middle of this discussion, Finn avoided saying, 'Don't worry your mother till she's back on her feet'.

"Today and tomorrow. That's all I'm asking," Finn pushed his point.

"Okay." Jason shrugged.

For Finn, the gesture, mimicked perfectly, was the best compliment he'd had in weeks. He let out a breath. "Thanks."

On the ride to school, Finn, victor of this small skirmish, offered no advice on cleaning off sugar and milk moustaches. In the mustard-yellow classroom, he inserted no corrections as Jason expanded on falling off his pony, going to the hospital, then sleeping on the barn floor after Finn, covered in scratches, came back with Jessicat.

"And," Jason concluded, his little chest puffed out, "my mommy hurt her toe so bad she can't wear a regular shoe."

"Oh, my goodness." Including Finn in her warmth, Ms. Forrest smiled reassuringly. "You really had an exciting and interesting vacation, didn't you?"

Stoked with sugar, optimism on the rebound, Finn dawdled a little longer before leaving Jason's classroom and facing Kelsy. On a perfect, cloudless day, he felt more alive just being outside. Since going undercover, he now believed that walls had ears. Remembering he couldn't be too careful, he moved away from the school building to make his call to the San Mateo Division of the Highway Patrol in Redwood City. He identified himself immediately and asked the status of the hit and run in Half Moon Bay.

He tilted his head, caught a few rays of sunshine and waited on hold, loosening his grip on the phone. On the second recorded announcement, he was transferred to the investigating lead, Officer Scott Ryder. Once he confirmed Finn's identity, Officer Ryder had no problem sharing info with a local cop.

"Especially since we caught the SOB," Ryder boomed.

"You're sure?" Finn, who believed in coincidence until it figured into a crime, kept his heart rate level by quietly inhaling three times.

"No question we have the right guy," Ryder insisted. "At two o'clock this morning, the lab made a perfect match with blood from under our guy's right bumper."

Of its own volition, Finn's heart went through his skull. "That's—that's great! Congratulations."

"Thanks." Ryder sighed. "We can't take all the credit." He paused and Finn, ready to hang up and dance through the streets, said, "Why not?"

"Oh, we'd've found him sooner or later. His name's on our STOP LIST."

Finn swallowed and focused on the playground. "I heard you had a list."

"Shorter than it was, but long enough to keep us busy for a couple more days."

"Someone turned him in?"

"His wife."

"His wife?" *Must've been one ticked-off wife.* Finn stared at a circle of flowers planted by five-year-olds.

"Can you believe it?"

"What happened?" Seeing the similarity with him and Kelsy, Finn made no effort to hide his impatience.

"They had a big argument Saturday night. Hubby took off. She called us late yesterday afternoon. And here I thought marriage was based on trust." Ryder laughed.

The cynicism rubbed Finn the wrong way, but he said tightly, "Maybe there were extenuating circumstances."

"Oh, definitely. Apparently last Tuesday our guy was in bed in La Honda with his wife's best friend."

"No shit?" The taste of sugar, sickeningly sweet, filled the back of Finn's throat. La Honda was fifteen, twenty minutes inland from The Ritz, the date-place with Perfect Gentleman Dane Jensen.

"Life is stranger than fiction." Ryder chuckled, as if he'd just made up the cliché. "Surprise, surprise. The wife threw hubby to the dogs after he finally admitted where he'd been."

Ryder went on for a few more minutes, but Finn tuned him out. *Life is stranger than fiction.* He and Kelsy laughed about this cliché all the time. Except when it came to infidelity and male mid-life crises. Those clichés cut a little too close to the bone for her to laugh. The knot in Finn's stomach tightened around a ten-ton ball of pure sugar. How much of what he'd learned from Ryder should he tell Kelsy?

None. His first instinct.

All. His wimpy second instinct.

The sun, hot enough to roast chickens, scalded his scalp and brains, making both conclusions doubtful. What did make sense, even with sweat dripping off his eyebrows into his eyes, was telling her all the facts. Something she wouldn't get from the media. On the other hand, she might not thank him, either.

Too bad women don't come with a roadmap. Pulling his stuck shirt away from his sweaty back, Finn interrupted Ryder's rant on guys who can't keep their Johnsons at home.

"When're you releasing the story?" He opened his car door, but stood on the asphalt till the blue wave of heat inside ebbed.

"Last I heard, today at noon. It's the media's story *du jour.*" Ryder snickered. "Except you gotta remember in TV-land, *du jour*'s about two minutes. Soon as somethin' else happens, off the talking heads go—hounds after the fox. Go figure, right?"

"Go figure," Finn agreed, realizing he should've defended Kelsy's chosen profession out of loyalty to her. Worried there'd now be a news leak before he got back to Risa's, he said firmly, "Thanks for your help."

"No problem," Ryder said. "I'll share a final insight if you've got a minute."

"Sure." Finn shook off his resentment for being held longer by Chatty Scotty.

"The moral to this story? Don't ever piss a woman off. They never forget—or forgive—when we betray them."

Finn grunted, then hung up. In the 'Vette, he immediately flicked the radio to KGO, San Francisco's premier talk station. Commercials droned on, then came the news at the top of the hour. Nerves twanging, Finn turned up the volume.

"Yesss!" He smacked the horn. He'd scooped the media. The music swelled as he pulled into Risa's driveway.

An announcer with a deep baritone boomed, "Late-breaking news in the hit-and-run case in Half Moon Bay last week . . ."

Chapter 20

"You probably figure a good lay would cheer me up, right?"

Kelsy sat at the kitchen table undisturbed by her snarky tone, her hair wild and messy and her toe purple, ugly, and repulsive.

"Never entered my head." Finn eyed the muted TV.

She wagged a finger at him. "Cops shouldn't lie, you know."

He flushed, his features sharp in the sun-filled room. "You make me sound as if I think with my dick."

"Still no reason for lying." She nodded at the TV. "I assume I'm now off the CHP's Most Wanted List."

"You were never on their Most Wanted List." Mouth rigid, Finn eased into the chair across from her as if it was electrified. "Sorry I wasn't here when you heard the good news."

Shrugging, her breath shallow, she shoved the empty coffee mug to the center of the table. "You have absolutely no reason to feel guilty."

"You're not going to trot out that crap about me being a saint, are you?" He tugged at his rooster's tails, then took her hands and held them between his. "God, you're freezing!"

"Risa says I probably have an infection. I think I— why didn't you come back downstairs last night?" She tried not to whine, but she was scared now that she'd made up her mind to tell him about Dane as well as everything else.

"I thought we both needed a little space. Besides, by the time I got off the phone with Ma, it was too late."

"That's a rationalization, isn't it? Or maybe a white lie?"

He flinched, but didn't let go of her hands.

"A *little* white lie." Unsure where she was going, she made a face. "That's how I started, you know. *Little* white lies and fibs. A couple at first, then at least one every day, sometimes two or three a day."

"Kelsy!" His look of worry almost derailed her till she realized she was counting on exactly such a reaction.

Shouldering away the tears on her chin, she said, "I moved on to half truths, lies, and whoppers. Till the accident in Half Moon Bay, I convinced myself they didn't matter. I didn't get caught, and no one got hurt. The truth? It was out there, but I didn't look very hard. Probably wouldn't have recognized it anyway."

She knew what he was thinking. That she exaggerated. He didn't know what to do, so he shook his head and squeezed her hands tighter. "Did Risa say you should go to the doctor?"

Kelsy laughed. "Sure did, and she said I should wait to 'confess' till I had my head examined, as well as my toe."

"Risa usually dispenses pretty good advice." Finn inched his fingers under Kelsy's sleeves, sending an army of goose bumps down her back.

"Usually." Heart thudding, Kelsy nodded. "Not always. Not this time. Be-because I'll wiggle off the hook if I don't tell you." She sighed. "I went to Half Moon

Bay because I think—I'm sure I want a career. Full time."

He stared at her. "You what?"

"You heard me. I want to be someone. Someone with influence. The influence of Savannah Jones and B. J. Thomas."

There, she'd finally said it. Out loud. Without apology.

"Savannah Jones and B. J. Thomas," he murmured, then added disbelievingly, "You mean the TV personalities?"

"They're not personalities! Savannah—B. J., too— they've interviewed some of the most important people in the world: Donald Trump. Martha Stewart. Julia Roberts."

"People who make a difference." Finn looked dazed, so his sarcasm caught Kelsy off guard.

Impatiently, she said, "Dane Jensen offered me a job in Seattle. I'll do two specials—"

"In Seattle? That's a thousand miles from here."

"Duuuh." She felt a spurt of anger. Did he think she didn't know Seattle wasn't in the next county?

Frowning, he opened his hands wide. "How can you and I have a life with you working a thousand miles away?"

"We'd have to work it out."

"Now there's an idea I hadn't considered." His mouth twisted.

To her surprise, she didn't feel offended. "Lots of people do this—have long-distance marriages."

"Really? How many?"

"Risa and Ben." Exasperated, she sighed. "I don't have an exact number—"

"How about a general, ballpark figure?"

"Why?" She tucked her icy fingers under her armpits. "Do you have a figure in mind that equals *a lot*?" Mildly ticked, she put quotes around "a lot" with her fingers.

"If my figure doesn't match yours, does that mean that very few people have long—"

"I don't know what it means, okay?" He pushed his chair away from the table. "You said *a lot of people do this.* I'm interested in knowing how many is a lot. That's all."

"I don't think so." She put her hand under her thigh and hoisted her foot to the floor. "I think you have in mind that I should forget a career, hang around the house and become a baby machine."

"A baby machine?" Holding onto the back of his chair as if for support, he stood. "What the hell does that mean? I said I'd like to have a couple more kids. How does that make you a baby machine?"

"Are *you* going to carry them for nine months?" The pain in her foot hurt worse than labor. "Are *you* going to take care of them twenty-four/seven?"

Finn opened his mouth, but Kelsy talked over him, her voice rising. "God forbid we feed them from a bottle. Are *you* going to eat enough for an elephant, gain as much weight as an elephant so you can breastfeed them?"

"Yeah," he drawled, his eyes half closed. "I can probably do that. Especially since it sounds like you're gonna nail my balls to the wall."

Kelsy snorted, throwing her hands in the air. "Why does it always come back to men's cojones? How about my chance at a life, a career while I'm still young and don't have to tuck and suck the major parts of my anatomy?"

"You'd do that?" Finn exploded, his face livid. "You'd go under the knife because—because why, for God's sake?"

"Because I'd had three kids and was ninety-three years old and wanted to be competitive in TV news." Kelsy blotted spit in the corner of her mouth. "And I don't expect you to understand any of this. You're a guy. You think women truly want to stay at home barefoot and pregnant, then die."

His eyes widened, then he hooted. "You are puttin' me on, right? This is to get back at me for not coming back last night and begging you to forgive me?"

"In your dreams. You could have crawled on your belly—"

"Men are idiots." Without warning, he dropped down on one knee, his hands under his chin. "I am a man. Ergo, I—" His mouth twitched.

Unamused, Kelsy jerked away from him. She said, "How do I set a laser printer to stun?"

"Huh?" Then, he nodded and laughed. "Round One to Kelsy."

"Game to Kelsy. You have the right to remain silent, so please *shut up*." She nudged him till he got to his feet, then returned to the chair he'd vacated.

Through her teeth, she said, "I want you to listen."

Without missing a beat, he made an X across his mouth. "You've done this before, I see," Kelsy said, imagining him a small boy in deep maternal trouble.

No muscles twitched in his face. *Smart man*. Ears ringing, she said slowly, "I don't want to get married—"

His eyes bulged. Before he could ask, *What?* Kelsy rushed on. "I already said this. I'm rethinking having two more babies right away after we get married. I've got a chance at being someone important. More than a mommy and wife."

Holding up his hand like a schoolboy, Finn said, "May I leave the room and come back in? I think I've stepped into a parallel universe."

"You haven't." She softened her voice, but clasped her hands in front of her.

"Okay. Then, I've lost it."

Do not touch him.

"Finn." She longed for a romantic movie moment.

She'd lay a finger on his lips, absorb his body heat, lean closer, feel his breath on her face as their desire pulsed to moody strings in the background. "This has been coming for a while. *Before* the divorce, if I'm . . . totally honest."

He twisted the rooster's tails. "You just said you don't recognize the truth anymore."

"I recognize the truth here." She swallowed. "Trust me."

He could've laughed, but he looked ready to cry. "I've always trusted you."

Her heart tap-danced so fast she felt lightheaded. "I know. You and Risa almost make up for Sam and my mother. I don't think either can spell *trust*."

"That must've been tough."

She wrinkled her nose. "I'm not blaming them. I became an accomplished liar all on my own."

Finn squinted against the sun. "I don't believe that, but I can see you do." He sighed. "Where does that leave us? You in Seattle with Mr. Big Shot, me down here with . . . exactly what? Memories and a fuckin' broken heart?"

Heat stung Kelsy's ears. She demanded, "Are you trying to make me feel guilty?"

His eyes blazed, held hers and turned hard. "Why not? You know what they say."

"Oh, goody. A test." Tensing, Kelsy felt a sting under her ribs that raced down her leg, settling in her toe. "What do *they* say?"

"Misery loves company."

Cranky from fighting the pain in her toe, Kelsy said, "After ten years with Sam, I've already paid my misery dues. Buying into more babies, going along with your view of domestic bliss? I'd say I've paid an overabundance of misery dues, so—"

"Wait a minute." Finn slammed his hands down on

the table. "You're saying I'm at fault here? From Day One, I tell you what I want, honestly and up-front, but now I'm the bad guy."

"No, you're not the bad guy. You just assumed I wanted exactly what you wanted. It never occurred to you I might want anything different."

Finn looked at the ceiling. "So why didn't you tell me?"

"News update." She put her hands on either side of her mouth. "I lie. I do not tell the truth. Not even to myself. I do not readily admit what I need or want."

"Now you tell me," he said as if he hadn't heard a word she'd said. "Why the hell do you keep jiggling your foot?"

"I have a broken toe, in case you hadn't noticed."

"Maybe we should take it to the doctor, then pick up this-this discussion when you feel better."

She closed her eyes against the sting of tears. "I don't think I'm going to feel better for quite a while," she whispered, her heart aching far more than her toe.

Mad as hell, Finn paid twenty bucks to get rid of the taxi driver Kelsy had called while he took Jason to school. Over her protests, he drove her to Urgent Care at El Camino Hospital. She adamantly refused to let him go into the examining room with her. Since he didn't feel like a confrontation with Security, he stayed in the waiting area, smoke coming out of his ears. The TV played on mute. Four Spanish-speaking women, three kids, and a Gen X guy with a bald head, ignored the idiot box. Eyes stinging, Finn hated the smell of alcohol mixed with phony pine-scented disinfectant. To avoid biting his tongue in two, he called Risa.

"They'll probably give her a heavy-duty painkiller," Risa said. "She needs sleep. She told me she was awake all night."

Guilt slammed Finn in the guts. "Typical male, I went to bed and thought she'd call me if her toe hurt."

"She told me you two had a fight. *A major fight*, she said."

"Not as major as the battle we had an hour ago." Finn nodded at one of the women trying to corral two of the kids.

"Did you reach an . . . understanding?"

"Yes, that I fell into the gene pool when the lifeguard wasn't watching."

Risa didn't cough up a lung laughing, but she chuckled. "Sometimes I think men and women trying to understand each other is a spiritual test."

"Funny, I was reminded of a dog-and-cat fight."

"Believe it or not, I think that's a good sign. Kelsy never fought with Sam while they were married." Risa paused, then continued quietly. "Her mother never let her forget she had no value except as a rich man's wife."

"I never realized Hungary was another planet." Finn dangled his keys in front of the toddler, who waved at his mother across the waiting room.

"My mom says they had it pretty tough before they escaped to the U.S. Kelsy would kill me if she knew I'd mentioned Monica."

"Got it. Here comes her doctor. Call you later."

The middle-aged doctor slapped one fist into his palm, then repeated the same action in his other palm. Looking down his nose at Finn, he stayed within an arm's length of the swinging door and never made eye contact during the three-second update.

"Miz Chandler reminded me you aren't related to her," the twit said. "Patient privacy comes first, I'm afraid. So there isn't much else I can tell you except she can leave."

Asshole. Thinking "spiritual test," Finn said, "Now?"

"She asked a CNA to call her a taxi."

CRRRAAACK! Finn smacked a fist into his palm.

"And I bet she wants to wait in the examining room till the taxi gets here, right?"

The doctor eyed the door, pivoted slowly, then paused on the threshold. "We put in the record that she ran into a piece of furniture. I certainly hope she doesn't run into anything else for a while."

The door flapped behind him. Choked by the cuss words stuck in his throat, Finn stared after Dr. Moron, felt his brain shift back into think mode, then pushed the door open.

The doctor whirled around. "You can't come in—"

"I'm not," Finn said. "I just wanted to thank you for doing your job." He backed out into the waiting area. The doctor's bedside manner sucked, but it took balls to imply Finn had caused Kelsy's accident.

Twenty minutes later, a CNA rolled her wheelchair right up to the taxi. The driver remained in the front seat. The CNA helped Kelsy into the back and dragged the seatbelt across her chest, then slammed the door. Edgy, but resigned, Finn stayed inside till the taxi pulled away from the curb. Then he jogged across the parking lot, jumped in the 'Vette and pulled in behind the cabbie at the end of the block.

They must've given her a hyperdose of mind candy, Finn thought, watching her bob from side to side as the taxi moved forward. Damn, the woman was stubborn. A quality, he admitted grudgingly, he happened to admire.

The driver turned right, and Kelsy swayed right, then left as the cab moved into the left lane. Finn ground his teeth and felt a flash of sympathy. No way she was comfortable. But he'd fix that as soon as they got back to Risa's. He'd treat her royally. Massage her other foot. Fix her favorite foods. Help her to the bath—

Reality smacked him between the eyes. Breaking his cardinal rule—no cell calls in the car—he called Risa, who confirmed his hunch. Kelsy would hate having him see her drugged and dopey. She never wanted anyone to see her at less than her best.

"What about Ma?" Finn asked, already knowing the answer, but making the case anyway. "They bonded last year when the flu nailed Kelsy."

"After the major battle you two had, I'd say no."

"What about Jason? Kelsy shouldn't be alone with him."

"I'll call my office nurse, Em, see what her schedule is tonight, then I'll talk with Ben. If he can manage the kids, I'll come down tomorrow. By Wednesday, Kelsy should be fine physically."

Finn felt as if he'd been rear-ended. "I report for work at five tonight. Maybe I can stop by on Wednesday morning before I crash."

"Mother Risa suggests later. After you've had some sleep. In the meantime, can you pick up Jason at school today?"

As much as Finn wanted to stay with Kelsy, he figured the best thing he could do for her was take care of Jason. Ahead of him, the taxi turned into the hills. They'd be at the house in less than five minutes. He ran his idea by Risa. Why not take Jason to Ma's after school? "Em can pick him up there. I'll hang at your place, find something to do so Kelsy can sleep for the rest of the afternoon."

"Sounds good as long as Kelsy doesn't veto the idea."

"I'm confident I can persuade her." Scared as he was, he wasn't above begging.

After Finn paid the taxi driver, settled Kelsy on the sofa, reviewed the plan for Jason, and got her buy-in, her cell phone rang. Ignore it or give her hell about the cab?

Head back, eyes closed, she wasn't comatose, but she wasn't legally conscious either. Forget the taxi. She made no movement toward the phone. He glanced at the LED. He blanked on the area code, but his suspicions immediately unleashed gallons of testosterone into his veins.

He snarled into the mouthpiece, "What the hell do you want?"

For a heartbeat, all he heard was white noise. A small voice said, "This is Victoria Moreno. I'm calling Kelsy—"

"She's unavailable!"

Whether it was the ice in his tone, his pointed delivery or something else altogether, Miz Loony Tunes said quickly, "I'll call later."

"Not today!" A dial tone buzzed in his ear.

"Phone?" Kelsy tried to sit up.

"I took care of it." Gently, he plumped the pillows behind her till she relaxed against them, then he repeated his lie. "I took care of it. Now, go to sleep."

Sighing, she closed her eyes again, murmuring. "Thank you."

"You're welcome." His heart melted like wax, and he leaned over and kissed her.

She smiled vaguely, but didn't open her eyes.

I love you, he thought, admiring her need for independence, then letting the magic of his love flow into him and over her.

The vague tightness in the pit of his stomach eased as he watched her sleep. Maybe under torture, he'd feel guilty about kissing her. At that moment, he regretted only that Miz Loony Tunes hadn't been that bastard Jensen. *You'd be dead Jensen.*

Ready to climb the walls from sitting around watching Kelsy sleep for two hours, Finn jumped at the chance to go pick up her prescriptions when the neighborhood drugstore called.

He bent over her before he left. Her eyelids didn't flutter, and her pulse didn't miss a beat. If she was playing possum, she was damned good. He scribbled a note with the time and his destination and laid it on top of her chest.

Tempted to kiss her again, he whispered, "Stay put."

Halfway out the front door, he trotted back into the family room. He grabbed her cell phone and muted it, plus the other phones in the family room and the kitchen. He'd be gone ten, fifteen minutes max, he rationalized. Why gamble that no one would call?

Red and bronze leaves, a cloudless blue sky, and the manicured lawns, lush with yellow and purple mums, taunted him. He felt edgy, borderline ticked. Why didn't Mother Nature blot out the sun, kick up a wind, and dump an early rainstorm on this piece of Paradise?

In no mood for chit-chat, Finn paid for the prescriptions and stalked back into the fucking perfect outdoors. He passed a tanned and buffed woman in lime-green leotards with matching sports bra. Her black Newfie, about the size of Ole Paint, barked twice before she shushed the dog. Looking at Finn, who scowled, she moved closer to her canine protector.

Loud enough that people in the next state could hear, she said, "I'm okay, Baby. That man didn't hurt your mommy."

Finn snorted, but kept on truckin'. God save him. He'd read about women and their cats and dogs. How more than half of them chose their four-legged companions over a red-blooded, lusty male. Another study he'd read said forty-seven percent of all women in the U.S. would rather sleep than have sex. He started the 'Vette and glanced back at the woman, one hand on her hip, the other on her dog, still staring after him.

Hell, who was he to doubt scientific studies?

His mood improved as he caught the lights at Foothill Expressway and headed into the hills. The last of the morning fog had burned off, and the smell of eucalyptus cleared his head. It was too early for the lunch crowd so he had Santa Ysabela Road to himself.

Cool it, he thought. Stop driving yourself nuts. You'll figure something out.

Next to him, Kelsy's cell interrupted his churning thoughts. He choked the steering wheel. Blind curves didn't make Santa Ysabela a good place to reach for the damned phone.

Don't even think about answering.

What if it was Jensen?

Sooner or later, that bastard would call.

By the third ring, Finn spotted a pullover area. Heart pumping, he careened off the road and grabbed the phone. "Jensen?"

"Who is this?" The plumy baritone Finn remembered from Montana scraped his soul.

"Who is this?" Finn mimicked, killing the engine.

"Ahhh, now I recognize that hick accent."

"Ahhh, now I recognize that pompous accent," Finn countered. "What the hell do you want from Kelsy?"

"From?" The bastard laughed. "Don't you mean *for?*"

"Whatever. She's not interested," Finn barked.

"Unless you have her locked in a tower somewhere, I believe I'll wait for Kelsy to tell me that herself." The edge in Jensen's voice sharpened.

"Then you'll wait till hell freezes over."

"Oh, how original."

The condescension froze Finn's brain in lame-mode. He snapped, "I don't have to be original. She loves *me.*"

"And what is it you want *from* her?"

Finn reset his brain to DANGER. This bastard was a rattler, ready to strike just because it was his nature. "I love her." The sun scalded the back of his neck.

"Of course you do. That must be why she told me so much about you on Tuesday night. I think it was a passing remark between the appetizer and soup."

Blood boiling, Finn lied, "In the past four days, she hasn't mentioned you at all. Appetizers and soup didn't figure into our agenda. Don't blubber if I don't mention you called."

"I have no doubts Kelsy *will* call me very soon."

"I bet you believe in Santa Claus, too, don't you?"

Jensen chuckled. "Did you mention what you do—besides run Kelsy's life? I bet you're a stand-up comic." His pause, less than a heartbeat, didn't give Finn enough time for a comeback.

Too cool for school, Jensen added, "Not a very good stand-up comic, I'd bet. Otherwise, if Kelsy weren't ashamed of you, why didn't she sing your praises?"

The question hit too close to Finn's heart, about to break a rib if he didn't get a grip. "It's been nice." Damn, he longed for a lightning-bolt zinger.

"Hasn't it? I bet your knuckles are hardly bloody at all."

"Asshole!" Finn squeezed the cell harder and harder, fighting for breath, squeezing, squeezing till his knuckles turned white and his nails bit into flesh.

Calm down, calm down. Reason echoed all the times he'd spouted the same advice to drivers choked by road rage. This isn't helping. What would help? His eyes stung as he fumbled his sunglasses out of the glove box. Memory flooded him.

A five-year-old kid, bullied and taunted by older brothers, pushed to tears before he figured out what they wanted: to see him so frustrated and furious that he cried.

So, he stopped crying in front of them.

But sometimes, when he was alone, when he longed to grow up and stop the bullies in the world, he cried for the little boy inside him.

Not for hours or even minutes.

Just long enough he felt ready to stand up against his six brothers again.

Pulling himself back from the past, blinking till his eyes were absolutely dry, Finn put his sunglasses on. He tossed the cell onto the passenger's seat, rubbed his hands together and laughed. "Too bad I'm not five years old anymore, Jensen."

Chapter 21

Fully awake at 2:30, working up her courage, Kelsy
had been watching Finn through her lashes for half an
hour. God, he was easy on the eyes.

A golden bubble of afternoon sunshine encircled
him, barefoot in the leather recliner, a laptop on his
knees. Faded jeans hid the muscles in his strong run-
ner's legs. Her fingers burned with the memory of
touching those legs, traveling up them to a spot behind
his knees.

"Like what you see?" Finn ran his hand through his
ultra-short hair. "I'm not wearing too much Old Spice,
am I?"

Kelsy flinched, then blushed. "I was-I was thinking
about getting up."

"Without help?" He shut the lid on the laptop.

"If I need help getting off the sofa, I'll call a Boy
Scout."

"Boy Scouts help *old* ladies." He flashed her a very
non-Boy Scout grin. The gap between his front teeth
still fascinated her.

"I'll be thirty-eight in January—in case you've forgotten."

"I haven't forgotten . . . anything." He set the laptop on the floor and folded the footrest on the recliner.

Afraid he'd close the distance between them before she finished, Kelsy held up a hand. "But do you know thirty-eight's beyond old?"

He snorted, an expression of disbelief rather than derision. "You and I'll probably live to be a hundred."

Kelsy shuddered dramatically. "Thirty-seven's still old. It's ancient."

"Ancient." He wiggled his eyebrows.

And suddenly, in the unforgiving sunshine, Kelsy felt ancient and ashamed because she simply didn't peel away the layers of melodrama and cut to the truth. "Thirty-seven's too old to have more kids," she blurted, then amended, "For *me* to have more kids."

"Great segue," he said, then clicked his tongue. "I'd about decided I'd have to drag us back to our unfinished business."

Her heart fluttered, then raced. "No, I always intended to finish the argument about Dane Jensen's offer."

"Would this be a good time for me to report he's called three times in the last two hours?"

Kelsy swallowed. "What-what'd you say to him?"

"Not much." Finn paused. "I gather I wasn't the main topic of your rendezvous in Half Moon Bay."

"It wasn't a *rendezvous!*" Kelsy moved her toe, pleasantly surprised after her first dose of antibiotic that her toe no longer resembled a purple submarine.

"Sorry. Must be that green-eyed monster I try not to feed or water more than once a decade. Drowning him in Old Spice usually shuts him up."

"I told you there was nothing sexual going on—" Confused as much by her thudding heart and defensive tone as by a flash of guilt, she stopped. "I love you," she whispered, wishing he'd come closer so she could inhale his scent.

"Which isn't to say you can't be tempted. If Jensen reeks rattler on the phone—"

"He's not a rattler!" Kelsy gripped her hands. Aware Finn hadn't mentioned love, she insisted, "He's not Sam's clone. Don't you think I'd recognize a snake *before* I picked him up?"

Stone-faced, Finn said, "I don't know, Kelsy. You say you want to feel important. Earn the big bucks, I assume. Why not take the job The Loony Tunes offered you, then?"

Pride bolstered her self-control so that her jaw didn't drop, Kelsy said, "Those jokers. They belong on reality TV. Are you crazy?"

"Terminally so. Right now, I want to jump out of this chair, charge over there, kiss you, then rip your clothes off and—" Palms up, he held his hands out. "Yes, I am insane. I still believe in the power of true love."

Her throat closed, and her breathing became shallow before she regained control. "In real life, I don't think it's simply a question of sex."

"You're right. In real life the question isn't sex. The answer is sex."

"Clever." She found herself imagining him buck naked and pursed her mouth. God what was wrong with her? The world was filled with women who'd kill for Finn.

Grinning as if she'd collapsed in laughter, he said, "Life beats fairy tales every time in my opinion. Wait till we're married. You'll see."

"I did that the last time. I waited, and I saw Sam and me drift so far apart that we were living on opposite sides of an ocean." Mouth quivering, Kelsy hugged her waist.

Finn put his feet on the floor, but she quickly waved him away. He said softly, "I believe in the power of my love for you and yours for me, Kelsy. Excuse the cliché, but I'm don't think I can improve on the idea or the words."

"What if I don't want more kids?" She focused on the ceiling, her hand on the pounding pulse in her throat.

A single blip of silence, but enough to turn her stomach inside out. "It's not a macho thing, is it? I mean, suppose I couldn't get pregnant again? It took almost three years with Jason."

"Yeah, but Dickhead's too dumb to breed."

Kelsy gasped, then laughed, knowing she should feel guilty for laughing at such a snide remark. She shrugged. "I think it was me. I wasn't sure I wanted to get pregnant."

"Why? You've told me you hated your weather reporter job."

"I did. I worked for the money. Not that we needed more money. I knew zip about being a good mother, but I knew I carried Monica's genes."

"You're not your mother." He streaked across the room, fast as a panther in the jungle. He perched on the edge of the sofa, but didn't touch her. "You are a wonderful mother, Kelsy. Risa must've told me dozens of times how great you are."

Blinking tears, Kelsy sniffed. "She is my best friend."

"I don't care if she's your identical twin. She'd never say you're a great mother if she didn't believe it. Remember all the hell she gave Ben with Molly?"

"Poor Ben." Kelsy loosened the hold on her waist as her insides heated up. "But not even an endorsement from Risa means I can mother three kids by two fathers."

"You don't have to do it by yourself, Babe. I'll be there with you every step of the way. You know I love Jason."

"Yes, I know." Kelsy felt herself wavering, but blurted, "Monica was thirty-nine when I was born. Six months later, she had to have a complete hysterectomy. She told Risa's mom she always wanted another baby."

A boy. Kelsy looked into the middle distance, trying to imagine life with a brother, but memories of Risa and Mom Taylor exploded, overlaying the faceless images.

Next to her, Finn shifted his weight, and Kelsy picked up the thread of her story. "Monica blamed my father for the surgery, saying if they'd had more money, better doctors, better insurance, she could've avoided the operation. Almost everything for Monica comes back to money. If you don't have it, marry it."

"Which you're not doing, so you have to get a big job with big bucks?"

Kelsy drew in a sharp breath.

"And you thought I was just another pretty face." Finn crossed his eyes, but she didn't bother trying to force a smile. She was afraid her face might fall off. She said, "I want to be someone in my own right. Do something important. Make a difference."

"So do I, Babe." He reached or her hand, but she drew it back. "So do most of us with more than a low-level pulse, in my opinion. But here's the question. Why do you have to live and work in Seattle to do something important? You don't want to work in San Jose? Last I noticed, San Francisco—"

"Owwww!" She spared a thought to wonder if Finn thought she was acting.

The invisible gila monster clamped down harder on her toe. She squeezed her eyes shut. "Ohhh, my God!"

A wave of Old Spice floated closer. Finn tapped a pill into her hand, helped her steady the water glass and waited till she swallowed before he sat down.

He took her hand, folding her fingers over his, and kissed her knuckles. As if sensing he couldn't fill the hole in her chest, he said, "You can run, Cinderella, but I will follow."

* * *

At Kelsy's insistence, Finn left at 4:30. He drove too fast but still showed up for duty five minutes late. Olivia, settled behind the wheel of a '99 Mercedes, said, "I thought you were supposed to come back from vacation looking rested and relaxed. You look like hell."

Still fuming over the stalemate with Kelsy, he said, "If you start with me, Olivia, I will cut you off at the knees."

"Beautiful day, isn't it?" She stuck her head out the window. "Look at that sky. Azure. I think that's more accurate than blue, don't you?"

He climbed into the car. "I think you'd better listen to what I said." Adjusting the seatbelt, he said, "Anything happen while I was gone?"

"Yep."

He stared at her. She started the car, checked over her shoulder and pulled away from the curb. Through clenched teeth, he said, "Yep?"

"They cut the grass at our guys' apartment." She giggled.

Finn's fingertips twitched with an electric current that ran from his wrists. "I'm not in the mood."

"Great!" She tapped the horn at the car in front of them. "Twelve hours with a catatonic partner. Ever think about staying on vacation?"

"Ever think about keeping your eyes on the road? You almost ran over that little old lady."

"I'm driving, Partner. You're over the line."

Pissed because she was right—cops didn't criticize their partners' driving—he groused, "Sorry. I was over the line."

They gave the day-shift guys the high-five sign and pulled into a parking spot near the park entrance. Olivia cut the motor. "One thing, then I'll shut up."

Before he could say, *Hell no*, she said, "Are you ticked because I gave you that heads-up about Kelsy's license?"

His guard went up, but he exhaled. "No, they found the driver."

"So Kelsy wasn't in Half Moon Bay?"

"I can still count to two, Olivia." Damned if he'd fall into that trap. "Either fill me in on the case or shut up."

A little surprised by his own hostility, Finn stared out the windshield and prayed Kelsy was okay alone till Em showed up at six. His green-eyed monster was out of the box again. He suspected Kelsy wanted him gone so she could call Jensen.

Logic said she had to call the bastard sooner or later.

Jealousy whispered she should call when Finn could hear what she said.

At this point, he didn't have a clue whether she was going to Seattle or staying in Cielo Vista and marrying him.

"Sonuva—" Olivia hissed so loud Finn jumped. "That's Javier Sanchez Olmeda!" She punched a PDA, and a picture of the man with the bulging garbage bag she'd spotted came up on the LED.

"Damn!" Finn sat up with a jerk, a flash fire in his veins. "This could be it."

"Maybe." Olivia scrolled down the PDA, then handed it to Finn. In a level voice, she said, "It could also be a trap. Apparently, Señor Olmeda's suckered cops in at least three states by appearing out of the blue with a garbage bag full of *basura*."

"Think this means he's spotted the stakeout?"

"Don't sound so disappointed, Partner. If he has, it means you and I can go back to the lives we once held dear."

Focused on Olmeda, Finn said, "I'm ready, but I don't want this scumbag to sniff us out. Let's see if we can mess his head up a little."

"I'm gaaammm—"

Finn grabbed her. Agreement or disagreement didn't matter to him. A plan had already played out in his brain. He pulled her across the leather seat. He kissed her, eyes wide open. They each stared into the other's eyes and tried to watch Olmeda at the same time. Which was impossible since the guy was about a quarter of a mile away.

Out of breath, Finn finally came up for air. Still playing out the plan, he left his arms around Olivia's neck. He explained, "For all Olmeda knows, we've stopped by for an after-work tryst."

"Tryst?" Olivia repeated, her eyes glazed over.

"You know. Romantic interlude." Impatient with her sluggishness, Finn turned his head so he could keep one eye on Olmeda.

"He's headed for the dumpsters."

"If you'd let up on the back of my neck—"

"Sorry." Finn still didn't release her, but he did lighten the pressure. "He could be playing us, or he could be dropping a million bucks of stuff they've sat on for six weeks."

"He's taking a big chance," Olivia said. "A neighbor could dump more garbage on top of his bag."

"The dumpster he drops that bag in won't have room for a crushed water bottle—let alone another bag of trash."

Olivia turned her head and her hair grazed Finn's cheek, bringing a memory of Kelsy in his arms. "What's he doing?"

"I can't see." Finn jerked his arms back to his sides, feeling awkward when Olivia flopped back against the seat. The air in the car was too close, too hot. He was sweating.

Sitting up straight, upper lip and forehead sweat free, Olivia said, "He's sure taking a lot of time with a bag of *basura*."

After another decade of pushing and stuffing the bag, then opening and closing the lid, Olmeda brushed his hands together and strolled back to the building.

"Think we'd better go back into tryst-mode?" Olivia asked. "Just in case he notices us here." Her gaze dropped to Finn's mouth.

"I don't think he's paying attention to us."

This time, Olivia threw her arms around Finn. He felt like a wrestler in a headlock. Which may've been her intention, since she didn't kiss him. After they sat there nose to nose for another decade, Olivia slumped. His heart banged as he scooted to his side of the car.

Back under the steering wheel, Olivia said, "Old Spice. My favorite. Funny I never noticed before."

Dane Jensen answered his cell on the first ring with elaborate detachment. Despite her hangover from the painkiller, Kelsy smiled. So Finn had hurt his feelings. She snuggled into the sofa, waiting for a thaw.

Instead of a thaw, Dane gave her silence. Edgy from the argument with Finn, and in no mood to nurse a wounded male ego, she stated the obvious, "You called me."

A heartbeat, then he said, "Yes. I had a very unsatisfactory conversation with . . . your friend. What is he? A gorilla?"

"He's worried. About my toe." *About you. About me.*

An undercurrent of dismay went through her when Dane didn't ask, "What's wrong with your toe?" What kind of newsman was he? Didn't he have any curiosity?

"Are you coming to Seattle this weekend?"

No sympathy or curiosity, but a one-track mind about the job.

Which is all that matters, she thought, saying brightly, "I think that's a definite possibility. You'll fax me a copy of the proposed contract first, of course."

A statement to which there was only one response in Kelsy's mind, and he gave it, spouting her fax number so quickly she wondered if he'd memorized her business card. After Kelsy verified the number, he said, "What's wrong with your toe? Would you be more comfortable staying at my place instead of at a hotel?"

Elaborate solicitude now replaced his elaborate disinterest. Kelsy's mouth went dry. Not totally whacked out of her mind, she knew she'd stepped into quicksand. She swung her feet onto the floor. The flash of pain in her toe focused her. She said, "Thanks, not this time."

Not ever, unless Finn was with her.

She added, "I'm bringing my son with me, so a reservation at the Four Seasons lets me use their babysitting services."

Since Dane was picking up her expenses, she'd let him know she expected first class—just like him and Sam and all the other men out there, who thought luxury was their birthright.

To Dane's credit, he didn't miss a beat. "I'll have my secretary make the reservations. What time can you leave on Friday?"

Five more minutes and they settled the details. He wanted to chat about the places they'd go, the things they'd see, but Kelsy found herself put off by his assumptions. How he thought he knew what she would and would not like dumbfounded, then irritated her. The guy acted as if he was a force of nature.

Please, she hoped, don't let him expect her undivided attention the whole weekend. *Maybe he thinks he's cheering you up.* With that thought in mind, she broke into one of his monologues. "I have to go now. Time for my antibiotics."

The lie was out of her mouth in a rush. She could've added she didn't have to hang up at that precise moment, but she let the opportunity slide. Her shoulders drooped with relief.

Would Finn appreciate her gesture?

* * *

For an hour after Javier Olmeda returned to Apartment 301, Finn and Olivia hunkered down and strategized about seizing the trash bag. They threw ideas at each other faster than bullets. The staccato give and take of brainstorming energized Finn, took his mind off Kelsy and pushed the kiss between him and Olivia to the back of his brain.

Tense, edgy, and funny, she took the disconnected banter in stride. A human tape recorder, she kept repeating, "Everything should be made as simple as possible, but no simpler."

They laughed every time she said it, as if the stupid comment was a profound secret they, and they alone, shared. By the time the sun went down at 6:32, they agreed they had a plan.

"Your mission, should you decide to accept it . . ." Olivia intoned.

First, Olivia called Lieutenant Matthews. Finn deferred to her rank without resentment. Those were the rules. The senior partner made these kinds of calls. Too bad, Finn thought as he watched the TV flicker in Apartment 301, most of life came without a rule book. About halfway through, you realized it was a "do-it-yourself" kind of thing. Which was why finding love helped. Doing it yourself sucked.

The longer Finn watched the TV flash in the upstairs apartment, the more depressed he felt. God, what a waste. Watching TV ranked up there with watching paint peel, in his mind. And Kelsy wanted to be part of a world as alien to him as life on Mars. Worse, she wanted to live on Mars. He wondered how she'd react if he said he wanted to live in Montana. His heart missed a beat. When had they taken different forks in the road?

Disgusted by his lack of answers, he turned his head from side to side, massaging the tops of his shoulders.

Random images of Kelsy working the same spots surfaced. Her touch was magic. In less than ten minutes, she could turn his tight, aching muscles into mounds of Jello.

Taking a deep breath, he shoved the memories away. Lack of sleep and too much adrenaline left him wondering if his muscles would ever unkink. If he didn't watch himself he'd start complaining to Olivia how Kelsy didn't understand him.

"We're in!" Olivia smacked him on the shoulder and jerked him off the cusp of self-pity. "Matthews okayed the plan. You leave here no later than four A.M. The garbage truck meets you on Soledad Drive at four-thirty with a uniform. Backup arrives same time. You come in the garbage truck at five, pick up Olmeda's bag, then ride out on the truck. You and I check out the bag, see what we've got, then go from there."

When she finished her recitation, she gave him a high-five. "Damn! Talk about simple."

"Okay!" Finn went for enthusiastic, but Olivia said, "What's wrong? It's exactly what we wanted. You even get to be the cowboy."

Without warning, his body turned on him. He flinched, then immediately laughed. "And when I come ridin' out on my two-ton garbage truck, I won't even have a horse to kiss."

Olivia stared.

Hellooo, Stupid. Praying he could breathe and therefore speak without his voice cracking, he said, "I suppose now's as good a time as any to clear the air about our . . . kiss."

She laughed, sounding marginally amused. "What's to clear? All in the line of duty, right?"

"Absolutely."

"Lots of cops probably kiss in the line of duty," Olivia said in the reasonable tone Einstein probably had used.

"Sure." Just because this was a first for him and Olivia didn't mean it didn't happen.

"Tell Kelsy."

"Uh. . . ." His heart slam-danced against his rib cage, and he stifled the urge to cuss.

"Or not," Olivia said airily. "I don't intend to bring it up the next time we review the case with Matthews."

"Me, either." More comments would send this conversation into the realm of dicey, so Finn said, calmly, coolly, "Let's go over it one more time. Make sure we haven't missed something."

After that, they went over the plan again and again, till Finn felt his mind numb out. Later, when he thought about it, he was grateful to Olivia for keeping his mind off Kelsy, and off the stupid kiss between them, and off his denial about its importance.

Chapter 22

Kelsy had forgotten what a yakker Em was. But she was also efficient. While she gave Jason his bath, Kelsy called Risa and stated, "Don't come back a day early."

Risa protested; Kelsy insisted. "I'm going to work, and I'm not teething. So I won't need a babysitter. Em and I have already agreed she'll spend tomorrow night again and get Jason off to school on Wednesday."

After four or five iterations, Risa finally agreed, adding, "When will you see Finn?"

"No idea." Kelsy stared at the recliner, remembering him there only a few hours earlier, pushing all her buttons about Dane.

"He's at work, I suppose?"

"He hasn't called." A bitter taste filled Kelsy's throat.

"Ben says this is a very big case. If they crack it, Finn hopes he'll get a promotion in Traffic again."

"And then he'll get about a-dollar-a-month raise."

"So the money's not a reason to break into cheers."

"Don't lecture me, La Ti Da!" Kelsy bit her bottom lip. Her toe felt as if she'd stuck it in the microwave, but she didn't want to call Maeve Bishop about arrangements for Jason, or think about sleeping, or go to work feeling so physically and emotionally rotten. Mostly, she didn't want to think. Period.

"I know I'm shallow as a saucer, La Ti Da, but I won't morph into a deep, mature, contented woman tonight."

"Oh, Kel. That's why I should come down."

"No!" Kelsy gritted her teeth. "You can't grow up for me. I have to do that on my own. I'm too needy and too angry right now. You'd probably lose all respect for me. If you haven't already."

"Are you fishing?"

"Shameless, right?" Glad Risa couldn't see into her twisted heart, Kelsy made a noise she hoped passed for a chuckle. "Respectable people don't fish."

Risa tsked. "You haven't lost my respect. I love you. You saved Harry's life."

"Okay, so my oxygen shouldn't be rationed. I have one redeeming quality."

"Stop that! If you hadn't turned heaven and earth upside down and come to Nashville—Kelsy, stop beating up on yourself. You're generous and loving and loyal."

"And you are the most objective, unbiased, fair-minded—"

"Kelsy! Are you crying?"

"No. I'm cursing. I bumped my toe." The truth was, she'd bumped into the coffee table on purpose so she could hang up and bawl her eyes out.

Before she indulged in that therapy, she called Maeve Bishop. She'd already figured out how she'd end this conversation. *And it's not even a lie.*

Taking baby steps around the family room, listening to Maeve's phone ring, Kelsy told herself her toe felt better. By tomorrow she might not be tap dancing, but she figured she could get to the studio in her pink fuzzy slippers.

Out of breath, Maeve came on the line. "I'd given up."

Who thought caller ID was a good thing? "I'm sorry, Maeve. I should've called sooner."

"No, Darlin', it's all right. I was just worried about you. How are you feeling? How's your toe? Have you and Finn made up yet? Am I being nosy?"

In the volley of questions, the last two smacked Kelsy between the eyes. *Foul*, she wanted to cry even though she should've expected both. She swallowed, "Finn and I need more time to work things out."

"And you don't need advice from me, right?"

"Show me a burning bush or some other kind of sign, but hold off on the advice, okay?" Kelsy crossed her fingers and went on. "You have been so wonderful to me and Jason, taking us into your heart. I know you're cheering for me and Finn. Until we figure out what to do, I don't want to put you in the middle."

Maeve didn't, for one minute, like the idea of Nurse Em as a substitute to care for Jason in the mornings. She liked even less hearing he might spend some afternoons in day care if Kelsy had to work. To Kelsy's amazement, Maeve said, "The only advice I was going to give you, Darlin', is listen to your heart. You know how to reach me, and no matter what, I'm here for you."

Kelsy heard Jason's footsteps on the stairs and quickly wiped away her tears. *Now for the fun part.*

Mercifully, Em busied herself in the guest room while Kelsy sat in the recliner with Jason in her lap. Certain he could feel her pounding heart, she started out slowly. First topic, his broken arm.

No problem. His friends thought the cast was cool. Weren't the pictures they drew on the cast neat-o?

Everyone laughed when he told about the plastic bag he used in the bathtub.

How much longer did he have to wear the cast?

Reassured that La Ti Da would know, he said, "I

dropped some doughnut crumbs down it this morning, but Finn fished them out. It tickled. Finn's real smart, isn't he, Mommy?"

At the mention of Finn, her heart tried to bang its way out of her chest. *Careful, careful.* For all she knew, Jason had picked up on something wrong between her and Finn.

"Yes, sweetheart. He's real smart." Her heart fluttered. She could not tell a lie.

"I'll be glad when he lives with us. Him 'n me can go for Krispy Kremes every day."

Put in her place, Kelsy hit the wrong button on the recliner's remote and nearly sent them into outer space.

"Do that again, Mommy!"

The screech nearly shattered the enamel on Kelsy's front teeth. *A small price for distracting him.* Not willing to risk losing any teeth, she clamped her jaw shut and shifted the remote into high-fly again. And again. And again.

Dizzy, wondering if she was demented for competing with Finn at such a juvenile level, she said, "Enough. Let's talk about this weekend. We're going on another trip."

"Is Finn coming with us?" Despite the cast, Jason threw his arms around Kelsy's neck and smiled at her as if she carried a magic wand and could make all his wishes come true.

His excitement caught Kelsy off guard. *I'm an idiot,* she thought. "We're not going back to Montana," she said, hoping Jason didn't notice she hadn't answered his question.

"Please, Mommy, please." Cheeks scarlet, eyes shining, Jason hugged the breath out of her. "Finn 'n me have the bestest times."

"I know, Sweetheart, but—"

"Please, Mommy, please, Mommy!" Jason jumped up and down in her lap. "I want Finn to go with us."

Resenting such devotion, she said, "I hear you, Sweetie."

"We'll have lots more fun if he comes with us."

This Kelsy doubted and she spared a second to wonder where she'd lost control of the conversation. Doesn't matter, she thought. There's only a second before things fall apart. Throat tight, she decided. "Finn isn't coming. Not this time."

Set Jason straight. "It may be a while before we see him."

"But why?" Jason pushed away from her, and his cast dragged down her neck.

"Ouch!" Kelsy rubbed the tender spot.

"Why won't we see Finn for a while?" Jason stuck out his chin and glared at her.

Still rubbing her neck, not wanting to lay a guilt trip on her son for such a small scrape, she tried to rein in her impatience. "First, he's working a lot." *Do not lie.*

She took a deep breath. "Second, I didn't ask him to come with us."

"Why not?" Jason frowned, and Kelsy could read the confusion in his eyes. "That wasn't very nice," he stated.

The comment smarted more than she wanted to admit, and her patience almost skidded out of control. Quietly, she said, "Finn doesn't go with us everywhere, you know. I'll be busy most of the time so I wouldn't see him much anyway."

"But what about me?" Jason tapped his chest. "Who'll be with me if you're busy? If Finn went with us, he—" Jason sniffled.

Tears rolled down his cheeks, and sadness gripped Kelsy with razor-sharp teeth. "Sweetheart."

"Don't call me that!" His mouth tightened.

Gently, she put her arms around him. He went rigid. "I want to stay here," he wailed.

"You can not stay here." She held her breath. Please, please, don't let him suggest staying with Maeve.

"I don't want to go with you." Face dark, he shut her out.

"I won't take that personally."

"I think you're mean." His defiance shot that idea to hell.

"I think I got that." She managed to lift her top lip in a pathetic imitation of a smile as dread warned her what would come next.

"I hate you!" He'd only hurled those words at her once before, during an argument about the divorce. She didn't cry then or now, but she felt herself plunging down that black, endless hole again.

Hugging her chest, she said thickly, "Okay, but just for the record: I love you."

"I don't love you. I love Finn!" He scrambled off her lap, stomped across the family room and didn't turn around when she called his name.

"My, didn't that go well?" Kelsy eased out of the recliner, her toe protesting every movement.

In the kitchen, Em opened and shut the fridge. Wanting to call for help, Kelsy bit her lip. *It's your mess.*

She took ten minutes to regroup. Full of sympathy and words of encouragement, Em cheerily agreed to make a pot of hot chocolate and bring it up to Jason's room. "Give me nine minutes, max," Kelsy said. "I doubt we'll achieve world peace, but maybe we won't be at war, either."

Em chuckled. "And people think mothers couldn't run the world."

By the time Kelsy reached the top of the stairs, her toe felt bigger than a rhino. Her heart was going a hundred miles a minute, and she breathed through her mouth.

Thank God, Jason's door was at the top of the stairs. She probably would have to crawl to the master bedroom at the end of the hall.

Wouldn't Finn pay to see that? The thought came out of nowhere. Her skin tightened with goose bumps, then she felt her mouth twist, caught herself and stopped. Forget Finn. She had to get Jason settled, then figure out how to get to work. After the fiasco with CHP, driving wasn't an option. Finn might arrest her himself if he suspected she'd gotten behind the wheel.

"Sweetheart?" She pushed open Jason's door. Her mouth dropped. *Seeing is not believing.* "What in the—"

On top of the covers, an ankle over his bent knee, cast above his head, Jason held her cell against his ear and ignored Kelsy. He spoke into the receiver, "But I don't wanna go, Finn."

"Finn?" Feeling suddenly weightless, Kelsy said the name as if she'd never heard it.

"I wanna stay here with you," Jason said.

"Please give me the phone, Jason." Kelsy held her hand out as she clumped across the room.

"No." Jason turned on his side and tucked the phone between his chin and shoulder.

"Jason Andrew Chandler." His failure to hand over the phone immediately didn't surprise her. He so rarely heard his full name, he probably didn't recognize it.

Her legs buckled. She shrieked. Arms flailing, she collapsed on the bed. Jason didn't even glance her way, but he exhaled a ragged sigh.

What's going on?

Don't tell me Finn didn't hear me screech?

A light went on in her brain. She didn't know how she made the connection, but she said softly, "Jason, I know Finn's not on the phone."

"Is too." He laid the cast across his chest.

Tears closed her throat. *No one told me lying's genetic.* She shook her head. "No, Sweetheart. He's not."

Her heart fired rapidly. Against her better judgment, she said, "But we can call and leave him a message."

Finn sat in the dark at 7:59, aware of every breath Olivia took. Which might explain why he didn't notice the red voicemail light on his cell as soon as it blinked on. When he did see it and came out of his trance, his stomach pitched. *Kelsy.*

"I've got a phone message," he said, his skin too tight, too chilly in the balmy air.

As if she didn't hear his panic, Olivia yawned. "Break time. You go first."

They never took a break before ten, but Finn wasn't about to correct her. Not after receiving his first phone message in six weeks of undercover duty.

"I owe you." He lurched out of the car, dragging the key out of his pocket, and jogged toward the restrooms.

Everyone—Ma, his brothers, Kelsy, Risa—knew the rules. No calls except in an emergency. "Emergency" he'd defined as life and death.

Shiiit. *The best laid plans . . . .*

The sultry, sweet scent of jasmine perfumed the night air. Or maybe the scent smelled so strong because he smelled so sweaty. For two cents, he'd say screw going into the cement restroom and use his cell right there on the path. So what if Olmeda and his boosters intercepted his call?

Six weeks of work down the drain. Along with his career.

Huffing, he slammed the key in the restroom lock. Without a moon, he couldn't see his hand in front of his face. He shoved the door open, pushed the LED light on the phone, then smacked FASTDIAL for messages.

"Hello, Finn. Jason and I are fine, but he'd like to talk with you tomorrow when you get off duty."

There was a blip of white noise, then the love of his life continued in a bossy tone that frosted his short hairs. "Please call him on my cell at eight-thirty."

"What the hell?" Finn replayed the message twice, but each time he felt more confused than he had the first time.

According to schedule, Jason should be in school at 8:30. Ma picked him up at noon. Kelsy usually showed up two, three hours later, depending on what kind of stories she caught and taped for other editions of the news. And, oh by the way, how could she drive to school during rush hour with her toe?

"Jesus!" He smacked the cement wall with his open palm.

After the third replay of the tape, a spurt of anger zipped through him. The garbage bag bulged at the seams. How long they'd need to sift through its contents was anybody's guess, but Finn didn't see them being finished in less than two, three hours. If they found something—anything from microchips to diamonds—in the bag, he'd never have a minute to call Jason.

What is this? A setup? Kelsy's way of flippin' me the bird? He sighed. Deep down, he didn't, wouldn't believe that.

Sure he wouldn't get another break that night, he was standing in front of the head when the cell vibrated. As he fumbled to zip his jeans without dropping the phone, a mental headline flashed. COP CAUGHT IN COMPROMISING SITUATION IN PUBLIC RESTROOM.

"We've got action!" Olivia whispered.

"I'm halfway there." He yanked the key out of the lock and took off at a full sprint.

"No! Stay back. They're out by the garbage. They could spot you."

His leg muscles burned. "Don't get out of the car, Olivia."

"Get off the phone, Bishop."

"No heroics, Stuart."

"You either. Hang up."

"What're they doing?" Chest tight, mentally kicking himself for leaving his partner alone, he ducked behind a huge, twisted live oak.

"I can't see, dammit."

"What? They told me you have eyes like Super-woman."

"Yeah, well, they lied."

Lotsa members in Kelsy's liars' club. Carefully, Finn peeked around the tree and stared into the darkness. "Now you tell me."

"Don't you want to know what else I lied about?" Her tone teased.

Straining because he couldn't see or hear anything but his own heart thumping in his ears, he said, "Another time."

"You're no fun." She sucked in a breath. "I saw a light. A match, I think. At the dumpsters."

"I'm coming back." Bent double, he stepped out from behind the tree.

"Negative!" Her voice blistered his ear.

"Too late." In case a shooter with a night scope watched, Finn dodged across the grass, pretending he was a downhill skier, running blind.

Olmeda had to be up to no good, Finn reasoned. Otherwise, why prowl around the dumpsters in the dark without a flashlight?

Lots of people take their garbage out after dark.

In which case, they use a flashlight in the open.

Confident of this logic, he cut a few more switch-backs. If the guys at the dumpsters were up to no good, it only made sense they'd have lookouts for him and Olivia. The skin on the back of his neck crawled. Using a silencer, they could—

"Shiiit!" He was down.

Ass over teakettle.

Not a bullet, he realized, coming upright with his hands on his knees, his head spinning.

"Sonuvabitch!" What the hell was wrong with him, tripping over his own damned feet?

Nothing broken as far as he could tell. Clumsy oaf, he'd knocked the breath out of his lungs and bruised his ego. A galaxy of stars cha-chaaed in front of his eyes. Tough. Get back to the car.

He bent over to do his dart and dodge routine. "Damn." Fire ignited in his side.

Kneading the spot, he took a step, realized too late he didn't have his cell, then heard a crunch.

Guess who's it, stupid?

Two more steps, and he decided he was turned around. At least he thought he was turned around till he heard another crunch. Either the dark or the jasmine had messed up his internal radar. *Wouldn't count on that promotion soon, Stu.*

Surrounded by trees, he looked up. Years as a Boy Scout came back. He sighted the North Star and saw the Merc in his mind's eye. If he used a modicum of common sense, he should make it back to the car without any more slapstick.

There was one problem.

He had to figure a way not to get shot by Olivia.

Without his cell to warn her he was headed back to the car, he couldn't just sneak up on her and say, *Boo!*

Ten, fifteen feet from the Merc, Finn froze. Just as he began to doubt his eyes, he saw a flash. Light, down by the dumpsters. Voices. Intermittent, but voices, he was certain. He cocked his head waiting for the light breeze to carry the sounds closer.

Then silence, thin and vibrating with stillness. About to admit Olivia had planted suspicions in his mind,

Finn took a step, and the light went off, then on again. A yelp. Darkness.

Exhaling, Finn stared into the void. First, Olmeda dumped his overflowing garbage bag. Less than four hours later, strange goings on at the dumpsters. Were both he and Olivia making something out of nothing? Wouldn't apartment occupants with legitimate business keep their flashlights on while dumping their trash?

"Bishop!" A hiss. "Can you hear me?"

"Olivia!" He turned, saw no one, but smelled the scent of lilacs she always wore.

"Where the hell are you?" she growled.

"Where the hell are you?" he growled back. "Be careful, our friends at the dumpster are headed back inside."

"Good! Let's head back to the car."

He jumped, heart too fast, the skin on his arms tight. "Since you can, apparently, see me, just give me directions."

She did, quickly and precisely. As if walking arm in arm, they arrived at the back bumper of the Merc at the same time.

"You are an idiot!" she said in his ear.

"Just don't blame my mother. She raised me to come in out of the rain, dress myself, go to the bathroom by myself—"

"Ha!" Olivia crouched and waddled to the front bumper.

"I know," he whispered, following her. "The jury's still out on that one."

"Are you okay?" She stopped, and he ran into her backside.

Blood boiling, he leaped back. A snapshot of Kelsy exploded in his head. "Fine!

Something wasn't right in his side, but he wasn't about to admit it. Stupid he might be, but a wimp he was not. "What do you see?"

She handed him the night glasses. Three Eskimos trudged toward the main door of the Nimitz Park Apartments.

"Damn! Wanna bet they're each carrying a hundred pounds of merchandise?"

"No bet," Olivia said. "These guys are smart crooks, though. Can you see a face?"

"Nope. I bet their own mothers wouldn't recognize them."

"Which makes it a little awkward. We can't charge in there and do a body search on three people who happen to dress funny."

"For all we know, they're foreign diplomats from Iceland."

Lame as the comment was, Olivia laughed. Surprisingly, the laugh—light and thin compared to Kelsy's elegant guffaw—triggered an image of her. He felt his heart catch. He hadn't thought of her since he'd left the restroom. A first, since she always occupied space in his head. She was his sun, and he could no more slip out of her orbit than a magnet could shun metal.

"The Crooks R Us think they're so much smarter than us dumb cops, why don't they come downstairs and flash us?" Dammit, he wanted to catch these guys, put them away for a long time and make the world a better place so he, Kelsy and Jason could enjoy the good life.

"I like it." Another laugh rewarded his wit.

Outwardly joking, inwardly fuming, Finn felt the adrenaline burn through him. Standing there, doing nothing, was no longer an option. He said, "Get back in the car. Let me borrow your cell. I have to call Kelsy."

It was against all the rules but, wisely, Olivia didn't point out that she called the shots. She said, "Doesn't look like any of our guys are leaving any time soon, so take your time."

Finn made it to the restroom in record time. Out of breath, he dialed Kelsy's number. "Is this a pervert?" she demanded, starting to sound feisty.

"Yes," he said. "And I love you. Sweet dreams."

Chapter 23

He loves me, he loves me. Finn Bishop loves me.

Next morning on the set, the air around Kelsy vibrated with nervous energy. She personally felt as if she'd been struck by lightning. Finn loved her, and the world made sense again.

Thirty seconds before her opening billboard, she understood the source of everyone else's nerves. She could feel Brad Hall standing behind her. She turned away from the camera and stared over her shoulder. Sure enough, he skulked in the shadows like Dracula. He gave her no sign he'd seen her even though they'd made eye contact.

Why am I surprised? she thought. Why do I care? Secure in believing Finn loved her, she didn't care if Brad swooped across her desk with fangs bared.

A laugh got away from her at the image. Just in time, she remembered her mike was live and rearranged her face to serious because the lead story was still the hit-and-run in Half Moon Bay. Most of the forty-five-second segment was taped, but even so, Kelsy felt her stomach clench as she looked into the camera and read her prompter script.

After all the lies she'd told, Finn's unwavering faith in her innocence still amazed her. Quickly she dabbed a tissue under her lashes during the taped portion.

After her outcue, the credits, and the montage for the next show, she removed her lapel mike and pushed away from her desk. Brad was on her instantly, sticking with her as she hobbled off the set.

"Brilliant, Kelsy!" he boomed and got hisses from several people.

"I'm in a hurry, Brad." She glanced at her watch and crossed her fingers the cab she'd ordered would be on time.

"Those tears." Brad put his hand over his heart.

She recoiled in distaste. "Get away from me, Brad."

Apparently struck deaf, he disregarded her order. He shook his head. "That sincere but objective emotionalism's why you're goin' far, Baby."

"I had something in my eye," she lied automatically, caught herself and felt a twinge of guilt, but Brad was already yapping at her. "You can't fake that kind of emotion, Kelsy."

"I wasn't faking, Brad." At least this was the truth.

"Why didn't you call me last night, let me know you were coming to work today?" He walked on her right, which made her very nervous. She wouldn't put it past him to step on her toe.

"Why would I call you to tell you I was coming to work?" She put her hand on her hip, jutting her elbow, as she walked.

"I haven't talked to you since Thursday. You left so fast the smoke alarms went off."

Blushing at his snide reference to the interview with Victoria, her heart galloping a mile a minute, Kelsy said, "So?"

"So did Victoria Moreno and Steele contact you?"

They'd reached the glass lobby. Kelsy bit back a

scream. No cab. "Yes, they contacted me," she snapped. "I should sue you for giving them Risa's address."

Casually, he lifted one shoulder. "Sorry, but they are persistent."

"They're-they're demented."

"What'd you tell them?"

Since he persisted in getting up too close and personal, Kelsy stuck both hands out and held him at arm's length. "And that would be your business because?"

"The walls have ears." He pointed at the guard, Nick, who was in his mid-seventies and wore two non-functional hearing aids. "Let's go to my office for privacy," Brad whispered.

"I have a previous appointment."

Brad made a production of looking at his watch. "I believe your time is my time till noon," he said edgily.

"Not today. Today, my time is Jason's." She switched her gaze from looking for the taxi to dead-on Brad. "In case you've forgotten, I've given—and I mean *given*—you a lot of time in the past eight months."

"Yes, but yesterday—"

"Yesterday was a mental health day. Arranged and agreed to in advance." In the distance, Kelsy saw a flash of yellow and limped to the doors. "Get off my back, Brad."

He slithered along beside her. "Teamwork, Kelsy. TV's a small world. Word gets out you're not a team—"

"Give me a break." Adrenaline kept pumping nonstop, directly into Kelsy's mouth. "You can't spell team, and teamwork is a concept as foreign to you as astrophysics."

The way he squinted made her think of a snake about to strike, and she shivered. Where the heck was that cab?

"Some station managers might consider that insubordination," Brad said.

"You're kidding." Kelsy smiled at Nick, who had gotten up and stood holding the door open for her. Over her shoulder she said, "I'm so lucky you're a nice guy, Brad."

"I'll match my rep with anyone's. Give me an hour after your show tomorrow, Kelsy. That's not negotiable."

Could he know about Dane? Kelsy wondered as the cab pulled away from the curb. Had Dane contacted Brad? He said he hadn't, but what if he'd lied?

Not everyone lies.

Shaken by this realization, she gave the cab driver the address of Jason's school, adding, "I'm late, so I'd appreciate it if you could hurry."

"Hey! You're gorgeous. You could probably sweet-talk the devil out of his pitch fork. But I ain't burnin' rubber just to get you there, since I'll get the ticket."

At 8:00 A.M., knee-high in garbage strewn around an empty warehouse near the dump, Finn said to Olivia, "How about breakfast? My treat."

Stripping off her latex gloves and orange coveralls, Olivia said, "You don't have to ask me twice, but McAfee's will be mobbed."

"I'm thinking some place in Los Altos." Finn tossed his coveralls on a chair.

Olivia stared at him. "Los Altos? The way we smell?"

"Okay, how about we drive through Krispy Kreme in Mountain View?" Finn ushered Olivia into the sunshine and clean air. Both inhaled deeply at the same time.

"Krispy Kreme, here we come." Olivia stretched, and her black shirt rode up, revealing a flat stomach.

The woman is in shape. As if unaware he was staring at her from behind his shades, she scratched a spot above her belly button. Without any signs of self-consciousness, she tucked her shirt into her jeans, then started for the car. Finn fell in step, telling himself men were visual creatures.

He was male, ergo, he'd committed no crime.

"I will never look at garbage the same way again for the rest of my life," Olivia declared.

Glad for a distraction, he laughed. "How'd you look at it till now?"

"Like it was sanitized!"

They both laughed. Then she said, "Sifting through that muck's a waste of our time, isn't it?"

"I do believe Olmeda's conned us."

"Jokester." As usual, she went for the driver's side.

Finn said, "Mind if I drive? I want to make a stop first. Ten minutes, max."

"Nothing takes ten minutes, but sure, why not?" She tossed him the keys to the Mercedes. "You going to tell me where we're stopping, or is it a surprise?"

"It's a surprise." He got in and rolled all the windows down. "I'm going to surprise Jason."

"Jason?" Her surprise came out as a yelp. "Didn't you see him two days ago?"

"Uh-huh. But I told you he broke his arm, and I'd guess the novelty's worn off. He's apparently feeling a little down."

"As down as you?" Olivia turned a little so that the wind ruffled her short hair.

Surprised she'd pegged his mood, Finn zipped through a yellow light, and Olivia grabbed for the door handle. "Watch it," she warned. "Think how 'down' a ticket will make you feel."

"Frowning's the way you get that line between your eyebrows, you know." Olivia pulled the visor down.

Finn snorted. "Lines between my eyebrows are the least of my worries." Why hadn't Kelsy put Jason on the phone last night?

"You say that now. But someday, when you're top cop—"

"Honest to God, Olivia!" Finn felt his cool slip. Eyes straight ahead, he said, "How do you have time to do your job and listen to gossip?"

"You call it gossip, I call it networking. When I'm a hot-shot DA, my bros in blue will remember me. Fondly, I hope. In the meantime, I never break a confidence."

"Me, either," he said, thinking how easily he could betray Kelsy by baring his soul to Olivia.

"I mean it, LB—Finn. Once my mouth is sealed, it'd take dynamite to force it open."

"I'll remember that." Tempted by her offer of consolation, he hoped she understood his words as refusal.

He enjoyed a nanosecond of feeling proud. He could resist temptation. He gave a signal to the taxi behind him. To his surprise, they both turned in to the school.

The parking lot was a maze of arrows and lines directing traffic, but Finn kept his eyes glued to the rearview mirror. The last problem he needed—was getting rear-ended in the car they used for an undercover operation.

"You didn't say Kelsy was showing up, too," Olivia said.

"That's because—" Finn switched his gaze from the taxi driver to his passenger.

Her silver-blonde hair, aflame in the morning sunshine, lit up the back of the taxi. Finn caught his breath, remembered Olivia sat next to him, and tried to bring his pulse down to a gallop.

"Jesus," Olivia said as Kelsy extended one long leg from the back of the taxi. "She is one sexy female."

"There is that."

Rolling her eyes, Olivia said, "I'm surprised you don't have to beat bigger guys off with a stick."

"Bigger guys don't scare me," he growled, then felt his face and ears heat up. He regrouped by laughing.

Olivia arched a brow. He cut the engine and grinned at her. "Big guys don't scare a wanna-be top cop."

"Ah, yes, there is that." Olivia tilted her seat back and stretched out. Her shirt rode up again, but Finn paid no attention.

"Take your time, but pass by the car with Kelsy when you leave, will you?"

Anxious to get to Kelsy, who had gotten out of the taxi without a glance at the Mercedes, Finn opened his door. "The purpose being?"

"Maybe some of her incredible sex appeal will waft through the air and into my body while I grab a few z's."

Calling himself a fool for falling for Olivia's bait, Finn slammed the door, then leaned back through the window and waited till she opened her eyes. When she didn't, he said, "Jealousy doth not become thee."

"Go away," she said. "You'll give me bad dreams."

At first, when Finn called Kelsy's name, she was sure she was dreaming. Then, the scent of Old Spice floated toward her, telegraphing trouble. Not fun trouble. Bad trouble. He'd insist they talk.

Damn, it's not a dream. It's a nightmare.

Her toe messed up her sense of balance so she couldn't pivot around to greet him. At least that's the lie she told herself. As soon as she realized her denial, she waved, wiggling her fingers. Heart stuttering, she didn't turn around, but held her head higher and concentrated on getting to the front door. She moved as if in a dream. She couldn't seem to control the way her hips swayed with him behind her. With his long legs and her limp-and-hobble gait, why didn't he catch up?

Because he's taking a picture. The prickle on her neck reinforced this feeling of being watched and measured. The sun burned through her hair, down to her scalp, but she slowed her step, then stopped and stared at the purple mums the kids had planted near the door. Jason didn't need a scene at his school, and she didn't either. Finn was never reasonable, but if she didn't provoke him, he might at least play fair.

To show her willingness to abide by the unwritten rules, she said, "This is a surprise."

"I bet." Slowly, careful not to touch her, he came around to her left side.

Shocked by the lines etched around his mouth and the network of wrinkles across his forehead, Kelsy sucked in a breath. "You look tired."

"Nothing a few hours in bed won't help." He flicked his tongue in the sliver between his teeth. "How's your toe?"

"My-my toe?" Lust rolled off him, stunning her.

"The one you hurt?" The way he said *hurt* made her want to kiss him till her breasts stopped aching.

"Oh, nothing a few hours in—" Face on fire, she caught herself, swallowed, then shrugged.

"Nothing a few hours in-in the recliner won't help." Irrationally, she wanted to forget their differences and drag him into the bushes.

"That's a great chair. Molds to your body perfectly."

Calling up willpower she didn't know she had, she tore her gaze away from him. "We should go," she said shakily. "I'm sure Jason's waiting."

White-edged desire uncurled in the pit of her stomach. Terrified their hands would brush, she said, "I called the school from the cab. Jason should be in the director's office by now."

"Is it just us guys—or are you sticking around?"

Determined not to go with her first instinct and lie, saying her foot hurt too much to stick around, she said thickly, "I think it's better if he talks to you without me."

"I know that's tough," Finn said, his voice soft as the old flannel blanket she'd carried around till she was nine. "I wish I could tell him we'll have our lives back, but I can't."

Overcome by sadness, she opened the door and cool air washed over her. "I know," she whispered. As far as she knew, Finn had never lied to her or to Jason. "It's not your fault, you know. You have a job, a career. You can't always work when you want. You don't have to ask permission to do what you love. Opportunities come along and if you don't take them . . ."

She heard the words as if she swam underwater, knowing she spoke as much about herself as about Finn and thinking, again irrationally, about the desire which hadn't asked permission to wash over her in the brilliant morning sunlight.

"You okay?" Finn asked from another planet. "You look sorta dazed." He touched her elbow, and she heard a sizzle.

"Too much-too much sun." She didn't gasp, but the smoky rasp in her throat sounded funny. "Come on inside. You have to register."

So did she, and her hand shook so badly she could barely hold the ballpoint. The clerk, obviously used to the brilliant yellow, green and purple walls displaying student artwork, shot her a look. But Finn was laying on the charm, praising the color scheme, and Kelsy faded into the background. She cleared her throat. The clerk reluctantly broke away from Finn and invited Kelsy behind the desk. The director, with Jason at her side, answered the tap on her door immediately. Jason saw Finn and pushed past Kelsy as if she were invisible.

"Finnnnnn!"

Without flinching, the object of his affection went down on one knee, bracing himself. Jason hurtled toward him with the cast straight out in front of him like a hockey stick. Kelsy opened her mouth to warn Finn, but said nothing when Mrs. Albin, white-haired and comfortably round, offered her a tissue.

Kelsy's heart twisted. Was there a worse mother on earth? Finn's schedule didn't make it impossible for Jason to stay with him, but what about her trip? She could postpone going to Seattle. If she waited a week and played up all the advantages of Seattle, Jason would beg to go with her. Maybe, in a week, Finn could go. . . .

Lost in her fantasy, she managed a teary smile as Mrs. Albin led Finn and Jason to a conference room next to her office.

Kelsy refused the director's offer of coffee in the teachers' lounge, but Mrs. Albin insisted. She said quietly, "We can use the time for a quick conference."

"Of course." Kelsy's heart beat high in her chest as old memories surfaced. School conferences had always meant trouble for her.

"Prevention of a problem is preferable to treating it later, don't you agree?" Mrs. Albin moved at Kelsy's snail pace.

"Of course." Although Risa could defend herself against taunts about her weight, Kelsy had always felt the need to show her support.

"I don't think we have a problem . . . yet." Mrs. Albin ushered Kelsy into a large room with several chintz sofas and overstuffed chairs. Mercifully, the walls were a pale melon.

"With Jason, you mean?" Disdainful of Risa's ventriloquism which had nearly always stopped the taunts, Kelsy had resorted to more primitive action.

"Yes," Mrs. Albin spoke in the tone used with mentally challenged adults. She selected two straight chairs in a corner.

Busybody, Kelsy thought. Name-calling had sent her to the principal's office more times than she could remember. But she wasn't in trouble today, so she said, "Jason talks about school all the time."

"I'm not surprised. He's doing very well. He misses

Molly Macdonald, of course, but I think he's making new friends."

"That's wonderful." Kelsy let her shoulders relax. "But, I don't understand?"

"The potential problem?" Mrs. Albin smiled. "Has he told you about Parent-Career Days?"

Flooded with relief, Kelsy nodded enthusiastically. "I've heard about Mitch Brown's astronaut father for at least a week."

"Yes." Mrs. Albin nodded just as enthusiastically. "Lieutenant Brown even excited the girls. Next week, we have Zoë Zuckerman's mother. She's an evolutionary biologist who spends every summer in Kenya observing baboons."

"That'll be a hard act to follow," Kelsy said, thinking, *all I want to do is go to Seattle and work at a TV station.*

"Our thought exactly. Which is where our potential problem comes in."

"Potential problem with Jason," Kelsy cued, anxious to get back in case Finn and Jason had finished their talk.

"Yes." Mrs. Albin glanced at the old-fashioned clock on the far wall. "Luci will let us know as soon as Sergeant Bishop and Jason leave my office."

"Great!" Ready to scream in frustration, Kelsy eased back in her chair. Some people would not be hurried.

"I'm sorry I'm taking so long." Mrs. Albin didn't pause for reassurance, probably because she saw no such emotion in Kelsy's face. She sighed, then said, "We arrange the bi-monthly Parent-Career Days by alternating between the beginning and the end of the alphabet."

In a nearby window a fly buzzed against the pane. The sound, plus the overheated room, made Kelsy drowsy. Determined to hang in with Mrs. Albin, she said, "Sounds workable."

"Yes, well, we do it that way . . . I won't go into why. I'll simply say that Jason's name comes up in a month. When we talked to him about what your career is, he was quite adamant."

"Adamant about me being on TV? Why?" Kelsy felt her mother's claws come out. "Did you think he was lying?"

"Oh, no!" Mrs. Albin's eyes widened. "Nothing like that. A few of the teachers have seen you on the news. Jason's intransigency stems from *whom* he wants here on Career Day."

Kelsy's heart plummeted. "You mean he wants his father?" *A skirt-chasing, money-grubbing, cradle-robber? What a role model for kindergartners.*

"No, no," Mrs. Albin said. "He wants Sergeant Bishop."

Unnerved by the merciless look of sympathy in Mrs. Albin's brown eyes, Kelsy took a deep breath and lied through her teeth. "I can understand that. What's a TV anchor compared to a cop?"

"In Jason's eyes, Sergeant Bishop regularly leaps tall buildings in a single bound. When, of course, he's not catching criminals—here in Cielo Vista and around the world."

Kelsy didn't know whether to laugh or cry. She closed her eyes, opened them and met Mrs. Albin's gaze. "Charisma is Finn's middle name. His admiration for Jason is mutual."

Before Kelsy could agree or disagree, she said quietly, "Our potential problem is—technically—Sergeant Bishop isn't a parent."

Too late, Kelsy saw the freight train roaring right at her, but she couldn't get off the track.

"In rare cases," Mrs. Albin continued, "we've let grandparents substitute for a parent. That has happened exactly twice in my twenty years as director."

"What about working parents? Parents for whom it's a hardship?" Kelsy demanded hotly.

"We make *every* accommodation so a parent can come to class and stand in front of his or her child's classmates. We do this even though we recognize times and families have changed."

"They certainly have. What if I was a single mother and worked in Kenya with those baboons year round?" Knowing she was being ridiculous, Kelsy couldn't let it go. "Then what would Jason do on Parent-Career Day?"

"Would your parents be living in Kenya with you?"

The soothing tone the director used with preschoolers didn't comfort Kelsy, but she said, "Not my parents. They live in Sarasota, Florida, but could probably sub for me on Career Day. I'm sure the kids would love hearing about the excitement of retired life."

Briskly, Mrs. Albin said, "How shall we handle this? I'm sure you'd rather talk with Jason about it first."

I'd rather kiss a snake. Kelsy said, "No, I wouldn't, but I will—after I leap my first tall building."

Chapter 24

Finn wasn't surprised Kelsy was waiting when he and Jason left the director's office. He was surprised she didn't ask what they'd talked about once Jason returned to class. But she had thrown them a smile. Finn felt the bright edge of hope spike. He took her hand, shocked by its iciness.

He stated the obvious. "You're freezing."

She shrugged, but didn't remove her hand. "I'm tempted to go with the cliché: my heart feels frozen, too."

Her lifeless tone squeezed his own heart. He said, "I could administer mouth-to-mouth." When she stared at him, he said, "Or, I could kiss you, tell you I still want to celebrate our fiftieth anniversary together and—"

"And I still want . . ."

They stopped at the front door, and he glanced past her at the car. Olivia was probably wondering if he'd stopped a holdup in progress inside the school.

"What's going on, Kel?" Finn rubbed a spot over his heart.

"I've been thinking." She twisted the ring he'd given her.

"Oh, shit." Screw Olivia. Screw no profanity in an elementary school. "About what? About giving my ring back?"

"As a matter of fact . . ." She twisted the ring off, left it at the first knuckle, then wiggled the gold band completely off, laying the ring in her palm.

Sunlight bounced off the sapphire, throwing a blue pool onto Finn's tennies. Dry-mouthed, he stared at it. "I hate sentences that start with *as a matter of fact*."

Tears spilled down her cheeks. "As a matter of fact, I still love you," she whispered. "But I've figured out one thing. Loving you doesn't mean I'm ready to marry you."

Neck muscles knotted, Finn watched her fingers open and close over the ring. "Let me get this straight. First, loving me means not having more kids—not turning into a baby machine, I think you said."

Her mouth tightened till her lips disappeared, but she kept opening and closing her fingers over the ring. A high-octane surge of adrenaline zapped his brain. "Now, loving me means, after ten months together, you don't think you're ready to marry me. Call me dense, but I don't get it."

She shot him a look that said he was so dense light bent around him. She skewered him for ten seconds, then said, "If I were ready, I'd have told you the truth. About everything." She held up her index finger. "About wanting a career. About making out my résumé. About shopping it around. About making an appointment with Dane Jensen." She ticked off the reasons and flinched at his curled lip when she mentioned the bastard he now hated for no other reason than he was a bastard.

Without giving him a chance to say anything, she started ticking off more reasons. "I'd have told you about interviewing with Dane."

Dane this time, instead of *Dane Jensen*. Finn growled.

Whether Kelsy heard him or not, she didn't miss a beat. "About getting stopped by the police. About spending the night at La Lunada. Instead, I went to bed with you in Montana and pretended the world hadn't slipped off its axis."

She took a breath, and Finn went for cute. "Think of me as your priest at first confession."

Cute earned him a look that almost charbroiled his cojones.

"I'd have told you about the TV interview with The Loony Tunes instead of falling into bed with you and pretending I was fine."

"Yes," he agreed. "You should have told me. You didn't. I hope you've learned—" Sweat dripped into his eyes. Shoveling coal in Hell couldn't be any hotter than the glass lobby.

"That's the problem, Finn." Kelsy made a fist with the hand holding the ring. "I've learned that lies catch up with us sooner or later. Duuuh, right?" She whacked the side of her head. "Here's the truth. I want to go to Seattle. I'll never know if I want the job unless I go up there."

Finn's pulse spiked, and the lobby spun a couple of rotations. The sun kept right on blazing through the glass, making it clear to Finn what his choice was.

"All right then, you have to go." He swallowed, wanting a fight, but his heart wasn't really in it.

"Thank you for understanding."

"Sure." He tasted bile in the back of his throat. "You'll still wear your ring, right?" The way Finn saw it, understanding should result in more understanding.

"Do you want the truth?" The sadness in her eyes brought back memories of Ma about to give him a long time out.

Hundreds of hot needles stung his scalp. "This a test?"

"Do you want the truth?" Now, she sounded mad.

In a flash of resignation, he knew that in the name of truth and honesty, Kelsy was going to rip his fucking heart out. "I want the truth."

Without a visible drop of perspiration on her, she said evenly, "I don't think so."

His jaw cracked in protest, but she went on. "If I wear it, I'll be constantly reminded of you—your dreams, your needs, your wants. I'll focus on *us*, instead of on me."

"God knows we wouldn't want you thinking about *us*!" he exploded, not bothering to soften his sarcasm.

"Exactly why I told you I'm not ready to marry you."

"Sorry. I forgot." His throat tightened. Dammit. He couldn't stand giving up on them, letting go of his fantasy of their fiftieth anniversary, their grandkids, their love.

A bell clanged. Any second they'd be surrounded by hordes of five- and six-year-olds with the same focus on freedom as Kelsy's. Instinctively, Finn took her arm, pushed the door open, then guided her into the scalding sunshine.

With only a second before they reached the taxi and he went back to sorting garbage, he blurted, "Is there anything between you and this bastard Jensen?"

"No!" Kelsy missed a step, but Finn saw no telltale flush.

"Why not? He's not dead. And I know this fact because I've talked to him on the phone. Is he gay?" Time was running out.

"How would I know?" She jerked her elbow out of his hand.

"Is he blind?"

"Blind?" Her tone warned her patience had worn thin.

"Blind. You know . . . can't see you. Which could explain why there's no chemistry—except blind people compensate with smell and touch. You telling me he never touched you?"

"I'm telling you . . ." She stopped, then slapped her hands on her hips. "He kissed—*bussed*—me good night. On the cheek, okay? I got in the car and drove away. Because," she dragged the word out, "because, I love you."

"Were you wearing my ring?"

She didn't miss a beat. "No, I took it off before I got in the shower. I was late. I forgot it."

"Musta made it easier not to think about *us* though."

"Truthfully?" She waited while he opened the taxi door and panic kicked him in his gut. She said, "It didn't."

Against her better judgment, Kelsy went back to KSJC. She had almost no personal items there, but she was certain that no matter what happened in Seattle, she no longer had a future at KSJC. In her present mood of taking no prisoners, she actually looked forward to telling Brad where to shove her job.

He was on the phone with the door closed when she went by his office. As soon as he saw her, he hung up, tore across the carpet and ripped open the door. Insisting she sit in a wing chair, he parked his rear on the edge of his desk and asked about her foot, staring at it as if he could make her toe okay.

Totally calm, Kelsy ignored his hypocrisy and took control of the conversation. "I'm here to give my notice, Brad."

"Before you find out how you like KSWA?"

Kelsy raised her eyebrows. "So the walls really do have ears," she said. So Brad really was smarter than a speed bump.

"They do." Brad rocked off the edge of his desk and took the wing chair across from Kelsy. "Believe it or not, I've been thinking about your career for a while."

"Why?" Kelsy stretched her legs in front of her and wiggled her toes. Definitely less pain.

"Because I don't want to lose you." He sounded marginally sincere to Kelsy. She frowned, and he continued. "You're a very talented anchor, and you're an asset to KSJC."

Surprised, wishing Finn was there to hear this, Kelsy said, "Life is a timing problem, Brad. Yours is off, since you figured out I'm an asset the day I'm leaving."

"Reviewed your KSWA contract yet?" He crossed his legs.

"No." She didn't soften her answer because he didn't need to know Dane hadn't faxed her the contract yet. Which didn't matter. Her new contract was none of his damned business.

"Let's see if I can guess what's in it—besides the basics." He tilted his head back and looked up at the ceiling.

When Kelsy didn't take his bait, he stared harder at the ceiling and hummed—as if he'd forgotten the apple he'd dangled in front of her. Teeth gritted, she said, "Go for it."

And he did. He recited verbatim, including the two specials, what Dane had promised her. More amazingly, he didn't gloat or outwardly delight in having dropped the snake in her small Garden of Eden. As her mind raced, he anticipated her questions, asked them in a logical fashion, then answered them. Sick to her stomach, Kelsy wanted out of his office. Finn had implied Dane had a sexual agenda. Now, Brad was implying . . . what? She couldn't sort it out.

Brad said, "I told you the TV world is small."

"Yes." Kelsy wondered if he was rubbing her nose in it. Sure he wouldn't tell her, she asked, "Who told you about Dane?"

"Victoria Moreno. She described Dane right down to the ice cubes in his baby blues."

Fury mixed with relief hit Kelsy. "Dane didn't call you?"

"Oh, no. Dane travels in a brighter galaxy than mine. His rep precedes him. He's offered that same contract in the past to several of my best people."

Now, pure relief flooded Kelsy. "It's a damned good contract. At first, I thought it sounded too good to be true."

Brad nodded, his smile almost as stiff as his moussed hair. "You know that old saying—"

"Of course." Kelsy slid forward onto the edge of her chair. "In this case, the deal's too good for me to pass up. I have to think about my future. I'll never get another chance like it."

Brad straightened the crease in his pinstriped pants. "Suppose I offered you the same deal?"

Kelsy laughed. "Uh-huh."

"Same salary?" Brad met and held her gaze.

"Uh-huh." Too bad she didn't believe him.

"Same perks? Better work schedule?"

"Ooooh, good things in life should be savored," Kelsy said. "I ought to say yes and watch you squirm, Brad."

"You wouldn't watch me squirm. You'd watch me jump up and down. Erica's pregnant."

"Preg—" A tingle of excitement stopped Kelsy from repeating Brad's announcement. Pregnant. Who'd have thought?

"Says she already knows she wants to stay at home with the baby," Brad sounded confused, but his face remained blank.

"Good for her." Kelsy meant it. She'd never regretted staying at home with Jason. Not till he'd started kindergarten and Finn had gone undercover. Would Erica's husband help with the baby?

"Grace Liu's also leaving. Stanford Law School."

"What a great opportunity." At twenty-six, Grace was

the youngest on-camera anchor at KSJC. On her worst day, she looked about fifteen, and Kelsy had heard that viewers doubted her credibility with serious stories.

"You see where I'm going here?" Brad asked.

Kelsy felt dazed. "Let me think about this, Brad."

Squared for battle, Finn sorted garbage with Olivia till noon. By then, they both had trouble with basic motor skills. Talking was a challenge, but they agreed Olmeda had played them. They staggered to their cars and went their separate ways for four hours of sleep till their next shift. Before he fell into bed, Finn tried Kelsy, got a busy signal and vowed he'd call back. The numerals on the digital clock on his bedside table blurred. His eyelids felt like lead curtains. He fought sleep for a couple of heartbeats, then sank into darkness with his cell on top of his chest.

Dry-mouthed, feeling more asleep than awake, he got up late, passed through the shower and rushed out of the house, cursing his lack of follow-through with Kelsy. *The road to Hell . . .*

The cliché tempted him to call from the car, but he realized the traffic and his slow reflexes demanded his full attention. With luck, he'd call while Olivia got them to the Nimitz. But Olivia shoved the keys to the Mercedes at him, confessing she wasn't fit to drive. Not about to whine that he'd blown his best option to take care of his personal life, Finn drove.

Another flurry of activity at the stakeout kept him and Olivia occupied till their shift ended. Neither so much as took a potty break or drank a cup of coffee. The next morning, bleary-eyed, both agreed breakfast held zero appeal. Knowing Kelsy was on the air, Finn swore he'd sleep till seven, then call her. He woke to Ma's taps on the door at 3:30 Thursday afternoon.

Throwing caution to the wind, he called Kelsy from

the car. No answer at Risa's. Voice mail on Kelsy's cell phone. With six minutes to spare before his shift started, he called Risa at her office. Of course, she was with a patient. Nurse Em refused to interrupt, and he had to hang up when Olivia arrived. Over her protests, he spent the first hour of their shift cussing because he hadn't reached Kelsy. Then, he switched to cussing because she hadn't called him and left a message that she and Jason were okay.

At 6:47 P.M., dressed in black from head to toe, Olmeda and three companions strolled out of the Nimitz Park Apartments and climbed into his 2003 seamist Avalon. Pushing Kelsy to the back of his mind, but also thinking the stakeout could soon be over, Finn rode shotgun while Olivia tailed the boosters. Three hours later, the pursued and their pursuers returned to the Nimitz, where the TV still flickered in Apartment 301.

"My, my, wasn't that fun?" Olivia grumbled as Olmeda parked the Avalon. "I love feeling so . . . D-U-M."

Nervous Olmeda would—uncharacteristically—take off again when one of them was on break, they agreed to go another whole shift without one.

By 5:00 on Friday morning, Finn could barely walk to the 'Vette. When he slid under the wheel, his bladder screamed. Pretending he was Dirty Harry didn't help. He had to stop at the nearest service station. When he returned the restroom key, he bought a pack of Dentyne because he was so damned embarrassed.

The small TV next to the cash register was tuned to KSJC. A young Asian man read the news.

So, Finn thought despondently, she went to Seattle.

The flight to Hell, Kelsy thought, patting Jason's knee at 8:32 on Friday morning. Teeth gritted, she repeated the mantra she'd started five minutes after take-off. "Sweetheart. Please. Stop kicking the seat."

Any minute, she expected the businessman in front of her to call the first-class cabin attendant and demand that Kelsy and Jason be thrown off—preferably from their cruising altitude of thirty-five thousand feet.

"How much longer, Mommy?" Jason's whine pushed all of Kelsy's buttons—right down to her toe. It had started throbbing when, like the dumber one of the ugly stepsisters, she'd forced on a pair of open-toed pumps at dawn, ignoring Risa's comments that Kelsy was nuts-o.

Praying for patience, Kelsy said, "I'm not sure, Sweetheart." Probably another lifetime.

"Ask how long, Mommy." Jason thumped his cast against his window, and the businessman nearly gave himself whiplash whirling around to see what was going on.

My fiancé's a cop, she almost said, but let common sense reign. "Sweetheart, our cabin attendant's busy."

"Ask her anyway, Mommy."

Kelsy tapped his cast. "She's going to bring us breakfast."

"Yuck." Jason gave one more thump with his cast. "I don't want breakfast. I wanna go home. I wanna talk to Finn."

Finn's under his skin. Kelsy clasped her hands together till her nails bit into her palms. *God, grant me—*

"Cantcha call Finn, Mommy? He said I could call him any time." Jason jerked the window shade down hard, and the man in front of him swore.

"Let's change seats, Jay." Kelsy unbuckled her seatbelt with shaky hands.

"No!" Jason slammed the window shade up. "I wanna sit where I can see."

"There's nothing to see, Sweetheart." Nothing but gray clouds and raindrops sliding down the window.

"I wanna talk to Finn." Jason snapped the buckle on his seat belt, then wrapped the strap around his cast.

"I'm sure he's asleep." No use mentioning the call would cost more than a week's salary and wouldn't be paid for by KSWA. Or that she didn't think she could talk to Finn without crying.

Lowering his seat, Jason said, "Can we call him when we get to Seattle?"

A deep inhale soothed the frayed edges of Kelsy's nerves. Perseverance is a positive character trait, she reminded herself.

She took Jason's hand, so small in her own, smiled, then said, "We can call Finn as soon as we get inside the airport. Deal?"

"Deal!" he shrieked, giving her a clumsy high-five.

The man on the aisle across from her looked up from his laptop and grinned. "Traveling alone with enthusiastic kids is sure fun, isn't it?"

"I'm trying to remember when I've had so much fun." Kelsy flashed the man one of her Nicole Kidman enigmatic smiles.

Jason leaned across her lap. "I'm calling Finn soon as we get to Seattle," he announced in a loud whisper.

"That won't be too long now," the man said. "Wanna come over here and show me your cast? Then, I'll show you a couple computer games my six-year-old son really, really likes."

When Jason returned to his seat for the landing, Kelsy shook hands with Brett Trimble, thanking him for his help. "My pleasure. My wife and son live in Raleigh, and I'm living in Tacoma till we sell our house. After six months apart, I need my kid-fix regularly or I can't keep going."

A believer in cosmic signs, Kelsy listened attentively to Brett lament about being separated from his family as they stood in the aisle, then walked through the jetway and into the concourse. There, they shook hands, and he pointed out his favorite place to call his son on the way back to Raleigh.

Taking his suggestion, Kelsy and Jason stepped into a deserted nook. After dialing, she handed the phone to Jason. Tears blinded her when he shrieked, "Finn! Did I wake you up?"

As much as she wanted to listen to every word Jason said, she gave him some space. He'd earned it. She stared out at the gray landscape and shivered. Last night when she confirmed her arrival with Dane, he'd sworn the sun had shone all day.

For cryin' out loud. Don't read too much into the weather.
Or meeting Brett.

Or the ache in her heart that sharpened every time she thought about Finn.

Jason tugged her hand. "Finn wants to talk to you."

Goosebumps skied down her spine. She wiped her hands down the front of her wool trousers. Face bright, Jason stared up at her. "Hey, Finn!"

"Careful, the phone lines might melt," he drawled. "And I'm not too sure I won't turn into a puddle my-self."

Her heart jammed her throat. "There you go, being eager."

"Why are you crying?"

"Because . . ." She swallowed. Terrified that if she started telling him why, she'd turn around and get back on the plane, she said, "I love you."

He didn't miss a beat. "I love you, too. I want you to be happy. I hope this weekend goes the way you want. I'll be here when you get home."

After Finn hung up, Kelsy floated next to Jason on a technicolor cloud. He kept asking why she was smiling, and she kept saying she was happy, happy, happy.

Happy he'd called Finn?

Happy as a fool in love with the man of her dreams, the dream man she was destined to love throughout eternity.

"I'm sooo happy you called Finn." She hugged Jason.

"He was happy, too, Mommy."

"Yes, he was." Over-the-moon happy, infectiously happy.

Kelsy smiled. At Jason, at arriving and departing passengers. Whether her smile scared them, surprised them or amused them, the passengers gave a wide berth to a limping woman and a boy wearing a cast on his arm. At the exit, Dane pulled her into an embrace. *Rhett Butler and Scarlett on the stairs.* Dane smelled quietly of Chanel for Men.

Except, down at their knees, Jason tried to shove himself between her and Dane. "You let go of my mommy!"

"It's all right, Jay." Recovered from her mind blip, Kelsy pushed against Dane, but a man racing through the concourse stepped on Kelsy's toe. Moaning, she fell back into Dane's arms. *Please, don't let me faint . . . or throw up.*

Dane's Viking DNA must have kicked in. Without so much as a grunt, he scooped Kelsy into his arms, ordered Jason to stay close, and carried her through the crowd—a Viking hero one step ahead of the arriving enemy.

My God, Kelsy thought, her face hot and sweaty, terrified Dane would drop her, was she out of her mind thinking about old movies and ancient history?

"Jason!"

"I've got him." Dane stopped, shifted Kelsy into one arm and hoisted Jason onto the opposite hip. "The limo's at the curb."

Despite this good news, Kelsy's heart lurched with every ten-league step Dane took. "Jason? Are you holding on?"

"Uh-huh." He sounded so sullen, Kelsy said, "I can walk."

"Not necessary," Dane whispered.

"It's necessary for my pride," Kelsy said. "I make judgment calls on my own."

He arched his reddish-blond eyebrows and smiled. "Don't feel the need to express gratitude."

"I don't. So put us down. Now."

"Yeah," Jason piped up. "Put us down."

"Let me get through—"

"Now," Kelsy repeated. A crowd was behind them.

"Okay." He swung Jason off his hip like a baby chimp.

Through clenched teeth, Kelsy said, "Did you ever do that to your son?"

"Sorry." Dane gave her a look that was marginally contrite. "It's been a long time. I'm out of practice."

"Don't drill with my kid, okay?" She started to slip out of his arm, but he put his hands around her waist and held her at chest level for a heartbeat.

"Put. Me. Down." As if they were tango dancers, Dane slowly lowered her down the length of him. Finn's voice hammered in her ear. *You telling me he never touched you?*

"Let's go, Mommy."

"I need to think for a minute, Sweetheart." Tempted to smack Dane, Kelsy flexed her fingers. *Go home.* So what if she went back humiliated, her pride shredded?

"Careful," Dane winked. "We could make the nightly news."

With both feet on the floor, Kelsy said, "I will kill you."

"Kelsy?" Her name echoed across the concourse as if magnified.

"Briana!" Jason screamed, and Kelsy froze.

"Jesus!" Dane clapped his hands over his ears. So did half a dozen other people who glared at Kelsy.

Cute as a leprechaun, but vicious as a pit bull, Briana Bishop charged forward, tousling Jason's hair, her green eyes narrowed, her lips a thin, red slash in her pale face.

"Small world, isn't it?" Staring at Dane, she hugged Kelsy.

"Tiny." Kelsy licked her lips. "I have a job interview."

"What're you doing here?" Jason demanded.

"Met with my advisor at UW. Didn't my favorite brother-in-law tell you I was here?"

"No," Kelsy said, taken aback, fighting anger building in her chest. Had Finn sent Briana to the airport to spy?

"Who's your favorite brother-in-law?" Jason asked.

"Finn, silly." Briana focused on Dane. "Kevin's his big brother, remember?"

"Sure," Jason stated, though Kelsy was pretty sure he didn't because the seven Bishop brothers bore an uncanny resemblance to one another. She was also pretty sure Finn hadn't sent Briana because they'd never discussed an itinerary. She sighed. *You are insane.*

Watching Kelsy, Briana said to Dane, "Have we met?"

"No." Dane extended his hand and introduced himself, adding, "I'm the reason Kelsy's here."

Briana's eyes widened. "Is the job here, in Seattle?"

"Seattle's not Siberia," Kelsy snapped. "You come up often to meet with your advisor, don't you?"

"Once a month." Briana shrugged. "Up one day, back the next. But you'll work more than one day a month, won't you?"

"That's why Kelsy's here." Dane smiled at Briana as if he'd known her since birth. "So we can work out the details."

"I'm bored," Jason announced.

Within seconds, Dane took charge, reminding Kelsy the limo driver would pick up her luggage as soon as they gave him her claim checks. Grateful he short-circuited Briana's curiosity, Kelsy smothered her fury at him, but refused his arm.

Just in case any news hawks hovered in the wings, they'd have their come-to-Jesus meeting in private.

Chapter 25

Between Jason's non-stop questions, the constant rain, and endless caravans of big rigs on busy Interstate 5, Kelsy wanted to scream. Her outrage—intertwined with helplessness—filled the limo with explosive tension. Dane, apparently deaf, blind, and stupid, had nonchalantly taken a call in the limo at the airport. Despite her smoldering rage, he talked on the phone for the thirty-minute ride into downtown.

Probably faking, Kelsy thought. She'd used the trick often enough.

At the Four Seasons, Dane hustled her and Jason into the lobby. "I'm sorry," he said, "an emergency. I have six people waiting at the station. I'll check back with you around four."

Sending Jason to help the bellman count their luggage, Kelsy drew Dane aside. No scenes, she told herself. Pulse pounding, she shoved her left hand under his thin, patrician nose, amazed her hand didn't shake as she pointed to Finn's ring. "See this? I'm deeply engaged. Do not ever touch me again."

He smiled coolly, arching his damned eyebrows a

fraction of an inch, and Kelsy felt her own cool heat up. "Should I have let you fall on your beautiful nose? Get trampled? Maybe mess up that lovely, TV-genic face?"

"Yes." She spit out the single word. Whether he'd had his emotional lobotomy long ago or recently, she wasn't going to argue with him.

"You certainly didn't object to my *touching the merchandise* at The Ritz."

Heat flooded her neck and face. "A mistake on my part."

"I see." He stared past her as if she wasn't there, and she didn't care what he looked at as long as he saw she wasn't backing down. Not even with hot needles piercing her toe.

Face blank, he brought his gaze back to her. "There's a problem with the story I wanted you to do on the Six o'Clock News tonight. If I get it fixed, I'll pick you up at five. Otherwise, we'll have to find a spot for you on the Late News."

"No." Kelsy shook her head, gearing up for battle. "I'm not leaving Jason alone that late."

"All right." His shrug surprised her. *Maybe he's a quick learner.* "I'll call you between two and three. In the meantime, why don't you and Jason take the Monorail, then have a great lunch on KSWA?"

"Great and expensive." Kelsy deliberately didn't point out it was raining and that a ride on the Monorail lasted ninety seconds start to finish.

"Have fun." He waved jauntily, then pivoted on the balls of his feet.

Kelsy let him get two feet away before she called, "Dane? The contract? When Jason takes a nap, I'll review it."

The expression on his face didn't change much, but then, she supposed icebergs didn't show much change either. There was, she thought, a dark hardness to his

Viking blue eyes. **Determination** stopped the shiver halfway down her spine.

He said, "The contract's in my office."

Uh-huh. "I'm sure a courier can bring it over," she murmured, her heart beating too fast.

Without missing a beat, he said, "I'll ask my secretary to handle it since I've got this three-alarm fire to put out."

In Kelsy's stomach, a three-alarm fire was fast on its way to becoming four-alarm. Don't jump to any conclusions, she told herself, limping toward the elevator. You just kicked the guy in the cojones. Why shouldn't he be a little edgy?

While Jason watched a video in his adjoining bedroom, Kelsy called Finn's mother. She listened without interruption. Kelsy finished and Maeve said, "Guess who's picking up Briana at the airport?"

Kelsy's heart fluttered, but before she could accept this easy out, she said quickly, "I don't want to put you in the middle, Maeve. Briana will tell Finn or she won't. I'd like to give him my side first . . . but—"

"At least let me help you out there. Finn should roll out of bed around three. With a few well-chosen questions over a leisurely lunch, I'm pretty sure I can keep Briana occupied till four. Finn leaves at four-thirty."

Blinking back tears, Kelsy closed her eyes. "I owe you."

"Yes, you do," Maeve declared. "You and Finn belong together. The past few weeks, you've hit a bad patch, but you have the rest of your lives to work it out."

"I hope . . . you're right." The tightness in Kelsy's chest closed her throat.

"Corny as it sounds, hold on to hope," Maeve said.

"And love, of course. Love and hope will surprise you every time."

Dry-mouthed, Kelsy stared out at the fog curling around the windows as if looking for a crack to get inside. "How can I feel so blessed having Finn in my life and resent having him in my life at the same time?"

"Don't know. Psycho?" Deadpan, knocking the breath out of Kelsy. Maeve laughed. "Being psycho's part of being human."

"Yes, but—"

"No buts. As long as you don't stay in Cuckooland twenty-four/seven, you're normal. End of pep talk. Time to go."

As she hung up, Kelsy thought, time to stop feeding your self-pity. Playing in the rain could be just as much fun as playing in the sun. "Hey, Jason. Let's go do something."

On the fifth Monorail trip to the Space Needle, they got off, found a small restaurant, then walked in the rain till Jason admitted he was tired. Although he was almost asleep on his feet when they entered the hotel, she stopped by the front desk.

Surprise, surprise. No contract.

In the elevator, Jason sagged against Kelsy, who crooned to him while she mentally blistered Dane's ears. She and Jason staggered into their suite at 2:25.

Surprise, surprise. No flashing red light. Dane hadn't called.

Teeth gritted, Kelsy read *The Cat in the Hat* to Jason, his eyes drooping. By the end of the second page, he was snoring. As she studied his damp hair, crimson cheeks and grimy cast, she felt her pulse spike. The spike intensified as she limped out of the bedroom, into the huge, ornate bathroom.

Forget Dane Jensen. Think about Finn. Mind-lessly, she applied a few drops of L'Air du Temps, his favorite perfume.

She twisted her hair into a chignon, applied fresh lipstick and stared into her own eyes. Decide now what to tell him.

The truth.

Anybody home? Her stomach knotted. The truth made her look like an idiot. Her eyes got hot.

The truth was she'd ignored all the signs that Dane was scum. She'd really thought she was different. An important addition to KSWA. Her bottom lip trembled.

The truth was Dane thought she'd fall in bed with him on the promise of a job. She bit her lip to keep from crying and faced the harshest truth of all.

She'd jeopardized a meaningful life with Finn to chase an illusion. With no one to blame but herself, she now expected Finn to welcome her back with open arms.

"You are an idiot," she muttered. If she and Finn changed places, how generously would she behave?

The phone rang before she reached an answer. Mad and sad and humiliated and hurt, she grabbed the phone near the bathtub. Dane's secretary identified herself immediately. Since Kelsy had been out, the courier hadn't left the contract. Dane suggested they review the specifics during dinner.

"Around seven?" the secretary chirped.

Hating her vulnerability, Kelsy asked, "Is he expecting me at KSWA at five?"

A pause, just a heartbeat, then the secretary said, "I believe there's still a problem. He's in conference. Out of the building, in fact."

"That's a crock." Kelsy glanced at her watch and added, "Tell him I expect a phone call if he won't be here by seven."

Holding her breath, she immediately called Finn. He didn't pick up. Her heart dropped. Dammit, he must be in the shower.

"Call me, please. I love you." She left the number, closed her eyes and fantasized standing in front of him under the pulsing water. Her body tingled as she remembered his tongue down her back, between her legs . . . . Light-headed and on fire, she placed a second call in case he hadn't noticed her message.

No answer.

"Damn!" She squeezed the receiver, replaced it, then limped into the sitting room.

Six calls later, at five till four, she gave up. Damn, damn, damn. He must've gone to work early. He was so conscientious, and what he did mattered so much. Her anxiety mattered zip, and her bruised ego sure wasn't an emergency.

Jason woke up at 4:00 and wanted to ride the Monorail. Glad for an excuse to get out of the luxurious suite, Kelsy ignored the rain and said yes. She could stuff her suspicions about Dane.

Half an hour later, Jason said he didn't like the rain. Kelsy echoed his sentiment. Why, she wondered, even if there was a KSWA job, would she want to adapt to sunless days? Why would she want to see Finn only on weekends when she could sleep with him every night in Cielo Vista?

Because you could go big-time from here.

Her stomach clenched. Big-time meant New York. Half a continent away. New friends and new schools for Jason. Major adjustment for Finn. Why would he actually go through with a long-distance marriage?

Daydreaming, and umbrellas carried by nearly every pedestrian hurrying in the downtown district, made walking hazardous. Twice, Kelsy banged into someone and got cold water down her back. Jason barely smiled when she danced wildly around on the sidewalk. Hoping to ward off an impending attack of self-pity, she suggested hot chocolate and cookies at the hotel.

Although Jason's spirits rose marginally, she thought dry clothes might help more. Jason agreed, then wanted to open their door. Glad such a small thing made him happy, she gave him the electronic key. As soon as the door swung open, the scent of roses drifted into the hall.

"Are those from Finn, Mommy?"

Those were dozens of red, white and yellow roses in a bouquet of lilacs, baby Iris, furled tulips and flowers Kelsy didn't recognize because she was in a state of shock.

"Are the flowers from Finn, Mommy?"

"I-I—" Finn would have to sell his Corvette to buy this bouquet fit for a king's funeral. "Let's see."

"Who'd send you flowers besides Finn?" On tiptoe, having trouble with his balance because of his cast, Jason peered over her shoulder at the small white card.

"Sorry for . . . miscommunication?" she read aloud.

"Who's Miz Communication?" Jason demanded.

Kelsy laughed, saw his face fall and regrouped. "Miscommunication isn't a person, Sweetheart. It's a word that means two people didn't understand each other."

"'Cuz they had an argument?"

Kelsy nodded. "Sort of. Dane and I had a misunderstanding this morning."

"I don't like him!" Jason jutted his jaw.

Kelsy bent and kissed him. "I know, Sweetheart. But he sent these flowers . . . so what do you think of him now?"

"I hate him!" Jason stomped off to his bedroom.

* * *

Fifteen minutes before the licensed sitter's scheduled arrival, Kelsy posed in the door that connected the sitting room with Jason's bedroom.

"What do you think of my dress, Sweetheart?"

"I don't like it." Cheeks crimson, eyes glazed, his cast on top of the satin covers, Jason looked lost in the king-size bed.

"Too red, huh?" The perfect tomato red for her blond hair, but too low-cut, not to mention too body-hugging.

"You only wear that dress when you go out with Finn."

Surprised he'd noticed, she blushed. "Yes, he likes this dress a lot." *Not as much as he likes it on the floor.*

So you brought it why?

Face burning, Kelsy inhaled the heady scent of roses. Her eager conscience kicked her in the head and gave her an earful. *You are so pathetic. You wanted revenge. Make Finn squirm, you decided. Bring the dress and play Little Red Riding Hood to Dane's Big Bad Wolf.*

Damn, the truth is ugly. She inhaled again, and her boobs rose till she thought they'd pop out of the skimpy bra.

Between yawns, Jason said, "You should wear a different dress."

"I didn't bring another dress."

"Wear . . . what . . . you wore on the plane."

"That's too casual, Sweetheart." But Jason, who *never* commented on what she wore except at Halloween, had a point.

"I could wear my navy Armani," she said. She'd planned to wear it on the news show, but she'd brought a second gray suit.

"What's your navy Army?" Jason yawned.

Smothering a smile, she said, "A pantsuit, Honey."

Fine for the dining room downstairs. If Dane didn't like it . . . she unzipped the dress. She could wear overalls and Dane would look at her like the Wolf.

Most women find that kind of appreciation flattering. Kelsy stared at her reflection. Flattering was always so predictable. Finn, on the other hand, never failed to surprise.

Disappointment burned the back of her throat. If only she'd caught him at home. Surprised him after he'd just gotten up. A few minutes of sexual bantering with him would've chased away her loneliness. Then, a million roses could never have influenced her to put on her red dress. Damn, why hadn't she brought a hair shirt to wear with Dane?

Gripping the zipper, she crossed to the bed. "Sleepy, yet, Sweetheart?"

"Huh-uh." Jason sat up straighter in the bed. "Why do you hafta go out, Mommy?"

"I'll just be downstairs, Jay." They'd gone through this during his bath, but Kelsy sat down on the edge of the bed and rezipped her dress. "Remember where we went for hot chocolate?"

"I just 'member the Monorail."

"What a surprise." Kelsy chuckled, and her stomach stopped burning. She'd done one thing right. They'd had so much fun. They'd always had fun—before she started lying.

Speared by guilt, she tickled Jason's ribs lightly. "How many times did we take the Monorail?" She put a finger on one cheek and rounded her eyes.

"Seventeen!" Jason sat up, his blue eyes the size of saucers. "Can we go again tomorrow? Pleeeeze, Mommy!"

Silently, she inhaled and mentally counted to ten. Dry-mouthed, she took Jason's hand. "Remember, Dane's picking us—"

"I don't wanna ago with Dane! I don't like him."

Jason jerked his hand out of hers. "He doesn't like me, neither."

"That's not true, Jason." Kelsy hoped she sounded calm.

"Uh-huh!" His bottom lip stuck out a mile, his eyes flashed and fury radiated off him.

"I think he's just not used to little boys—"

"I'm not a *little* boy."

Kelsy flinched, and her stomach contracted. God, he sounds exactly like Sam. Disdainful. Dismissive. Disrespectful.

"I-I meant . . ."

Surprisingly, she felt tears sting her eyes. She swallowed hard. "I should've said young, Jason. Dane's not used to young boys. He has an older son. He's eighteen—"

"I don't care!" Jason rolled onto his side, away from her. "I'm not a little boy. You shouldn't have dinner with him. I'm telling Finn."

The higher his voice rose, the lower Kelsy's heart dropped. Without thinking, she blurted, "Finn knows." Guilt flashed through her. God, she had the integrity of an eggplant.

"He does?" Jason turned over and sat up, peering into her face, vulnerable as a small animal separated from its mother.

Unable to lie so brazenly again, Kelsy said, "Honey. Going out to dinner with Dane is business." She lowered her voice as if sharing a secret with her best friend. "Finn trusts me."

Her tongue burned, and she half expected smoke to come out her mouth. Jason gave her a long, appraising look, then said, "Ooo-kay. If you're sure, Mommy."

"I am very sure you and Finn are the only men in my life." Her ears rang with each syllable.

Unbidden, her mental VCR rolled out a movie that started up when she least expected it.

Kelsy outside the E-Z Sleep Motel. Pawing through the trash. Fishing out six empty condom wrappers. Holding them to her heart.

Scene shift. Kelsy in Risa's master bedroom. Putting the wrappers under her pillow. Lying on the pillow. Dreaming about a church, the minister, Finn. Finn offering great sex instead of marriage.

Offended, Kelsy stalks out of the church.

A fast-forward. Kelsy, an old lady in the park. Finn—still young and gorgeous—driving by in his squad car with Olivia, also young and gorgeous. Flashing a gold ring. . . .

This last frame went into a loop that wavered and faded in and out of focus. Kelsy felt panic swallowing her.

"Mommy, Mommy!" Jason was shaking her arm, his eyes wide, scared. "Don't you hear the doorbell, Mommy? Are you okay?"

"Yes, Sweetheart, yes. I was thinking about Finn." Laughing and crying at the same time, she stumbled to her feet.

Hysterics or a heart attack?

"I'll be right back. Then, I'll give you the best back rub ever," she called over her shoulder.

Dane could wait. Or not.

The mousy thirty-something babysitter couldn't believe Kelsy's offer of Dane's bouquet. When Kelsy insisted, she gladly took the damn flowers in their Orrefors vase and only charged a hundred bucks for unrendered services. By rights, Kelsy should've put the babysitting fee on her room, but warning bells started clanging in her head when Dane didn't call from the lobby during the transaction.

Half an hour after the sitter left, he still hadn't

called. By eight, Kelsy realized that for the first time in her life, she'd been stood up. Ticked at first, then humiliated, she finally saw the humor and fell on the sofa laughing till tears ran down her face. The jerk ditched her before she dumped him. She imagined calling him at home, disguising her voice and leaving the kind of anonymous message she'd left for Rob Parker in high school, but logic prevailed.

"He is soooo not worth it," she said to the ceiling. Wait till she told Finn. She smiled, then decided silence didn't, in this case, constitute a lie.

The earliest of early birds, Jason refused to get out of bed the next morning at 4:45. A sliver of light came through the cracked door to the bathroom, but he put his cast over his eyes as if warding off light from a 747.

"I don't wanna go." He tossed his head back and forth on his pillow.

But you will. Kelsy's heart fluttered, and she couldn't keep her excitement in check any longer. She whispered, "Wake up, Honey. We're going home. We're going to see Finn."

Chanting, "We're going to see Finn, we're going to see Finn," Jason dressed with the speed of Clark Kent in a phone booth.

By the time the limo pulled onto the rain-slick I-5 half an hour later, he momentarily forgot his mantra and asked anxiously, "We won't see Dane, will we?"

"Nope." Kelsy pulled Jason closer, double-checking his seatbelt, adjusting it over his cast. "Dane's no longer in the picture."

"What's that mean?" In the soft glow from the side lights, Jason's face was pinched. "Don't you like him anymore?"

"No, I don't like him anymore." Kelsy figured Dane wouldn't like her very much once he saw the five-hundred-buck surcharge she'd blithely put on her KSWA tab. Changing tickets to return home a day early cost a bundle.

No more than dinner would've cost last night, she thought. It's cheap for standing me up.

"I'm glad, Mommy." Jason put his hand in hers. "And I bet Finn will be glad, too."

Kelsy gave him a high-five. "I bet you're right!"

The limo driver reassured them the rain wouldn't ground their plane. Tired, but relaxed for the first time in weeks, Kelsy listened to Jason's plans for surprising Finn. Since he probably had to work, they'd have to enlist Maeve's help.

"Let's call Gramma Bishop now."

"I think we should wait till the birds wake up," Kelsy joked. "We'll call from the airport. Before we get on our plane."

"Okay, but what if Finn goes to work before we get home?"

Kelsy reassured him they should get into San Jose long before Finn got up. "Let's hope he got home on time so he won't mind when we wake him up early this afternoon."

"He won't mind, Mommy. I'm sure."

Throat tight, Kelsy nodded, impatient to see Finn, to set things right between them. She glanced at her watch. Almost six. If Finn was home, he probably hadn't gone to bed yet. Why not call him instead of waiting? Tell him they'd see him later? She ran the idea past Jason.

He shrieked, "Yes, yes! Call now! Let me talk to him!"

Using the microphone, the limo driver asked, "Is everything all right, madame?"

Everything was perfect, and since they'd already entered the airport departure lane, Kelsy suggested they call from inside. "Then we can talk without any interruptions."

Check-in was a snap, but Jason's patience was clearly wearing thin. He wanted to talk to Finn—give him something to dream about till they got home. Kelsy felt his euphoria lift her heart. Or maybe it was her toe. She was barely aware of it as she and Jason went through security, then headed for their gate at a slow trot. Jason was intent on talking to Finn immediately, if not sooner. Happier than she'd been for weeks, Kelsy stopped at the first waiting area. Jason couldn't stand still while she placed the call to Finn's cell.

"Hello," Maeve said almost instantly.

"Maeve?" Surprise muddled Kelsy's brain. Maeve never answered Finn's cell.

"Let me talk, let me talk." Jason tugged at Kelsy.

"Kelsy, darlin'."

"You said I could talk." Jason looked ready to cry.

Was Maeve crying? Dry-mouthed, Kelsy held a finger up to Jason. "Is Finn in bed already?"

Maeve's pause yawned into a black hole filled with nothingness. "Where are you, darlin'?"

Not an answer, Kelsy realized, fear building in her chest. "At the Seattle airport. Jason and I leave in about ninety minutes. Is Finn asleep yet?"

"Not . . . yet."

Kelsy's pulse kicked up. Staring past Jason who had gone still as a statue, Kelsy said, "Maeve? What's wrong?"

She heard the rest, ears ringing, heart pounding, like part of a dream. A shooting. Finn in CCU after removal of a bullet in his left shoulder. Barring infection, a full and quick recovery expected. Olivia in surgery. Olivia seriously hurt.

Kelsy couldn't swallow. Fighting tears, she beckoned Jason to her. Eyes huge, he came immediately. "What's wrong, Mommy?"

"I'm in the CCU waiting room with Sean and Kathleen. Everyone's on the way. Someone will pick you up. What time?"

There was a frantic moment when Kelsy couldn't find the tickets and still couldn't talk. Jason's scared face didn't stop her hands from trembling, but she regrouped, found the tickets and read the flight number and arrival time to Sean.

He said, "Ma wants to talk to Jason, but she figures you need a minute with him first."

"Yes." Her throat tightened again. "We'll call you back."

As she snapped the cell shut, Jason opened his mouth in protest. Kelsy opened her arms. "C'mere, Sweetheart."

She took him on her lap and looked deep, deep into his clear blue eyes. As her mind churned, Kelsy thought nothing in her life had prepared her for this moment. Then, images from Nashville came back. Jason and Molly had gone to Nashville with her. They'd loved the triplets long before their scary birth. They'd been there for the duration, including Harry's first surgery. Risa swore that their unconditional love and trust got her through the worst of the endless nights. They had accepted her tears of sadness and fear and frustration without judgment.

Feeling tears start down her own cheeks, Kelsy said, "I need to tell you something before we call Gramma Bishop back."

Then, without melodrama or unnecessary detail, determined not to terrify him, she told him—with what she hoped was the right mixture of hope and sympathy.

"You think Finn will have to wear a cast?" Jason asked. "I can tell him all about casts. They're not so bad."

"Sweetheart, I don't know. You can ask Gramma Bishop, but she may not know yet."

"Okay. But if she's too sad, I'll tell her about the Monorail. When Finn's better, let's come back to the Monorail, okay, Mommy?"

Infected by his unbending optimism, Kelsy blew her nose, then said, "I bet Finn would love riding the Monorail with us."

Chapter 26

On the trip to San Jose, Jason sat in Kelsy's lap except for take-off and landing. At one point, the man in front of them turned and said what a pleasure it was to travel with a well-behaved child. Under the circumstances, Kelsy wouldn't have objected if Jason had kicked both seats to pieces. But, sure she'd need her energy later, she thanked the man and went back to mindlessly stroking Jason's hair.

They stumbled off the plane and into Tad Bishop's open arms. A stockbroker, he'd managed to persuade security to allow him to meet Kelsy at the gate.

"A little hard to say no since Finn's a cop." He guided Kelsy to a wheelchair, setting Jason on her lap so they could get outside as quickly as possible.

No need to wait for her luggage. He'd arranged for the airline to send it to Risa's house. Despite strict parking restrictions, his car waited at the curb.

"The sun's shining!" Jason shouted.

"I ordered it special after I read the Seattle weather."

"It rained and rained," Jason said from his car seat in the back.

Tad shot Kelsy a glance, but spoke to Jason, "Finn

and I always liked playing in the rain. We never got much rain in San Jose, you know."

Gratitude filled Kelsy for Tad's recollections, but she listened with only one ear. Hugging her waist, she turned her face to the windshield. The sun blinded her, but threw off no heat. She closed her eyes and tried to shake off the memory of the polar temperature in the CCU.

Thanks to the wonders of technology, a cell phone call from Tad as they pulled in front of El Camino Hospital, Maeve was there to meet Kelsy and Jason. Despite the strain in her face and eyes, she was smiling.

"Finn's awake and wants to see you both."

Kelsy felt her legs wobble, but she took a deep breath and felt her head clear. "We're ready." No matter what, she'd be there for Finn.

"Let's go," Jason said quietly, apparently remembering Kelsy's instruction on the plane to speak softly. Critical Care rules were being bent for a child under twelve.

The Bishop clan made way for Kelsy and Jason as if they were royalty. Even Briana, whose puffy eyes welled with tears, squeezed Kelsy's arm with what Kelsy believed was genuine warmth.

"I'm glad you're here," Briana said.

"So am I." Breathing hard, Kelsy felt lifted up by this truth.

"Remember, he's a little pale." Maeve rang the bell on the door that led into the CCU.

Kelsy's heart caught, but she forced a smile. "Pale makes it easier to count his freckles. I love his freckles."

Inside the icy room, awash in blue from the overhead fluorescent lights, Jason squeezed Kelsy's hand so hard bones in her fingers cracked. *Hold on as hard as you need to, Baby.* They followed the nurse, padding ahead of them on cat's feet, to a curtained-off area. Heart pounding, Kelsy licked her lips.

"Hark! Who goes there? Speak the secret word." Finn's voice, thin and unusually high, Kelsy noted, floated through the curtains in a raspy whisper.

"Fizzlerizzlerazzledazzle," Jason whispered, then threw a triumphant grin at Kelsy.

"Okay, nurse. Let 'em in."

"Finn." A whisper, but Jason rushed the bed, side-stepping machines and IV stand with the agility of a downhill skier slalomming around moguls.

"Hey, Jason."

Shocked by his drained whiteness, Kelsy thought, it's the lighting, and leaned against the foot of the bed in relief that more of him wasn't wrapped in bandages.

"Hey, Babe." They looked at each other, and Kelsy felt her insides melt from wanting to hold him.

She tossed her head. "You really didn't have to go to such extremes to get us home. I was on my way."

"Being eager, were you?" He took Jason's hand.

"Silly me." She hardly recognized her voice.

"I'm glad we're here," Jason said.

"Me, too." He sounded tired, and Kelsy felt her pulse drop. She'd never seen him physically vulnerable, and it scared her silly. *In sickness and in health.* . . . A challenge that, after rethinking her whole life, she looked forward to accepting.

"We wouldn't be anywhere else," she said. "Rest, now. We'll be outside." Dizzy with love for him, she brushed his lips carefully with hers. "We don't want your heart rate too high," she whispered.

He laughed. A single sound, but a laugh. "Braggart."

For the next three days and nights, Kelsy and the Bishop clan stayed in the CCU waiting room around the clock. Risa arrived late that afternoon with Molly, Ben, and the triplets. As always, Molly took care of Jason while Ben took care of all five kids so Risa could stay at the hospital with Kelsy.

Most of the time Finn slept, exactly what he needed,

according to his surgeon. Risa agreed with this opinion, but Kelsy still hated visiting him when he was asleep. As impatient as Jason, she wanted him back in the real world so they could make up for lost time. Lost time she'd racked up chasing a goal that now baffled her.

Olivia joined Finn in the CCU after eighteen hours of surgery. Her two ex-husbands were remarried and they provided the CVPD no help in locating her family. During the times Kelsy waited her turn to see Finn, she went to see Olivia, who was in an induced coma because of post-surgical trauma.

"I just talk to her," Kelsy told Risa. "Whatever comes to mind. I hope she knows she's not alone."

"Okay, okay. I can take a hint."

One by one, the Bishops started dropping by as well. Olivia remained unconscious. Finn, on the other hand, was now awake for longer and longer periods. He repeatedly asked about Olivia, calmed only when Kelsy reassured him his family was watching out for her.

Four days after he was shot, Finn was transferred to a regular surgical ward. Pointing out that he was out of danger, he ordered his family and Kelsy to take a break and let the hospital staff take care of him.

"I'm staying with you," Kelsy said.

"You'll make yourself sick." He laced their fingers.

"Then we can share a bed here in the hospital."

"Don't be ridicu—" Apparently seeing her face, he changed his mind. "What about Jason? What about your job? What—"

"What about you shut up and get out of here so we can get married and live happily ever after?" Fiery hot from lust, as well as the desire to prove she loved him, she kissed him on the lips with such passion she was afraid she'd sucked the oxygen right out of him.

When she released him, his head sort of flopped back against the pillow, and his eyelids fluttered. Her heart lurched. "Finn?"

He opened his glassy eyes, but they focused on her hotly and he said, "Shut the door. Then, get in bed with me."

"Good things in life deserve to be savored," Finn announced to Kelsy at the end of his first week of excruciating P/T. Exhausted down to the cellular level, he studied the ceiling in his hospital room through half-closed eyes. "You've got a life. Go savor it. Make a deal with Brad. Or The Loony Tunes."

"Did that bullet hit you in the head?"

"No, and it didn't hit you either." He patted the bed next to him, then winced when she sat down. "You don't have to throw yourself on the funeral pyre to prove you love me, Kelsy."

"I'm not! I'm sticking with you—through thick and thin. You never gave up on me when I went to Seattle. You let me come back—"

"Let you come back?" Moving his head, he stared at her. "I was ready to say yes to the long-distance marriage, no to more kids and anything else you wanted as long as you didn't kick me out of your life."

"And that's my point." She shifted her butt on the bed, and he bit back a moan. "You were willing to make any sacrifice, so why shouldn't I come to the hospital every day? It's not that big a deal."

"It's a very big deal. You gave up your chance of a lifetime in Seattle for us, but that doesn't mean . . ."

She flinched, and tears filled her eyes. Sure she hated him, he wanted to shake her because he felt so defensive. "Dammit, I didn't ask you to give up Seattle."

"I never said you did. I'm very aware you didn't. You were a saint, trusting me, watching me play with fire."

Ahhh shit. "Wrong!" he yelped. "I wanted you to give it up. Sooner or later, I'd have done something stupid. Said, 'me or the job in Seattle'." He thumped his chest, but stopped because his heart was pounding so wildly.

Kelsy opened her mouth, but fed up with this saint crap, Finn added, "Now, does that sound saintly?"

She shrugged. "Probably not. But I don't want you thinking I made any sacrifices in Seattle." She waved him to silence. "I didn't even get a look at the contract."

"Why not? Because you came home early?"

She snorted, a noise that grated his ears. "I doubt there was a contract. You were right about the Viking. He's scum, but I was lying to myself and wouldn't admit I loved his garbage."

"Oh, Babe." He drew her into his arms. "I can tell you how sorry I am Sam and your mother did such a number on you. Or, I can tell you to go out there, find a job, work, get over Dickhead and the divorce and then decide if you're going to be happy married to a cop. Not a big-shot lawyer. A cop."

"Reality TV in the corporate world," Victoria Moreno said to Kelsy over coffee at Starbucks. "Write your own deal, because we want you."

Optimistically suspicious, Kelsy found a lawyer, wrote the deal, took it to Brad Hall, wheeled and dealed and divided her eggs into two baskets, since she still wasn't sure *By the Skin of Their Teeth* would make it in the reality-TV world.

If that show failed, she'd still have the daily talk show she'd re-envisioned. Brad was so glad to have her, he let her walk all over him. Having power, she decided, definitely beat not having power.

Blowing on her hands, Kelsy leaned against her open front door the night of Finn's discharge from El Camino. "Brrrr. I am freezing."

Before Finn could act on this sign of encouragement or point out the unseasonably warm temperature, she unbuttoned his top shirt button. His core body temp shot up at least eighty degrees. "You, on the other hand—" She dragged a fingernail along his collarbone, making him shiver. "You are hot enough to melt polar ice caps."

"That's pretty hot." Scared to move, maybe turn her off because he was already hard and admittedly nervous after three weeks in a hospital bed, Finn forgot everything he'd ever learned in the Academy about breathing, and held his breath.

"So hot you look feverish—as if someone struck a match and lit a fire inside you," she whispered.

"Probably a pyromaniac." A heartbeat from asphyxiation, Finn prayed she didn't stop her finger dance on his collarbone.

"You think?" She rubbed her back against the door, reminding him of a cat, and he almost grabbed her right then, but he didn't want her to think he lacked self-discipline. Even if waiting killed him.

"Who do you think lit my fire?"

"Now there's a mystery." She finished with the last button and slowly pulled out his shirt tail. "Need help searching for the maniac?"

His heart went into orbit. "You volunteering?"

"Unless you think I'm too . . . old to be helpful." Her hand rested on his hip, searing denim and bone.

"You're not too old, but you could be too distracting."

"You think?"

Clumsy as a teenager, he grabbed at her, missed her mouth by a mile and ended up kissing a panel of etched glass on the door.

Disappointment didn't get a toehold. Swaying, she turned her luscious mouth to his and guided his hands to her waist. "Unzip me, so you can decide how distracting I really am."

"That swaying's distracting enough for me to arrest you right now."

"Arrest me for what? I've got my rights."

Most of which he planned to violate right there in the entry. "As a public nuisance."

She laughed. He slid the belt over her undulating hips. "Minor point, Sergeant Bishop. We're not in public."

"Thank God." He lifted the tiny zipper on her dress, and she unbuckled his belt, momentarily stunning him.

"Oh, I don't know." She splayed his shirt open. "Personally, I think fucking in public sounds exciting— something I'd like to try before I die—unless it's against your oath of office."

"Can you wait till June? Till I finish law school?" He leaned into her, amazed at how soft she was. He'd finish law school just in case he got tired of being a cop.

She slid a hand inside his jeans. "Depends on what you have in mind in the meantime." Their mouths collided again, and thought evaporated.

Her fingers moved under his shirt, caressed bare skin, then she gasped, but said quickly, "I bet this is 'nothing'."

"That's right." He guided her fingers away from the scar, still tender. Meeting his gaze dead on, she laid her free hand between his legs. "This, however, is not nothing. This is something very, very big. Speak now or forever hold your peace."

"I think you're already holding it," he said.

"I love you," she said. "Will you marry me on June first?"

"Huh?" he said, brilliantly.

She explained that Jason's last full day of school was June tenth and she hoped Finn would make them legal so he could take the last slot for Parent-Career Day.

Grinning, he drawled, "I believe I'm up to that."

* * *

On June first, having received the minister's blessing to kiss the bride, Finn removed his top hat, rolled back the fake sleeves of his fake tuxedo and lunged for Kelsy. She looked hotter than a hot tamale in her sequin-studded, red, one-piece bathing suit.

"Kiss her, Finn! Kiss her," Jason yelled.

"What're you waitin' for, Bro'?" Big brother Sean taunted.

For my head to clear, Finn thought, staring down at Kelsy's inviting smile.

Despite the A/C in the wedding tent, the Las Vegas sun was hot enough to broil chickens. Of course, Kelsy was Miz Cool. Cut high on the thigh, low in the back and lower in the front, her suit couldn't be tighter if she'd sprayed it on. The gauzy, white micro overskirt, gathered on a ribboned waistband, opened up the middle and knocked her sexiness quotient off the scale.

Wild applause threw Finn into a deep state of discombobulation. Add Kelsy laughing up at him, and he wondered if wearing an electric blue Speedo showed good judgment on his part. But then, he hadn't counted on his bride giving a little shriek when he tilted her backwards. Her veil grazed the floor and Lucky Prince snatched it off her head. For some reason Finn couldn't explain, her second scream made him instantly—and publicly—hard.

Behind him, he heard Ma gasp. Out of the corner of his eye, he saw Sean wrestle the veil away from Lucky Prince. Kelsy lay in his arms and laughed convulsively. "Thank God, I warned Ma our wedding would be unforgettable," he mumbled.

"Hurry, Finn," Jason shouted. "It's hot. Me 'n Molly're burning up. We're ready to go down the water slide."

The titters among the guests rose to laughter. Hotter

than a fried lizard, Finn muttered to Kelsy, "Whose idea was it again to get married at Niagara Falls of the West?"

"I believe it was a mutual decision." She stuck her tongue out at him, bringing back memories of the torrid, creative months it had taken them to resolve this disagreement. Secretly, Finn had loved every minute of their negotiations. He and Kelsy *negotiated* for weeks her stipulation that Lucky Prince accompany Jason, the ring bearer, down the aisle. Most of all, Finn enjoyed the pretense that he'd never consider getting married in the biggest, gaudiest, wildest water park in Las Vegas.

"Hey, Big Boy." In real time, Kelsy kicked one long, gorgeous leg up over their heads, wiggled her crimson toes in her new, red Manolo Blahniks and whispered, "Don't tell me you've got cold feet at this late date."

Finn laughed. Then for the hell of it, he dropped her head an inch lower and grinned insanely as she yipped. "You know," he said right in her ear, "this isn't legal till I kiss you."

She grabbed his red bow tie. "C'mon then, we've got a show to tape. Olivia doesn't know she's catching my bouquet."

Behind them, TV cameras zoomed in. "I am the luckiest guy in the universe," he said.

About the Author

In high school, Barbara wrote a weekly column for her Southern Missouri hometown newspaper. Later, teaching adolescent boys, she put writing on hold. She acted in melodrama for stress relief. As a marketing specialist for IBM, she developed high tech materials that really honed her fiction-writing skills.

Besides living in Kansas, Missouri, Florida and North Carolina, she has lived in Mexico City, LaPaz (Bolivia) and Buenos Aires. She currently lives with her husband and two cats in the heart of Silicon Valley.

Visit Barbara online at http://www.barbaraplum.com.

Contemporary Romance By
Kasey Michaels

__Can't Take My Eyes Off of You
   0-8217-6522-1   **$6.50**US/**$8.50**CAN

__Too Good to Be True
   0-8217-6774-7   **$6.50**US/**$8.50**CAN

__Love to Love You Baby
   0-8217-6844-1   **$6.99**US/**$8.99**CAN

__Be My Baby Tonight
   0-8217-7117-5   **$6.99**US/**$9.99**CAN

__This Must Be Love
   0-8217-7118-3   **$6.99**US/**$9.99**CAN

__This Can't Be Love
   0-8217-7119-1   **$6.99**US/**$9.99**CAN

Available Wherever Books Are Sold!

Visit our website at **www.kensingtonbooks.com**.

By Best-selling Author
Fern Michaels

Weekend Warriors	0-8217-7589-8	$6.99US/$9.99CAN
Listen to Your Heart	0-8217-7463-8	$6.99US/$9.99CAN
The Future Scrolls	0-8217-7586-3	$6.99US/$9.99CAN
About Face	0-8217-7020-9	$7.99US/$10.99CAN
Kentucky Sunrise	0-8217-7462-X	$7.99US/$10.99CAN
Kentucky Rich	0-8217-7234-1	$7.99US/$10.99CAN
Kentucky Heat	0-8217-7368-2	$7.99US/$10.99CAN
Plain Jane	0-8217-6927-8	$7.99US/$10.99CAN
Wish List	0-8217-7363-1	$7.50US/$10.50CAN
Yesterday	0-8217-6785-2	$7.50US/$10.50CAN
The Guest List	0-8217-6657-0	$7.50US/$10.50CAN
Finders Keepers	0-8217-7364-X	$7.50US/$10.50CAN
Annie's Rainbow	0-8217-7366-6	$7.50US/$10.50CAN
Dear Emily	0-8217-7316-X	$7.50US/$10.50CAN
Sara's Song	0-8217-7480-8	$7.50US/$10.50CAN
Celebration	0-8217-7434-4	$7.50US/$10.50CAN
Vegas Heat	0-8217-7207-4	$7.50US/$10.50CAN
Vegas Rich	0-8217-7206-6	$7.50US/$10.50CAN
Vegas Sunrise	0-8217-7208-2	$7.50US/$10.50CAN
What You Wish For	0-8217-6828-X	$7.99US/$10.99CAN
Charming Lily	0-8217-7019-5	$7.99US/$10.99CAN

Available Wherever Books Are Sold!